THE MOUNTAINS OF ALLAH

Paul Chavchavadze

THE
MOUNTAINS
OF ALLAH

DOUBLEDAY & COMPANY, INC., GARDEN CITY, NEW YORK

THE MOUNTAINS OF ALLAH

Part One
The Lover

1   "There is nothing more aggravating, more exasperating than
to be a widow at twenty," Zoë wrote in a leather-bound
notebook she called her *Book of Stray Thoughts*. She underlined the
words "widow" and "twenty," adding four exclamation marks to
strengthen her plight. Her small hand, with a white widow's cuff
around the wrist, darted to the day-by-day calendar on the desk, and
three little beaklike fingers plucked off the top leaf, much as a bird
might pluck a worm off a garden lawn. The new date, so suddenly
revealed, stared up at her—February 1, 1854. Six months to the
day since René had been laid to rest in his father's country place
outside Paris. Such a foolish, unnecessary death! She had begged
him, pleaded with him that afternoon not to tackle the big stone
wall, but he had laughed and had spurred his horse on. . . . She
had watched him gallop away, anxious, frightened. She could still
see his horse rising from the ground to the stroke of his whip. A

breathless moment, and all was over. With horror frozen in her eyes, she had stared down at the tall lanky body flung across the meadow, the head bent at a terrifying angle, a narrow streak of dark blood trickling slowly out of a corner of the mouth. René, the young husband, who had been so ardent a lover for so short a time. Less than eight months.

"Why, then, should I no longer understand the despair I felt at the time? Why does it seem as if a load had fallen off my shoulders!" Zoë had put these questions to herself many times in the past few months. She had loved René, or at least she thought she had, stirred as she had been by his youthful passion. Even now she could almost feel the tingling thrill of his burning lips upon her breasts. She closed her eyes and shook her head. "I must not think of that! That is dead and gone!" She sighed a little, moving closer to the window and looking down into the quiet little street, in which the modest house of Mesdemoiselles Chabout—her maiden aunts—was but one of a long line of modest houses. "Death came before its time, but it released me from a trap!" She frowned in a vain effort to scold herself, but her heart sang of rejuvenated life, and hope, and love, as she gazed at the warm, springlike day outside. Her lips tightened. "He is dead, but I am alive! And, oh God, how I want to be loved!"

When Zoë had first married René she had passionately wanted a child. Now she was glad her wish had not come true. Today a child of his would have meant years of bondage to René's parents, to the ridiculous pomposity of Papa Duval and the sanctimonious selfishness of his mother. Prematurely old, disillusioned, bigoted, and hopelessly possessive about René, her only son, Madame Duval had taken an instantaneous dislike to Zoë. Had Zoë been, like herself, a product of middle-class wealth and austerity, things might have gone better. But there she was, "A penniless daughter of an obscure Napoleonic general, and with an air of gaiety about her that is positively obscene!" the old lady had said repeatedly when René was out of earshot. But as long as René had been there, a semblance of mutual civility had been maintained between the Duvals and Zoë. With René gone, the whole artificial structure came crashing to the ground.

Actually it crashed sooner than Zoë had expected. They had just returned from the funeral. Overcoming her personal dislike, Zoë had gone up to her mother-in-law with outstretched arms, but the other had waved her away in a frenzy of hate and fury. "Murder-

8

ess!" she had screamed, her voice rising to a high pitch, her eyes bulging. And clutching at her heart, she had crumbled to the floor in a dead faint. While friends and relatives busied themselves over her, Papa Duval took Zoë aside. "My poor child," he said, patting her hand. "Believe me, I feel deeply for you, but you must understand, my wife is not herself. She does not what she is saying. She thinks you should have curbed poor René's passion for horses. In a month or so, when the violence of her grief dies down, she will be all right again, I assure you." He wiped the perspiration off his forehead with a large handkerchief bordered with black. "I am sure, my dear little Zoë, in your sorrow and your loneliness you would much rather be in Paris with your own family."

Zoë pulled her hand away sharply. She gave no thought at the time to her family, which consisted of three eccentric old aunts she did not like. She just wanted to get away. Very calmly, very coldly, she told Monsieur Duval she was going upstairs to pack and asked him to order a carriage to take her back to Paris. Thinking of it now, she marveled at her own calm. Her rage must have drained her sorrow, leaving her cold and dry-eyed.

Monsieur Duval saw Zoë off. He looked so crushed that for a moment she had felt sorry for him. "When we return to town, you must come to our Sunday family dinners. Promise me you will, my child." He hesitated, shifting heavily from one foot to the other. "Conventions demand this of us, you know."

Something snapped in Zoë. "I would sooner die!" she cried.

She never saw him again. And now, with her thoughts still on Papa Duval, she suddenly knew what had stood between René and herself. René had loved his middle-class moorings. Fun, adventure, travel, all the things she had always craved had meant nothing to him. Outside of his horses and his father's business he had had no interests in life. Even the delight he had found in her would have died away in time, giving place to something terrifyingly solid and immutable. Zoë guessed rather than knew that René would have wanted it that way out of deference to the narrow world in which he had been born and bred and which, fundamentally, he had respected and admired above all else.

Zoë could remember well the doubts that had assailed her at times when René, exhausted and happy, slept peacefully at her side. Somehow those doubts were closer to her now than his love. She could see herself lying very still, hardly daring to breathe, her eyes wide open, staring into the dark, while thoughts, like big black flies, went

9

buzzing through her brain. Had she made a mistake in marrying him? Could she love him all her life? Could she . . . And finally she would find herself dreaming. It was always the same dream—the face of a young man. She did not know how tall he was, nor what his hands were like, nor what kind of clothes he might wear, but his face she knew by heart, with its sharp, regular features and hazel eyes. She felt disturbed by the patience and resignation in those eyes, but the profound understanding she found in them brought her a sense of peace. And when his lips began to move silently, every word resounded deep in her heart. They were always the same words—"Take courage. I am watching over you."

Zoë smiled to herself. "I feel better for having thought of him!" And she threw a sidelong glance at herself in the cheval glass across the room. What she saw there pleased her, especially the golden-brown ringlets peeking from behind her ears, and the large, luminous eyes topped by smooth, even eyebrows. They were eager, provocative eyes, yet strangely innocent. "And my waist," she murmured. "The strong hands of a man could enlace it." She measured it with her own small hands and her fingers almost met. Pleased, she laughed at her own reflection, at the garlands of rich black crepe and the lovers' knots of the same fabric that decorated her hooped skirt. "A bit frivolous for a widow, but I had to put them there to enliven this horrible black dress! Oh, it is cruel, unnatural for a woman of twenty to be wrapped in black crepe for two whole years. I want color, music! I want life!"

Zoë bit her lip and bent over the desk to read the daily motto on the calendar. It said: "Do not put off until tomorrow what you can do today."

"And who said I would put it off!" She was addressing the calendar now with a scornful look. "Such nonsense, I do declare! Last night I came to a decision, and it is irrevocable. I shall declare my intentions to my aunts!" She placed the palm of her hand on the calendar as if to hush it. "Isn't it strange, though, that I dreamed of him again last night! I had not seen his face since René's death. 'Take courage. I am watching over you.' He had said it again!" Yes, and the words had brought her determination and courage. She would discard her widowhood together with her dull life. She would turn her back on this house; leave France, never see her mad old aunts again. . . .

But here her thoughts came to an abrupt end. Her aunts. They were waiting for her downstairs in the parlor. Hurriedly she picked up her reticule and glanced into it—the letter was there. She patted her hair and smoothed her dress in front of the cheval glass and stepped out of the room.

For a brief moment she paused on the landing, sniffing the air with distaste. "What a deadly place, with its smell of vinegar and dust! Away, away, away!" She closed her eyes to shut out the dreary sight of a worn-out stair carpet and an ugly wooden banister. Instead, a vision of distant mountains, of a sunlit, semi-tropical land rose up in her mind and made her heart beat faster. "There I will find my romance. *Ma grande passion!*" And laughing lightly, she ran down the stairs, thinking of everything under the sun except the one thing that preoccupied the thrifty minds of her three aunts. For Zoë was facing life penniless and destitute.

2   An ominous silence greeted her when she entered the dingy little parlor. The old ladies occupied an entire corner of the room, their wide black skirts spreading over the plush-upholstered furniture. They looked like three huge cats in crinolines. Emilie, the eldest, was the angry black cat with bristling hairy growths at the corners of her mouth; Clotilde, once upon a time the white pussy with round blue eyes, had dissolved into layers of fat; while Roxane, the youngest, was the aging alley cat, all bones and angles. She sat pondering over mysterious back-wall struggles of her own, though her strange smile was in no way a reflection of her thoughts —nature had shaped her large crescent-like mouth into a perpetual smile. Emilie and Clotilde stared at Zoë, but Roxane paid no attention to her. She was gazing across the room at a china statuette of Napoleon on the mantel and at an oil painting on the wall above it, in which Zoë's father was portrayed in the full regalia of a French general of Napoleon's days.

Zoë settled down in a stiff chair at the opposite end of the room, feeling uncomfortable under Emilie's critical eye. She sat very straight and tense, bracing herself for a possible battle. To anyone else she could have unfolded her plans, but in this household everything was done according to age precedence, and Emilie would have thrown a fit had Zoë been the first to speak.

"A new dress!" Emilie exclaimed at length. "Garlands and lovers' knots! How shocking!"

"Lovers' knots!" cried Clotilde ecstatically. "Ah, but Emilie, my darling, they might be very apropos!"

11

"Hold your tongue, Clotilde! I will speak of that later. First I want to know who paid for that dress!"

"I did," Zoë said. "I had a little money left."

Emilie looked at Clotilde with raised eyebrows. "She had a little money left, so she bought a new dress! More like her mother every day!" And to Zoë, "Young lady, we cannot support you at this rate!"

Zoë tried to master her rising anger. "I have made plans for my future, you won't have to support me any more."

"Plans! Plans indeed! We have plans for you, Clotilde and I!" Emilie was speaking very fast now, her eyes shining with suppressed excitement. Zoë heard the words "seductive offer," "a man of means," "asking for your hand," and then suddenly, "Don't stare at me like that when the whole of paradise is falling into your lap!"

In her surprise Zoë had indeed opened her eyes wide, trying to figure who could have made such an offer. And it was Clotilde's small cry of ecstasy that gave her the answer. Monsieur Auguste Tresor, a bald little man with a paunch and a weedy semblance of an imperial on his chin, who lived in a big ugly house around the corner. The idea was too preposterous. She tossed her head and laughed, a loud throaty laugh, contagious to a degree.

Emilie stamped her foot. "How many times have I told you, such loud laughter is vulgar! And what is wrong with Monsieur Tresor, may I ask? He is only fifty, and his six children will keep you out of mischief when he is away!" She leaned forward, wagging her finger fiercely. "Someday, a few years from now, you may be sorry you turned him down!"

Zoë's laughter died away. Emilie might be right, she thought. Five or ten years from now she would be growing old. A comfortable income. A big ugly house. Security. Hadn't she better dangle him for a while? And aloud, blushing a little at herself: "I cannot consider marriage for another two years at least."

"Why don't you tell him so?" Clotilde exclaimed. "He might consent to wait a little longer."

"Oh no, Aunt Clotilde, I would feel much too embarrassed!"

"Oh, fiddlesticks!" Emilie exploded. "You are no more embarrassed than the Shah of Persia is in his private cabinet! Such crass ingratitude! And after all we have done for you! Remember, your mother deserted you after your father's death. She eloped with a musician of no importance and squandered your father's inheritance. And we! We with our poor meager resources had to bring you up!"

Zoë closed her eyes. In her childhood she had felt lashed by

Emilie's cruel words; she had wept bitterly over her mother's disgrace. But now she experienced nothing but a vague impatience as she sat there waiting for the panegyric about her father which was bound to follow.

Emilie pointed to the portrait above the mantel. "There was a man for you! Jean-Désiré Chabout! A soldier of our great Emperor! A colonel at twenty-seven and a general at thirty! A man of duty and honor! And you, insignificant as you are, you bear his name, *Zoë-Jeanne-Désirée!* Yet you have never tried to live up to your memory of him!"

"Memory!" Zoë cried. "What memory! I was a few months old when he died!"

"Ah!" Clotilde raised a finger, a sly look creeping into her small eyes. "You don't know what things one *can* remember when one has a memory like ours! Emilie here remembers how she was born, and I remember the taste of our saintly mother's milk! Ah! Could anything be sweeter!"

Zoë tried not to listen to these vagaries. She glanced in Roxane's direction, hoping against hope that help might come from that quarter. Roxane had not said a word; she had sat aloof and unheeding. But now, as Emilie turned to her, asking how far back she could remember, she tore her eyes from the opposite wall and looked straight at her eldest sister. "I remember how our father whacked you once," she said in hollow, measured tones. "I wish he had whacked you more often."

For once Emilie was winded. Profiting by the short silence that followed, Zoë asked if she could tell them about her plans, but Emilie brought a heavy fist down on a nearby table. "Hold your tongue, you ungrateful wretch!"

"Hold your tongue yourself," Roxane said in that rusty voice of hers. "Let our niece speak." And turning her strange, dull eyes on Zoë, she added: "Tell us about your plans, Niece."

Zoë drew a sharp breath and clenched her fists. Emilie could fume and rage as much as she liked, nothing would make her change her mind now. "I am going away," she said; and encouraged by the clear steady sound of her own voice, "I am going to a place you have never heard of—a town named Tiflis."

Emilie stared back at her vacantly, Clotilde blinked several times, but Roxane said, "I know all about Tiflis. It is the capital of the ancient kingdom of Georgia." Zoë's eyes widened with surprise as Roxane turned to Emilie and Clotilde. "Sisters, Georgia is located

13

in the south of Russia, south of the high chain of Caucasian mountains."

"Our brother got his feet frozen in Russia," was Emilie's somber comment.

"But our niece will not. Tiflis has a mild climate."

"But why go so far in search of a mild climate?" Clotilde exclaimed in dismay.

"There is a position waiting for me there, Aunt Clotilde!" And to forestall further arguments, Zoë drew a letter from her reticule. "It's from Thérèse Michot, do you remember her? She was my teacher at the Pensionat."

"A shady character, I believe," remarked Emilie.

"Not at all! She was the most popular young teacher we had. She left of her own free will to establish herself in business."

"How shameless of her!" This from Clotilde.

"All right, Niece," Roxane cut in. "Tell us about her offer."

Zoë told them what she knew. Thérèse Michot had drifted from place to place until she had finally settled in Tiflis, where she was now well established as a fashionable dressmaker. Zoë had kept up a steady correspondence with her. She had written Thérèse a few months ago telling her of her strained financial circumstances as a result of René's death, and Thérèse had responded with an offer of a job and a promise of a future partnership. "Listen to what she says," Zoë exclaimed, unfolding the letter. She scanned the written pages for a moment in silence and then began to read aloud: " 'My clientele is among the wives of Russian officials here who have plenty of money to spend on clothes. Most of the local Georgian aristocracy is impoverished by devastating wars with Turkey that raged in the preceding century, before Georgia joined the Russian Empire, and, furthermore, most of the Georgian ladies wear their national costume—little headbands with white tulle veils, and flowing silk robes tightly fitted at the waist. Graceful and picturesque, but quite outside of my competence.' "

"How I would like to see those costumes," Roxane said musingly.

Zoë smiled at her. "I hope to see them soon, Aunt Roxane. Thérèse is very anxious to have me with her. She says . . ." Zoë turned a page and read aloud again: " 'Ah, my charming Zoë, I wish you would pluck up sufficient courage. Do not shudder and say no! Do not turn down my offer without first giving it a careful thought! This is not a bad place; it only seems so very far away. My French friends, Monsieur and Madame Tollet, who have a pros-

14

perous confectionery business here, will bring you this letter, and they will be glad to bring you back with them when they return to Tiflis.' " Zoë folded the letter and looked at her aunts. "I have an appointment to see Madame Tollet tomorrow!"

Clotilde, who had been growing more and more agitated during the reading, leaned forward now, trembling all over, clasping and unclasping her fat little hands. "No, no, no!" she piped. "The daughter of Napoleon's great general cannot go into trade! Never! I would die of shame!"

She moaned and whimpered a little, while Zoë tightened her lips. She, too, had thought of the social stigma attached by her contemporaries to women in trade, but she had fought it all out with herself the night before. She looked hard at Clotilde, ready to speak up for herself, when Emilie patted Clotilde roughly on the shoulder. "Hold your tongue. Remember, our niece is a pauper!"

And Roxane said, "There is nothing shameful about being a dressmaker. I would rather see her independent, well established in an honest trade, than serving as a menial in some rich household."

A sudden wave of affection for this ugliest of her three aunts filled Zoë's heart. She would have liked to express it in a word, in a gesture, but she was shy of her. It was easy to talk back to Emilie and laugh at Clotilde, but Roxane's aloofness had built a wall between them. And so she just looked at her with softened eyes. Roxane saw the look and turned her head away. "Isn't there more to that letter, Niece?" she asked gruffly.

"Only a description of Tiflis, Aunt Roxane."

"That is what I want to hear."

"Why, of course . . . Let me see . . . Tiflis . . . Where is it she writes about Tiflis?" She glanced through the pages of the long letter and her face brightened. "Ah, here it is. 'Tiflis is very colorful and picturesque, situated between high mountains on the banks of the fast-flowing river Kura——' "

"Known to the ancients as the Cyrus," Roxane's rusty voice cut in on the reading.

Struck again by Roxane's wealth of knowledge, Zoë looked up at her in surprise. Roxane was looking the other way, deliberately so it seemed. Zoë's eyes searched her face for a moment and then went back to the letter. "Where was I? . . . Ah, yes! '—high mountains on the banks of the fast-flowing Kura. One bank is dominated by an old castle, the former residence of the kings of Georgia, while on the other stands the ancient Cathedral of Zion below the present street level, so that it looks half buried in the ground. Narrow, tortuous streets wind themselves around it, in which Armenian and Persian merchants display their goods to the passers-by; and sometimes you can see a caravan coming in from the south.' "

"That is very beautiful," Roxane murmured dreamily, half to herself.

New and heretofore unsuspected sides of Roxane's nature were unfolding themselves in a slow and wondrous metamorphosis. Zoë laughed happily, waving the letter in the air. "But wait, Aunt Roxane! Tiflis offers contrasts! Thérèse says: 'Do not imagine for a moment, my sweet Zoë, that everything here is wild and barbaric. Tiflis has a modern European section, too, with broad avenues, fine-looking buildings, and pleasant homes, where life is gay and carefree, and lilacs often bloom at Christmas!' " Zoë folded the letter and clasped her hands together. "Ah! It all sounds just too ravishing for words!"

"That's all very well," Emilie broke in like a cold shower, "but who will pay for the journey?"

"I will!" Zoë had no money, but she owned a few valuable pieces of jewelry. There were the diamond earrings René had given her on their wedding day, and the diamond brooch, and the necklace. "I will sell them all," she said, looking down thoughtfully at the large diamond ring sparkling on the third finger of her left hand above the gold wedding band.

"Not that," Clotilde cried in a tearful voice. "Not your engagement ring!"

Zoë closed her eyes, and for a moment René's pale face with its soft brown eyes and blond mustache stood out clearly in her mind. It brought no sorrow, only a greater urge to do the things she could never have done with him. "Yes," she said, "I will sell it!"

Roxane stood up, moving her chair back noisily. Her great height always gave one a shock when she got up suddenly like this, for seated she appeared comparatively small. She came up to Zoë with her heavy tread and laid a large angular hand on her shoulder. "Brave heart!" she said, pressing Zoë's shoulder, while her dark eyes warmed up with inner flames, like black opals caught in a ray of light.

16

3   The appearance of Roxane's bedroom was as peculiar as that of its owner. Zoë had not been in it for more than a year, not since before her marriage, and that afternoon she examined every detail with a newly awakened interest. One side of the room nearest the wide massive bed bore a martial appearance, with weapons of all kinds, epaulets, shoulder knots, army buttons, insignia, badges, and army decorations that once had belonged to Zoë's father, forming on the wall an intricate star-shaped pattern around a portrait of Napoleon; while the other side was all fluff and bric-a-brac, with old pieces of Louis XVI furniture, a few Saxe figurines on the tables, and a couple of Watteaus on the wall. And Roxane, with her perpetual smile, sat in a severe, stiff armchair next to a dressing table decorated with frills and lace, saying to Zoë, "After your mother left I went around the house collecting all the things that had belonged to your parents. I have lived with them ever since."

"But why did you do it?" Zoë exclaimed in surprise. "They are so ill assorted!"

"So were your parents, yet they loved one another."

"Did my mother really love him?"

"Of course she did! She eloped with him, a man thirty years her senior! True, she couldn't have had him any other way, and he was pretty dashing—didn't look a day over thirty-five! But then, you see, the granddaughter of a peer of France was not supposed to marry a Bonapartist. A parvenu, they called him, and they never forgave her for it!" Roxane frowned and picked up a well-worn book from the dressing table. "I did not invite you here to talk about your parents," she said sharply, opening the book at a marked page. "I have something more important in mind."

For years Roxane in her loneliness had collected books on travel, reading them from cover to cover, living in them the life she was never destined to lead, and of all the distant lands she had thus discovered, the Caucasus stood out foremost, calling and beckoning to her. And here, she said to herself, this foolish niece of hers was to see it all with unseeing eyes, with no real perception. To Roxane this amounted to a sacrilege. "Niece," she said abruptly, "I will read you a passage about the Caucasus. Listen carefully and remember— to read is to behold!"

Zoë leaned back in her chair with a little sigh of resignation. She did not want to listen to the reading, she wanted to hear more about her parents, but gradually, as Roxane's rusty voice droned mo-

17

notonously in her ears, strange, exotic names began to capture her fancy. "Elbrus and Kazbek . . . Djing-Padishah, or Great Spirit of the Mountain." And before she knew it, she was all attention.

" 'Elbrus raises its two-humped peak far above all else for thousands of miles around,' " Roxane read, her long bony finger following the printed lines. " 'And Kazbek lords it over the rest of the snow-capped mountains, a thousand peaks in all. This range of granite, known as the Caucasus, springs forth on the shores of the Caspian and stretches in a straight line westward for almost a thousand miles, where it ends abruptly in the Black Sea, as if saying to the world, "Thus far and no farther!" And the sea, ever anxious to destroy, lashes the formidable rampart, dashing its spray against the immense stems of the blood-wooded taxus, while the red and almond-leaved willow sweep with their branches the foaming waves.' "

"It must be a magnificent sight," Zoë said in a low voice.

"It is," Roxane agreed. "And it is the cradle of man's inspiration and hope. Listen to this, Niece: 'Noah's ark is said to have grounded on Mount Elbrus before reaching its final resting place further south, on Mount Ararat in the lesser Caucasian range; and it was on Kazbek that Prometheus was chained to a rock for having stolen the fire from the gods and given it to mortals. In the land of Colchis, Jason and his Argonauts carried off the Golden Fleece, and Cadmus reaped a harvest of armed men from sowing serpents' teeth in furrows turned by the fire-breathing bulls of Vulcan. And finally, in the heart of the mountains existed, so say the traditions, the gallant state of the Amazons, until the heart of their otherwise unconquerable prophetess was taken by Thoulme, Chief of the Circassians.' "

"What a fantastic world," Zoë murmured, a faraway look creeping into her eyes. "Who wrote that?"

"An American traveler, but I don't remember his name—the front page is missing. Your aunt Emilie in a moment of rage laid her hands on this book. I have never invited her into this room since!"

"Oh, please!" Zoë cried. "Don't bring her into this picture! Not after Prometheus, Jason, Cadmus, and the heart of the Amazon!"

Roxane was looking at Zoë now with approval. "You are right, my niece. She has no place among these noble, unconquerable cliffs, for listen to this: 'The ancient Persians gave to the Caucasus the name of Seddi Iskander, or the barrier of Alexander, who here met his first check in his attempt to subjugate the world. Attila, Genghis Khan, and Tamerlane swept their victorious career along the base

18

of these ramparts of freedom; the Persian and the Turk have waged occasional unsuccessful wars with Caucasian tribes; and it is the Muscovite Empire alone which has ever succeeded in throwing the shadows of imminent subjugation over the landscape of these sunny vales.' "

"Aunt Roxane!" Zoë exclaimed suddenly. "I am not going into those mountains! No, no! God forbid! I'm going to Georgia, a Christian country. The mountains are in the hands of savage Moslem tribes!"

Recently Zoë had read a short article in the press about a man named Shamyl, the Imam, the holy leader of these tribes, who had been waging war on Russia and on Georgia for many years now. But Roxane insisted that Georgia was an integral part of the picture. The ancient land of Colchis, the land of the Golden Fleece, was supposed to have been in western Georgia, in a small principality now known as Mingrelia. "No," she said in a firm tone. "When you get there, Niece, wherever you turn, you will be surrounded by those ramparts of freedom!"

"Oh, you are wonderful!" Zoë cried, jumping to her feet and running toward Roxane. "Why didn't I know you before? Why didn't you reveal yourself to me sooner?"

"*Mea culpa*, Niece, *mea maxima culpa!*" Roxane clasped and unclasped her big bony hands. "You seemed so ordinary, so uninteresting a child for two outstanding people to have left behind. Your aims and interests in life appeared to me banal and dull, and I never bothered to find out. That was very selfish of me. I forgot it was up to old age to discover youth." Roxane rose to her full height, towering over Zoë. "I would like to atone for it now." She picked up a jewel case from a shelf and opened it. Inside, on a background of dark velvet, lay a pendant formed of two tiny miniatures surrounded by small diamonds and rubies; a gold chain with a ruby-and-diamond clasp was attached to it. "Your parents," she said as Zoë leaned forward to look at it, her eyes glued to the picture of her mother.

"I never knew what she was like," she said after a while. "She must have been very lovely!"

"She was. You have her eyes—brown with violet streaks in them."

"You do not hate her like Aunt Emilie does?"

Roxane shook her head. "She was the most enchanting creature I have ever known!" She took the pendant out of its case and held it against Zoë's black bodice. She scrutinized the two miniatures

19

for a moment and then clasped the chain around Zoë's neck. Zoë ran to the dressing table. She leaned forward to admire the pendant in the mirror while Roxane watched her, a sparkle of amusement in her dark eyes. "Always take what Emilie says with a grain of salt, Niece. Your father was a spendthrift. There was not much of his inheritance left for your mother to squander. This pendant was one of his follies. Poor Jean-Dé." Roxane came a step forward, frowning. "You inherited your extravagance from him. You might as well have his folly—I give you this pendant."

Zoë turned around swiftly. "Oh, you darling!" She threw her arms around her aunt's neck and kissed her several times in succession. Roxane stood leaning forward patiently, her arms dangling at her sides, but when Zoë let go she moved quickly out of reach. "Your mother," she said, "was the only woman who ever kissed me that way. I suppose I must tolerate it from you now!"

"You must, you must!" Zoë laughed. "And I promise I will never part with this. I will wear it tomorrow when I go to the Tollets'. Widows are not supposed to wear fancy jewelry, but I don't care a fig for that!" She looked up at Roxane, defiant, half expecting to be scolded. But Roxane only shrugged her shoulders.

"Wear it, of course. I don't suppose you will be masquerading as a widow much longer."

Zoë blushed. Roxane's insight into her state of mind disconcerted her. Confused, she murmured, "I was thinking, perhaps half mourning would be more suitable to my new position in Tiflis."

"Bright colors, Niece! Bright colors suit you best! And don't pretend you want my opinion on the matter. You will do it whatever I might say or think. I am beginning to see you have a little of your mother in you after all!"

Zoë tossed her head and laughed. "You know me too well, Auntie! Ah, but I wish I had known my mother!"

"She had greater depth and more heart than you. But as long as there is time, there is hope." Roxane drew Zoë's chin up and looked deep into her eyes. "Yes, there's hope, there's hope," she whispered almost inaudibly. "Someday you, too, may develop depth, but not until you have suffered much. Suffering alone will crack that silly shell of yours."

20

4   Madame Tollet, small, round, and middle-aged, had retained
a certain freshness and sweetness, not of spring flowers,
of course, but of fresh candy laid out in neat little boxes among
crisp paper frills and small paper doilies cut out to look like fine lace.
Monsieur Tollet himself could have passed for the stick of sugared
orange peel usually found near the edge of the box and placed
there for those who preferred a touch of tartness to their sweets.
There was, in all, an affinity between the Tollets and the confec-
tioneries for which they had become famous in Tiflis. Even their
speech was sprinkled with appropriate metaphors borrowed from
their trade, such as, *"C'est du praliné ça,"* when they wished to
stress the high social standing and fine moral qualities of an individual; and Monsieur Tollet in moments of great tenderness would
press his plump little wife to his breast, exclaiming, *"Ah, ma bombe
au chocolat!"*

The simple kindness and the artlessness of the Tollets had attracted Zoë the moment she had laid eyes on them. At first they had
spoken of Thérèse Michot's prospering business, of Zoë's future
plans, of their departure for Tiflis, which Monsieur Tollet had set for
the fifteenth of February. And now Zoë sat enthralled, not noticing
how the time slipped by, listening to Madame Tollet's gay prattle
that brought distant, exotic Tiflis into these furnished rooms only
a few minutes' walk from the Champs Elysées. Madame Tollet
spoke Russian fluently and had a smattering of Georgian, that difficult, guttural tongue of the Near East that sounded harsh in the
mouth of a stranger but flowed like a babbling brook when spoken
well by a native; she understood the people she was describing;
she told her stories well. Men of fierce dignity, clutching the gold
or silver handles of their daggers; women, graceful and indolent in
their white tulle veils and long flowing robes; *kintos,* the street
vendors, mischievous and shrewd; long-nosed, oily-eyed merchants
of the Near East—all seemed to crowd around Zoë, moving to and
fro, until Monsieur Tollet's high piping laugh suddenly broke the
spell. He slapped his lean thigh. "Look at Madame Duval, *Bonbon
chéri!* Look at her! She is fascinated. I can see it in her eyes!"

"I am," Zoë exclaimed, "but do my eyes betray me so?"

"Your eyes are a dead giveaway, madame!" And Monsieur Tollet
chuckled over Zoë's blushes.

"Stop teasing the child!" Madame Tollet scolded him. "She has
lovely eyes!"

"And who said she hadn't? Now that I come to think of it, they

21

are just like our cherries in brandy the Princess of Mingrelia likes so much!"

"The Princess of Mingrelia!" To Zoë the name evoked all the wonders Roxane had read about the day before. "Like a myth!" she cried. "I can just see her handing the Golden Fleece to Jason and his Argonauts!"

And again Monsieur Tollet laughed. "Only the Argonauts in her case are the Tiflis merchants." And Madame Tollet broke in, anxious to tell the story herself. "Ah, *mon Dieu*, that princess is lavish with her money, and when she comes to Tiflis it's a red-letter day for us shopkeepers. She is the regent of Mingrelia—regent for her small son—and such a great lady! Beautiful, too! She has a *faux air*, you know, of our Empress Eugénie, only many years older and perhaps . . . Oh, how should I put it? Perhaps a trifle too proud in her bearing. But she dresses to perfection, almost as well as the Empress!"

"What?" cried Zoë. "Doesn't she wear her national costume?"

"Oh no, no, no, no," Madame Tollet burst out, shocked where Zoë had been disappointed. "The Princess of Mingrelia, her sisters and her brother, Prince David Tchavchavadzé, are highly civilized, very refined people—they speak French as well as you and I!"

This was a different picture from the one outlined in Thérèse Michot's letter, but, "You will find all kinds in Tiflis," was Madame Tollet's final comment. Neither Zoë nor the Tollets had noticed how dark it had grown until a maid brought in two lamps under pink lamp shades that cast a soft glow on the heavy plush furniture. And Zoë suddenly realized it was time to leave. Madame Tollet laid a dimpled hand on her arm. "Don't go yet! Stay and have supper with us—we eat at six."

Zoë hesitated, and the Tollets, having taken a fancy to this spontaneous young creature with her bright, luminous eyes and her loud, contagious laugh, did their best to talk her into staying. They told her they were expecting another guest for supper, that she should stay to make up a foursome, the other guest being a certain Captain Novoselsky, a young Russian, whose acquaintance they had made on their way from Russia to Paris. He belonged to a prominent and wealthy family, *"du praliné jusqu'au bout des ongles, celui-là,"* to use Madame Tollet's own words. The dashing young captain, an officer in the Russian Imperial Guards, had come to Paris on a visit to his sister, the Countess Koramzine, whose husband was stationed at the Russian Embassy here. The countess herself, Madame Tollet explained, was a popular figure at court, having been a personal friend of Eugénie de Montijo before the latter's recent marriage to the Emperor Napoleon III. Zoë felt dazzled. She was not accustomed to hearing big names handed around in such a casual way. Even Monsieur Tollet's damper, when he said, "Oh, that dashing young captain would not be coming here if he hadn't a favor to ask of us," did not diminish the glamour of it all. She was aching to meet the young Russian nobleman, and only the thought of a possible scene with Emilie made her hesitate.

"You would be wise to stay," Monsieur Tollet was saying in the meantime. "I hear the Russians don't issue entry permits easily these days. Captain Novoselsky, with his high connections, could get your passport visaed in no time."

"My passport!" Zoë sat up, staring at them in dismay. "Why, I had not thought of a passport!"

The Tollets laughed. The idea of anyone going to Russia without a passport struck them as exceedingly funny. And Zoë stood up, a little confused and embarrassed. Madame Tollet was stretching out a retaining hand when a loud knock on the door sent Monsieur Tollet scuttling into the small vestibule. "Ah! That must be Captain Novoselsky!"

The two women stood in silence, listening to Monsieur Tollet welcoming his guest. Zoë, her heart beating a little faster, found herself straining an ear to catch the first sounds of the newcomer's voice. So far Monsieur Tollet alone was talking: "Allow me to help you off with your coat. Oh, it's wet! Is it raining?"

"Pouring!"

The answer came in a rich, vibrant voice, and the short low laugh that followed re-echoed pleasantly in Zoë's ears. "If he does not live up to that charming laugh," she said to herself, "I will leave at once."

The young man walked into the room, tall and broad-shouldered. In repose his dark face had a moody, brooding quality to it, but when he caught sight of Madame Tollet, it lit up with a bright, boyish smile. "Twenty-six or twenty-seven, not a day older," Zoë thought, watching him unobtrusively out of the corner of her eye. She saw him shoot a glance in her direction, one of those all-embracing "what have we here?" glances. He seemed surprised but not otherwise impressed, and she felt let down.

Novoselsky bent low to kiss Madame Tollet's hand, and she, flattered by this attention, kissed him, Russian-wise, on the forehead. Zoë noticed that his waist was slim and his hips narrow. His

23

brown suit, however, though impeccable in cut and style, did not seem to belong to him somehow. "When he walks, his suit walks along with him," she smiled to herself. But unwilling to find fault, she added, "He is a man accustomed to wearing a uniform. How splendid he must look in one!" And when Monsieur Tollet took him by the arm and led him up to her, she noticed his eyes. "As blue as cornflowers! And all fire and kisses!"

Abashed at her own thoughts, she turned quickly to Madame Tollet. "I really must be going . . ." Then hesitatingly, addressing no one in particular, "Is the weather really so bad?"

"Appalling!" Novoselsky replied. "But my carriage is at your disposal, madame." He spoke French fluently and well, ending his sentences abruptly, as though a little weary of words.

"Oh no, no," Madame Tollet cried. "We want Madame Duval to stay for supper!"

There was a touch of speculation in the look he gave Zoë. "The carriage can take you home at any time." It was a kind of acquiescence, a princely permission to stay. But he did not press her, and she felt disappointed.

"He should always smile. He looks sulky when he does not." Suddenly her mind was made up. "I will stay and make him smile for me alone!" And aloud she said to Madame Tollet: "If you really want me to stay, I will. I would so like to hear more about Tiflis and Georgia. And about Russia too." She did not look at Madame Tollet when she said this. Instead she smiled straight into the young Russian's eyes, and the look of astonishment in them was quickly replaced by a responsive twinkle. Zoë felt satisfied for the time being. She had scored.

"Wonderful! Wonderful!" cried Madame Tollet, placing an arm around Zoë's waist. "And now, my dear child, I am sure you will want to take off that sad little bonnet of yours. Come into the bedroom, I have a large mirror there." She picked up one of the lamps and turned to her husband. "Tell the maid we will be four for supper. And tell her to bring a few more lamps. It is so dark in here."

In the bedroom Madame Tollet placed the lamp on the dressing table and Zoë sat down, taking off her bonnet with its long crepe veil and shaking her head slightly in front of the large looking glass. Madame Tollet chatted away—"When you get to Tiflis, always remember, my dear child, most Georgian men are attractive, with much temperament and little money!"—but Zoë was listening with one ear. Her thoughts were in the next room, hovering around the handsome young stranger, going over every detail of his person —his dark wavy hair, his tufts of side whiskers; the moody face, the boyish smile, the blue eyes, and the strong but sensitive hands. They pleased her more than she cared to admit.

Madame Tollet was saying, "There was a Georgian once who paid court to Caroline, my daughter. He was a prince, an authentic one, but like so many of them, *pas un sous!*" And Zoë thought, "The young Russian is very distinguished-looking; he might be a prince too. There is a glitter about him—diamonds and deep blue sapphires!"

Madame Tollet, uninterrupted, went on with her story: "I took Caroline to the country. I invited the son of some well-to-do Swiss people we knew. And, my dear, there we stayed, the three of us, for two whole months, until she changed her mind and fell in love with the young Swiss. They are happily married now!"

"At least she had her Swiss," Zoë said to herself. "She had a man, lucky girl!"

Physically awakened but spiritually still dormant, Zoë at that period of her life was a problem to herself. For weeks now, in her idle loneliness, all the young men in her street attracted her, even the butcher boy with his round face and fleshy body and the milkman with his long nose and sensuous mouth. She wanted them to drop whatever they were doing and look at her, admire her, even follow her perhaps, without, however, touching her. But when she smiled at them in passing by, they would bow to her solemnly, respecting her deep mourning, with not a sparkle, not a gleam in the eye. She had begun by blaming it all on her black crepe. It made her look ugly, old, hideous, she kept repeating to herself over and over again, until the thought had finally taken root, growing into an obsession.

She leaned forward in her chair and looked at herself closely in the mirror. "He will admire me now without those horrid widow's weeds. He will smile at me!" She thought again of his deep blue eyes and his brooding face. They looked lonely, too, she thought, and closing her eyes, she let her fancy guide her hand through his thick black hair, her fingers toying with a stray lock. She shook her head. "Silly woman! Madwoman!" And aloud she said, "Why does Captain Novoselsky look so sad? Has he had a tragedy in his life?"

Madame Tollet, caught unawares in the middle of a sentence, remained with her mouth open, and Zoë, catching sight of her reflection in the mirror, swung around impulsively. "Oh! What are

25

you going to think of me! Here you have been entertaining me, and I have done nothing but weave silly fancies around a man I do not know!"

Madame Tollet smiled. "I am not surprised. He is attractive. But, my dear child, beware!"

"Beware of what? *'Grattez le russe et vous trouvez le tartare,'* as they say?"

"No. It's just that he might misunderstand your candid ways."

"Oh, I don't know what my ways are! I only know that to be a widow is horrible, lonely, disgusting! Like being locked up in a nunnery all of a sudden! Some women may have a calling for it. I do not!"

Madame Tollet patted her on the shoulder. "Of course not! You were not born for a nunnery. You are much too pretty, much too vivacious. But don't let Captain Novoselsky fall for your charms!"

"He hasn't even noticed me!"

"Oh yes, he has! Trust my experienced eye! I don't know him well, but I know his kind. Accustomed to easy conquests. Such men are dangerous. Mark my words!" She made a wise face. "They can be faithful only when a woman is unattainable. Out of sheer obstinacy, you know!"

"Easy conquests! How shocking!" Zoë threw up both her hands. "But to be unattainable—God forbid!"

Madame Tollet rippled over with laughter. "No, no, of course not! Who wants to be unattainable! But all the same, remember, you have great powers of attraction. So just be on your guard!"

She bent down and kissed Zoë on the cheek, and the two women smiled at one another in mutual approval and satisfaction.

5   Madame Tollet's warnings did not influence Zoë in the least. She was determined to captivate the young Russian. She did not stop to think of the consequences. All she cared for at the moment was to prove to herself that life had not passed her by, leaving her buried alive under a heap of black crepe. And of course there was her vanity. Novoselsky was good-looking, sophisticated, worldly, rich. It would be exciting to lead him on a bit and then snap her fingers in his face.

She entered the living room on wings, Madame Tollet's words ringing in her ears—"Remember, you have great powers of attraction!" But Novoselsky, engrossed in his conversation with Monsieur

26

Tollet, did not even notice her. He was saying, "You really think, then, that France and England will declare war on Russia?"

Zoë stopped dead, waiting anxiously for Monsieur Tollet's answer. The latter pursed his lips and stuck his head a little to one side. "Frankly," he said, "the situation worries me. And if war broke out while we were still in Paris, we couldn't return to Tiflis. My daughter and all my business interests are there."

"*Crème de pistache!*" Madame Tollet exclaimed indignantly, and Monsieur Tollet turned around and twitched his thick eyebrows, knowing this to be a sure sign of her displeasure. "What nonsense is this? There will be no war!"

Zoë was alarmed, not so much by the possibility of war—she knew nothing of war; France had been at peace during her lifetime —but at the prospect of having all her plans upset. She moved closer to Madame Tollet and touched her hand.

"Do not worry, my dear!" the other said. "Wars do not affect individuals of good standing. In Tiflis we live surrounded by wars— war with Turkey, war with Shamyl! Does anyone care? Certainly not! We are living in a civilized age!"

"But if it broke out while we were still here!"

Zoë wondered what would happen to her if she were forced to remain in Paris. Would she be forced to marry Monsieur Auguste Tresor? Mercy, no! Not with the Russian's slim waist and handsome thighs in front of her! She even shuddered a little and looked up at Novoselsky for encouragement. His eyes were laughing into hers. And when he spoke she thought she detected a note of mockery in his voice. "Do not be afraid, madame."

She tossed her head a trifle too disdainfully. "Afraid! I am not afraid. I am merely vexed!"

He raised his eyebrows, shrugged his shoulders, and turned deliberately from her to Monsieur Tollet. This did vex her. With another angry toss of her head she followed Madame Tollet across the room to the small dinner table the maid had laid out for four. Madame Tollet went out into the pantry, and Zoë roamed aimlessly around the table, rearranging a knife and a fork here and there or moving a glass a little to one side. But all the time she was listening intently to what the two men were saying.

Novoselsky's voice seemed to hit all four corners of the room at once. "My brother-in-law is in a position to know. He admits there is a diplomatic tension, but could anyone in his sound mind imagine England and France, those two proverbial enemies, coming to an

27

understanding? And don't forget the strong coalition on our side. First there is Prussia. Well, as you know yourself, the King of Prussia's sister is Empress of Russia. Then there is Austria-Hungary. What have we there? The Emperor Francis Joseph owes his throne to the Russian Emperor. If Emperor Nicholas had not sent his armies into Hungary to crush the rebellion of 1849, where would Francis Joseph be today, I ask you!"

Monsieur Tollet's high voice rose and sank in an even cadence. "Does that constitute in your opinion a good reason for a monarch to remain loyal and grateful?"

Novoselsky laughed. "I see you are a bit of a cynic, monsieur!"

"Oh, not at all! It is just that fear is a great driving force. England fears Russia's possible expansion in the East and will do everything in her power to prevent it. As for France . . ." Here he twitched his eyebrows again and looked up slyly at Novoselsky. "Ah! In France we have a few personal reasons. Should a war be successful, it would solidify the new Bonaparte throne. And don't forget, when Charles Louis Napoleon Bonaparte became Napoleon III, Emperor Nicholas addressed him officially as 'My Friend' instead of 'My Brother.' That hurt, you know. To the Emperor Napoleon it was a slap in the face. It sounded like, 'Hello, you parvenu'!"

"Well, all I can say is this," Novoselsky burst out, his voice ringing with suppressed indignation. Zoë, glancing at the back of his neck and his well-rounded head, was struck by the youthfulness of their appearance. They seemed unprotected, vulnerable, disclosing as it were a secret which his face and eyes concealed so well. "He can be very helpless," she thought. And all desire to snap her fingers in his face vanished at the sight of that boyish nape. "If he looks at me now," she said to herself half in jest but hoping secretly that her wish would come true, "if he looks at me now, this very minute, then he will be mine!" He did look around, flashing a smile. It left her breathless. Her lips parted, her eyes melted into a velvety softness, and she leaned her elbows on the back of a chair, reveling in the sound of his rich, vibrant voice.

"Well, all I can say is this! Emperor Nicholas is seeking to protect some of the Christian population of Turkey. Surely under such circumstances Queen Victoria and Emperor Napoleon would not side with the Turks! No, Monsieur Tollet! This is just another international bluff!"

Madame Tollet had returned from the pantry. She was standing beside Zoë now, shaking her head at the two men with disapproval.

28

A disheveled maid in a shabby dress and a patched-up apron brought a steaming earthenware pot into the room, placed it on a sideboard with a good deal of clatter, and scurried back into the pantry, throwing a careless *"Madame est servie"* over her shoulder. And Madame Tollet rapped a knife on a plate. "Messieurs, enough of this foolish talk about war! Supper is served."

Zoë sat opposite Novoselsky at the narrow table. She ate in silence the *coq au vin* Monsieur Tollet had served her, listening to Novoselsky and studying his face. As Monsieur Tollet had predicted, he had come to ask a favor. His sister, he explained, had some valuable lace she wished to send to their cousins in Tiflis through safe hands, and he hoped Madame Tollet would consent to take it. His face was serious now, and Zoë, looking at it, realized that, while his smile was endearing, it was the brooding quality around the corners of his mouth that stirred up deeper emotions in her. "Many women must have raved about him," she thought. "I wonder whom he loves! Whom he is fond of?"

She heard him say, "I am deeply devoted to my two cousins in Tiflis—Princess Anna Tchavchavadzé and Princess Varvara Orbeliani. They are the ones I want you to take the lace to."

"Two of our best customers!" Monsieur Tollet exclaimed. "Princess Orbeliani—*truffes au chocolat;* Princess Tchavchavadzé—*marrons glacés!*" He slapped his thigh and let out a squeaky laugh.

"Their favorite sweets," Madame Tollet hurried to explain.

Novoselsky seemed genuinely amused. "Truffes au chocolat! Marrons glacés," he repeated. "Why, they suit their dispositions perfectly!"

"He has strong family ties," Zoë thought. "He is fond of his cousins, and his cousins have wonderfully exotic names!" And aloud, looking straight into his eyes, she tried to pronounce the two difficult names that had fascinated her: "Or-be-lia-ni and Tcha-tcha . . . Or-be-lia-ni and Tcha-tcha . . ."

A mocking smile hovered around Novoselsky's lips, but his eyes were soft and tender. "Tchaf-tchaf," he corrected her, "and then Adzé."

"Tchaf-tchaf-and-then-adzé," she repeated mechanically.

"In this case 'and then' is *de trop!*" And his eyes added, *"And then* the Tollets are de trop, too, aren't they? *And then* we shall meet again, and again, and again, won't we?"

Zoë blushed. "How silly of me! But I can pronounce it! Just wait and see! Tchaf-tchaf-adzé." And to Madame Tollet, "Isn't that the name you mentioned when you spoke of the Princess of Mingrelia?"

"Why, yes! What a memory! Prince David Tchavchavadzé is this lady's husband." And to impress Zoë she added: "The two ladies we are speaking of are sisters, the granddaughters of the last reigning King of Georgia!"

"Born and bred in Moscow, though," Novoselsky put in, "where their mother comes from. Their mother is a Russian. The Tsarevna Anastasia, as she is called, is my mother's first cousin. That's how we happen to be related. Besides, we were childhood friends."

"Don't tell me," Zoë exclaimed, disappointment depicted all over her face, "that these ladies do not wear the Georgian national costume either!"

They shook their heads at her and laughed. And she joined in the general laughter, leaning a little forward, making it clear to Novoselsky she was laughing with him alone. He raised his glass to her. His eyes above the glass of red wine were hot and caressing, full of secret queries and promises which she mistook for candid admiration. The evening was becoming enchanting, thrilling. A giddy, happy mood took hold of her. She raised her own glass. And when she put it down again, she sighed with contentment.

"I want to learn to speak Russian," she said. "Monsieur Tollet! Madame Tollet! Won't you please teach me during our voyage? You said we would be almost two months on the way!" And while the Tollets promised her they would, she glanced at Novoselsky out of the corner of her eye, daring him to offer his services.

He did not miss the opportunity. "In the meantime," he said, "would you allow me to give you a few lessons here in Paris? And later, in Tiflis—I go to Tiflis sometimes, you know—we will continue them."

"Oh, in Tiflis you won't even want to know me," she replied in a bantering tone. "There I will be nothing but a modest little dressmaker!"

"Wonderful! A modern Eve! Eve, after all, was the first dressmaker, wasn't she! And I will be a modern Adam admiring all your creations!"

"As for me," Monsieur Tollet piped out, having emptied his fourth glass of wine, "I would much rather be the old serpent. He wound himself around Eve long before she knew what it was all about, the sly old devil!"

"Pistache!" cried Madame Tollet, scandalized.

Monsieur Tollet's head shrank into his shoulders. He twitched his eyebrows guiltily, glancing in turn at his wife and at Zoë. But Madame Tollet, refusing to be placated, shook a reprimanding finger at him.

Zoë and Novoselsky exchanged an intimate smile. He leaned forward, his elbows on the table, his eyes mischievous and merry. "Dear pupil, I am about to give you your first lesson!"

"Yes, *Monsieur le Professeur!*" She, too, leaned forward, sitting on the edge of her chair. Their faces were less than a foot apart. Their eyes met and mingled, hers searching for devotion, his promising an early intimate seclusion. The Tollets faded momentarily out of the picture.

"Your first difficulty," he said, "will be with Russian names and nicknames. I will therefore begin by teaching you mine. My name is Alexander, or Alexandr, as we pronounce it in Russian, but my intimates call me Sasha."

Sasha! She repeated it to herself several times, turning it over on the tip of her tongue. It sounded like a lover's happy sigh.

He continued: "Strangers call me neither Alexandr nor Sasha, they call me Alexandr Dimitrievitch because my father's name was Dimitri. Sounds quite different, doesn't it? But remember, whether Alexandr Dimitrievitch or Sasha, it's always me!"

"And what would I be called? I have three first names—Zoë-Jeanne-Désirée. My aunts call me Zoë-Jeanne."

Monsieur Tollet's chuckle came as a sharp, tingling impact, so completely had they forgotten about his presence. Quickly they settled back in their chairs with as much decorum as they could muster.

"Zoë-Jeanne!" Monsieur Tollet exclaimed. "Why, people will love that in Tiflis. Won't they, Bonbon chéri?" He ignored his wife's warning frowns. "It sounds like Zoë-*djan*. In Georgian 'djan' is an endearment. Like saying—Zoë darling!"

"Zoë darling! Zoë-djan!" Sasha repeated in a low voice. "Delightful!"

Zoë did not trust herself to look at him. "My father's names were Jean-Désiré. So what would I be called in Russian?" she asked the Tollets, but it was Sasha who answered her question. He raised his hand, pondering over the matter as though it were of primary importance. Finally he said, "Désiré won't do. It does not exist in Russian. Jean is Ivan. As for your own three names, I prefer Zoë—Zoia in Russian. We will make it Zoia Ivanovna, if you don't mind."

31

Zoë repeated her new name slowly, "Zoia I-va-no-vna! Yes, I like that!"

"Very well then! From now on you will be Zoia Ivanovna to me. Except when I am thinking of you." And turning to Monsieur Tollet, "Would you blame me if I thought of her as Zoë-djan?"

Zoë felt swept away completely. It never occurred to her that he was playing a very ordinary, banal game. True romance had come into her life at last. Love at first sight, to be followed by a beautiful, formal courtship. And it was characteristic of her to have forgotten altogether how deliberately she had set out to captivate this man.

From here on Sasha took over. He planned things for them to do in the next few days—sight-seeing, rides in the country—in which the Tollets were but vaguely included. His eyes were innocent now, his smile disarming. He talked, he laughed, he charmed them all, finally obtaining the permission of the Tollets to give a farewell party for them in their apartment, just for the four of them again, ten days from now. "I will have a special dinner prepared, and my man Poushka will serve it!"

Zoë laughed. "What a funny name—Poushka!"

"Ah, Poushka is quite a character! He has been with me all my life. He came to us as part of my mother's dowry."

"A serf!"

"He was until lately. At my request my mother gave him his freedom as a present for his fiftieth birthday. He is very useful around here; he can even speak a little French! A funny kind of French he picked up during his trips abroad with our family. So you see, we will have Poushka serve us, and there will be champagne, and I will bring a guitar so that we can sing after supper! Do you sing, Zoia Ivanovna?"

A wistful look crept into Zoë's eyes. "Alas, no! I wish I could! To possess a beautiful voice must be so inspiring!"

"Inspiring!" Sasha looked puzzled. "No! Just pleasant." He laughed.

They had all risen from the table. Monsieur Tollet hurried out into the pantry to tell the maid she could go. Madame Tollet excused herself and went into the bedroom. Zoë and Sasha were left alone. She moved toward the bedroom door but stopped in the middle of the room. He was standing close behind her, so tall that she knew he would be looking down at the top of her head. Her heart was pounding. Now was the moment for the first romantic declaration. He would tell her how adorable she looked, how much he longed to kiss

32

the tips of her fingers and gaze into her eyes. He was bending over her. She could feel his breath close to her ear, and she heard his voice, low and caressing: "I know a secluded little spot where we can have a private room and a bottle of champagne. My carriage will take us there in no time!"

A blow, a punch in the back could not have stunned her more. The blood rushed to her face and tears filled her eyes. Easy conquests! Easy conquests! The words burned through her brain. And with a smothered gasp she tore herself from her place and ran into the bedroom.

Her hands trembled as she picked up her bonnet; and Madame Tollet, alarmed, came hurrying to her side. "What happened, dear child? What is it?"

Zoë opened her mouth and shut it. Her pride would not let her tell Madame Tollet nor ask for advice and help. She must handle this alone. Hurriedly she put on her cloak and bonnet, anger replacing her first anguish. She would put him in his place, out, out of her life for good. But when she returned to the living room, she found it harder to do than she had expected. Sasha was standing in his overcoat, cool, unruffled, handsome, holding his brown top hat in his hand. He was saying good night to Monsieur Tollet and telling him he could arrange to have Zoë's passport visaed. And Zoë, trying to appear calm and composed, took leave of her hosts.

Sasha caught up with her in the small vestibule. She stopped, rigid, the top of her bonnet barely reaching above his shoulder. And she heard the mocking note in his voice as he said, "My carriage is at your disposal, Zoia Ivanovna."

She tossed her head angrily. "In that case, monsieur, you will have to walk!"

"Oh, I can always reach my destination!" And in a low whisper, offering her an arm, "You are adorable when you toss your head. Like a little pony asking to be patted!"

Speechless, she tossed her head again without knowing it and swept out of the room, ignoring his arm.

Madame Tollet sighed and shook her head, while Monsieur Tollet slipped his arm around his wife's waist. "Come, give your old caramel a kiss!"

"That man is after little Zoë-djan!"

"Of course he is, and she gave him plenty of encouragement too. Oh, leave them alone. They will only be young once." And his hand pressed her side lovingly.

33

Madame Tollet smiled up at him, laying a plump finger on his chin. "You will never grow old, Marzipan! Still, I can't help it! I am worried about that child! She flirts, but she does not know!"

"Well, I have no cause to worry!" Monsieur Tollet replied with a chuckle. "That young Lovelace will never know how wonderful *you* are!" And he gave his fat little wife a tender squeeze.

6   The carriage lanterns, placed on a level with the coach box, shed a few rays into the night, and cold sharp raindrops flashed by them like tumbling needles. Seated inside the carriage, Zoë had but one thought in mind—to get rid of Sasha as quickly as possible. Coming down the stairs, he had held her by the elbow, making her conscious of the pressure of his fingers; and when she had hastened her step, he had had the effrontery to laugh and say, "Don't be in such a haste, my dear. A little decorum is always necessary." She had stopped then and had looked him straight in the eye. "I want you to understand, monsieur, I am going home!" He had bowed stiffly and had helped her into the carriage. And now, as he leaned through the open door, throwing a fur-lined robe over her knees, she stretched her hand out and he took it in both of his. "Good night, Monsieur Novoselsky!" But seeing that he was about to say something, she added impatiently, "Upon my word, monsieur, all I want now is to go home!" She leaned forward and called out her address to the coachman.

Sasha smiled, or at least she thought he did. He said he would tell the coachman to whip up the horses, and when he stepped out into the street she quickly closed the door. Through the patter of the rain on the roof she heard the coachman crack his whip, and a moment later the carriage was on its way. But she hardly had time to settle back in her seat, complimenting herself on the clever way in which she had handled the situation, when the opposite door flew open and Sasha jumped in. Slamming the door, he almost fell into the seat beside her. She heard her new name whispered into her ear—"Zoë-djan!"—and her gasp left her breathless.

She shot forward in her seat. "No, never, never, never! Madame Duval! Madame Duval! Always Madame Duval!" In her panic she found herself repeating the same words over and over again, and she clutched her hands tightly together inside her little muff in an effort to regain her composure. It was very dark in the carriage; only the lights of occasional street lamps wandered leisurely through it. And

34

Zoë sat stiffly on the edge of the seat, staring at the blank wall in front of her. When finally she trusted herself to speak, she said without turning her head, "This may be customary in St. Petersburg, but it is not done in Paris!"

"What isn't done in Paris?" The question came from somewhere out of the darkness behind her.

"Jumping into carriages and attacking young ladies!"

She heard him laugh. "But I have not attacked you yet! And, Zoë-djan, to prevent any further misunderstandings on the subject, I might as well tell you—in St. Petersburg, as in Paris, it isn't customary for a young man to jump into a lady's carriage, nor is it considered proper for a young and unattached woman to travel alone with a man, especially at night. So now go ahead, scold me, lecture me! Get it off your chest! I will listen!"

He leaned back, waiting for her reproaches, knowing from past experience that women felt better, more pliant, having once proven to themselves that they were not too willing. For Sasha was still full of confidence that she would change her mind and let him take her to the small hotel he knew. Her eyes, he said to himself, had promised him that much earlier in the evening. But Zoë remained silent. Perched on the edge of the seat and bounced a little now and then by the movements of the carriage, she felt at a loss what to say or what to do.

The light of a street lamp fell on her head and shoulders, and Sasha caught a glimpse of her neck. It looked so small and white and tender against the black crepe of her veil. Hot flames shot through him. "Darling little neck," he whispered, "darling little neck!" He was drawing her to himself now, his lips searching for the sweet softness; but with sudden strength, surprising in so small a woman, she freed herself from his grasp and pushed him away. Her arm shot out, and before he knew it her muff had hit him squarely in the face. His hat fell to the floor. His hand flew up to his cheek, and he stared at her, more puzzled than angry. "What is it you want? What kind of new coquetry is this?"

She turned on him furiously. "How dare you call me a coquette! I am nothing of the sort!"

"And what would you call your behavior earlier this evening, may I ask!"

"You are behaving like a cad, sir, reminding a lady of—of what she prefers to forget!"

"That," he said sardonically, "amounts to a confession."

35

Suddenly Zoë felt spent. She knew she was to blame for it all and she leaned limply against the side of the carriage, staring at the dull rain-spattered windowpane. "You could never understand my behavior," she said with a sigh. "You are not a young widow. If you were, you would know what all this black crepe meant to a woman!"

"Oh, I see. You felt stale. You needed a little practice, and you chose me as your subject!"

She straightened herself and looked in his direction. "Yes, if you must have the truth—yes! That is what I did. That is exactly how I felt. At first."

"And now?"

He leaned forward, his curiosity aroused by her unexpected candor. She looked the other way. "Now I am sorry I created a wrong impression. No man has ever made love to me except my husband."

"Judging by the garlands and lovers' knots on your dress and the frivolous pendant around your neck, you are not a heartbroken widow."

"You are impertinent, sir, but you are right!"

Her answer delighted him. He chuckled and edged a little closer. "Have you ever thought of looking for happiness outside of marriage?"

"What! In my present unattached condition? Why, I'd sooner die!"

Sasha slapped his knee and threw his head back. His loud peal of laughter hit the upholstered sides of the carriage and fell back flattened and muffled. "In other words, find me a husband first and then come knocking at my door!"

Zoë sat bolt upright. "Oh, how shocking! That is not what I meant at all!" She opened her mouth to say more and shut it again, struck by a sudden thought: "You would throw the door wide open if you were married to Auguste Tresor and Sasha came a-knocking!" Annoyed at herself, she stamped her foot. "Stop laughing at me!"

Sasha found it difficult to analyze his feelings. Where he had expected to find a pleasant little mistress he had discovered a woman, or a child—he did not quite know which—whose frankness and naïveté he found intriguing, refreshing, amusing. He was seized with a momentary longing to protect her. But this last feeling he did his best to crush. To make a fool of oneself over a woman was, in his opinion, the great, the unforgivable blunder. And aloud he said, "Perhaps I am laughing at myself, Zoë-djan."

"Oh no, you are not!" She stumbled a little over her words. "I want to take all I can from life, but I am afraid to do it. And you have guessed it, and you are making fun of me, and you are treating me as if—as if I were an easy conquest! And—and stop calling me Zoë-djan!"

"No, Zoë-djan. I think you are a child who should not be allowed to run unprotected all over the face of the earth."

He had not intended to say this. He sat back now, surprised at himself, watching her in his embarrassment. A street light flashed across her face. It looked sullen and almost plain. The eyes seemed enormous and the mouth had grown too large. Yet somehow he liked it better that way—there was more character, more personality to it.

Zoë in the meantime had been strangely moved by his last words. She dared not look at him. And when she spoke again there was a slight catch to her voice. "I am not a child. I was very brazen tonight when I made you suggest Russian lessons."

"You were! And so was I when I jumped into the carriage! That makes us even." She heard his low laugh again. "You know what I like about you? You don't flicker your eyelashes when you try to fascinate a man!"

"They are too short to be flickered."

"Yes, I noticed that. I noticed a few more things too." The mocking note was in his voice again. "When you look sullen, your mouth grows very large. Your face becomes all eyes and mouth. And your neck is so thin it makes me think of a chicken."

"How dare you!" she cried. "You with your big sulky mouth, and your hair that looks like twisted wire, and your infantile nape!"

The light of a street lamp traveled through the carriage and they saw each other's faces plainly. They looked at one another, a merry, tingling sensation rising up in their throats. And suddenly they burst out laughing. The snows melted and little tufts of grass sprouted from the face of the earth. Little tufts of well-rooted feeling.

"Zoë-djan," he said at last, and this time she did not protest. "Give me your hand to show that we are friends." He tugged at her wrist, finally extracting her hand out of the muff. He raised it to his lips, and when he dropped it again the carriage had come to a full stop.

It was no longer raining. The street lamp on the corner shed a dim light on a vast expanse of mud in which Sasha had to stand to help Zoë out. She paused on the carriage step, looking down hesitantly. Suddenly he gathered her up in his arms and carried her to the front door. "Careful!" she cried, trying to hold her hooped skirt down with her hand, but he held her crushed against his shoulder. He set her down roughly on the ground. Her skirt billowed up, but he advanced on it fiercely, almost savagely, crushing it, pinning her arms back against the door. And swiftly he kissed her three times around the mouth without touching her lips. "There! That will teach you to play with fire, you little madcap!"

Zoë gasped. "You unspeakable brute!" she cried. "I never want to see you again!"

He was beside the carriage door now. "I will send Poushka in the morning to find out how you are."

"No!"

"And at five I will come myself."

"No! No! No!" She stamped her foot. He waved to her, and she heard him laugh as he jumped into the carriage, slamming the door behind him.

Zoë watched the receding carriage, a soft warm happy glow melting her anger away. "Zoë-djan, you are a child who should not be allowed to run unprotected all over the face of the earth!" She smiled and turned slowly to the door, giving the brass handle of the doorbell a sharp tug.

7   A feeble tinkle resounded inside the house, and a minute later a heavy footstep was heard in the hall. The door flew open, and Emilie's belligerent bust appeared silhouetted against the light. She frowned at Zoë and moved back to let her pass.

Zoë braced herself for a scene, but it did not come. Her decision to go to Tiflis had had its effect on Emilie; she was beginning to respect her niece. "An invasion of the Caucasus!" she had exclaimed, looking with pride at her sisters after Zoë had left the room. "That chit of a girl might yet add a leaf to our laurel wreath!" And now she was actually smiling. "We have company tonight," she explained as Zoë, surprised, listened to the sound of voices coming from the parlor. "Monsieur Auguste Tresor!" With an impatient shrug Zoë turned toward the stairs. "Don't be so uppity, my girl! Monsieur Tresor is either a great gentleman or a great fool. Perhaps both. When we gave him your answer this evening I thought he would cry. But a moment later he offered to help you get a passport."

"A passport!"

In a flash Zoë was at the parlor door. But the look on Emilie's face reminded her of the rules of precedence in the household, and she opened the door, stepping aside to let her aunt sail in.

Monsieur Tresor, hardly more than five feet tall, came hurrying up to Zoë on tiptoe, which was the way he always walked in an effort to appear a little taller. A blissful smile spread over his bald and shiny countenance, and he clung to Zoë's hand, not daring to kiss it. "Ah, dear Madame Duval! How happy you have made me this evening by not refusing altogether—I mean by saying that per- haps—— Oh no, that's not at all what I want to say! What I mean is—— If I had known sooner of your brave, your glorious decision, I would have offered you my humble services long ago!"

Zoë saw fifty years of innocence reflected in Monsieur Tresor's little round eyes and, touched, she gave him her best in the way of a smile. Small beads of perspiration stood out on his smooth and un- wrinkled brow. "Ah, my dear and exquisite young lady! You over- whelm me! Do not refuse me the pleasure of going with you—I mean, going on your behalf—— No, that's not at all what I mean. What I want to say is—I would like to help you with your passport!" He paused for a moment to dab his forehead with his handkerchief. "One of my best friends—that is, a man who has been an intimate friend—— In fact——"

Roxane stood up and, crossing the room, took Monsieur Tresor firmly by the arm. "Do not work yourself up so, it is bad for your health," she said.

"Ah, dear and kind Mademoiselle Roxane! You must not worry about me!"

Roxane showed such possessiveness as she led him toward the settee and settled down on it herself that for a moment Zoë thought she might dandle him on her knee. But instead Roxane made him sit down beside her. "You have a brother-in-law in the government circles, isn't that it?"

"That's it! That's it! And he wields a great deal of power—I mean influence——" He cut his sentence short, looking at Zoë, who was hurrying across the room toward him. She sat down on his left, thanking him for his kind offer to help. "Ah!" he cried. "Now I have an aunt on my right and a niece on my left. I could almost make a wish!"

"Don't," Roxane said gruffly. "You would make the wrong one and it would be wasted."

Monsieur Tresor bowed his head obediently and then gave a short outline of what he called his "plans of action." He would speak to his brother-in-law about Zoë's passport, and later he hoped to have the honor and privilege of escorting her to his brother-in-law's office, if her presence there were found necessary. "But!" And here he folded his hands together. "Have you seriously considered the matter, madame? The Caucasus! Oh, it sounds so far away and so wild! Aren't you afraid?"

"I will have you know, monsieur," Emilie cut in, "fear is not one of our family possessions!"

"We belong to General Chabout!" cried Clotilde.

"Ah! Mademoiselle Emilie! Mademoiselle Clotilde! I know, I know!"

But Clotilde interrupted him. "Are you aware, monsieur, that our great Emperor pinched the general's ear not once, not twice, but on sixteen different occasions?"

"Let us not exaggerate!" Emilie reprimanded her. "He pinched it six times! And that," she added, turning to Monsieur Tresor, "is more than the average Frenchman can boast of!"

In his confusion Monsieur Tresor began to stammer again. He assured them over and over of his esteem and admiration for General Chabout's glory and for his bravery, as he saw it reflected in the members of his family, until Emilie relaxed and Clotilde began to coo with pleasure. "And yet," he continued, "the Caucasus seems such a formidable place for so lovely and delicate a person as Madame Duval. Why, I have been told there are dangerous, fierce brigands there, known locally as 'shamyls'!"

"You have been misinformed, Monsieur Tresor," said Roxane. "There is but one Shamyl, and he is a war lord, a religious leader of the Moslem tribes that inhabit the heart of the Caucasian mountains."

"But aren't you worried, Mademoiselle Roxane? This Shamyl and his hordes might become a living threat to your charming niece!"

"I am not worried," Roxane said in hollow tones. "Wherever she will be, those mountains will be near her, with their ancient legends, their fierce independence, and their faith. They have brought inspiration to others, and to her they might bring a revelation, for the Spirit of the Almighty dwells unimpaired in mountain fastnesses, and the truth that escapes us can often be found among lesser tribes!"

Roxane sat there, looking like a grotesque prophetess, her long index finger raised, her perpetual smile curled around the base of her thick, upturned nose; but her dark eyes had grown resplendent with inner fires. Monsieur Tresor lowered his head as though listening to

40

a holy sermon, Clotilde clutched her heart and emitted a birdlike cry, while Emilie stared at her youngest sister in perplexity, a furrow drawing her thick eyebrows together. And as Zoë gazed into Roxane's strange, opalescent eyes she felt an emotion stirring within her, obscure as yet and intangible, but which, she sensed it from afar, lay dormant in her, waiting for the spark that ignites.

8   Zoë spent a restless night. Strange half-conscious dreams, nebulous and yet disturbing, had hung over her until the wee hours of the morning, and it was not until ten o'clock that she found herself fully dressed. She was wondering, as she put a few finishing touches to her plain black dress with its little white collar and cuffs, if Sasha had really meant what he had said about sending Poushka and coming himself to call, when she heard the tinkle of the front doorbell. She opened the door and stuck her head out, listening intently. "If that is Poushka, then Sasha will be my husband!" The thought made her smile, but it was forgotten a moment later when a wild shriek resounded through the house.

Rushing down the stairs, Zoë caught sight of Marguerite, the little maid of all work, dashing into the kitchen with a scared face, while in the front hall Roxane alone faced the street door that had been left wide open. On the bottom step Zoë stopped, stunned by what she saw. A man stood on the threshold, truly fantastic in appearance as well as in size, holding a large cardboard box in his hands. His dark green coat reached to the ground, making him seem even taller than his six foot six, and the short cape on his coat that should have reached halfway to his elbows barely covered his huge shoulders, sticking out half an inch on both sides, as if the tailor, having run out of cloth, had left it that way in despair. The small old-fashioned three-cornered hat he was wearing looked odd perched above a big bushy beard and a pair of thick eyebrows that at the moment were closely knit over a small round nose, and his blue eyes squinted at Roxane with suspicion. "Why do you smile?" he said at length in broken French. "I am not funny."

"Who are you?" Roxane exclaimed, regaining her powers of speech.

"Klementi Poushka! Russian! Humble servant to the highly well-born Captain Novoselsky!"

"You are a giant, my man!"

Poushka assumed a modest air. "No, no! In Russia I very, very

41

small!" And he spread his right hand out on a level with his knee to show how small he was.

Zoë laughed. She descended the last step and joined Roxane. Poushka was looking at her with undisguised admiration. "Little lady, she Zoia Ivanovna?" he asked, and beamed in response to Zoë's nod. He took a few steps forward and handed Zoë the box with a low bow. "Flowers! With the compliments of the highly well-born Alexandr Dimitrievitch Novoselsky!"

Giving Zoë no time to answer, he whipped out of his coat pocket a large and rather soiled handkerchief, the four corners of which had been tied into knots, with an additional knot in the center. "This is the first knot," he said, brandishing one of them. "He asks—how you feel this morning?"

"Oh, very well, thank you."

"So . . ." Poushka untied the knot and held up a second one. "This . . ." He looked at it thoughtfully, scratching the back of his head. "No, not this one!" He held up a third knot. "This is second knot. He asks—do you need help with passport?"

"No, not right away, thank you."

"So . . . So . . ." He undid the second knot and hesitated among the remaining three. "Hah!" he cried at last, holding up one of them. "This is he, the rascal! He asks—do you need carriage this afternoon?"

"Oh no, thank you——"

"Oh yes, please!" came unexpectedly from Roxane, and to Zoë she added: "You should have one to carry your diamonds around from jeweler to jeweler. After all, you are not going to accept the first price offered!"

Poushka smiled approvingly at Roxane. "What hour you need carriage?"

"Oh, I suppose around two," Zoë muttered, embarrassed.

"So . . ."

The third knot proved to be stubborn, and while Poushka labored over it, trying to get it undone, Emilie's angry voice reached them from the kitchen. "And what did this villain do to you, Marguerite?"

Zoë looked around and saw her two other aunts coming toward them, followed by the maid. "He scowled at me, he made a ferocious face," Marguerite whimpered, casting a furtive glance at Poushka. "He stamped his foot and made a dreadful sound in his throat!"

Emilie turned on Poushka angrily. "Explain yourself, you, whoever you may be! What did you do to frighten this poor girl when she opened the door?"

Poushka shrugged. "Poor girl very dark here!" He tapped his forehead with his finger. "Also very bad manners—stare at me like little wolf! So! I stamp my foot and say 'Brrrysss!' In Russian it means 'Away!'" Poushka feigned a lunge in Marguerite's direction that sent her scuttling back into the kitchen with a frightened cry while he turned to Roxane. "More great ladies!" He jerked his head in the direction of Emilie and Clotilde. "But you, madame, most greatest!"

Emilie demanded to know what it was all about, and Clotilde gazed up at Poushka, mumbling to herself, "So big—it's formidable! So big it's formidable!" And when Zoë had explained, Poushka drew himself up to his full height. "I Klementi Poushka! Russian! And you who, madame?"

"This lady is my aunt," Zoë said severely, "and so is this one, and so is that one. And you should take your hat off when you speak to ladies!" She frowned and pointed her finger at the absurd little three-cornered hat he was wearing.

Poushka grew very red in the face. He tore the hat off and bowed low to Zoë. "Excuse my peasant darkness, Zoia Ivanovna!" And then, drawing himself up once again, he held up the fourth knot. "This knot says—the highly well-born Captain Novoselsky come here at five!" He dangled the handkerchief by the remaining knot. "This one not for you, Zoia Ivanovna! This one for the washerwoman!" And with that he bowed and ran out of the house.

Flushed with excitement, Zoë carried the box into the pantry. Marguerite hovered around her, exclaiming under her breath, and when Zoë had opened the box, she squealed with joy at the wealth of flowers it contained. Zoë looked at them spellbound. She had never dreamed that a man could send so many flowers to one woman. Had she really captivated him? She picked up a few camellias and pressed them to her cheek. To her they breathed romance. "These," she said to Marguerite, "will go into my room." They busied themselves arranging the other flowers in vases. Several vases went into the parlor, two were sent up to Emilie's and Clotilde's bedroom, another to Roxane's room, and one vase was placed on the landing outside Zoë's door. All morning Zoë walked on air. Wherever she went she was reminded of Sasha. And at two o'clock she and Roxane rode off in Sasha's carriage, carrying Zoë's jewel box with them.

They returned home at a quarter to five, somewhat exhausted by the shrewd bargaining Roxane had put up at every jeweler's store they had visited, and Zoë ran up to her room to collect herself before the approaching meeting with Sasha. Something Emilie had said about only women of the demimonde receiving so many flowers from their admirers had upset Zoë, arousing her suspicions. Perhaps Sasha was still thinking of the private room and the bottle of champagne and this was just another way of dazzling and inveigling her. Somehow she could not bring herself to believe it, but she stiffened, remembering how rudely he had treated her at the front door. "At my own front door, too!" she exclaimed indignantly, addressing her reflection in the cheval glass. "He should be put in his place for that! Perhaps an air of utter indifference on my part would do the trick." She made a few faces and struck a few poses of utter indifference in front of the cheval glass, but they only made her laugh. She frowned. That would never do. " 'Zoë-djan, you are a child who should not be allowed to run unprotected all over the face of the earth.' Oh, that was sweet of him! He would never have said it if his intentions were not honorable!" And leaning against her desk, Zoë was lost in a pleasant reverie. A loud knock on the door brought her back to earth. She heard Marguerite's excited voice announcing that the Russian captain was waiting in the parlor. Zoë got all flustered. "What am I to say? How am I to act? Oh, I will be distant! Cold, distant, and indifferent! At least at first. And I will wear a couple of his camellias." The idea did not strike her as inconsistent. She pinned the camellias to her dress and ran to the door. But there she stopped. She had read somewhere that sophisticated, worldly women always made their lovers wait. And a friend had once told her, "A woman who appears too keen inevitably loses her man!" Slowly she retraced her steps. She sat down at the desk and forced herself to remain there, glancing every other second at the clock. It was the longest quarter of an hour of her life.

In the meantime, downstairs in the parlor, her aunts were entertaining Sasha, and things there were taking a strange and unexpected turn. "I'll be damned," Sasha had said to himself as he sat down opposite the three old maids—Roxane placid and silent as usual, Emilie eying him critically, and Clotilde babbling away about nothing in particular. And finally, profiting by a short silence, he had turned to the portrait of Zoë's father, asking who it was. Immediately Clotilde's frills and ruffles began to flutter, and Emilie's proud bust swelled up visibly. "That is our brother, monsieur. The General Jean-Désiré Chabout!"

"Chabout!"

Sasha gazed at the portrait in wonder. The name brought back to him his whole childhood and the many stories the old housekeeper and sometimes even his mother had told him about the great war of 1812 and especially about the man who bore that name. It had happened in the days of Sasha's grandparents, when Napoleon's army was retreating from Russia, and the peasants had brought a captured French officer, a young colonel, to his grandfather's country house. The Frenchman was very weak and his feet were badly frozen. And as Sasha began to relate the tale the three sisters stared at him, incredulous. "Your grandparents' name," snapped Emilie, "what was it?"

"Romantzeff. They were my mother's parents."

"Count and Countess Romantzeff!" she cried. "Why, of course!" She stood up, her face flushed, her right arm extended in a gesture of classical welcome. "On behalf of the late general I am happy to welcome you to our humble home!"

In the twinkling of an eye the three sisters had pounced on him from all sides, Clotilde as tall as himself, Emilie half an inch taller, and Roxane towering above them all. They were patting him on the shoulders, shaking his hands, and Clotilde kissed him on both cheeks. "Ah! Young and delicious enemy!" she sighed before kissing him a third time. And when Zoë entered the room she found the four of them lined up at attention in front of the portrait. She noticed with gratitude that Sasha's face remained serious when Emilie put her hand to her mouth and produced a good imitation of a bugle call, a thing she did on rare and solemn occasions.

The ceremony over, Roxane hurried out of the room, calling out to Sasha over her shoulder, "I must show you one of my valued possessions—a letter your grandfather wrote to my brother!"

Sasha's face brightened when he caught sight of Zoë, but Emilie thrust herself between them. "For everything your grandparents did for our brother, *mon capitaine*, allow us to offer you a glass of wine!"

"Yes," said Clotilde, "the very, very best!"

"Oh no, Clotilde, not the very, *very* best!" Emilie hesitated. "Have we any left?"

"Indeed, indeed we have!"

Emilie gave it another thought, finally nodding a reluctant consent as she and Clotilde left the room. Zoë was so surprised that for a moment she forgot all else. "Have they gone mad?" she cried, opening her eyes wide. She opened them still wider when Sasha told her what had happened. "Count and Countess Romantzeff?" she murmured. "How very strange."

How very strange indeed, he thought, that she should be Colonel Chabout's daughter. The hand of destiny had suddenly dropped her into his own past, making her a part of an intimate pattern, and the desire to protect seemed no longer out of place. "Don't you think this should bring us closer together?" he said, looking into her eyes. But Zoë, remembering her decision to be cold and distant, moved away toward the settee.

"That man of yours—Poushka. Oh, what a funny, funny man!" she exclaimed a little too smoothly. "When he told Aunt Roxane that in Russia he was considered small, I thought I would die laughing!"

"Did he say that? Oh, Poushka never misses an opportunity to impress foreigners with the greatness of Russia!" He laughed. Then his face became serious again, and he pressed her for an answer: "Don't you think the daughter of General Chabout and the grandson of Count and Countess Romantzeff should get to know each other better?"

"Not—necessarily."

He looked at her in dismay. It was as though she were refusing to remain where she belonged. He smiled to release the tension around his mouth. "And why not?"

"Because, monsieur, you are a man a young woman cannot trust."

He was no longer smiling; his eyes looked solemn now. He sat down beside her. "I want you to trust me, Zoia Ivanovna."

In an instant her air of indifference vanished. "If you want me to trust you, you must change your whole attitude. You should not jump into carriages! You should not attack me in the recesses of front doors! You should not treat me as if I were an easy conquest!" She saw him smile again, and she finished in a huff: "I have nothing more to say. Except that you make me think Russians are not nice people at all."

"Oh, that!" A mocking note had crept back into his voice. "Poushka thinks all French people are horrid, but he thought the world of you. And when Poushka offers his devotion, it's for life!"

Zoë made a last stand. She arched her eyebrows and looked at him coldly. "For life! That is hardly our case, monsieur."

Sasha sprang to his feet, annoyed. "What is the matter with you today? Trying to be a little lady! I like you better when you are natural!"

"And I will kindly ask you to keep your likes and dislikes to yourself!"

She had flared up, and her mouth had grown larger and her face had become plain. Yet he felt happy again—it made her look real; alive and pulsating. "But I can't." He laughed. "Take the dress you are wearing, for instance! I like it much better than the one you had on yesterday. This one suits you to perfection!"

"Oh?" She smoothed her skirt out, trying not to look too pleased.

"And I see you are fond of camellias."

"Oh!" It came almost as a groan. She had forgotten to thank him for the flowers. Horrified, her fingers flew up to her mouth, but he gave her no time to speak. "Since you like them so well, you will get a few every morning. And that reminds me of Poushka—he will be the one to deliver them to you. I must tell you, the poor fellow was very upset today. He said he was so impressed by the appearance of your aunts that he forgot to take off his hat, and you scolded him."

"Oh, I hope I did not hurt his feelings."

"You don't know Poushka. He respects you all the more for it. He said you were an imperious young lady worthy of his master."

Zoë blushed to the very roots of her hair. "That is servants' gossip, monsieur! I don't care to hear it!"

"No? Well, I will tell you something else he said. He said when you were surrounded by your aunts you looked like a darling little kitten dropped among large feather beds."

Sasha smiled. It was one of those boyish smiles she liked best, and the thin little coating of ice she had managed to muster around herself with so much trouble melted then and there. And Roxane, returning with the letter, found them laughing merrily together.

9   From that day on Sasha became very assiduous in his attentions, and his attitude toward Zoë underwent a drastic change. Even Emilie could find nothing wrong with his courtship—it was so dignified and proper, like a boy-and-girl affair in the grand old style. Every morning Poushka appeared, bearing gifts of flowers and sweets for the aunts as well as for Zoë, and every afternoon at five Sasha would come in person. He entertained the old ladies with stories of Russia and of his childhood in Romantzevo, his mother's ancestral home near Moscow. And then came an evening when the old maids, mollified and flattered by his attentions, invited Sasha to

47

dinner and he described to them in detail the room in Romantzevo in which their brother had lived and which had not changed since the days of his grandparents. It was the contrast of the gloomy little Chabout dining room, with its dark brown walls, its heavy oak dinner table, and its massive sideboard with an artificial marble top to it, that brought back to Sasha's mind the big bright room in Romantzevo, all blue and white and airy. And he told them how he and his sister—Hélène ten years old and Sasha six—used to sneak into that room to play a game in which Sasha took the part of Colonel Chabout and Hélène that of the Countess Romantzeff, who had nursed the young Frenchman back to life. Sasha would stretch himself out on the huge bed, and Hélène would rub his feet that were supposed to be frozen, and while he, pretending to be writhing in pain, called out in an agonized voice the names of Napoleon's great battles—"Austerlitz! . . . Jena! . . . Eylau!"—she kept repeating, "Borodino! Borodino! Borodino!" And the game always ended with Sasha's complete recovery, after which the children would jump up and down on the bed, shouting somewhat inconsistently, *"Vive l'Empereur Alexandre! Vive Napoléon!"*

"It is a great pity," said Sasha when the ripple of laughter subsided around the table, "that today the relationship between our two countries should undergo again such a strain!"

"Indeed, indeed, indeed, mon capitaine!" cried Monsieur Tresor, who was also present that evening. "I had much difficulty—I mean I had trouble—— No, that's not at all what I want to say! What I mean is—there was some doubt in the minds of our officials as to whether a passport for Russia should be issued today. My brother-in-law, of course, at my instigation, overcame all such opposition and, if I may add, prejudice! But do tell us, *mon très cher Capitaine Novoselsky"*—in the kindness of his heart Monsieur Tresor had accepted Sasha without bitterness or rancor as the inevitable and more desirable rival—"tell us truthfully, is it quite safe for Madame Duval to go to Russia at the present time?"

"Of course it is!" Sasha exclaimed. "You don't seriously think France will ally herself with England!"

"Avec la perfide Albion!" Emilie snorted, digging her fork into her roast chicken. "Never!"

Zoë, touched by Monsieur Tresor's solicitude, wanted to console the little man. "In Tiflis," she said, repeating Madame Tollet's words, "people live surrounded by war and they do not care! There is a war there with the Turks and a war with Shamyl!"

"Ah, Shamyl!" Monsieur Tresor rolled his eyes in terror. "His name alone gives me the creeps!"

"Now, now, Monsieur Tresor, do not work yourself up," Roxane said, giving his arm a gentle pat. "Remember that kind heart of yours is still needed by your friends."

"Ah, dear and excellent Mademoiselle Roxane," the little man murmured as Roxane turned to Sasha and asked, "Have you ever been to the Caucasus, mon capitaine?"

"I spent a few months there last year when I was attached to the staff of the former Viceroy."

Roxane leaned forward in her chair, her dark eyes aglow. "Tell me, is it as beautiful as they say?"

"Stupendous, mademoiselle! Breath-taking! Next to the Caucasian mountains, the Swiss Alps seem frivolous!"

Sasha described at length the forbidding granite cliffs of the Caucasus and the mellow valleys of Georgia. It was obvious to all that he had a real flair for that country, and when he spoke of a certain part of Georgia, known as Kahetia, a dreamy look crept into his eyes and he waxed lyrical. "A beautiful green valley, lying at the very foothills of the snow-capped Caucasian chain. A happy land of peace and plenty, where wine is good and men are carefree . . . Ah, Zoia Ivanovna! I hope you will see it someday! My cousins, the Tchavchavadzés, have a lovely estate there called Tsinandali—a perfect little paradise! And incidentally, Monsieur Tresor, Tsinandali is closer to Shamyl's domains than Tiflis, and even there they are not afraid of being attacked by his mountain tribes!"

Monsieur Tresor seemed satisfied there was no imminent danger there for Zoë, but Shamyl must have still weighed heavily on his mind, for he wanted to know more about him—"What is the monster like?"

"That I could not tell you! Very few Russians have seen him. His origins were humble, I'm told, but through his courage and his religious fanaticism he has become a proud leader of savage men." Sasha smiled as he added: "Strange that his son should be so different. A more tolerant, a more peace-loving man I have seldom known!" Noticing the surprised looks around him, he hurried to add: "His name is Jemaleddin. We call him Jemal for short. He is one of my best friends."

His listeners stared at him in blank amazement. "But how could that be?" Roxane asked at length. "That Shamyl's son should be your friend, I mean?"

Sasha had forgotten that no one at the table knew that Jemal was an officer in the Russian Army. Cornet Jemaleddin Shamyl was his official name. And in a few words Sasha told them how this had happened. In 1839 Jemal's father—Shamyl—had been faced with temporary defeat. The Russians had laid siege to Ahoulgo, his *aoul*, or mountain village, perched so high up on a cliff that it seemed impregnable; but the Russians managed to undermine it and were blowing it up in sections. To save his own life and that of the rest of his family, Shamyl had been forced to give up his eldest son as hostage to the Emperor Nicholas. The little boy—Jemaleddin, that is—aged eight, was brought to St. Petersburg, where he lived for a while in the Winter Palace as the Tsar's ward, later receiving his education in a cadet school.

Zoë, fascinated, had listened to the sound of Sasha's voice rather than to the words he was saying. As on the first day of their acquaintance, its rich quality set her all astir, and for a wild moment her eyes had clung to his lips. Tearing them away, she now caught onto the strange name he had pronounced. "Jemaleddin! It sounds like the *Arabian Nights!* What is he like, this Jemaleddin?"

Sasha did not answer at once; instead he half closed his eyes, a habit with him when concentrating. "You know," he said at last, "I find it difficult to describe him. He is about my height, only much slimmer, and he has a striking face. By that I mean a face one doesn't forget easily. He is quiet, serious, reserved. In fact, he has all the qualities that usually go to make a young man thoroughly unpopular among his fellow officers. But Jemal is very much loved by his comrades. As one of them once said, 'When I get drunk and get into mischief, I always know Jemal is there, sober and strong, like the granite rocks he comes from.'"

"But doesn't he ever want to go back to them?" Roxane asked.

"No. He is just another Russian officer like myself."

"Oh, how very muddling!" cried Clotilde.

"Very muddling indeed," Emilie agreed. "I would just as soon stay right here in Paris!" And with that she got up and led the way into the parlor.

On the rare occasions when Zoë and Sasha found themselves alone he dropped his bantering tone and, what was more, he never made love to her; instead he would teach her a few words of Russian —unromantic words, such as "bread" and "water" and "How much does it cost?"—and would also give her details of her forthcoming voyage. Zoë would travel by rail through France and most of Germany, but once in Russia, he told her, it would be the slow way—by horse and carriage; and in Odessa, on the Black Sea, she would embark for one of the Caucasian ports. Zoë, on the other hand, had told him about her life with René, about René's death and the painful scene that had followed with her parents-in-law; she was beginning to feel as if she had known him for months instead of days, and at times she felt impatient about his reticence. On one occasion only he had hinted at his feelings for her. It happened the afternoon he came early, offering to take Roxane and Zoë for a long ride. It was an unusually warm and balmy day for February, and they were sitting alone in the parlor waiting for Roxane.

"This is my lucky day!" Zoë exclaimed, for that morning her diamonds had been sold at a good price, thanks to Roxane's shrewd bargaining. To this money her aunts had added a thousand francs of their own. They had done it in a little ceremony in front of the portrait, and Emilie, incapable of being gracious to the end, had handed her the gift, saying, "Who knows, you may perish in the wilds. Here is part of what would come to you if you outlived us."

When she told him about it, Sasha sighed. "If only I could provide you with all you needed in life. But alas! I know you would refuse me that right." He gave her no time to answer. An almost mischievous smile replaced the momentary wistfulness in his eyes. "Today I found something that will bring me luck. I found it in my sister's greenhouse." His strong agile fingers searched through his wallet, bringing out a four-leaf clover.

"I didn't know you were superstitious," she murmured just as Roxane entered the room announcing that she was ready.

"Only when I'm in love," he whispered back, offering her his arm and following Roxane out of the room. And Zoë found herself wishing Roxane would change her mind and let them go alone for the ride.

Zoë had grown listless in the last few days. She needed some tangible assurance of Sasha's love. Sharp doubts were beginning to assail her from time to time. And the day before Emilie had made matters worse by saying pointedly, "Captain Novoselsky has not introduced you to his sister yet. Why?"

"Why, why indeed?" The question had flashed through Zoë's mind, but aloud she had said, "There is plenty of time for that, Aunt Emilie."

"Oh? I should have thought Countess Koramzine would be

anxious to meet General Chabout's daughter. After all, she, too, has heard of him all her life!"

There was acid to Emilie's words that had stung a little. Zoë knew Sasha was making arrangements for Madame Tollet to see his sister, then why not for her too? Madame Tollet, it's true, was not going to pay a social call; she was going for the sole purpose of collecting the gifts Hélène Koramzine had prepared for her cousins in Tiflis, and yet . . . Zoë frowned, shrugged her shoulders, and deliberately plucked the thorny question out of her mind. "He will," she said to herself, "when the time comes. But oh, if only he would hurry up and say the word. If only he were not so reticent and calm about it all!"

But Zoë was wrong. There was no peace and calm in Sasha's mind. Every morning since he had met her he had awakened with a sense of guilt. "Today I must tell her. I can't let it drag any longer. It's unfair." He would roll over on his side and look through half-closed eyes at the far corner of the room. Yes, it was there, always with him. The mad folly of his early youth, the years of dissipation that followed, and now this love for Zoë that had sprung on him out of nowhere, bringing with it a half-forgotten element of purity. He tried to be deliberately cynical about it. "I am soaring high for a change— lips and eyes instead of hips and tits!" But cynicism toward women, acquired through the years, fell flat in Zoë's case. Her courage and her candor brought delight; her artless, unsophisticated nature touched a tender chord in him, while the feeling of destiny he had experienced when he had learned about Colonel Chabout seemed binding. "Little darling. Angel," he would whisper, stretching himself languidly, half hoping that his outstretched arm would find Zoë sleeping by his side. Then he would sit up in bed. "Besides, the little angel is devilishly proud. She might send me to the devil! No, not today, tomorrow will do as well!" And his nature, forever shunning the unpleasant, would turn a deaf ear to reason. Poushka would be dispatched in the morning with the gifts, Sasha would follow in the afternoon on his daily visit, and thus the days had slipped by one by one. The farewell party Sasha had arranged at the Tollets' was upon them, and still he had not spoken.

When Zoë reached the Tollets' shortly after six, she found their dowdy boardinghouse room transformed beyond recognition. An abundance of flowers stood everywhere in vases and in fancy baskets, and the dinner table, covered with a spotless white table-cloth, had been laid out with fine crystal and silver. Sasha was already there. "Zoia Ivanovna," he said, "allow me to present you with the keys of Russia!" He held out the passport, pointing to the official endorsement. "And that, I declare, calls for a celebration!" He clapped his hands and called for champagne, while Zoë, smiling, slipped the passport into her reticule.

A moment later they heard a cork pop, and Poushka appeared in a white apron and chef's cap, bearing a bucket of ice into which a bottle of champagne had been stuck at a rakish angle. Poushka was obviously the main prop of the party. The sloppy maid who had served them on the previous occasion was nowhere to be seen, though from time to time one could hear Poushka giving her orders out in the pantry in a rich mixture of meager French and colorful Russian. And when it came to serving the supper, it was Poushka who did it. Having discarded the chef's cap and the white apron, he now appeared in the livery of Count Koramzine's household, as much out of place on him as a saddle would have been on a buffalo. But he served at table in the manner born, seeing to it that the champagne glasses were kept constantly filled to the brim. And this he kept up after supper, too, his own face growing redder all the time, a veritable glow spreading over his short nose. And around eleven, when Sasha, a guitar on his knee, was entertaining his hosts and Zoë with French and Russian songs, Poushka suddenly flew into the room, beads of perspiration standing out on his forehead. "For God's sake, Alexandr Dimitrievitch," he cried in Russian, "get that maid out of the pantry, quick! The champagne makes her look attractive!"

Zoë's loud, throaty laugh resounded through the room when Sasha had translated Poushka's words. The champagne was having its effect on her too. She found herself talking too loudly and laughing far too boisterously. She even tried to sing, ending up with a flat croak.

Suddenly she grew very quiet. Her eyes grew big and her mouth seemed to spread. "Oh, that dreadful voice of mine! It's a devil's curse!"

Sasha laughed. "But why, why do you take it so to heart?"

She turned to him, her face earnest. "If I had a beautiful voice I would never feel lonely. If I had a beautiful voice I could rise above things. If I had a beautiful voice——"

"You have everything else," he cut in. "Look at yourself! You are full of grace! Isn't that so, Monsieur Tollet?"

"A muse of grace!" Monsieur Tollet exclaimed, blowing a kiss.

Zoë beamed. The champagne carried her from despondency to

elation. She got up swiftly and took a few impromptu steps, and Sasha on his guitar played a sedate minuet. Her movements were slow and graceful, almost professional in their precision and timing. It was a formal, conventional exhibition of mutual harmony and rhythm. But gradually Sasha began to play faster, changing the melody, modulating the tempo, accelerating, until almost imperceptibly the sedate minuet was transformed into a series of chords, loud and passionate. His eyes never left Zoë's face. His mouth was drawn, his nostrils dilated. The wild chords and the savage rhythm were like burning physical caresses. Zoë stood still for a moment, her eyes melting into his, and then her whole body responded, giving itself to the dance with abandonment, to which her severe black dress added piquancy. And once again, as on the evening when they first met, the Tollets faded out of the picture.

Suddenly, as though the tension were too great, a string snapped with a whining twang and the dying sounds of a broken chord vibrated feebly through the room. Sasha passed his hand over his eyes. Zoë sank limply into a chair. Very slowly she was coming out of a sweet trance. The voices of the Tollets reached her from afar and she was about to say something, when she saw Sasha standing over her, his hand outstretched, his eyes weary.

"Come! It is time to go," he said abruptly.

She rose, obedient, to her feet.

Madame Tollet's face clouded. "My old caramel will accompany you home," she said, coming between Sasha and Zoë.

While Zoë searched her mind for an excuse to get rid of Monsieur Tollet, Sasha took the matter in hand. "Do not worry, madame. Poushka will be our chaperon."

"Oh well, if Poushka will be with you . . ." Madame Tollet conceded, kissing Zoë good night.

Zoë and Sasha stood outside the house waiting for the carriage. She glanced up at him. He was looking across the street, his face set, and the light of a street lamp cast dark shadows around the corner of his mouth, giving him a look of bitterness she had never seen there before. She moved closer to him, sliding her arm into his.

"Why is the highly well-born Alexandr Dimitrievitch so solemn?" she asked in a whisper.

Sasha shook his head, as if shaking himself free of depressing thoughts. He smiled down at her, and there was tenderness in his eyes that filled her whole being with happiness. She could not say a word; she could hardly wait to be alone with him in the privacy

54

of the carriage with not even a street lamp for witness. And when the carriage drove up she paid scant attention to Poushka, who was seated on the box, holding the reins and grinning at them through his beard.

She slid into the carriage. Sasha seemed to hesitate, finally jumping in after her and closing the door behind him.

The horses started off at a lunge, throwing Zoë closer to Sasha. "Zoë-djan," he began in a hoarse whisper, intending to say more, but the way she whispered back his name—"Sasha"—chased all other words away. His arms closed around her and their lips met.

That first kiss went through Zoë as no kiss had ever done before, and her lips responded instantly, demanding more, and more, and more. With one quick movement he undid the ribbons of her bonnet and his hand went through her hair. He kissed her again and again, tenderly on the eyes, scorchingly on the neck and ears, but always returning to the lips with renewed passion. And with every kiss a new wildness swept through her, spreading in spirals, until she lay limp and breathless in his arms, while the carriage circled through the streets of Paris, Poushka losing his way at least a dozen times before he brought it to a final stop in front of Zoë's house.

10   Despite the cold weather, small beads of perspiration stood out on Madame Tollet's upper lip. She was running down a crowded street, carrying a parcel wrapped in tissue paper. She did not notice how the passers-by stopped and stared at her in surprise. She was muttering to herself, "It's past noon and my *boule de gomme* will be waiting for me for dinner! But this is so important, so dreadful, he will just have to wait for once!" When she saw an empty cab she stopped abruptly, almost knocking a man off his feet, and, the time element having overcome frugality, she hailed the cab, giving the coachman Zoë's address. Once there, she refused to wait in the parlor and followed a disapproving Marguerite up the stairs. And no sooner had the latter opened Zoë's door than Madame Tollet, her bonnet askew, precipitated herself into the room, crying, "Ah, my poor, dear child! Here I am! Ah, how I wish I were not!"

Alarmed, Zoë jumped to her feet, insisting on having her unexpected guest settled in a comfortable chair. "You look so upset, what is the matter with you? Calm yourself, dear Madame Tollet, please calm yourself."

"Ah no, dear, sweet child! I should be the one to calm you!" And without further preamble Madame Tollet blurted it out: "I am the bearer of terrible news—Captain Novoselsky is a married man!"

"Impossible!" The cry was torn out of Zoë, but Madame Tollet raised a warning finger. "Ah! He is a wicked philanderer! I suspected it the very first time he met you! His intentions were low, very low, my child! He wasn't after your hand at all!"

Zoë was too steeped in the visions she had woven around herself and Sasha to take it all in, and "Who told you such a lie?" was all she managed to say.

"His sister told me! The Countess Koramzine! You know I went there this morning to pick up the gifts." The parcel which Madame Tollet was still holding trembled slightly in her hand. "Ah, my dear, never, never have I seen such beautiful lace!"

Zoë interrupted her almost rudely. What did she care about the lace? She wanted to know what the countess had said. Madame Tollet breathed heavily, gathering her thoughts together. "She said—— Why, she said: 'Madame Tollet, I want to thank you for all your kindness to my brother. He tells me he has had a wonderful time with you and your husband. He needs it so, the poor boy! He is so unhappy in his married life.'"

"Married life, married life! Easy conquests and a married life!" Suddenly Zoë felt her knees giving way under her. She sat down abruptly on the edge of the bed, while Madame Tollet, not daring to look at her, carried on: "I think the way he has treated you is outrageous, positively outrageous! I will tell him so when I see him, you can count on that! But then, dear child, all men are alike. Even my old sugarplum, who has been as faithful as faithful could be, once cast an eye on a Georgian princess. Ah, she was so beautiful, so young, so poor! Well, do you know what I did? I closed our shop, I took him to the country, and there I sat over him for two whole months until he said, 'Oh, ma bombe au chocolat!' And I knew he had forgotten the princess. Ah! What we women won't do to hold a man."

Zoë's voice suddenly cut in, cold and lifeless: "I do not understand why you are telling me all this! I have no man to hold!" And seeing that Madame Tollet was about to retort something, she interrupted her again, determined not to show how deeply she had been wounded. "I thank you for taking it so much to heart, but honestly, I don't see why all this fuss. Captain Novoselsky paid me a little court during the last two weeks, but there was nothing serious about it. Of course, had I known he was married, I would never have

56

allowed it, but then . . . Well, there's just nothing more to be said."

"Except that you look so pale, my poor child."

"I am tired. All this packing and the last-minute errands . . . Besides, I'm nervous, I'll admit it." She attempted a smile. "It's a long way from Paris to Tiflis."

The kind old busybody was not taken in at all, but she played up to Zoë. "Oh, I am so happy it's that way! I was afraid——" And taking a hurried leave, she rushed out of the room, refusing to let Zoë see her downstairs.

Zoë turned the key in her door, a bitter lump rising in her throat. It was all quite clear to her now, why he had not introduced her to his sister, why on that first evening he had hinted at happiness outside of marriage; and again the other day he had spoken about "having no right." It was all very clear now—he wanted her as a mistress, not as a wife. Oh, if she could only forget him, throw him out of her life! But the thrill, the secret passionate longing for his kisses were with her, stronger than ever now. She clenched her fists and closed her eyes. "I must not think of that! That is dead and gone!" Running across the room, she threw herself on her bed, burying her face in the pillow.

She did not cry. She lay there for an hour or more, chasing all thoughts away, for every thought was a stab. But she sat up, her eyes wide open, when Marguerite knocked on her door, calling out that the Russian captain had arrived. He had come. Then it could not be true. A wild hope surged up and, brushing away a wisp of stray hair, Zoë unlocked the door and ran downstairs. "If he kisses me before saying anything, then it's a mistake," she said to herself as she entered the stuffy little parlor. But Sasha did not kiss her. And the violence of the short scene that followed swept over them like a sudden whirlwind.

Alarmed by Zoë's distracted look, he had taken a step forward and she had caught him by the hand. "It isn't true, is it? That you are married?"

His smile vanished. Bewilderment, bitterness, anger shook his face. "Who told you?" he almost shouted, pushing her hand away.

"Then it is true!" Her eyes scanned his face, and she sank limply into a chair. "Does it matter who told me?"

Sasha was standing over her, his fists clenched. "It does matter, it does! I came here to tell you, and you will never believe me now. I want to know who told you."

A thousand bitter reproaches were crowding the tip of Zoë's

57

tongue, but they were checked by the fury she saw in his eyes. "Who told you!" he thundered for the third time.

"Your sister told Madame Tollet."

"My sister! Hélène!" He seemed to shudder. "I don't—I don't believe it! . . . Oh, damn her!" And turning abruptly on his heel, he rushed out of the room.

11   "Marriage is an insurmountable barrier whichever way you look at it," Zoë wrote in her *Book of Stray Thoughts.* "I knew he loved me the moment he lost his self-control, but alas, of what avail is such knowledge, since he belongs to another woman!" She underlined the words "he belongs to another woman," and added four exclamation marks to heighten the poignancy of her torment; and after a moment's thought she added as a postscript: "I forgot my bonnet in his carriage. He has not returned it!"

A loud knock on the door made her blot the lines in a hurry and close the book. A starry-eyed Marguerite appeared, holding a calling card gingerly between thumb and index finger. On it Zoë saw, *La Comtesse Koramzine, née Novoselsky,* engraved in delicate letters.

"Is she here?" Zoë murmured, taking the card, her heart beating a little faster. "Where is she?"

"Ah, madame! In an elegant carriage with four white horses, a liveried coachman, and a beautiful flunky!" Marguerite pointed to the window, adding in an awed whisper: "Is she really coming in, madame?"

"No! I mean yes! Show the countess into the parlor. Tell her I will be down in a few minutes. And wait! Tell my aunts I wish to be left alone with this lady; she has come to see me on a matter of great importance."

Marguerite had kept repeating, "Yes, madame . . . Yes, madame," and now she dashed out of the room. Zoë looked down thoughtfully at the visiting card, turning it over in her hand. A matter of great importance, she had said, but how important? And of what use now? Her first impulse—to refuse to see Hélène Koramzine—had been quickly crowded out by her curiosity to see Sasha's sister. And now, hiding herself behind the curtains, she peered out of the window into the street below.

Zoë was not the only one to watch Hélène Koramzine's progress from her carriage to the front door. Emilie and Clotilde were at their window, and in the houses next door and across the street neighbors were peering out of theirs when the liveried footman opened the door of the carriage and Hélène stepped out. She was dressed according to the latest fashion, her crinoline far larger than any yet seen in that neighborhood; and her long sealskin coat, tightly fitted at the waist, covered three quarters of her bell-shaped skirt. A bonnet trimmed with black fur and ermine sprigs and a small sealskin muff completed the picture. She moved gracefully forward, her light, springy step making her hooped skirts billow about her. She smiled at Marguerite as the latter, her face flushed, stood on the threshold, bobbing in front of the glamorous countess.

Wherever Hélène went she created an impression of glamour and brilliance, yet actually she was a rather simple-minded person well trained in the ways of the smart world she lived in; her emotions, like her life, were smooth and well rounded, with a sincere regard for her husband and a tender care for her two little girls. Only her love for Sasha had an explosive element to it that made it soar high above all else; there was nothing she would not do for him.

Hélène entered the parlor and looked at the portrait over the mantel with undisguised curiosity. "The colonel himself—a legend suddenly come true!" she said to herself. Only a day had gone by since she had first heard of Zoë, when Sasha had come to her late at night seeking her advice. At first she had laughed. He might as well have told her he was in love with the daughter of *Le Bon Roi Dagobert*. But when she realized how serious he was, she had taken it to heart, and yesterday, when he had stormed into her room, accusing her of duplicity and perfidy, she had felt deeply distressed. Hélène had not expected Madame Tollet to rush straight to Zoë, but she knew that by giving Sasha's secret away before he had had time to speak of it himself she had failed him for the first time in her life. And now here she was, calling on Zoë, bringing her a message from Sasha, and not a little curious herself to see what this "daughter of a legend" was like.

Zoë, on the other hand, felt distinctly ill at ease when she entered the room. She greeted Hélène awkwardly and dryly, and despite the latter's graciousness, or perhaps because of it, she remained uncomfortably conscious to the end of being made to feel at home. The fact that Hélène, too, felt embarrassed never occurred to her, for Hélène hid it well under a cloak of easy chatter about Zoë's father, at the same time giving Zoë a quick mental appraisal: "Luminous eyes . . . Slender neck . . . Good figure . . . Will still look well at

59

forty . . . Sasha always had good taste in women!" And aloud she remarked, "You look far too young to be Colonel Chabout's daughter."

"Madame," Zoë said abruptly, "I don't think you came here to speak of my father," and then in a much smaller voice, "Oh, I am sorry. I did not mean to be rude. I am not very happy."

Hélène leaned forward in her chair impulsively. "I understand so well. Would it help you to know that Sasha is miserable too? You would know it if you saw him."

"I never want to see him again!"

"Oh yes, you do. Of course you do. I don't know what Sasha would say if he thought this was the end."

Zoë opened her eyes wide. "But he is married, madame. There is nothing more to be said."

"Oh, but there is. That is why I am here. You don't know all the circumstances."

"He should have told me he was married in the first place."

"It was wrong of him not to," Hélène admitted earnestly. "He was afraid you would refuse to see him; he kept putting it off. It was my fault you found out the way you did. I should never have told Madame Tollet."

"No."

A short silence fell between them.

"I will begin by telling you that Sasha has not lived with his wife for seven years," Hélène began at length. She looked down at her hands and toyed with the rings on her fingers. "His wife is insane, hopelessly insane!" And noticing a new interest in Zoë's eyes, she unfolded the whole story. A mad boy-and-girl affair, ending in an elopement at the age of nineteen. A few months of happiness, and then strange symptoms developing in the young bride which finally culminated in a permanent derangement of the mind after their child had been born dead. "There was insanity in Natalie's family all down the line," she said. "Her grandmother had died insane. The old lady used to lock herself up in an old bathhouse, refusing to come out for days on end. She said she was hatching eggs!" Hélène smiled. "I know it is a crime to make light of such matters, but it does sound ridiculous, doesn't it? But Natalie never thought so. Even as a girl she used to say her grandmother was wise to try to forget she was a human being! Well, to make a long story short, Natalie is well taken care of now in Romantzevo, my mother's country place near Moscow. She is harmless most of the time. Only when she sees Sasha she becomes violently agitated. She calls him 'The Living Death.' "

Zoë's hands trembled a little and she swallowed hard. To her the story was both repulsive and pathetic, gruesome, and so very pitiful. But why was Hélène telling her all this? Was she here to ask her to become Sasha's mistress? Someone had once told her that Russians were amoral. She gave Hélène a quick searching look. She saw a pair of clear gray eyes and a gentle smile, and she looked away again, ashamed of herself. She caught a few disconnected words—"Sasha," "suffering," "he loves you so." And then one sentence rang out sharp and clear: "Sasha has decided to obtain an annulment. Of course he must first discuss it with his mother. But then our mother, though she is reputed to be severe, is really a very understanding woman at heart."

Bitter lines appeared at the corners of Zoë's mouth. Was there to be another mother-in-law who did not want her? A rich, aristocratic, powerful, far more formidable mother-in-law than Madame Duval? She was looking at Hélène with resentment now. "She takes it for granted I want to marry Sasha," she thought. "They think all they have to do is beckon to me. Another form of easy conquest!" And when she heard Hélène say, "Sasha considers himself pledged to you," she jumped to her feet, her face flushed. "Oh no, no! I cannot accept such a pledge!"

Hélène had risen too. She could not understand Zoë's refusal. The pledge did not bind her in any way; it concerned Sasha alone. But Zoë was not listening. She repeated the same words all over again, as though trying to impress them upon her mind. "No! No! I cannot accept such a pledge!" And then, drawing herself up, "Tomorrow I am leaving for Tiflis. That is all there is to it, madame."

"But won't you let him see you before you go?"

"No!... Oh no!... No!"

The words shot out of their own accord. She felt like crying out in pain, but she could not retract them. The stubborn, unseeing half of her nature had gone on a sudden rampage, running wild, dragging the other half, helpless, along with it. Another minute and she would have burst into sobs. Forgetting all else, thinking only of escape, she turned her back on Hélène, flung the door open, and ran out into the hall. She did not notice Marguerite and the handsome flunky jumping apart at her sudden appearance, nor did she see them watching her in dismay as she ran up the stairs. She had but one thought in mind, to get away and cry her heart out.

61

Zoë's rude, abrupt departure had unexpected results, for she had done the one thing that established her sincerity beyond all doubt in Hélène's mind. "Unsophisticated," she said to herself. "Unpolished, but not scheming. That young woman is not after position and wealth!" And with such thoughts in mind Hélène walked out into the hall, where the tall footman stood in readiness, holding her fur coat.

In the meantime Zoë had broken every rule and precedent of the household by storming into Roxane's room unannounced. She flung herself on the big hard bed, sobbing loudly. And through her sobs she told Roxane for the first time all that had happened since Madame Tollet's visit the day before.

"What are you crying about?" Roxane asked when Zoë had grown calmer. "You refused to see him. You did right. You have nothing to offer him."

"But I want to see him and I don't dare see him. If I saw him again I might be sorry afterward."

"Stop sniffling!"

Zoë blew her nose, stunned.

"I am not sorry for you. I am sorry for Captain Novoselsky."

Zoë stared at her for a moment, bewildered. "Oh, you are cruel and hard!" she cried out at last.

"And you are a lonely little animal in heat."

The words were said in such a quiet, even tone that at first their meaning did not reach Zoë. When it did, she jumped up, trembling with rage. "Oh, you horrid, dreadful woman!" she screamed. She ran to the door, but Roxane seized her roughly by the arm. "Stay!" she said. "There are a few things I must tell you before you go." She pushed Zoë back on the bed, laying a restraining hand on her shoulder.

"Haven't I suffered enough without your insults?" Zoë cried.

"You have suffered great pangs of self-pity. You thought you had found a husband, a permanent security, and now you have lost them. Mind you, I don't blame you. Your whole childhood was insecure. I am to blame for that. And that is why I will be patient with you now." Zoë sat gazing up at her aunt, fascinated in spite of herself. "Think back, Zoë-Jeanne. It was insecurity that drove you to René. And with Novoselsky, was it any different? You did everything in your power to lure him, thinking only of his love for you, never of your love for him. Now take my advice. Go your way. Try to find yourself, Niece. Your real self, I mean. And never think

62

of marriage again until you know you could give your love to a man, whatever the circumstances might be."

Zoë felt shattered. "But," she said in a weak voice, "that would be immoral!"

"Your mother did it."

"My mother abandoned me!"

Dangerous flames flared up in Roxane's eyes, but she mastered herself and said in a hollow voice, "There you go, thinking of yourself again. Think of her for a change. Emilie has reviled her, and you are like Emilie. When your mother knew how much he needed her, she gave herself to him willingly. Then the inevitable happened. She went away with him, intending to take you later, after the birth of their child. But she died, and her son died with her."

Tears were streaming down Zoë's cheeks. Roxane patted her head with unexpected tenderness. "There now, there now. Everything will work itself out in the end. I suppose you've given up all thought of Auguste Tresor?"

Despite her misery Zoë could not help flaring up with indignation. "Auguste Tresor!" she cried. "Oh, Auntie, how could you!"

"I just wanted to know." Roxane clasped and unclasped her big angular hands. "Because if you don't want him, I will take him myself."

Zoë didn't know whether to laugh or to cry. "You? You, Aunt Roxane!"

"Yes, Niece." Roxane's tone was matter-of-fact. She was fed up with her sisters, she said. Auguste Tresor's children needed a mother, and Auguste himself needed taking care of, for rumors had it that his business had declined since the death of Clementine Tresor. "I am the kind of woman who has to make the first advances," she said, "and I am old enough now to do it. I will start courting him tomorrow." And for once Roxane really smiled. It was a wet, glistening smile in which tongue and gums participated freely, as though rejoicing at their sudden liberation, while the smile itself spread over her face, wonderfully mischievous and quite devoid of malice.

Zoë stared at her aunt, finding no words in which to express her surprise. The genuine smile vanished from Roxane's face, and she pushed Zoë toward the door. "Go now. You have had enough. You are replete."

She closed the door behind Zoë. Hurrying to her desk, she scribbled a few hasty lines and ran downstairs, sealing an envelope

63

on the way. In the kitchen she hailed Marguerite. "Drop everything! Take this letter to Countess Koramzine's house. And hurry!"

Roxane did not have to repeat it twice. Excited at the prospect of seeing the stalwart footman again, Marguerite dashed up to her attic to get her coat and bonnet.

12 On that last night in Paris, Zoë was unable to fall asleep for a long time. A muffled longing to see Sasha again mingled with a secret dread of a new life in a mysterious, distant land, while the words Hélène and Roxane had spoken returned to haunt her. And gradually her thoughts became all jumbled—Sasha, a "living death," pledged himself for life, while she marched up a steep slope, looking like Emilie, but she would be like her mother when she reached the summit; and because her mother had a son who died, she might perhaps bring happiness and inspiration to Sasha someday.

Zoë sighed as a deep, heavy sleep closed in on her. Next morning she woke up bright and early, and during a brief moment of half consciousness the hazel eyes of her dream fled away and the words, "Take courage. I am watching over you," rang in her ears. And a great calm descended upon her.

Zoë's room was all topsy-turvy: the wardrobe with its door ajar, the dresser with empty drawers half pulled out, an open portmanteau, a packed trunk that looked as if it could never be closed, and a mass of discarded belongings heaped pell-mell all over the place. Zoë glanced at them from time to time as she washed and dressed, surprised to find herself a little sorry to part with them.

She was fully dressed and was giving herself a last glance in the cheval glass when Marguerite brought a letter. There was a new light in Marguerite's eyes and a new look about her that bespoke newly born ambitions and aspirations. She had scrubbed her cheeks until they looked like two red apples, her hair was tidy and her hands unusually clean, and she did not hold the letter between her thumb and index finger, as she would have done the day before; instead she had placed it on a small silver tray, face down, so that she could admire the engraved crest on the back of the envelope. And she tilted the tray slightly to show it to Zoë, saying with pride: "This is the way Casimir does it!"

To the accompaniment of Marguerite's idle prattle about the "calves of Casimir," which she said were not straw but real, honest-to-God, well-rounded muscle under his silk stockings, Zoë tore the letter open. It contained a short note from Hélène and another unsealed envelope.

"People around us talk so much about the possibility of war," the note began without any preliminary form of address, "that I can't help feeling a bit worried, even though I do not believe in its eventuality. I am therefore taking the liberty of enclosing a letter of introduction to my cousin, Princess Anna Tchavchavadzé, knowing how useful she and her husband, Prince David, could be to you with the great influence they have in Tiflis. I hope that in all events you will call on them when you get there. . . ." Zoë paused in her reading, vaguely irritated by the patronizing tone she thought she detected in the letter, but the last paragraph served to dispel this impression. "I sincerely hope," it said, "that life will bring us together again sooner than we think and for a long time. In the meantime, bon voyage and good luck!" It was signed simply "Hélène." A subtle hint at the close bond that united them. This touched Zoë, and she hid the two letters in her bag, noticing for the first time that Marguerite was still there, staring at her with doleful eyes. "Ah, madame, it is so sad that you should be leaving us! Now I may never have another chance to get instructions in proper deportment from Casimir! He's the countess's beautiful flunky, you know. And—— Oh, I want so much to be a personal maid to some lady of quality!"

Zoë smiled wistfully. Cupid had been busy with his darts around this household, she thought. "And they can all get together with the men they have chosen, Marguerite with Casimir, and Roxane with Auguste Tresor. Only I . . ." She sighed a little and sat down at her desk to write a hurried note of thanks to Hélène. "Take this to the countess," she said, sealing the envelope and handing it to Marguerite. "And when I am gone," she added, pointing at the heaps of discarded belongings, "you can take all this away and pick out what you like for yourself." Marguerite trembled from head to foot with suppressed joy; she even curtsied to Zoë, a thing she had never done before, and, clutching the letter to her heart, ran out of the room just as Roxane stuck her smiling face through the door.

"Tresor is here," she said, "with two carriages and his two eldest sons. They will help with the luggage. And come downstairs quickly, I have prepared a big breakfast for you."

The atmosphere of sustained excitement and animation usually connected with a departure reigned in the entire household that morning. Marguerite was dashing all over the place, carrying out useless orders issued by Emilie; Clotilde fluttered aimlessly around, and Roxane, with Monsieur Tresor's help, packed provisions into a basket. And while Zoë ate her breakfast in a hurry, the two Tresor boys, aged sixteen and seventeen, showered her with questions about her forthcoming journey and the strange land she was going to.

"Papa told us," said Auguste, the eldest, "you will travel most of the way by horse and carriage and you will cross the Black Sea in a ship!"

"Yes," echoed Clement. "He also told us the country you were going to, madame, was full of dreadful shamyls, whatever that may be!"

"A kind of camel, no doubt," said Auguste with an air of superiority, and, *"Espèce de chamyl, va!"* he added under his breath to his younger brother.

A few minutes later Monsieur Tresor marched upstairs to Zoë's room followed by his two sons, and to the sound of his repeated commands, *"Un, deux, trois, hop-là! Un, deux, trois, hop-là"* the boys bounced up and down on the lid of the trunk while he endeavored to fasten it. At last, with the trunk locked and strapped securely, Zoë's baggage was hauled downstairs and placed in one of the waiting carriages, together with the large basket of provisions prepared by Roxane. But Zoë's departure could not take place without the inevitable ceremony in front of her father's portrait, Emilie's bugle call and all, after which Clotilde embraced her several times, crying a little, and Emilie laid a hand on her shoulder, saying: "Brave girl, go your way, and never lower the standard of the Chabouts!" And finally, accompanied by Roxane, Monsieur Tresor, and the boys, Zoë left for the station, waving a last farewell to a weeping Marguerite.

The Tresor boys made up for Zoë's lack of interest in the railroad station and all its paraphernalia. The cars, in that transitory stage of the evolution of the railroad, still bore a resemblance to their ancestor, the stagecoach, but to Auguste and Clement they appeared as the last thing in elegance and modern design; and having inspected the plush seats and the dusty little red curtains at the windows of the compartment that by hook or crook Monsieur Tollet had managed to reserve for himself and his party, they ran off to inspect the locomotive.

Zoë, her face pale and drawn, stood by the open door of the compartment. She paid scant attention to the Tollets, nor did she notice how Roxane held Monsieur Tresor by the hand, like a huge nurse fearful of having her nursling trampled by the crowd. "Any moment now," she was saying to herself, "any moment now! They will order us into the cars and we will be gone. Oh, what a fool I have been!" And then her heart skipped a beat as she caught sight of a familiar three-cornered hat bobbing up and down above the heads of the crowd. Poushka was grinning and pointing in her direction, and Zoë could hardly believe her own eyes when she finally caught sight of Sasha coming toward her ahead of Poushka. Madame Tollet looked nonplused and Roxane's eyes twinkled merrily, but Sasha paid no attention to them as he strode up to Zoë.

"So you came . . ." she whispered.

"Yes, under orders from Mademoiselle Roxane." He smiled. "She sent me a note saying, 'Don't be a fool, come and see her off.' "

They laughed happily, foolishly.

"I want you to take this," he said, his face serious again, and he pressed a small envelope into her hand. "May it bring you better luck than it did me. I will keep your bonnet. And you will accept my pledge, Zoë-djan!"

She nodded in silence. Nothing more was said. Conductors came rushing by, shouting "*En voitures,*" and through the soiled windowpane of her compartment Zoë looked at Sasha, her eyes locked in his.

Tremendous sounds, undreamed of by its modern gargantuan descendants, were now issuing forth from the locomotive ahead. Great explosive puffs, prolonged wild hisses, and finally, with a deafening roar, it started off in a series of small jerks. Zoë lost her balance and fell into a seat, while the Tollets clung to one another and to everything else they could in order to watch the crowded platform that was gliding slowly by their window. Sasha, Roxane, Poushka, Monsieur Tresor had all vanished out of sight. And an avid future, forever anxious to swallow its prey—the past— moved closer in as Zoë sat gazing dreamily at a four-leaf clover in her hand.

Part Two
The Princess

1   By the middle of March 1854 England and France formed
        an alliance against Russia and the threat of war hung heavily
over Europe. Six more months were to go by before actual fighting
broke out in the Crimea, but in the meantime two hostile armed
worlds—the East and the West—faced one another in grim determination.

Zoë and the Tollets heard of it in April, when after many delays
in their journey they had finally reached Odessa on the Black Sea.
Monsieur Tollet twitched his eyebrows meaningly and said, "I told
you so!" All his predictions were coming true. The Austrian Emperor Francis Joseph had surprised even the western allies by joining their ranks, and the Prussian King, in spite of his sister's being
Empress of Russia, had turned his back on his brother-in-law's empire and was making overtures to the West, thus leaving Russia and
her Tsar in an embattled isolation.

68

Madame Tollet, the incurable optimist, brushed the whole matter aside with an impatient sweep of her fat little hand. And Zoë backed her with Sasha's words, "Just another bit of international bluff!" At heart, though, she no longer felt as confident as before. She hated to admit it, but the long, uncomfortable journey had begun to wear her down. Trains, stagecoaches, diligences, carriages with broken-down springs, and carts with no springs at all had been tried and had all been found trying. "Toughening up our buttocks for a good sound spanking," she had said once after they had been almost jolted out of a vehicle, and her touch of Rabelaisian humor had made the Tollets laugh. In Russia the swift sleighs, with their little bells on the harnesses ringing out through the clear frosty day, had given her a thrill; but the monotony of an endless expanse of snow and the filth of the smoky roadside inns had depressed her. Kiev alone stood out as a sparkling memory, the domes of its old churches and monasteries perched on steep hills overlooking the wide, sweeping bend of the Dnieper. Then came the little white-washed, straw-thatched houses of the Ukraine, cheery, no doubt, and pleasing to the eye in the flourish of spring, but looking sad and forlorn in the wane of winter; and finally Odessa, bustling, prosperous, new, with straight wide boulevards and a view of the sea. The sight of it had cheered Zoë. But it was here, while waiting for transportation to the Caucasian port of Sukhum-Kalé, that she first heard of the real threat of war. The prospect of finding herself completely cut off from the world she knew frightened her. And with every passing day she clung more fiercely to the memory of Sasha's pledge. In it she found strength and courage. "A few months with Thérèse Michot," she would say to herself, "and then he will come to claim me. In the meantime I can write to him, I can be in constant touch with him." Yes, and his four-leaf clover lay safely pressed between the pages of her *Book of Stray Thoughts*.

It was on a bright morning early in May that Zoë caught her first glimpse of the Caucasus. The little steamer, with its long thin funnel, throbbed from bow to stern to the thrashing of its large paddle wheels, and a cloud of black smoke trailed low over the sunlit waves behind it. Zoë's heart was throbbing too. In her plaid skirt and brown shawl and bonnet she stood on the deck, flanked by the Tollets, her eyes big with wonder. The Caucasus! There it was, just as Roxane had described it—the high, forbidding mountains rising out of the deep blue sea, a fringe of green, rich vegetation marking the short line. And when the steamer came closer to shore,

Zoë saw the willows sweeping the waves with their long graceful branches.

"Over there, to the east," she exclaimed, unable to contain her excitement any longer, "must be Mount Kazbek, where Prometheus was chained. And beyond it the Daghestan, the lands of Shamyl, whose son Jemaleddin is Sasha's friend. Isn't that so, isn't that so?" And the Tollets nodded their heads and smiled, amused and touched by her youthful exuberance.

There was none of the bustle and feverish activity of Odessa in the quiet little port of Sukhum-Kalé. Everything here was warm and mellow, and life seemed to flow in a well-measured tempo.

"Time is of no account to these dear Georgians!" Madame Tollet exclaimed a little impatiently, pointing out to Zoë the postilion of the stagecoach in which they were to travel from Sukhum-Kalé to Tiflis. A typical young Georgian with soft brown eyes and indolent, lackadaisical ways, he stood leaning against the coach in no apparent hurry to leave. Occasionally he exclaimed in mild annoyance at the *moushas*—the Georgian equivalent of oriental coolies—urging them to work a little faster. They were piling pieces of luggage on the top and at the rear of the coach and strapping them down. But the moushas replied with mildly indignant cries and went on working as slowly as before. And Zoë noticed that the postilion did not really care; he was merely asserting his authority in a vague and offhanded way.

Besides Zoë and the Tollets, there were three other passengers in the coach—an elderly Georgian couple and their young daughter. They sat in studied indifference, all three in a row, the daughter squeezed in between her parents. The man was wearing a dark *tcherkeska*—a knee-length tunic—strapped tightly around the waist with a narrow leather belt, a large silver dagger dangling in front. And his aquiline nose protruded grandly from under his fur hat as he gazed out of the window, munching his gray beard now and then. The two women, Zoë thought, might have stepped out of the pages of Thérèse Michot's letter, with their long silk robes and their little round headbands worn well over the forehead and their hair under their white tulle veils done up in long corkscrew curls. They, too, were gazing out of the window, a placid expression on their faces; only the smooth-rounded eyebrows gave them a look of mild surprise. "You see, local color for you from the very start!" Monsieur Tollet chuckled into Zoë's ear while she, fascinated, trying hard not to stare, took in every detail of their attire.

70

The stagecoach was on its way now, bouncing heavily over the bumpy road. Vine-covered valleys and ruins of old castles that brought an unexpected medieval touch to this distant land drifted slowly by Zoë's window. If only Aunt Roxane could see it all, she thought. And later, when they traveled through the domains of the Princess of Mingrelia, she could almost feel the presence of Roxane at her side pointing out invisible Argonauts, or the ghost of Cadmus plowing the earth with his fire-breathing bulls.

But gradually, as they traveled away from the sea, they left the ancient myths behind. Early eastern Christendom claimed the land now, with its old churches, severe in line but blushing warmly in the sunset. And on the third day, when they were nearing Tiflis, Monsieur Tollet pointed out to Zoë the ancient cathedral of Mtskhet. They had been traveling through a barren valley—a landscape of baked clay, Zoë thought—and the cathedral, of the same golden-pinkish tint as the earth around it, seemed to have sprung out of the soil.

"The sole survivor of past glories," Monsieur Tollet said. "Mtskhet today is a sleepy, half-forgotten little town, but up to the sixth century it was the capital of Georgia."

Profiting by a half hour's delay during which their horses were being changed, he took Zoë to visit the old cathedral. Here, he told her, the kings of the Bagratide dynasty had been crowned as late as 1800, when George XIII, the last King of Georgia and already a vassal of the Russian Tsar, had come there for his coronation, only to die a year later, leaving his country and his throne to the Romanoffs. This he had done following the policies and wishes of Irakli II, his father, nicknamed "The Lion of Georgia" by Frederick the Great of Prussia for the valiant way in which he had defended his small country against the Turks. For Turkey in those days had threatened to conquer Georgia in an effort to wipe out the ingrained Christianity of the Georgians and enforce the faith of Islam.

The old cathedral stood empty, immersed in silence and peace. Semi-darkness reigned in it, broken here and there by slanting shafts of light falling through narrow windows. In one corner stood a small chapel, built by St. Nina, the Roman matron who came to Mtskhet in A.D. 314, carrying a cross of vine twigs bound together with strands of her own hair. She converted the Georgians to Christianity and remained enshrined in their hearts as their patron saint.

Zoë felt deeply moved by the ancient rites and the solemn faith

71

of old that seemed to cling to this little chapel and to the many frescoes on the cathedral walls. She closed her eyes, giving herself up to the mood that had captured her. Peace without measure. A quickening of the spirit, an upsurge, seemed to carry her through the air, light as a wand. A vision of Roxane flashed through her mind; Roxane, her finger raised, her eyes resplendent with inner flames. For somehow this wonderful moment was linked with that other moment in the stuffy little parlor in Paris, when Roxane had spoken of "the truth that escapes," and Zoë had felt a vague stirring within her. The vision vanished. The link lay deep within her now. A fragrant flower had unfolded, holding its petals open for a fraction of a second.

"We must go now, Zoë-djan."

Monsieur Tollet's high voice broke sharply through the spell. Zoë followed him out of the cathedral, hurrying back to the stage-coach for the last short lap of her journey. And all her most mundane, most wishful thoughts rose up to avenge themselves for the lost moment. "At my journey's end I find a blessing. Everything will go smoothly from now on. Sasha will be with me soon. Two, three more months, perhaps, and I will be his wife!"

2   The stagecoach reached the top of a hill and Zoë saw Tiflis. It lay at the bottom of a wide caldron-shaped valley dominated by the sentinel mountain of St. David. She recognized the landmarks she knew so well by hearsay—the river Kura, the old castle on a cliff, the half-sunken Cathedral of Zion. She could hardly believe she was actually there; it was all so much as she had expected it to be. And she clutched Madame Tollet's hand to make sure she wasn't dreaming. But when they got to the crowded streets, her eyes ran wild. Colorful oriental rugs hung from second-floor balconies; beneath them idlers in bright native costumes wandered to and fro and merchants called out their wares, while the inevitable kintos, those peripatetic vendors, strolled around leisurely under the big flat trays they carried on their heads, showing off a little, as if saying to the world at large, "See what a fine bird I am!"

Half an hour later, preceded by five moushas carrying their baggage, Zoë walked between the Tollets down the Golovinsky Prospect, the chief modern thoroughfare of Tiflis. She was looking forward now to her meeting with Thérèse Michot and to a good night's

rest in a clean bed after the long, tiring voyage. She glanced somewhat absent-mindedly at the broad straight avenue paved with
cobblestones, at the neat two- and three-storied houses on either
side of it, and at the mountain of St. David in the background, rising
high above the city, bare-and bleak.

"Well, here we are at Thérèse Michot's," Monsieur Tollet said,
coming to a stop. "Strange! I don't see her sign."

But Zoë did not hear his last remark, for Madame Tollet had exclaimed at the same time, "Look, Zoë-djan! There goes Princess
Anna Tchavchavadzé. She is the one Countess Koramzine gave you
a letter to!"

"Where?" Zoë turned around quickly. An open carriage was
carrying two ladies swiftly by, one dressed according to the latest
Paris fashions, the other in deep mourning, her face hidden behind a
heavy crepe veil. "Which one?"

"The one you can see. The other is her sister, Princess Varvara
Orbeliani."

"Marron Glacé and Truffe au Chocolat!" Monsieur Tollet put in
with his high piping laugh. "You can see them in the flesh now.
Marron Glacé is yours!"

Zoë saw a proud profile, cold and delicate as a cameo, framed in
a bonnet trimmed with small ostrich plumes. And as she gazed at it,
a strange discomforting feeling came over her. It was as though she
were facing the inevitable, a challenge she would have to grapple
with sooner or later. Frowning a little in her perplexity, she turned
back slowly to Thérèse Michot's door, half expecting to see a smiling
Thérèse on the threshold. But the door remained closed, deaf to the
tingling of the bell and the blows of Monsieur Tollet's umbrella.

The next half hour remained forever dim in Zoë's mind. Monsieur
Tollet had run around to the back of the house and had returned, his
face a study in dismay. "She is gone! She has left Tiflis!" Zoë stared
back at him in blank amazement. Gone! Thérèse gone! The shock
was so great it left her numb. "I am not afraid," was all she was able
to mutter. Instantly Madame Tollet's motherly arm was around her,
and Monsieur Tollet grabbed her firmly by the elbow. Between them
they all but carried her along the street. She saw a young woman run
out of a shop to greet them—Caroline, with her father's twitching
eyebrows, her mother's round face, and her own demure little smile;
and her dark lanky husband behind her. There were hugs and kisses,
little cries of joy, and then Zoë was taken up a long flight of stairs
into a big bright room. She heard Caroline speaking in a high-pitched

voice like her father's: "Oh, Thérèse Michot. Such a scandal! It has shaken the whole French colony here. Just imagine, *Maman*, she turned out to be a *spy!* So unladylike! So shocking! And not in the pay of France, either, in the pay of *Turkey!*" A gasp of horror escaped the Tollets, and the word *"Turkey!"* re-echoed through the room. "It seems the authorities got wind of it, but she vanished before they could arrest her, no one knows where to!"

It was the pitiful look on Madame Tollet's face that brought Zoë out of her stupor. The little dumpling of a woman had crumpled into a chair, exclaiming pathetically, "To think she could have done such a thing! Compromising us all! To think, to think, to think! And *Turkey*, of all countries! Oh, horrors!" Her mouth sagged and her left eye went on a sudden rampage.

For a moment Zoë forgot her own troubles and fears. "Dear darling Madame Tollet, don't let it upset you so," she exclaimed. "Good riddance is all I can say! Good riddance!"

Madame Tollet stood up, her face flushed. "My dear brave child! To think of you consoling me! You who have nowhere to go now, no money left. Oh dear, dear me! But you will stay with us, won't you?"

"Of course she will," Monsieur Tollet piped out. "What room shall we give her?"

"Your study, Marzipan."

"How right you are! I hardly ever use it anyway. Isn't she always right? Always, always right, my little lozenge!"

Tears of gratitude came welling up into Zoë's eyes. "Oh, you are so kind to me." Her voice trembled a little. "Yes, I will stay with you if I may for a little while."

"For months!" Monsieur Tollet cried.

Zoë forced a smile. "For two or three months perhaps, until Sasha comes to fetch me."

Yes, she still had Sasha. She wasn't alone in the world, after all. It was just a question of time. She would write and tell him what had happened and he would hurry to her side. Her tears dried up, and for the first time she looked around the room with interest. She saw frills and flounces everywhere, and small tables and flimsy chiffoniers loaded with bric-a-brac. Small as she was, she felt like the proverbial bull, and her eyes rested with relief on a big massive couch, the one solid, substantial piece of furniture in the room. Above it on the wall hung a large oil painting of a rosy, chubby infant carried across a cloudless blue sky by a flock of cherubs. The infant looked surprisingly like Madame Tollet. Zoë refrained from asking questions. It might be a child they had lost, she thought, following Madame Tollet and Caroline out of the room.

The study they entered adjoined the living room, and for almost an hour the three women, with the help of a maid, busied themselves transforming it into a bedroom. They brought in a washstand and a towel rack; they made up the low divan into a bed and moved the heavy desk to one side, clearing it and turning it into a dressing table. Even its drawers were emptied for Zoë's use. And when they had finished and were surveying the room, Monsieur Tollet popped his head in at the door.

"I went to the post office and look what I found!" he cried, brandishing a letter over his head. "For you, Zoë-djan."

She rushed across the room and snatched it out of Monsieur Tollet's hand. She held the envelope up to look at it, her own hands trembling a little. It was from Roxane. She tore it open. She read the letter hurriedly and her eyes began to shine. Roxane, in a few brief sentences, had contrived to tell her everything she wanted to know. "Oh, do listen to this!" she cried, and read aloud: " 'Dear Niece, I have seen Captain Novoselsky twice since you left. He is leaving for Russia tomorrow. I do not know why the man loves you so, but he does. I showed him a miniature I have of you as a child and he grew all soft and sentimental. So do not be a fool! . . . After your departure Marguerite, the maid, acted very strangely—stupid and listless. Now she has run away. Personally I think she has eloped. Last night I proposed to Auguste Tresor and was accepted. At first he cried a little, but then he folded his hands together and thanked me in the most touching terms—"Dear and excellent Mademoiselle Roxane, I need you as a guardian angel!" He is a very sensible man. Your aunts are wild, but I am keeping them at bay. And I am waiting for a long letter with a detailed description of all you have seen. Your affectionate aunt, Roxane Chabout.' "

"Well, well!" Monsieur Tollet exclaimed when Zoë had finished reading. "Do you suppose he climbed on a chair to kiss Mademoiselle Roxane?"

"Oh no! Aunt Roxane sat down and offered him her cheek."

"Her *cheek!*"

They all laughed. Then very tactfully the Tollets withdrew, leaving Zoë to herself. Her eyes flew back to the letter. She read the sentences about Sasha over and over again, luxuriating in them, storing every word in her heart—"I do not know why the man loves you so, but he does. I showed him a miniature I have of you as a child and he grew all soft and sentimental. . . ."

"Zoë-djan, you are a child who should not be allowed to run unprotected all over the face of the earth!" She had closed her eyes and the lights of occasional street lamps were wandering slowly through the carriage. "I will keep your bonnet. And you will accept my pledge." And through the soiled windowpane of the railroad carriage her eyes were locked once again in his.

The memory of it all brought on a wave of unbearable loneliness. Quickly she folded the letter, slipped it inside her blouse, next to her heart, and ran out of the room. During the remainder of that afternoon she worked hard, helping the Tollets to settle down, keeping her mind safely fixed on her work. And it was not until after supper, when the Tollets were in the living room, that she left them to write a letter to Sasha.

She undressed in a hurry and slipped into a dressing gown. But when she had seated herself, pen in hand, at the improvised dressing table, she remembered with a sudden heart-rending pang that she did not know his address in St. Petersburg. A cord snapped. Alone, all alone at the wild ends of the world with only a couple of candy-makers to depend on! Stark, cold terror stared out of her eyes. She sprang to her feet, clutching at her throat. And with a cry she fell on the bed, sobbing desperately.

The door flew open. Madame Tollet appeared on the threshold. She ran up to Zoë, flinging her arms around her. "My poor darling! Don't! Please don't! We will take care of you." She went on speaking for a long time, and when Zoë had grown a little calmer, she said, "I have good news for you. Caroline just told me that Princess Anna Tchavchavadzé is looking for a French governess for her two eldest children. With Countess Koramzine's letter you could easily get the job."

Zoë sat up, her eyes big and frightened. She remembered the cold delicate profile, and once again an inexorable destiny seemed to be closing in on her. A menial in a rich household was what Roxane had said. And before she knew it she had cried out, "No! I can't! I won't do it! I don't want to see Princess Anna. Not until Sasha takes me to her himself."

Madame Tollet sighed. "Oh well, you don't have to think of it now. Tomorrow everything will seem much brighter."

A sudden panic seized Zoë. The Tollets were trying to get rid of her. "Dear darling sweet Madame Tollet, don't send me away. Don't make me go to Princess Anna!"

Madame Tollet gathered her up in her arms. "There now! Who said I was going to send you away? Such foolish talk, I do declare! There, there. I will keep you right here, and you will help me in the shop. I can do with an extra hand now that Caroline tells me she is going to have a baby."

She rocked Zoë gently. And when Zoë had cried herself out, she put her to bed and tucked her in. Zoë looked like a frightened little girl, lying very still, hiccuping ever so slightly, her face all eyes and mouth. Madame Tollet sat down on the edge of the bed. She patted her hands and stroked her hair, whispering a thousand tender, soothing words, until at last, still sobbing a little from time to time, Zoë fell asleep. Madame Tollet stood up and blew out the candle.

3   Rain fell overnight, washing the city clean. It looked bright and cheery in the morning sun; the air was fresh and cool. And Zoë's fears were washed away by a good night's sleep. She had found real friends, she had found work. And Sasha, she felt, would not be long now in coming to her. Only the thought of Princess Anna kept cropping up to challenge her newly found confidence. "It's as though she were calling out, 'Madame Duval, I need a governess for my children,' " she said to herself as she hurried downstairs to the shop. "Well, I can forget about her now." But in this Zoë was mistaken. A perverse destiny seemed to thrust Princess Anna on her all through the day.

It started in the shop around noon when Caroline suddenly exclaimed, "Maman! The tragic widow and her nieces have arrived!"

Madame Tollet looked flustered. "Oh! Her Excellency, Nina Alexandrovna Griboyedoff!" she whispered to Zoë. "I must attend to her myself. And, by the way, her nieces are Princess Anna's eldest daughters."

Madame Tollet's words came as an unpleasant reminder of the night before. "Oh, the two little girls who need a French governess," Zoë said coldly, stationing herself in a corner behind the counter. In spite of her blind fears, she was curious to see these children and even more curious, perhaps, to see their aunt. The Tollets had spoken of her during the journey as one of their important customers, and everything they had said about her had sounded so very sad. Twenty-four years of widowhood at the age of forty! Zoë shuddered slightly at the thought. Born Nina Tchavchavadzé, she had been married at the age of fifteen to a man almost twenty years her senior and already famous throughout the Russian Empire as a poet and playwright. A year later she had been left a widow, when Alexander Griboyedoff, her husband, then Russian minister plenipotentiary to Persia, had been killed by a rioting mob in Teheran. "She never married again," Madame Tollet had said, "despite her beauty and wealth. And yet not a breath of scandal has ever touched her name."

Zoë had half expected to find in this woman an aura of tragedy and renunciation. Instead she saw nothing but complete serenity reflected in her countenance, with its large brown eyes set rather wide apart and its small well-modeled features that still bore traces of great beauty. She had entered the shop preceded by two little girls, six and seven years old, dressed alike—lace pantaloons showing under their short crinoline skirts and a profusion of dark curls falling from under their small Highland caps.

"*Bonjour, Madame Tollet! Bonjour, Caroline!*" Nina Alexandrovna was saying with a smile that revealed a row of teeth amazingly white in a woman of her age. Madame Tollet bowed respectfully and Caroline bobbed a curtsy, while Nina Alexandrovna addressed her nieces in French: "Salome, Marie, go over to the counter and pick out some sweets for your aunt Varvara."

"For the Princess Orbeliani," Madame Tollet chimed in. "Ah, in that case it should be truffes au chocolat!"

The two little girls exchanged a solemn look and Marie, livelier and more enterprising than her elder sister, exclaimed, "Oh no, madame! I prefer marrons glacés!"

"Just like her mamma." Madame Tollet chuckled. "And what does the little Princess Salome like best?"

Salome's round black eyes wandered in Madame Tollet's direction. "I have no preference, madame," she replied with a reserve and an aloofness surprising in so young a child.

"Salome likes fudge!" Marie cried. "And I like marrons glacés! Aunt Nina, must we buy truffes au chocolat?"

"Yes, darling. Today is your aunt Varvara's birthday and you should buy *her* favorite sweets."

Marie pondered this for a moment and then ran precipitately across the shop. Leaning forward on tiptoe, she clutched the edge of the counter and peered at Zoë. "*Jolie madame*, will you please give us a box of truffes au chocolat with *one* marron glacé and *one* piece of fudge in it?"

General laughter greeted her words, and Madame Tollet solved the problem by presenting each little girl with a couple of her favorite sweets, while Caroline packed up a large box of truffes au chocolat.

Nina Alexandrovna in the meantime had said a few words to Zoë, and Madame Tollet hurried over to their side. She presented Zoë, laying stress on the fact that she was a personal friend of Countess Koramzine.

Nina Alexandrovna smiled. Nothing ever seemed to surprise her. "I have not had the pleasure of meeting the countess," she said quietly, "but I know her brother, Captain Novoselsky. He was stationed here for a while. A charming young man! Do you know him too, madame?"

"Yes, madame . . . I—I have met him."

It seemed strangely unbecoming to be speaking of Sasha in this casual and detached way, and Zoë blushed. She felt awkward; she didn't know what else to say. And it was Madame Tollet who spoke up, telling Nina Alexandrovna about Hélène Koramzine's gifts for Princess Anna.

"My sister-in-law will be at home at four," the other replied. "I am sure she will be delighted to see you. Why don't you come this afternoon and bring Madame Duval with you?"

Princess Anna was moving in closer. There was nothing Zoë could do about it. And aloud she murmured a few words of thanks.

Nina Alexandrovna had turned to the children, who were quarreling over the box of sweets. "Salome, you carry it to the carriage. Marie, you will carry it out of the carriage, and both of you will hold it when you give it to your aunt." And with a gracious *"A tout à l'heure"* that seemed to be addressed almost exclusively to Zoë, she swept out of the shop.

And so the die was cast. At four that afternoon, nervous and a little confused, Zoë found herself seated opposite Princess Anna in the latter's big drawing room. Nina Alexandrovna was present, serene and composed as usual, and a few other ladies sat chatting in different corners of the room, but it was Princess Anna who dominated the scene. Her face in the full bloom of her twenty-eight years looked like a Persian miniature, Zoë thought. And her waist was a true miracle of grace in a mother of six children. But her personality was unbending. She sat very straight in a stiff chair, two large diamonds sparkling in her ears, her big black eyes wide open, despite the fact that she was very nearsighted. Even after reading

Hélène Koramzine's letter she did not seem to unbend. She merely smiled at Zoë, saying, "I hope we will be seeing you often," and then turned to Madame Tollet. Her extreme reserve made Zoë tongue-tied. She had to clear her throat several times before answering a question, which made her feel even more uncomfortable. And when Princess Anna asked Madame Tollet to keep an eye open for a French governess, she felt she could stand it no more. She stood up abruptly to take her leave, and Princess Anna raised a lorgnette, leveling it in her direction. Formidable was the only word that came to Zoë's mind as she almost fled from the room, furious at herself and at this woman who could make her feel so nervous and gauche.

"What do you think of her, Zoë-djan?" Madame Tollet asked when they had left the house. She had lowered her voice, as though Princess Anna were still within earshot.

Zoë drew her shawl tighter around her shoulders and tossed her head. "She chills me! If she were my employer she would crush me! Never, never would I be able to face her again as Sasha's wife!"

Madame Tollet glanced at Zoë out of the corner of her eye. Then she said an unexpected thing: "Perhaps you will feel that way about all his relatives. It is the glamour with which our imagination surrounds these people that makes us poor little middle-class folk feel insignificant in their presence."

Zoë tossed her head again angrily and quickened her step. Madame Tollet's words had gone home.

4   To see Madame Tollet at work in her storeroom was to
      know her at her best. Here, in a subtle aroma of vanilla and chocolate, mocha and peppermint, she would lay her sweets out in neat boxes, using small silver tongs with gentle care, for to her all sweets were of the essence of angels, a blessing from the *bon Dieu* himself. Madame Tollet had a shadowless, innocent faith that had never changed since the day when, as a small child, her old French peasant nurse had called her to her side, saying, "Come here, my little Paulette, and I will tell you all about the bon Dieu!" Yes, the bon Dieu, she had said, sat on a beautiful white cloud supported by many shining angels, and around Him floated lots and lots of smaller clouds carrying all His pets; His pet dog, known as the *bon chien*, His pet cat, known as the *bon chat*, and many, many others; there was even a pet fish, known as the *poisson céleste*, that swam in a lovely crystal bowl, and a pet beehive made of pure gold that

hummed with the bon Dieu's own busy bees. And while the bon chien sat and thought of all the dogs on earth, and the bon chat of all the cats, and all the other pets were busy thinking of their own species, the bon Dieu sat and thought of human beings, especially of little Paulette. This is where the nurse's story had ended, but since then a new cloud had floated in with a clean little sweetshop on it that had pleased the bon Dieu infinitely. He would look at it and say to His cherubs, "Sweetness is part of your nature, my pretty ones, so fly over to that shop and eat those sweets to your heart's content." And in honor of this she had created "cherub wings," which had become very popular among her customers. They were made in the shape of two wings with a little round head between them, of a marshmallowy substance that melted away after one bite, leaving a refreshing, gentle flavor in one's mouth. They came in different colors and flavors—white peppermint and vanilla for our own children, she would explain; brown chocolate for the little Africans, yellow lemon for the little Chinese, and pink strawberry for "those poor Redskins in North America, who must have their own cherubs too."

Five days had gone by since Zoë and she had visited Princess Anna, and Madame Tollet was busy at the long table covered with sheets of clean white paper. It was getting close to suppertime and she was in a hurry, but she lined up her cherub wings in a box with as much care and tenderness as though she had all the time in the world. When Zoë blew into the room she looked up at her with a smile. "You are looking very happy this evening," she said, noticing the sparkle in Zoë's eyes.

"Yes, I feel happy! Happy and gay! May I have a cherub wing? A pink one, please. Mmmm! . . . Delicious!" She waltzed around the table, light and merry.

"And what makes you so happy, may I ask?"

Zoë laughed. "Oh, nothing in particular! Everything! Haven't you ever felt that way? When all is good inside? I am happy to be with you. I am happy to work here. And proud Princess Anna can look elsewhere for a governess! Tra-la!" She took two notes but clamped her hand to her mouth. "Oh no! Not all is good!" she cried in mock despair. "I had forgotten I had no voice."

Madame Tollet tried to look severe. "You cannot have everything you want, my child."

"Oh, but you don't understand." Zoë leaned across the table. "It would mean so much, so much. If I could sing, I know I could fly away. Up, up, up, to glorious, heavenly heights!"

81

"You don't need a fine voice for that, my dear. Not all the saints had fine voices before they went to heaven!"

"But I don't want to be a saint. I want to fly up to heaven and touch the angels, and then come back to earth again. It is so good to have a body! I don't want to lose it, or forget about it either." She shut her eyes tight and clutched her hands together. "Sometimes I think, if I were held in the deepest pit of despair and could sing, my song would carry me forth, way, way up, and out of my misery!" She opened her eyes and laughed. "Am I being very stupid?"

"Not stupid. A dreamer, that's all." Madame Tollet closed the box and put it aside in line with many others. "Come, let us close the shop. Caroline and her husband have gone out for the evening."

She led the way down the long corridor that separated the storeroom from the shop. Voices reached them from Monsieur Tollet's office, and Madame Tollet stopped, listening in alarm. "Wait a moment. I must speak to my caramel."

With that she threw the door open. She did not go beyond the threshold. She stood staring at a fat individual with an unusually long and fleshy nose who had stood up at her appearance. She acknowledged his bow with a curt little nod and then asked her husband to step outside. Monsieur Tollet came out, closing the door behind him. His eyebrows twitched nervously, and he said in a whisper, "It is a very big order."

"I don't care how big it is! You know what we know about his orders!"

"But, Bonbon chéri, that is only hearsay."

"Crème de pistache!" Madame Tollet exclaimed with unusual vehemence. "Hearsay or no hearsay, we cannot afford taking risks at this time. Remember Thérèse Michot. We might be under suspicion, for all we know! No! Tell him he can have his sweets if he gives us a written guaranty they are for himself, not for anyone else!"

Monsieur Tollet spread his arms out in dismay. "How can I tell him such a thing?"

"You can, and what's more, you will! If that man Spindarian"— here Madame Tollet's voice rose to a high pitch—"is buying our sweets for Daniel-Sultan"—she raised her voice still higher to be sure the man in the room could hear her—"and it was found out, we'd be in a fine kettle of fish!" She calmed down just as suddenly as she had flared up, and added in a low voice, "There. That should help you." And seizing Zoë by the hand, she scurried back to the storeroom, muttering under her breath, "Oh, my poor old caramel. He is so timid at times."

She flopped into a chair. "Oh, I am so upset, so upset! I must calm myself before I go to the shop."

Zoë had never seen her in such a state. "Who is this Spindarian?" she asked. "And why are you so afraid of his orders?"

"Spindarian! Why, he is one of the richest Armenian merchants in town. A most unscrupulous man! He does not care who he deals with so long as he can make money. Informed friends have warned us, he buys our sweets for Daniel-Sultan!"

The name meant nothing to Zoë, and Madame Tollet explained in a few words about Daniel-Sultan. The Moslem ruler of the sultanate of Elisou—a small principality in the Daghestan of strategic importance to the Russians and to Shamyl alike—he had served as a general in the Russian Army and had lived in Tiflis for a number of years. Infuriated by the steady refusal of the Russian authorities to recognize his status as a semi-independent ruler, he went over to Shamyl's side and gave his only daughter in marriage to Shamyl's son.

"Jemaleddin?" Zoë cried out in surprise.

"No, no! His second son, his heir, who lives with him in the mountains. I believe his name is Kazi-Mahomma."

But here she stopped suddenly. Heavy footsteps were coming down the corridor and a familiar voice was shouting in broken French: "Where Zoia Ivanovna? Where my young mistress Zoia Ivanovna?" Zoë had been sitting at Madame Tollet's feet. She seized her friend's hand now and looked up, her eyes shining, her smile uncertain, not quite daring to believe her own ears. "Poushka!" she murmured, and swallowed hard.

The door flew open and a gigantic bearded soldier stood on the threshold. Instantly Zoë was on her feet, running toward him. He kissed her hands and, straightening himself to his full height, made a broad sign of the cross. "Glory to Thee, God!" he exclaimed in his quaint French. "We are together again, and I find you looking well, my young mistress!"

He had said it again! Zoë's heart beat wildly. "Sasha must be free!" she thought. Poushka's short nose, his beard, all of his broad-shouldered immensity shone in her sight now. Elated, she raised herself on her toes and, flinging her arms around his neck, she kissed the rim of his beard, which was as far as she could reach.

83

Poushka's face grew very red. With a heavy thud he suddenly fell to his knees and, raising the hem of Zoë's skirt, he kissed it reverently. Zoë stood very still, her eyes closed, to accept the homage of Sasha's servant. Madame Tollet brushed away a tear and crossed her heart hurriedly. "Thank God!" she murmured. "The dear child's troubles are at an end."

If anyone had ventured to say to Poushka that he was in love with Zoë, he would have chased the blasphemer around the block. Yet in a sense it was true. Ever since that morning when he had first laid eyes on her in the narrow hallway of the Chabout house in Paris, he had worshiped her as he had never worshiped a woman before. His wife had been something to reach for; his three daughters had been the result. They had married early and had gone out of his life. But Zoë was there to be adored. And his adoration for her blended with his all-absorbing devotion to Sasha. All Poushka wanted now of life was to see those two married and to serve them for the rest of his days. He felt this more keenly than ever as he rose to his feet and looked sheepishly around the room.

"Where is Alexandr Dimitrievitch?" Zoë asked.

"With His High Excellency, the governor general. Alexandr Dimitrievitch had to report immediately upon arrival." Sasha, he told her, had left St. Petersburg at a moment's notice, sent as special courier to General Réad, the governor general of the Caucasus. They had flown, literally flown all the way, he exclaimed, making the trip in record time, in less than six weeks. They had arrived in Tiflis an hour ago.

"How long will he stay?"

"As long as His High Excellency will require his services. A month, two months, perhaps."

Zoë's eyes sparkled. "And when is he coming here?"

Poushka shook his head. "His High Excellency insisted Alexandr Dimitrievitch stay eat with him. And Alexandr Dimitrievitch said he come to see you chez Michot at nine. Now I must go tell him where you are. I went chez Michot—no one there. Then I say to myself— Tollets'! Hah! So I find you, Zoia Ivanovna. Now I must go." He bowed. "Good-by. Stay happy!"

Poushka was gone. And Zoë with a happy cry turned to Madame Tollet and hugged her several times.

5   He stood in the doorway, a glistening stranger in a hussar's
     uniform. She seemed like a stranger too. He had never seen
her before in anything but black, and now she was all dressed up in
his honor. He gazed in wonder at her evening gown—layers of tulle,
from pale pink to bright crimson, a crimson velvet sash around the
waist, and the jeweled miniatures of her parents around her neck.
"My sweet little posy," he whispered. And with a happy laugh he
swept her into his arms, almost lifting her off her feet.

"Damn, damn the general!" he cried.

"Bless him," she laughed back. "He is going to keep you here."

He covered her eyes and cheeks with little burning kisses. She held
him at arm's length and shook him happily. "I can't believe it! I just
can't believe it!"

"Believe it or not, I'm here." He pressed his nose against hers, and
his eyes blended into one big blue eye. It stared at her for a moment
and then vanished as his lips touched hers. She tore herself away.
"Come! The Tollets are in the living room."

Time seemed to be slipping back on them. It was their first meeting all over again at the Tollets' in Paris, with no narrow table to
separate them, but their eyes as eloquent as ever. They sat on the
couch, and she let the Tollets tell him the whole story. He listened
attentively. He looked a little startled when he heard about Thérèse
Michot, but he smiled at her reassuringly, while her eyes wandered
lovingly over his face, took in every detail of his uniform. "Mine! All
of him will be mine now for life!" Words said by the Tollets reached
her without registering properly, though she nodded to confirm them
every time he smiled at her. "Thérèse Michot . . . Turkey . . .
Turkey, of all countries! . . . Now we are all working together in
our shop." And suddenly—"Princess Anna"! Oh well, it did not
matter now that he was here. But a moment later she turned to
Madame Tollet with a frown. She had heard the word "governess."
"Let us not talk about that!"

"Why?" Sasha asked suddenly.

He seemed to be weighing the possibility of her becoming a
governess, and this annoyed her. "Because you can have your marron
glacé!" she said sharply. "She is a cold, haughty woman."

No sooner had the words escaped her than she felt ashamed. Less
than a quarter of an hour with him and she was speaking to him in
such a way. Tears of remorse filled her eyes and her mouth grew
larger.

Sasha laughed. He leaned forward and pressed her hand. "Come

85

now, eyes and mouth, cheer up!" And she smiled at him through her tears.

During the last minute or so the Tollets had been whispering to one another. They stood up now, and Monsieur Tollet led his wife out of the room. Sasha jumped to his feet, running after them to see them to the door. Zoë stood up too. She was alone with him at last. And a little scared, her heart beating wildly, she waited for him with bowed head.

He drew her chin up and looked earnestly into her eyes. "Zoëdjan, why are you afraid of Anna?"

"Oh, Sasha!" She hid her face on his shoulder. "I don't know how to explain. I don't mind working. Work is honorable. But to be a menial among your relatives—I couldn't stand it."

She heard his low laugh, slightly mocking, and then a tender whisper in her ear. "Little goose!"

"Oh, Sasha . . ."

He had intended to say more, but for the last three months he had been faithful, and he had been dreaming. He held her tight now, his body ripe, his lips hungry. And slowly, obeying his pressure, she sank to the couch. The rage of his kisses burned through her. Sensuousness and languor flared up into wild flames. There were no words left, only the inspiration of mad caresses. Impatient, frantic fingers searched for hooks and buttons that seemed to spring apart at their touch. The bodice of her dress fell open and he buried his face between her breasts. On his feet again, he drew her up roughly to himself. For a breathless moment he held her crushed, and she clung to him, her whole body craving, demanding. Swiftly he gathered her up in his arms and carried her across the threshold of her room. . . .

It was past five when Sasha slipped out of the house, trying to keep his spurs from clinking, and walked briskly down the Golovinsky to his hotel. His step was light, his heart elated. That night he had found a depth of satisfaction he had never experienced before. She had given herself to him with no reservations, no secret withdrawals, and with a purity of sacrifice that made his own self-immolation complete. He knew now that while she would go on giving he would remain forever her supplicant, for to survive with integrity he needed the tenderness she aroused in him, a tenderness that would outlast all earthly passions. Of the millions of God's creatures walking this earth, Zoë had been created for him and he had been allowed to love her. Sasha felt humbled. He would have liked to pray, except that prayer had always been a formal ritual in his life, unconnected with deeper emotions.

He entered the dark and narrow hotel hallway, hurrying past a sleeping porter and running up the stairs three steps at a time. But when he reached his room and found Poushka there waiting for him, a letter in his hand, he stopped and frowned.

"Don't you ever sleep?" he asked with annoyance.

Poushka looked at him gloomily. "We have our marching orders," he said. "We are leaving in a few hours. A carriage and post horses will be at the hotel at nine."

The shock was so great that Sasha sat down on the edge of the metal-framed bed. "Who told you?"

"The orderly who brought this."

Sasha snatched the letter and tore it open. Running to a big table near the whitewashed wall, he bent over a candle and read it. It was written in General Réad's own hand. "Alexandr Dimitrievitch," it began formally. "Alarming reports have just reached me from Kahetia. Suspicious movements have been noticed in the mountains among the Lezghian and the Tchetchen tribes, and a possible attack on Kahetia is feared. You will proceed at once to Telav, reporting to Prince Andronikoff, who is in charge of that city. He will provide you with horses and a guide. You are to visit the foremost outposts of our Lezghian Cordon, obtaining the latest information available from our scouts. You will then report your findings to Colonel Kulman, commanding officer of our regular troops in Kahetia, and remain attached to his staff until further orders from me. Godspeed."

Sasha's whole military training forbade him to consider the possibility of a delay, and he knew that whatever he wanted to do had to be done at once. "Heat up a samovar and bring me some tea," he said to Poushka.

"For God's sake, Alexandr Dimitrievitch, lie down and rest. We have a whole day's journey ahead of us."

"No, I will sleep on the way. There is much to be done between now and nine. A glass of tea will revive me."

"All right, all right! The samovar is all heated. How do you think I kept myself awake waiting for you!"

Poushka went out grumbling, and Sasha sank into a chair. He covered his face with his hands, pressing the tips of his fingers to his eyes. He was thinking, if war with France broke out while he was away, what would happen to Zoë, living here unprotected with a French family? Not that he had any misgivings about the Tollets—

their reputation in Tiflis was a solid one—but the story about Thérèse Michot had alarmed him. The police were sure to learn that Zoë had come to Tiflis at her invitation. For all he knew, they might be watching her even now. He shuddered slightly at the thought of Zoë in the hands of the police. Like most men of his day and class, he despised the police force, having no use for it except as a protection against thieves and robbers. Bullies, he called them, half-literate, uncouth ruffians who wouldn't know a lady when they saw one and wouldn't care whether the accusations against her were false. He saw it very clearly—it was up to him to protect Zoë before he left. For a moment he toyed with the idea of asking his cousin, Varvara Orbeliani, to take her as a companion, but he gave it up. It was too obvious; people might guess why she had done it. Once married, he could offer Zoë the protection of his name and of the high social position of his family, but until then the least said about it, the better. Higher authorities might get wind of his intentions and frown at the idea of a Russian officer marrying a Frenchwoman at this time. His other cousin, Anna Tchavchavadzé, was the only solution. She must be made to offer Zoë the position of governess. There was no other way, he said to himself, no matter how Zoë felt about it. In an instant his plans were made up. He would enlist Varvara's help. She was more understanding, more amenable, and together they would talk Anna into it. As for Zoë, he would find the proper words to make her understand.

Sasha looked up and smiled as Poushka came in, carrying a big samovar with a small round teapot perched on top of the funnel like a fat little bird in a nest.

"Won't you be reasonable for once and go to sleep?" Poushka said, pouring out a glass of tea for Sasha.

"No, I will go and wake up a few people instead."

"For goodness' sake, Alexandr Dimitrievitch, what do you want to do that for?"

Sasha sipped his tea. "Would you leave Zoia Ivanovna here unprotected? Would you hand her to the police, accused of being a spy?"

Poushka shook his head solemnly from side to side and crossed himself. "God forbid! Zoia Ivanovna is an innocent little tomtit sitting on a branch trimming her feathers. If anyone harmed her I would go out and kill!"

"Well then, you see!"

"O-och, Alexandr Dimitrievitch! If you had taken my advice in

88

Petersburg and had sent in your petition for an annulment to the Holy Synod, you might have been free by now to marry Zoia Ivanovna."

Sasha made an exasperated gesture with his hand. "Such a know-all! It takes longer than that to get an annulment. Besides, you know very well I spent those few days in Petersburg arguing with my mother. She said my marriage was my cross and I should bear it!"

Poushka sighed. "O-och! The lady Zenaida Pavlovna, for all her gentleness, can be mighty hard at times."

"She gave in in the end, didn't she? That is all that matters." Sasha looked at his watch. It was almost six. He got up abruptly. "Listen to me carefully now. I am going out. Pack up. Get the carriage here at eight-thirty and pick me up at Princess Varvara's house at nine sharp!" And grabbing his military cap, he ran out of the room before Poushka could say another word.

6 Sasha stormed into Princess Varvara's house, rousing the servants from their early-morning lethargy. Princess Varvara, alarmed and a little dazed—for until then she had had no idea Sasha was in Tiflis—came out into the drawing room to meet him in a dressing gown and a frilled nightcap. When she heard his story, however, she seemed to grasp at once all its implications. She lost no time in getting dressed and went with him to her sister's house.

Princess Anna proved to be more difficult. Her surprise at seeing Sasha hardly made up for her annoyance at being awakened at such an early hour, and it took a lot of arguing before she finally consented to accept Zoë as a governess for Salome and Marie. The whole situation, she said, would be a false one. She would find it difficult to impose her authority on Zoë, besides which she did not like to take such a step without first consulting her husband. And Prince David, she said, had already gone out for one of his early-morning horseback rides. But in the end Princess Varvara's gentle persuasions and Sasha's passionate outbursts and the quiet approval of Nina Alexandrovna, who had joined them, prevailed and she gave in reluctantly.

It was past eight when Sasha finally reached the Tollets'. He found Zoë alone in the upstairs living room, looking surprisingly prim and girlish in her plain gray frock with its white collar and white cuffs. When she heard the clinking of his spurs, she came running to him and pressed her cheek to his shoulder.

89

"I did not expect you so early," she murmured; and looking up anxiously into his eyes, "Has anything happened, Sasha?"

"Yes, darling. I have received my marching orders. I must leave at nine. I will be away for a month, maybe more."

She clung to him, trembling a little, while he held her tightly in his arms.

"Zoë-djan," he said at last, "I can't go away and leave you here with the Tollets. The way things are shaping themselves in the world, I want you in a safer place. I have made other arrangements for you."

She freed herself from his embrace and moved a step back. Her cheeks grew a shade paler. "What arrangements?" she whispered almost inaudibly.

Sasha took a deep breath. "Anna offers you the position of governess."

Her lips tightened and her eyes grew harder. She raised her hand as though to push away an unpleasant vision, then let it drop again. "I can't. I can't do it."

"You must, Zoë-djan." He began to speak fast, telling her of the inevitability of war with France and trying to explain the danger that might threaten her on account of her old friendship with Thérèse Michot. Besides all that, he said, Anna and her family would soon be going to their country home in Kahetia. He would be in Kahetia too. It would be easier for him to come and see her there. When he was through he took her hand. "Can't you see, my darling, it's the only way? No one will dare touch you in Anna's house. And if there were any trouble, she and her husband will protect you. You've got to accept the position."

Zoë looked away. "For how long, Sasha?"

He passed a helpless hand over his eyes. "I don't know. I really don't know. As soon as I can, tomorrow or the day after, I will mail my petition for an annulment." He saw her stiffen and hurried on, anxious to explain. "I didn't do it sooner because I wanted our married life to be a happy one, full of harmony in every respect. The few days I had in Petersburg I spent discussing the matter with my mother. At first she was against it. The idea of my having a wife in Petersburg and an ex-wife in Romantzevo went against all her principles. But in the end she understood. She has a kind heart."

"She doesn't want me," Zoë said in a flat voice.

"No, no! Don't get such notions into your head. She said the daughter of Colonel Chabout would be welcome as a member of her family. She told me to give you her love. She said her blessing would follow when I was free to marry you."

Zoë stood in front of him, her shoulders drooping slightly, her arms hanging helplessly at her sides. Madame Tollet's words about Sasha's relatives came back to her mind. She wanted to say something about it but changed her mind. The matter seemed too trivial to be discussed at a moment like this. A heavy lump was rising in her throat.

She crossed the room to the window and remained there looking out into the street. He followed her. Once again, as on that first evening in Paris, he was standing close behind her, so tall he could look down at the top of her head. Zoë froze. All too vividly she saw herself in Princess Anna's household, humiliated, trying desperately to assert herself, to fight the proud, domineering woman, yet getting more and more enmeshed in her own frustrations. The vision was like a physical stab; her whole nature seemed to revolt against it. Then she became aware again of Sasha's presence. She heard him sigh, and all the emotions of the night before came surging up. She could feel his breath close to her ear, and she heard him whisper, "You are my sweetheart. I need you. That is why you must accept. For my sake."

With startling clarity she had seldom experienced before, she sensed all the anxiety, all the love and care that had driven him to such frantic activity on her behalf. And what was her own love worth if she could not make this sacrifice? For his sake. She swung around, throwing her arms about his neck. "Oh, Sasha, anything you say, even if it hurts!"

He crushed her to his heart, then tore himself away. "Come! Varvara is waiting for us. I thought it would be easier for you if she took you to see Anna."

Poushka was waiting for them outside Princess Varvara's house. When he saw Zoë, he jumped out of the carriage and bent low to kiss her hand. "God help you, my lady Zoia Ivanovna," he said in his broken French. "When we come back, I bring a priest with me and two gold rings!"

His words broke the tension. Zoë and Sasha laughed. And in answer to Sasha's knock an old butler opened the front door.

"I will introduce you to Varvara," Sasha said, "and then I must go."

But Zoë stopped him. "No. After all, Sasha, I am a soldier's daugh-

91

ter. I should know where a soldier's duty lies. It is nine o'clock now. I will see you off and then I'll go and introduce myself."

Sasha did not trust himself to speak. Silently he bent over her hands, kissing them, turning them palm upwards and kissing them again. And when he went to the carriage, she pressed both her hands to her lips.

She stood there, looking very small, very lost, under Princess Varvara's big arched doorway, waving her hand and forcing herself to smile until Sasha's carriage had disappeared around a corner. Then she turned and walked into the house.

The old butler was bowing to her, pointing to a flight of marble stairs, and she went up slowly, bracing herself for the meeting with Sasha's cousin. She remembered the glimpse she had caught of Princess Varvara all wrapped in black crepe and wondered what she would find behind that heavy veil. Was it to be a second edition of Princess Anna? She hesitated before entering the drawing room, with its massive furniture and soft Persian rugs, and the sight of Princess Varvara coming forward to meet her was somewhat of a shock. "How very plain she is," she said to herself. A round face, big lips, and thickset features. But a few minutes later, seated in a big chair next to her hostess, she was indignant at herself for ever having thought this woman plain. In her way she was far more beautiful than Princess Anna. Intelligence, understanding, goodness were stamped all over her face and shone through her soft brown eyes. Zoë knew then why Sasha had arranged this meeting. The thought of Sasha brought the treacherous lump to her throat, and tears came streaming out of her eyes.

Princess Varvara patted her hand. "Every passing minute is bringing you nearer to Sasha," she said with a smile. She was leaning forward a little in her chair, as if to draw Zoë closer to herself, and for more than an hour they talked in low confidential voices of Paris and Zoë's family. Princess Varvara told her about George, her little boy of two, and about her husband, who had been killed recently on the Turkish front. She had a way of speaking about him that brought him very close, as though at any moment a door might open and he might come in. Never in her life had Zoë felt so much at ease with a stranger. Before she knew it she found herself confessing all her secret dread of Sasha's family and especially of his mother. She also told Princess Varvara about the experience she had had with Madame Duval after René's death.

Princess Varvara threw up both her hands. "Oh, Aunt Zenaida—

Sasha's mother, I mean—is not like that. I know why she was against the marriage at first. She is a woman who will never let herself be swayed by motives that might appear to her as selfish. You see, at heart she would like nothing better than to see Sasha happily married, with children of his own who would carry on her name. After her death Sasha is to add her name to his. He will become Count Romantzeff-Novoselsky. Didn't you know that?" Taken by surprise, Zoë stared at her, and Princess Varvara smiled. "Yes, he will. It was the dying wish of Aunt Zenaida's father, and the Emperor has confirmed it officially."

Zoë shook her head despondently. "I feel a little frightened. It all sounds too big, too grand for me. How will Sasha like it when in later years his friends and acquaintances refer to me as 'that Countess Romantzeff-Novoselsky, née Governess Chabout'?"

Suddenly Princess Varvara's face grew stern. "Never say that again!" she exclaimed. "As long as you think that way, others will too." Then her eyes softened and she leaned forward again. "Don't you know, my dear, that worldly differences of caste mean nothing to one who has true dignity? God created all men equal. That is a great, great truth, and all else is vanity. With it you can face a mighty emperor and know that he has his place and you have yours. And that both are good."

Zoë's deep sigh was a little tremulous. "I have so much to learn. My aunt Roxane told me so, and she was right. Oh, how I wish it were your children I had to take care of!"

There was an earnest appeal in Princess Varvara's eyes as she took Zoë's hand. "Don't be afraid of my sister. When you get to know her you will love her, I'm sure. Her shyness brings out the worst in her. She has a hard, glittering, sparkling shell into which she crawls when she is with strangers. But a woman of greater integrity, honesty, and faithfulness I have yet to meet." She stood up. "And now, shouldn't we go to her, my dear? She is waiting for us."

7   Zoë would have given much to be able to hide behind Princess Varvara's back as she entered Princess Anna's stiff, formal drawing room. The shiny parquet floor and the white walls, hung with portraits in heavy gilt frames, chilled her. She felt distinctly ill at ease. She saw three people standing at the far end of the room—Princess Anna, Nina Alexandrovna, and a man in a long dark green military tunic. She guessed that this must be Prince David,

93

Princess Anna's husband. He looked younger than his thirty-seven years, and although he held himself very erect, almost stiff, the frankness and informality of his manner helped to make her feel less shy. He shook her warmly by the hand and spoke in a pleasant, well-modulated voice. "Ah, Madame Duval! The kind young lady who has agreed to help us bring up our little imps. I can't begin to tell you how welcome you are to our family." And turning to his wife, "Anna, shall we present our children to Madame Duval?"

Zoë noticed two things about Princess Anna. She had laid both hands impulsively on Princess Varvara's shoulders, and her big eyes had lit up from within; and now, as she looked up at her handsome husband, they became soft and velvety. She said "Yes" with a smile that for a brief moment chased all coldness and hauteur out of her countenance.

Leaving Princess Varvara and Nina Alexandrovna in the drawing room, Zoë and Prince David followed Princess Anna through several rooms, down a long corridor, and into a big nursery where two nurses were taking care of four small children. Zoë saw two little girls playing in the middle of the room; two little beauties, one with golden hair and the other with thick black curls like her mother's— Elena, four years old, and Tamara, three. Sandro, fourteen months old, was the only boy of the family. He sat in his fat nurse's lap as straight as a little rod, watching a thin, dark nurse who walked to and fro in front of him, rocking his infant sister Lydia in her arms.

Elena and Tamara stood up, eying Zoë curiously. "Elena is almost old enough to be in the care of a governess," Princess Anna said, regaining her cold and distant air. "But she will be spending the summer with her aunt and cousins in Mingrelia, so we will have to postpone her education until the autumn."

"Yes, she is my sister Catherine's favorite." Prince David smiled. "Though why anyone should like a little yellow mouse so much I really do not know!" And he kissed Elena in the small of the neck, blowing out his cheeks to tickle her a little and make her laugh.

Prince David played with his children and fondled them, while Princess Anna pointed them out to Zoë in turn as if counting chicks. But when she came to little Lydia, her manner changed. She took the infant in her arms and pressed it close to her heart. "This one I am feeding myself," she said with pride. "It is the first time the doctor has allowed me to do it."

They made such a charming picture, all of them together, that Zoë could not help commenting on it. "Ah, but you have not seen

94

the pillar of our nursery," Prince David exclaimed. "Marina-gamdeli! In Georgian that means 'Marina the nurse.' Ninety-seven years old and still going strong! She nursed my father from the day he was born, and my sisters and myself, and now she still supervises the nurseries." He laughed as he added, "This year she said she was a little tired. So she accompanied my aunt to Tsinandali, our country home in Kahetia. I hope you will be there with us, madame. Then you will see her."

Zoë felt flattered. It was the second time Prince David had expressed his approval of her, and he had done it in such a charming way. Zoë liked this tall, debonair man with his highly polished manners and his deep-set eyes that seemed amused by everything they saw. *"Un grand seigneur tout fait,"* she said to herself, following Princess Anna into the adjoining room.

Salome was sitting on a small chair, looking bored, an old petticoat hanging from her shoulders in place of a mantle; while Marie, astride a small wooden rocking horse, was galloping vigorously, an old kettle on her head and a round lid from a hatbox slung over her left arm instead of a shield. When they saw Zoë, the two little girls came running up to her, exclaiming, "Oh, la jolie madame!"

"Yes. And now shake hands with Madame Duval properly," Princess Anna said, and Zoë noticed that she used a severe, distant tone with her children. "Just a shade less cold than the one she uses with me," she thought, while Princess Anna continued, "Madame Duval might consent to stay with us if you are very good."

"We shall be good if you will ride with me, madame," Marie cried, running back to the rocking horse and scrambling onto its back.

"Marie!" her mother called out sharply. "How many times must I tell you? Ladies always ride sidesaddle!"

Marie got off her rocking horse reluctantly. "But I am not a lady, Mamma! I am a knight!"

"Is that so?" her father inquired. "And what is the knight's name, may I ask?"

Marie pointed with pride to her shield, on which the name of the milliner was printed in large block letters—PETER TCHILINGA-ROFF.

"Peter Tchilingaroff! What kind of a knight is that?" Princess Anna exclaimed, suppressing a smile. "Peter Tchilingaroff is a milliner!"

"No he is not! He is a knight, and he is me!"

Prince David squatted down on his heels and put his arms around

95

his favorite daughter, drawing her closer to himself. "And where were you galloping to so fast, Sir Peter Tchilingaroff?"

"I was galloping all over the world, Papa, killing dragons. When I have killed them all, I will return and offer my hand to Salome. She is pretending to be a princess, you see."

"You mean you will ask for *her* hand?"

Marie looked at her father in surprise. "Oh no! That would be silly, wouldn't it?"

Outside the room, Princess Anna leaned against her husband's shoulder and laughed. It was a merry, silvery laugh. "Oh no! A knight called Peter Tchilingaroff! If you could only see the fat, unromantic Armenian who bears that name!"

She looked very feminine, very endearing at that moment. But the impression did not last. She was distant again, almost stern, when she took Zoë into her boudoir to discuss the terms of her employment.

That evening Zoë wrote in her *Book of Stray Thoughts*: "My Sasha is gone, and here I am, 'a menial in a rich household.' Oh, this Princess Anna! She makes me feel so small, so insignificant. Princess Varvara may say what she likes about her being shy, I think she disapproves of me in every way!" She underlined the words "in every way" and added several exclamation marks.

She felt unnerved; the ground seemed to be slipping from under her feet. And in bed that night she remembered her dream. She had not seen it since she had left Paris. She lay very still, concentrating her whole mind on it, trying to conjure up the hazel eyes and repeating to herself the familiar words, "Take courage. I am watching over you." But when sleep came to her at last it was dreamless.

8   Prince David and his family lived in a spacious two-story house high up on the slope leading to St. David's Mountain, at the top of a steep street that bore their name. It was a straight wide street that branched off the Golovinsky Prospect, and it had been named "Tchavchavadzé" in memory of Alexander, Prince David's father, an inspired Georgian poet who had played an important political role in Georgia in his day but had died young, killed in a carriage accident at the foot of this street.

Ordinarily by the first of June the big house stood silent and empty, the family having fled from the intolerable summer heat of Tiflis to the cool, shady house and the soft, refreshing breezes of

Tsinandali. But that year alarming rumors came pouring in from Kahetia. All minds were turned to the high Caucasian mountains in the north. Would Shamyl dare send his hordes into that peaceful province, people asked themselves, protected as it was by a line of Russian fortifications known as the Lezghian Cordon? And Prince David kept putting off the departure. Every day he went to General Réad's headquarters to find out the latest news, and every day General Réad, that good-natured Russian of Scottish ancestry, whose Scotch name of "Read" had been Russified into "Réad" or "Rayard" to give it a phonetic spelling in English, would say, "No, my dear prince. I know that the river Alazan will protect Tsinandali from any attack, but still, I beg of you not to take that charming princess and those beautiful children of yours so close to the mountains. Wait another day, we might get some reassuring news."

By the middle of June the heat had become oppressive. Nina Alexandrovna and little Elena left for Zugdidi, the residence of the Princess of Mingrelia, a mountain stronghold from which the Dadianis had ruled that small principality for centuries past. But the rest of the family still lingered on in Tiflis.

Zoë's spirits were at a very low ebb. The heat, the lack of news from Sasha, the delays in the departure which meant a longer separation from him, all combined to make her thoroughly miserable and sorry for herself. And worst of all, perhaps, were her relations with Princess Anna. Not that the princess was in any way unkind; on the contrary, in her own way she did her best to make Zoë feel at home, but the trouble lay in the fact that she did not know how to unbend and her manner always seemed to chill Zoë. "She is forever trying to put me in my place," she kept repeating to herself, and the knowledge that this was not really so only served to irritate her and make matters worse. In the end she found herself deliberately misconstruing everything Princess Anna said or did. Even when the latter made some amusing, trifling remark, Zoë perversely would say to herself, "Now she is making fun of me." Actually she would have liked to be friends with Princess Anna; her proud grace of carriage, the intrepid spirit she sensed in her were fascinating, but then they awed her, too, and Zoë's frustration had taken such deep roots she was incapable of shaking it off. She had buttressed herself against the princess, and nothing seemed to penetrate the dense walls, not even Princess Anna's clear, silvery laugh.

On the fifteenth of June, General Réad called in person on Princess Anna to give her the glad news of her forthcoming departure for

Tsinandali. "You may rejoice, Princess," he said. "Everything is under control. No danger threatens Kahetia any more!" He told her he had put her husband in command of the Auxiliary Militia in Kahetia. The members of the militia were stationed in private homes and would not go into action unless ordered to do so by Prince David. "And I predict," the general had said in conclusion, "that the prince will spend a quiet summer with his family, doing absolutely nothing!"

Princess Anna's joy was complete when Princess Varvara announced that she and little George would go with them. For once she shed all her reserve. She rushed into the nursery, her big eyes radiating happiness. "Madame Zoë-djan!" she cried, for Zoë's nickname had followed her into this household. "We are leaving on the eighteenth! Oh, I am so happy! What's more, we won't miss the twenty-fifth. That's my birthday, you know, and we always have open house that day in Tsinandali. Neighbors come from miles around!"

This was the moment to bridge the gulf that was widening between them so rapidly, but something in Zoë froze. "How nice," she said with a smile so artificial she could have kicked herself for it.

Princess Anna looked at her in surprise. With a barely perceptible shrug of her shoulder she turned and left the room. And later that day Zoë overheard her saying to her sister, "I really don't know what's the matter with that young woman! I have tried every way; nothing seems to get through that silly shell of hers. To think of her married to our Sasha!"

In a kind of haze Zoë heard Princess Varvara's quiet voice saying, "You know yourself, my dear, you have an unfortunate manner sometimes that chills and frightens people," but Zoë did not wait to listen to the end. She fled to her room, and that night she cried herself to sleep.

For the next few days excitement and activity reigned in the house in spite of the heat. When a large and wealthy family moved to the country, they did not just pack their bags and go; they took all their valuables with them, and a great part of their furniture, too, which had to travel the slowest way, in wooden two-wheel carts drawn by oxen and known as *arbas*. Almost a hundred miles separated Tsinandali from Tiflis, with a fairly high mountain range to be crossed on the way over which even horses traveled at a slow pace; and the arbas had to leave well in advance of their masters. The first convoy of arbas was dispatched on the sixteenth; the second left the following morning. They were guarded by mounted men with muskets, who had come specially for that purpose from Tsinandali and had been living in the house for the last fortnight, waiting for a word of command from Prince David.

And finally came the day of the family's departure. Everyone rose at dawn. It was not yet six when the entire family, including babies and nurses, had gathered in the large and now half-empty drawing room, where some of the older servants joined them for last farewells. Zoë, in her gray dress and gray bonnet, withdrew to a far corner of the room, holding Salome and Marie by the hand and doing her best to keep the two excited little girls quiet. And when Princess Varvara arrived, with her son George and his buxom young nurse, Princess Anna said, "We must all pray together now for a safe journey." For Zoë's benefit she added, "It is a tradition in our family."

It was really an old Russian custom acquired by Princess Anna during her childhood and girlhood days in Moscow. She had brought it with her when she married Prince David, and since then the entire household had observed it religiously. They all sat down now, including the servants, and bowed their heads in silent prayer.

Zoë sat with closed eyes, her hands folded in her lap, but no prayers came to her. Thoughts of Sasha, or rather of her own future, whirled through her mind. Would he ever be free? Would they ever get married? And would she ever be able to hold her own among his relatives? Self-pity is hard to bear. She felt tears tickling the back of her nose. She shut out all thoughts and became acutely conscious of the silence around her.

Prince David was the first to open his eyes and speak, his voice vibrating through the room after the prolonged hush.

"Tamara, you are the youngest here who can stand on your feet," he said. "Stand up now and cross yourself."

Tamara slid down from her mother's knee. Princess Anna took the child's hand in hers, folding the thumb and the two first fingers together, and then guided the little hand first to Tamara's forehead, then to her stomach, and then to her right and left shoulders, thus forming the Greek Orthodox sign of the cross. When this was done, the others stood up, crossing themselves devoutly. And they embraced one another, the male servants kissing Prince David's shoulder and Princess Anna's hand.

Two large open victorias and a *tarantas*, the ordinary type of carriage used for travel in Russia, stood outside the house, as well as

99

five saddled horses. Askar, Prince David's young Tartar valet, held his master's big black mare, which kept pounding the ground impatiently with her hoofs. A low cavalry saddle adorned the mare's glossy back, while the other four horses, smaller in size and a good deal stockier, were topped by high-pointed native saddles, well padded and cushioned in front and in back.

Ladies' dressing cases, small cases with jewelry and other valuables were packed at the last moment into the baggage compartments of the victorias, and the women and children settled down in the carriages. The two princesses sat in the first victoria with Zoë, Salome, and Marie opposite them, while the three nurses and the smaller children occupied the second one. The tarantas, which was heavily laden with baggage topped by a large zinc bathtub, had but one occupant—the imposing-looking Marfa, Princess Anna's Russian maid. She had served her mistress ever since the young princess had made her debut at the imperial court and in the social world of Moscow and St. Petersburg at the age of seventeen.

The butler, the chef, and a few other servants who were being left behind stood on the doorstep, surrounded by their wives and children, waving to the departing family. The big house in Tsinandali was serviced solely by women from the village, specially trained for the task, as their mothers had been before them. Those women would have resented the intrusion of other servants, with the exception of nurses and personal maids and valets.

Prince David swung into his saddle. Askar and the other three men, with muskets slung behind their backs, followed suit. Zoë looked at Princess Anna's proud profile framed in a straw bonnet and at Princess Varvara's kind face diffused behind her thick crepe veil. She thought of the Tollets, who the night before had given a little farewell party for her. She heard Prince David say, "Well, we are off!" And suddenly her heart quickened—she was on her way, going nearer to Sasha. A last farewell wave to the servants, and the little cavalcade started slowly down the steep incline of Tchavchavadzé Street.

9   The night was spent in a roadside inn, and next morning Prince David sent Askar ahead to announce to the inhabitants of Tsinandali that they would arrive around three in the afternoon. His timing proved to be correct. Shortly before three they were rounding the village of Tsinandali, its low whitewashed

100

buildings, its gardens and cemetery, and its old Georgian church occupying a small vine-covered plateau. Beyond it, across the river Tchobakhuri, they sighted a tower rising above the surrounding trees.

"Ah, there's our belvedere!" Princess Anna exclaimed, pointing in the direction of the tower.

There was no holding Salome and Marie now. They stood up, jumping and cheering, and it took all of Princess Anna's severest admonitions to get them to sit down again.

Ordinarily the Tchobakhuri, a small tributary of the Alazan—Kahetia's main river—ran dry at this time of the year, but there were a few streamlets running in its rocky bed that day. Prince David commented on this fact. It served to prove how high and impassable the Alazan was. "And when the Alazan is high," he said to Zoë with a short laugh, "none of Shamyl's men would dare cross it!"

The carriages moved slowly across the river bed, heaving and creaking over ruts and rocks, and when they began to climb up the opposite bank, Zoë saw the colonnaded house behind a high thick wall. As they passed under massive portals into a vast court, she noticed that the belvedere formed part of the house, its peaked roof glistening in the sun, its base hidden from view by dense foliage. The large three-story house had a façade of tall columns that rose from the second floor to the roof. It was built in a semicircle, linked at both ends to the high wall, forming a complete circle around the court, in the center of which stood an ornate well. "Why, one could stand a siege in here!" Zoë exclaimed, and Princess Anna replied, "I believe that is what Prince Garsevan had in mind when he built the house—he was my husband's grandfather."

The carriage came to a stop at the front door. An old lady in a wig that looked like a chocolate soufflé plunked on top of her head came down the steps to greet them. She was Prince David's maiden aunt, Princess Tinia Orbeliani, his mother's sister. But Zoë's whole attention was riveted to the nonagenarian nurse, Marina-gamdeli, who stood on the top step, surrounded by a dozen women and girls of all ages. She held a thick cane, but she hardly leaned on it. Prince David had been right, she looked like an ancient pillar, chipped a little here and there, but still standing firm and erect. Her face and hands were of the color of burned sienna, and her snow-white hair fell over her shoulders in long corkscrew curls from under her narrow velvet headband.

Prince David and the two princesses embraced her; the three

little girls, according to age, went up to receive her blessing. And Zoë noticed that when the three nurses brought up their charges, they paid homage to Marina-gamdeli by kissing her shoulder.

Zoë's turn came next. When Princess Anna had explained in Georgian who she was, the nurse inclined her head and mumbled a few words of welcome in her native tongue. Then she retired into the house, followed by the staff of female servants, and Zoë, turning around, found the court filling with people—the men of the village had come to welcome their master home. It was a simple ceremony, like the home-coming of an elder brother, impressive in its rural dignity and the total absence of servility. The peasants crowded around Prince David, asking after his sisters and their families and giving him their own news.

Zoë stood on the top step, captivated by this patriarchal scene. But she was not allowed to enjoy it. Salome and Marie were tugging at her skirt, and Princess Tinia was beckoning to her from a small garden gate concealed in the high wall.

Princess Tinia was small and ugly, with stooping shoulders and a head slightly bent to one side. She spoke French fluently and began every sentence with, "As my father, the sardar, used to say," sardar being the old Georgian title for a commander in chief of an army. The old sardar must have made a number of ambiguous remarks in his lifetime, for when they strolled through the shady park, he was quoted as saying, "Moss does not grow on the seat of my pants"; and later, when she took Zoë to the second floor of the house, to the big ballroom and the adjoining drawing room, it was, "As my father, the sardar, used to say, 'Our house is well organized —we have a room in which we dance, and a room in which we give ourselves to other pleasures'!"

In the ballroom Princess Tinia stopped in front of the mantel, pointing to a full-sized portrait of King Irakli II—"The Lion of Georgia"—in his oriental robes and a kind of feathered turban on his head. "That portrait was part of my sister's dowry. We, too, descend from King Irakli!" It was a dig at Princess Anna, Zoë thought, a hint that not she alone in the family had royal ancestors. But Princess Tinia's concluding remark seemed to put them all in their place: "As my father, the sardar, used to say, 'Anything can pop out of a king.'"

On the opposite wall were two portraits of Prince David's grandparents—old Garsevan, who had built the house, and his wife. They were represented wearing the old Georgian ceremonial robes of gold

102

brocade. Garsevan's head was uncovered, showing black, wavy locks, while his wife wore a many-pointed crown studded with precious stones. And two big flowers seemed to spring forth from one of the points of her crown.

"Take a good look at those flowers," Princess Tinia said. "They were a gift from Catherine the Great. Old Garsevan was Georgian ambassador to Petersburg, and Catherine was godmother to Alexander, his only son. The flowers are made of diamonds! I will tell my nephew to show them to you—they are the family's prize possession!"

For the first time Zoë listened with real interest. The story of the Empress's bouquet captured her imagination. And later, when they had all gathered on the balcony for tea, Princess Tinia mentioned it again. Princess Anna's large jewel case was brought in and the flowers laid out on the table in front of Zoë. They were life-size flowers, in which every petal was a diamond, every leaf an emerald, held together by thin, graceful stems of gold. Zoë had never seen anything like it. She gazed at them, lost in admiration. The children scrambled onto a chair beside her, and Prince David peered over her shoulder.

Peace and quiet reigned around them. The distant mountains looked innocent, almost dreamlike in the sunset. Nothing could ever happen here, in this peaceful place, protected by rivers, walls, and the devotion of its villagers. And Zoë felt very safe, very secure, when a little later she sat by the open window in her room, writing a letter to Roxane. "This is a real château that would do justice to any country, even our beautiful France! But here the setting is unique. Oh, Aunt Roxane, if you could only see it, I know how happy you would be! My description is a poor substitute, but I will attempt it all the same. Imagine for a moment the wide valley of Kahetia lying at my feet, and in the distance the mountains, from green foothills to snow-capped peaks, rising like eternal stepping-stones to heaven."

10 Next morning Zoë received a note from Sasha. The joy she experienced at the sight of it was quickly replaced by bitter disappointment. It was a short, almost impersonal note, obviously written in great haste, to tell her he hoped to come to Tsinandali before the end of the month, though he could not say when. And for almost a week after that there was no further news

103

from him. Zoë tried hard to rationalize and master her emotions, but disturbing fears kept creeping up. Was he growing indifferent? she asked herself. At night pangs of jealousy came to torment her, keeping her awake for hours. She lay very still, her heart dying within her as her sorriest fancies evoked visions of Sasha making love to some other woman, until, unable to bear it any longer, she would get up and wander restlessly around the room.

But on the twenty-fifth of June—Princess Anna's birthday—she got caught up in the general excitement, forgetting for a while her doubts and miseries. It was a lovely day. Salome, Marie, and Tamara woke up laughing and ran in their nightgowns to their father's study to see what present he had prepared for their mother. And together with him they gave Princess Anna a beautiful pigeon-blood ruby ring. Princess Varvara remained in her room, not wishing to participate in the festivities on account of her deep mourning, but the rest of the household was in a frenzy of activity. Loud voices came from the servants' quarters; maids rushed in every direction; Solomon Tchitchia, the gardener, mowed the lawns and trimmed the shrubs; his brother Adam, the house carpenter, repaired chairs and tables. Close to a hundred guests were expected for lunch. Behind the house, in a clearing in the park, long narrow tables were laid out, while beyond them, near the edge of a ravine overlooking the Tchobakhuri, the villagers built large bonfires over which they were roasting the carcasses of several sheep.

At noon the family gathered on the balcony outside the drawing room to watch the arriving guests, laughing and trying to guess who would arrive first.

"Look! It's old Goulbat himself!" Prince David exclaimed, pointing to a solitary rider who had emerged from the village and was crossing the Tchobakhuri in the direction of the house.

His words seemed to electrify all those present. The children fell silent. Princess Tinia clucked. Prince David dashed downstairs to meet his guest, while Princess Anna hurried through the drawing room and the big ballroom to the colonnaded balcony above the front door. And Princess Tinia hissed into Zoë's ear as they followed Princess Anna, "It is Prince Goulbat, the head of the Tchavchavadzé clan! In my youth he sought my hand, but fortunately my father, the sardar, had other plans for me at the time. Lucky, lucky me! Since then he has buried two wives and is tyrannizing over a third! And that is not all, my dear! The village is simply seething with his bastards!"

104

Princess Anna waved to old Goulbat from the balcony, and Prince David, followed by Askar, came out of the house to welcome him. Zoë stared at him in wonder. He was sitting in his saddle, his broad shoulders and slim waist encased in a white tcherkeska, the loose fur of his huge sheepskin hat falling over his brow, and his long, straight mustache sticking out a foot on either side of his thin face. The strength and virility of a man of forty were in his figure, and no one looking at him could have guessed that he was nearing the end of his seventh decade.

Prince David took the horse by the bridle, and old Goulbat jumped to the ground with amazing agility. A second later he stood towering over Prince David's six feet, his barbaric splendor offering a striking contrast to the well-polished elegance of his host.

"Greetings, kinsman," he shouted in Georgian. "I am glad you came home in time to celebrate your princess's birthday. But what kept you so long in Tiflis, eh? Don't tell me you were afraid of Shamyl, that old mountain goat! Ha, ha, ha!" And the roar of his laughter echoed and re-echoed through the walled-in court. It was a rare occasion when old Goulbat indulged in a hearty laugh, but when he did, it was always at his own jokes; he tolerated no levity in men younger than himself, considering such behavior a slight to his dignity. He clamped his hand down on Prince David's shoulder, pleased that the latter had limited his appreciation of the joke to a respectful smile, and walked toward the house, looking around provocatively, as though daring someone to come and step on his toe.

His wild and eccentric personality seemed to confirm all the sensational rumors that were spread about him. Half the products of his extensive vineyards, so people said, were consumed by Goulbat himself. His ability to imbibe was measureless, yet no one had ever seen him drunk; only the tip of his long pointed nose looked as if it had been freshly dipped in his favorite red wine. All the marriages in Tsinandali, people whispered in shocked tones, were consummated by Goulbat himself. He claimed what was called the *droit du seigneur*, and village brides were brought to spend their first night in his bed. And finally, strangers meeting old Goulbat for the first time, were warned not to proffer their hand, for he would then put his own hand behind his back, saying, "I do not know you. I cannot shake a hand that might be dishonest or unclean!"

Old Goulbat seemed to dwarf everyone he came in contact with. He always looked at people down his nose. When he saw Salome,

Marie, and Tamara lined up in the ballroom to greet him, he waved a deprecating hand. "Too many girls! I hear there's a new one now. This will never do. David! We need more boys to carry on the glory of our name!"

A sudden rush, and Marie stood confronting him, her legs apart, her arms akimbo. "What's wrong with me, Uncle Goulbat? I am a famous knight. I am Peter Tchilingaroff!"

Taken by surprise, old Goulbat examined her for a moment as though she were a rare insect. Then he burst out laughing. "Ohohoho! What an imp!" He picked her up and sat her on his shoulder. "I'll wager half my vineyards you are afraid of nothing!"

"Afraid? Of course not! You are my horse, Uncle Goulbat. We will go to battle and kill Shamyl and all his men!"

Princess Anna threw up both her hands in protest. "Oh, Goulbat! Don't encourage such unwomanly instincts in her!"

Goulbat swung around. "Anna," he said solemnly, "she has the blood of your illustrious ancestors mingled with the fearlessness of our clan. Who knows what lies in store for her? After all, the Amazons, they say, trod the soil of the Caucasus, and only the other day I heard a strange tale about a young girl who saved the ancient kingdom of France!" He looked straight at Zoë as he said this, and his gray eyes glistened. "Doesn't this young stranger come from the land of the French Amazon? Tell her I am glad to welcome her to our parts."

When Princess Anna had translated his words, Zoë blushed with pleasure and embarrassment. She bobbed him a small curtsy which seemed to please him, for he beamed at her. But Princess Tinia pinched her in the small of the back. "Be careful," she whispered. "The old satyr has noticed you!" And Zoë, confused, retired to the colonnaded balcony.

Guests were beginning to arrive, filling the big outer court and the house with their chatter and laughter. They came from Telav, from neighboring villages, and from beyond the Alazan, some of them having traveled all morning. The men, wearing either military uniforms or tcherkeskas of different shades and colors to suit the taste of the individual wearer, arrived on horseback; their womenfolk traveled in landaus, barouches, droshkies, and even in arbas upholstered for the occasion with soft cushions and rugs, the ladies reclining in them in their Sunday best. Over their flowing silk robes they wore *katibas*, or mantles, caught in tightly at the waist and made of bright-colored velvet, trimmed with fur and richly em-

106

broidered round the neck and down the front with silver and gold and seed pearls. Zoë, enchanted, looked at them all in openmouthed wonder, until Salome, with considerable foresight, said in her demure way, "Oh, Madame Zoë-djan, look out for the flies!"

At one o'clock Princess Anna led her guests to the improvised dining room under the shady trees of the park, and Zoë, the two little girls beside her, found a seat next to Princess Tinia, who, she knew, would be glad to explain all that was going on. Village lads served the guests, carrying roast lamb on long skewers and dishes of rice, while their elders crowded in a semicircle behind the tables, participating freely in the food and drink, taking an active part in all that went on, mingling now and then in the general conversation, and making their own observations and remarks. And once again, as on the day of her arrival, Zoë was impressed by the patriarchal spirit that permeated this colorful fairy-tale gathering.

No Georgian feast could be held without a *touloumbash*. The touloumbash was the great potentate of the feast, the high priest, the chairman, the moderator; announcer, toastmaster, commentator, master of ceremonies, cheerleader, promoter; the soul, the genius, the inspiration of the party. In short, he was the great impresario with the powers of a dictator thrown in for good measure.

The guests that day elected Goulbat as their touloumbash. He refused three times for the sake of form. And finally, with a gesture that was truly pontifical, he accepted the honor and immediately entered into his new role.

The feast never lagged once. The food was good and plentiful, the wine flowed freely. Many toasts were drunk, preceded by long flowery speeches. But gradually the individual toasts turned to mass toasts, sung in chorus by one side of the table and responded to by the other. And one thing leading to another, at a sign from Goulbat the shrill notes of a *zurna*—that distant cousin of the bagpipe—came floating from the ranks of the villagers to the regular beat of several small drums. The guests clapped in rhythm. The time had come for the *lezghinka*.

Old Goulbat pointed to a slim young man seated at the end of one of the tables. Immediately the man jumped to his feet, moving slowly forward in a rhythmic gait. He went around an imaginary circle within the open space between the long tables, one arm stretched out toward the center of the circle, the other folded over his shoulder. Gradually his movements became bolder, swifter, more precise. He pranced, he frisked, he lunged this way and that,

107

he stalked around, showing himself off to advantage, and having gathered momentum, his sharp young body went skipping in a straight line to one of the long tables in search of a partner. He paused in front of a handsome girl of twenty. He bowed stiffly, and by way of invitation he danced for her alone, his hands on his dagger, his feet moving rapidly in an intricate step, while she in her crimson katiba trimmed with sable sat with an air of studied indifference.

"That is Darico, old Goulbat's daughter. The apple of his eye," Princess Tinia explained. "They say she is the only one who dares talk back at him—a little!"

Broad-shouldered and slender, with Goulbat's features softened in the shapely oval of her face, Darico kept glancing at the young man from under her long lashes but gave no sign of accepting his invitation. After a while he danced away toward another table, pausing here and there in front of a young girl, but never for more than a split second, until finally he gave up the fruitless quest and returned once more to Darico.

At last, after a good deal of coaxing on the part of the other women at her table, Darico stood up. Her left arm stretched out in line with her shoulder, her head bent slightly forward, and her right hand shading her eyes in a gesture of bashful modesty, she glided away, the young man following in her wake. Her hips and shoulders never moved, though her feet performed a series of fast, complicated steps. They circled around several times, Darico and her partner, their every movement stressing the hidden meaning of the dance—man's eternal pursuit of the elusive maid. Darico danced beautifully. Her feet hardly touched the ground as she glided along, ignoring the man at her shoulder until suddenly he would bend forward and cut across the circle to confront her. Then she would turn abruptly and flee in the opposite direction. Time and time again he tried to take her by surprise, but she evaded him and danced away, elusive and unattainable. Finally, pretending to give up, the young man stepped out of the circle and stood clapping his hands in time with the music. And Darico, left to herself, became languorous. She swayed a little from the hips, ever so gently from side to side, her arms unfolding gracefully. She danced to the left and then to the right, only to come back again, searching, so it seemed, for the one who had left her so abruptly. But when he returned to the assault, circling around her like a bird of prey, Darico's hand flew up to shield her eyes, her body leaning slightly forward in an attitude of suspended escape. One moment she remained paused there, immobile, and in the next she had taken wing, darting back to her seat to the sound of general applause.

Zoë was no longer listening to Princess Tinia. Her whole heart was in this strange new dance, as old as the hills around her. She was out there, dancing with Darico, following her every step, her every gesture, and the pure delight that expressed itself in her eyes and face made people turn around and smile at her. And when the dance ended she sat with closed eyes, living it all over again. The long shadow of Goulbat brought her back to reality. He was standing behind her, saying something in Georgian.

"I believe he is after one of our little girls," Princess Tinia chuckled. And indeed, at his approach Salome had retreated behind Princess Tinia's back and Marie was about to do the same, when old Goulbat's harsh voice stopped her. "Oho! The bold and brave knight is afraid after all!"

"I am not!" Marie cried back.

"Prove it, then! Dance!"

Marie hesitated, glancing at the next table where her father sat, and then away she dashed, encouraged by his nod and smile. At first she tried to dance with decorum as Darico had done, but once out in the open, she began to imitate the young man, gamboling and frisking like a little pony. Cries of surprise and encouragement came from all sides, and old Goulbat's voice boomed above the others, "The little devil!" In his enthusiasm he tore his huge fur hat off and clamped it down on the little girl's head. The hat slipped down to her shoulders, where it remained propped up by her outstretched arm, but Marie went on with her dance. She might have gone on forever had old Goulbat not snatched up his hat again, leaving her dazed. She stood there, blinking, until he picked her up and kissed her. "This little one should sit in the place of honor!" he said, setting her down by her father's side. "And now watch!" he cried, turning to the guests. "After the young the old will do his share!"

"Oh, the old devil! Look at him," Princess Tinia gasped. She pinched Zoë again in her excitement. "No wonder he wears them out. Oh, lucky, lucky me!"

Old Goulbat's frame was heaving and tilting like a mountain suddenly come to life. But his step grew lighter as he got into the spirit of the dance with a kind of wild abandon. His body was no longer supple, but it had a certain savage grace. And he lunged to the right and left, looking fiercely in all directions. He did not prance like the younger man; he galloped down the line of long tables, eying the prettiest girls.

Zoë had watched him, fascinated, but when she saw him bouncing in her direction, she grew panicky. For a moment her heart stood still. Old Goulbat was stamping his feet and snorting in front of her, singling her out for the dance. "Hah!" he cried exultantly. "France had a heroic maiden once! We must do her honor!"

Zoë closed her eyes and shook her head when Princess Tinia had translated his words. She made old Goulbat return three times, not out of coyness but from sheer fright. "Come, Madame Zoë-djan," she heard Princess Anna call out to her with a laugh, "you cannot keep him jumping much longer. Remember, it is your privilege to stop dancing whenever you please." And Princess Tinia suddenly shoved Zoë off her seat.

She found herself standing alone with all eyes focused upon her. "Oh, my poor Jeanne d'Arc, help me!" she murmured, not daring to move. It was the panting of her host close behind her that sent her scurrying into the open. But once there, the spirit of the dance entered into her every limb. She glided forward, her white summer skirt billowing around her, long ribbons—the ends of her green sash—flying behind her like two gossamer reins; and where her memory of Darico's performance failed, her own inspiration stepped in. Her steps and the movements of her arms may not have been altogether orthodox, but they were full of rhythmic grace, disciplined, perfectly timed. And when all of a sudden she pirouetted right in front of old Goulbat's advancing nose and then flew to the other side of the circle, as though blown away by his puffing cheeks, enthusiastic cries broke out on all sides. Women wanted to know who she was, men stood up and clapped, and even from the crowd of villagers came shouts of approval: "This is a new dance, but it's a good one!"

Until then Zoë had given herself up to the dance completely, but old Goulbat stepped out of the circle now, and she found herself the sole performer. Stage fright suddenly gripped her. She stopped, looked around in dismay, and in her confusion swept a low curtsy right down to the ground. Thunderous applause broke out on all sides, and old Goulbat spread his arms out in ecstasy. "Wah! What enemy could withstand such grace!"

Young men gathered around her, escorting her back to her seat, all talking at once, interrupting one another and asking if she would dance with them when their turn came. Zoë did not understand much of what they said, but she felt carried away by her success. She came back to her seat, laughing up at the men, answering them in a mixture of French and badly pronounced Russian. Then she saw Princess Anna looking at her through a lorgnette. "That was very pretty, Madame Zoë-djan, very pretty indeed!" But she thought she detected sarcasm in the voice. All joy faded, the warm glow vanished, the sparkle died away. Her eyes grew larger, and so did her mouth. She sat down dejectedly, busying herself with Salome, paying no more attention to her cavaliers. They lingered for a while, looking down at her in surprise. They felt something had been lost. They did not know what. And finally they went away, feeling cheated.

But unexpected things were happening that drew the attention away from Zoë and cast a shadow on this gay and carefree gathering. No sooner had the applause died down than Prince David was seen to rise, a worried look on his face. Beside him stood Askar. They were about to leave, when old Goulbat stopped them. He refused to let his kinsman go without first being told the reason for his departure. At a word from Prince David, Askar stood at attention in front of old Goulbat and told him his story. A stranger, he said, claiming to be an Armenian merchant or peddler, had come to the servants' quarters asking for shelter overnight. The man had aroused his suspicions, and he had thought Prince David should speak to him and decide for himself. To refuse hospitality to a stranger was an insult to heaven in the eyes of every Georgian and mountaineer alike, and such a matter could not be dealt with lightly.

"Where is this man?" old Goulbat asked, and when Askar pointed to the house, he looked down at the young Tartar with a scowl.

"How do you know he is still there? If he is Shamyl's spy, he will have fled!"

"The Tchitchia brothers are guarding him, sir. Prince David's gardener and carpenter."

"Bring him here then! Let us see what kind of a bird he is!"

Prince Andronikoff, the commander of Telav, came forward, portly and a little flustered, to join Prince David and old Goulbat. Those among the guests who had overheard the conversation were craning their necks to get a good look at the stranger. He came, together with Askar, through the park, a slender man of thirty with a feline gait. This in itself aroused suspicion, for Armenian peddlers

111

did not usually walk that way. Also, his features were too angular, too sharp for an Armenian; nor was his proud bearing in accordance with his station—he had lowered his eyes out of respect for the noble gathering but had not bowed his head. And yet his long dark tunic was of the correct cut and he spoke Georgian fluently with a touch of an Armenian accent. When Prince Andronikoff, at old Goulbat's request, asked him a few routine questions about his name and his place of birth, he answered them simply and to all appearances truthfully. But in doing this he had given Prince Andronikoff and Prince David a sharp look out of the corner of his eye.

"Do you know us?" Prince David asked.

"No, sir, but I see you are Russian officers."

The man's look had aroused Prince David's suspicions. "Did you come to find out how many of us are here?"

"Oh no, sir. Of what interest are officers to a humble merchant?"

"I have been told Shamyl offers a moneyed reward for every Russian officer captured alive!"

"Three curses on his money!" the stranger muttered without raising his eyes.

"A peddler could make use of a few extra rubles, though."

"An honest merchant loves money but abhors war," was the reply.

Old Goulbat brushed all further talk aside. "You have come to the right place, my friend! Every guest is a blessing from heaven, be he a beggar or a prince. And let it not be said of any Tchavchavadzé that he does not do honor to his guests. Friend, you shall partake of our food and sleep in my kinsman's house, but first you must honor the princess on her birthday!" He clapped his hands, and three men came forward. One of them held a horn inlaid with silver and gold that could hold two quarts, while the other two filled it with wine out of a heavy leather container.

"Give it to our guest," Goulbat commanded. "He will drain it in honor of Princess Anna!"

The stranger looked at the horn, and the color receded slowly from his cheeks. "Spare me," he said in a hoarse whisper. "I have not the habit of wine."

"Oho! Listen to him! He has not the habit of wine! And why, pray, have you not acquired it at your age? Are you a Mohammedan?"

The man shook his head. "A Christian merchant should be abstemious if he wishes to run his business properly."

112

"A good Christian should drink and keep sober!" Old Goulbat narrowed his eyes. "Drink!" he roared. "Drink every drop, or I will hand you over to Prince Andronikoff here. He is the commander of Telav!"

Andronikoff tried to make his good-natured face look stern while the man took the horn that was being thrust upon him. He closed his eyes and raised it to his lips. He drank slowly, painfully, his Adam's apple heaving up and down with each heavy gulp. And when he paused for breath, old Goulbat's imperious finger forced him to go on. His eyes had become glazed and his face was drained of all color now. One . . . two . . . three more gulps, and his hands let go of the horn. He swayed and tottered, then crashed to the ground. A dagger fell on the grass beside him, and a small triangular silver object on a silver chain slipped out from under the edge of his tunic. The three men leaning over his prostrate form recognized it at a glance. It was a badge of honor given by Shamyl to his bravest warriors.

"He will sleep soundly tonight," old Goulbat said with a sardonic smile.

"He will," Prince Andronikoff agreed. "And with your permission, I will now have my men take him to my quarters in Telav."

But old Goulbat drew himself up sharply. "No poaching!" he shouted suddenly, glaring at Andronikoff. "This man was captured on our land! Tomorrow David will send him under special escort to General Réad in Tiflis, with our compliments!"

11 The peace of mind and the sense of security enjoyed by the inhabitants of Tsinandali were undermined by the sudden appearance of Shamyl's spy in their midst. The unconscious man had been carried to the house, where he had spent the night under lock and key. And early the next morning he was brought into Prince David's study. Looking a little pale after old Goulbat's treatment, the man stood in front of the desk, flanked by two armed members of the Georgian Auxiliary Militia. His arms were tied behind his back, but he held his head high and looked down defiantly at Prince David. He admitted being a Tchetchen, a member of the mountain tribe well known for its loyalty and devotion to Shamyl, and he said his name was Hadji-Kheriett. He told Prince David he had learned to speak Russian, Georgian, and Armenian in his early youth, when he had lived for several years on the shores of the Caspian Sea.

As to his present mission, he confessed having killed and robbed an Armenian merchant, in whose clothes he succeeded in crossing the Alazan. He gave the name of the fording place where peasants had guided him across the river, but beyond that he refused to commit himself. And when pressed for details of Shamyl's future plans, he only said, "Whatever the Imam's plans may be, they will succeed!" His eyes glistened with hatred. "If my hands were free I would kill you, David Tchavchavadzé! Today I have sworn vengeance on every man, woman, and child who bears your name, for it was the head of your clan who disgraced me and made me defile myself with wine!"

Prince David rose to his feet. "Hadji-Kheriett, you will have ample time to make plans for revenge and to forget them. You are a prisoner now, and I am sending you to our commanding general in Tiflis."

Zoë, returning from her early-morning walk, met the two militiamen and Hadji-Kheriett on the front steps of the house. Catching sight of her, Hadji-Kheriett stopped, paying no attention to the curses of his guards. "Is she one of yours?" he asked, turning to Prince David, who had come out of the house at that moment.

The latter smiled. "No, Hadji-Kheriett, your vengeance need not extend to her. She is the daughter of a French general."

Hadji-Kheriett had never heard of the French, but he did not trust Prince David. And Zoë confessed that the look he gave her as the militiamen led him away had sent cold shivers down her spine.

"You may set your mind at rest, Madame Zoë-djan. We have nothing more to fear from that man."

But all too soon Prince David found out that his confidence had been premature. The very next day the two militiamen returned, their heads bowed. Hadji-Kheriett had escaped. Passing by the home of some relatives, the indolent Georgians had dropped in for a glass of wine, leaving Hadji-Kheriett outside with the horses.

"By all that is holy, Prince," one of them exclaimed, "that man must be the devil incarnate. He had his hands and arms bound!"

"Some traitor must have unbound them," the other cried. "When we came out he was gone, and so was one of our horses."

They hung their heads in shame, waiting for the full blast of their commanding officer's fury. But Prince David was a man of action. He knew that to fume and rage was a loss of time. He sent out a searching party to scout the district, dispatching at the same time a full report to Colonel Kulman, with a recommendation that the ford

Hadji-Kheriett had crossed be well guarded at all times. The ford, Prince David said, offered no immediate threat to Telav and Tsinandali, but it gave the mountaineers an easy access to that part of Kahetia.

For three days the inhabitants of the big house lived in a state of suspense. They had no doubt now that Shamyl was planning an attack. To them it meant that Prince David would go to war, leading his militia across the Alazan to repulse the invaders. Only Marinagamdeli remained undisturbed. "In over fifty years those devils have not dared to cross the Alazan, and it will be no different now," she said, although no one had suggested such a possibility. "As for my David," she went on, "all he has to do is show himself, and the heathens will slink away in terror!"

Princess Anna did not share the old nurse's confidence in Prince David's powers of repulsion, but her natural reserve forbade her to display any emotion. Zoë marveled at her self-control. Only an occasional sigh or a rueful glance in the direction of the mountains when she thought no one was watching gave away her feelings. And on several occasions she remained closeted in Princess Varvara's room, deriving new strength and courage from her sister's calm and simple faith.

On the thirtieth of June, in the early evening, Zoë was in her room on the third floor. It was a corner room, in which one window offered a glimpse of the wide valley and the mountains beyond it and the other overlooked the front court. Princess Anna and Princess Varvara were playing a duet on the grand piano in the ballroom, and the sounds of a Beethoven sonata reached Zoë through the open window. She settled back in her armchair, her eyes half closed, her thoughts speeding to Sasha somewhere in Kahetia. Ah, if he would only come soon! All torturing doubts would vanish then. They would stroll through the park together; they would go horseback riding, galloping through the orchards and vineyards to the banks of the Alazan. She could hear the wind singing in her ears and the horses' hoofs pounding the ground in rhythm to the music. Suddenly she sat up. She listened intently. Those sounds were real. Horses were galloping, coming closer and closer. They passed under the heavy portals and clattered into the big court. She sprang to her feet. And leaning out of her window, she saw Sasha jump off his horse and throw the reins to Poushka. He ran into the house without looking right or left, but she noticed that his face was tense.

"Poushka!" she cried. "What news?"

Poushka looked up and grinned. "Ah! Zoia Ivanovna!" He saluted her and then bowed.

"What news?" She repeated her question.

Poushka screwed up his eyes. "Shamylka is descending," he shouted back in his bad French. "We go push him back! If we are lucky, we catch him. Phtt! The war is over!"

We! That meant Sasha too! Zoë's heart shrank into a tight little knot. "When?" she cried breathlessly.

"Tomorrow morning, Zoia Ivanovna, before the sun gets up!"

The music downstairs had come to an abrupt end, and Zoë's involuntary gasp relieved her tension. She ran out of the room and down the stairs; she raced across the ballroom. The door into the drawing room had been left ajar, and she could hear the quiet voices of the two princesses. On the threshold Zoë paused, her eyes wide, her lips trembling slightly. "Sasha," she stammered, fighting down the lump that had risen in her throat. "Sasha is going to war!"

Princess Anna gave her a caustic look. "I thought you were a soldier's daughter, madame!"

Her words were like a lash. Although Princess Varvara had taken Zoë by the hand and had made her sit down beside her, Zoë felt beaten. Her eyes wandered helplessly across the room to a large portrait of Prince David's sister, Catherine, the woman she had heard of so much and had never seen—the Princess of Mingrelia. But the proud-looking woman in the portrait, a wide red ribbon of the Russian Order of St. Catherine across her shoulder, stared back at her coldly as though she, too, were saying, "I thought you were a soldier's daughter, madame!"

Princess Anna was speaking again. "I am sorry. I did not mean to be rude and harsh. We are all rather jumpy this evening, aren't we?" Her warm tone and the note of apology in her voice brought tears to Zoë's eyes which she fought back, her head bowed.

The sound of men's voices and the clinking of spurs were heard outside. Zoë sat on tenterhooks. It was her first meeting with Sasha in the presence of his relatives, and she did not know what to say or what to do. But the situation did not seem to bother Sasha in the least. He smiled at her as he came in, and after embracing his two cousins he strode up to her and kissed her hand, murmuring her name under his breath. And she rose a bit toward him, her heart in her eyes.

"Well, my dears, tomorrow Sasha and I start off on our little campaign!" Prince David's voice came as a shock to Zoë—it was light,

116

almost flippant. "Colonel Kulman has sent him here as liaison officer." And his words were echoed by a loud exclamation from Princess Tinia, who had just entered the room.

"Ah, Alexandr Dimitrievitch," she cried as Sasha bent over her hand. "So you are going to fight Shamyl too! Bring me back his beard for my wig." She grinned, and her plain face became almost monkey-like, revealing a row of fan-shaped teeth.

"The old busybody is a soldier's daughter too," Zoë said to herself, marveling at the way the entire family reacted to the news, while the others laughed heartily over Princess Tinia's words.

"Dinner is served, my dear, and I am sure Sasha is famished after his long ride," Prince David said to his wife, at the same time offering his arm to his old aunt. Sasha offered his to Princess Anna, and Zoë and Princess Varvara formed the rear, walking in a leisurely procession to the dining room on the ground floor, as if hazards and dangers of war and battle were not hanging over their heads. And never for a moment throughout the entire meal did they allow this mood to escape them.

The dining room was low and vaulted and almost as large as the ballroom. Two silver candelabra on the dinner table and two more on the marble mantel threw a bright circle of light, beyond which the rest of the room remained in shadowy gloom. When they had settled down at the table, Sasha found himself facing the big picture that hung over the mantel. "Ah! The famous charter of the Georgian nobility," he exclaimed with a laugh. "I have not seen it in a long time."

The picture in question was a constant source of amusement to Prince David and his family; Princess Tinia alone took it seriously. The picture had come to Tsinandali as part of her sister's dowry. It was supposed to represent the first charter granted to the Georgian nobility, and in it the unskilled hand of a seventeenth-century artist had depicted a scene of the Great Flood. One green wave curled out of another the whole length of the canvas, and at one end Noah's ark stood solidly on top of the curly waves. Noah himself, in the stiff robes of a Georgian king, was leaning out of the ark, handing a scroll of parchment to a swimmer, who could be seen lying snugly among the waves, one arm outstretched toward the scroll.

"He must have been the greatest swimmer in the world!" Prince David said, pointing at the picture and looking mischievously at Princess Tinia out of the corner of his eye. "That's why he got the famous charter as a prize!"

117

"He was an Orbeliani!" Princess Tinia exclaimed, raising a warning finger.

"Oh, come now, Aunt Tinia! How do we know he was not *in* the ark originally with all the other animals?"

Princess Tinia scowled. "You always make fun, David, of things that should be sacred to you."

"But, Aunt Tinia, we all know how unruly the Orbelianis can be at times! This one must have caused an uproar, demanding to become a Georgian nobleman. Father Noah could not stand it. He threw him overboard and then sent the old parchment flying after him, crying, 'Here! Take your certificate!' "

"Very well, have it your way," Princess Tinia exclaimed, rising to the bait. "The fact remains, it was an Orbeliani who survived the Flood!"

"Oh, that's nothing! They have survived many worse things since!"

"Such Tchavchavadzé arrogance!" Princess Tinia cried, rapping her knife on her plate. "What, for instance? What?" And aunt and nephew made faces at one another across the table.

When dinner was over and Prince David and Princess Anna went upstairs with their aunt, Sasha whispered a few words to Princess Varvara and the latter hurried to Zoë's side. "It is so close indoors tonight," she said. "Sasha and I want to take a breath of fresh air. Won't you join us for a stroll, Madame Zoë-djan?"

They walked slowly down a gravel path that wound its way along the edge of the ravine. High above them myriad small lightnings flashed silently through the sky, forming patterns of flame that illuminated the entire firmament. "The heavens are on fire tonight," Zoë murmured in hushed tones. "Does that mean a storm, I wonder?"

"No," Princess Varvara replied, walking a little ahead of Zoë and Sasha. "Those heat lightnings never amount to much. But do listen to the nightingale!"

They stopped for a moment, holding their breath. Beautiful, lonely trills came to them out of the darkness that enveloped the park, and Sasha's strong, firm fingers closed over Zoë's hand.

12   They sat on a bench at the edge of the ravine—Sasha and
      Zoë. Princess Varvara had left them to go and pray in a
small chapel nearby. Sasha had whispered, "Tonight you are my

118

little sister," and Zoë had nodded her assent. After that he lapsed into silence, lost in deep thought. She kept repeating to herself, "Tomorrow he is going into battle; tonight he is holy!" But those were mere words. She was keenly aware of only one thing—he seemed oblivious of her presence. All the wretchedness of the past month surged up in her, and dark, destructive doubts came rushing back. Perhaps he no longer wanted her and "my little sister" was just a pretext. She felt an urge to break in on his thoughts, make him look at her, hold her hands, kiss her. She had an impelling desire for some tangible proof of his love. She cleared her throat. "The mountains seem so close tonight. Tomorrow they will be even closer to you, Sasha. Where will your headquarters be?"

Sasha pointed in the general direction of the Alazan. "Over there, across the river. In a place called Shildi."

His casual tone seemed like an insult. "He doesn't even look at me!" Offended, she sat stiff and silent by his side.

"Have you ever heard of Kazi-Mahomma, Shamyl's second son?" he asked suddenly.

"Why is he speaking of Shamyl's son? He must be thinking of his friend Jemaleddin instead of thinking of me!"

And Sasha went on: "They say he will be leading the attack. What an irony of fate if I were to kill Kazi-Mahomma—Jemal's brother!"

He had said it! A pang of jealousy shot through her. Hating herself for it, hating even more the honeyed tones in her voice, but feeling impotent to do anything about it, she said, "Ah yes, Jemal. Jemaleddin. You see, Sasha, how well I remember! Did you see him in Petersburg?"

"No. He is stationed with his regiment in Poland."

Even this simple statement seemed loaded—she detected in it a note of exaggerated regret. "What is there in this man to hold him so?" she cried out to herself. But aloud, still speaking too sweetly, "Tell me more about him, Sasha."

"I don't know what to tell you. It is just that I have never known anyone quite like him."

"And that includes me!" Her mind had shrieked it out, leaving her shattered by the onslaught of her jealousy. She shuddered slightly and closed her eyes.

Sasha was saying, "Someday you will meet him and then you will understand." He stopped abruptly, sensing the tension in her. He forced her chin up with his finger and looked into her eyes. "What is it, darling?"

119

Zoë shook her head. She swallowed hard. "Nothing, Sasha, nothing. I hope I will meet Jemal someday—and understand."

Princess Varvara's light step resounded on the gravel path. Sasha stood up, drawing Zoë with him. "I must see if my horse has been properly fed. Coming with me, Zoë-djan?" She remained silent and sullen, and he took her by the hand. "Come, my love!" He laughed. "Together we shall visit the noble beast."

Princess Varvara was walking ahead of them again. She was saying how sad and empty the Tsinandali stables looked since all but Prince David's two riding horses had been requisitioned for the wars. And Sasha swung Zoë's hand to and fro as they followed her. But she felt like a stranger at his side, excluded from a world she could not share with him. He was giving Princess Varvara tidbits of St. Petersburg gossip that meant nothing to her. And when they reached the stables and Poushka and Askar had sprung to attention, she snatched her hand away. Sasha glanced at her in mild surprise and went into one of the stalls. He examined his horse from its head to its hoofs, engrossed in what he was doing. Princess Varvara followed him and remained in the stall, conversing with him in low tones. "I am of no account," Zoë said to herself with bitterness. "I might as well not be here!"

She toyed with the idea of leaving, but the thought that he might not even notice it made her change her mind, and she lingered near the entrance, looking around despondently. A lantern, beside which Poushka and Askar had been crouching, stood on the ground, casting a dim light on the hindquarters of four horses and leaving a long row of empty stalls in darkness.

"Ach, Zoia Ivanovna!" Poushka exclaimed, noticing the misery in her eyes. "Do not fret! This war is nonsense! Alexandr Dimitrievitch, he come back to you without scratching himself!"

"I am not afraid," Zoë replied with a forced laugh. "I am a soldier's daughter, you know!" Her brave words brought no response from Sasha. And suddenly she was furious. "Good night, Poushka," she flung in a loud, hard voice, and dashed out of the stables. She heard Sasha running after her, but she refused to look back.

The big house was very silent. Everyone had retired early that evening. Princess Varvara left them on the third-floor landing to go to her own room, and Sasha took Zoë by the shoulders. "Zoë-djan," he said, looking deep into her eyes, "I know how it is. Very nerveracking. But in a few days I will be back, and we will have our fill of joy!"

120

Her distorted mind mistook his tenderness for condescension.

"No!" she cried, tearing herself away. "Don't return! Don't come back! I never want to love you again!"

She gasped at her own words. Her hand flew up to her mouth. And she turned and fled to her room.

She fell into the big armchair near the window, breathing heavily. How could she have said such a thing, mad creature that she was? A cold fear was tugging at her heart now. He could never love her after this. She had destroyed everything. And on this night of all nights!

Trembling, she flung her elbows on the window sill and rested her chin on her hands. Roxane's words returned to haunt her—"You have always thought of his love for you, never of your love for him. Go your way, Niece, and find yourself!" Yes, she was right! Yet it had been Roxane who had brought them together again. The crowded railroad station, the soiled windowpane, her eyes locked in his, and his four-leaf clover in her hand.

Zoë jumped up and lit the candle. She picked up her *Book of Stray Thoughts* and fingered through it until she found the right page. She sat down again, gazing at the little dry leaf that had brought him back to her. She closed the book and pressed it to her heart. It was Monsieur Tollet's study she was thinking of now, and flames shot through her, spending themselves in a moan.

She was on her feet again; she could not let Sasha go like this. The clock on her dresser said half-past eleven. The household would be fast asleep. She must stoop, humble herself, do anything to obtain his forgiveness; otherwise there might be no return.

She picked up the candle. Slowly she opened the door and listened. The big house was plunged in silence. She advanced stealthily along the landing that encircled the black chasm of the stair well, turned a sharp corner, and entered a long dark corridor. She had to pass by Princess Varvara's door, Princess Tinia's door, and the four nurseries before reaching Sasha's room. Those nurses, she knew, were light sleepers, and in front of every door she paused and listened. Her progress seemed endless.

At last she came to a stop, her heart thumping loudly in the dead silence around her. She hesitated, her hand raised, and her frightened fingers barely scratched his door. She knocked again, a little louder, and pressing her lips to the door, she whispered his name.

She heard the scrape of a chair being moved back and the soft tread of stockinged feet. What was she to say? How was she to act now that he was coming to her? Weak and frightened, she leaned against the wall. And very distinctly she heard the key turn in the latch.

Sasha had been sitting up, thinking of Zoë and wondering at himself. Her angry words and the scared look in her eyes had brought out his feelings for her in a new light. She had said, "I never want to love you again!" Silly, meaningless words of an angry, frightened little girl. He remembered the miniature Roxane had shown him: Zoë looking like a cute little pug with those big frightened eyes. It had made him feel all soft and tender inside. And now he knew it was for the specter of this little girl that all his tenderness had been preserved. It was the specter of this little girl that had lifted his love to a level he had never known before. He pressed the tips of his fingers to his eyes, hugging the vision to his heart.

He heard the scraping on the door, the knock, the whisper, but he did not trust himself to speak. Tonight that specter must reign supreme. One word, and it would be lost, crushed by an inevitable rage for possession. And when he went to the door, he turned the key upon himself.

He stood there, hardly daring to breathe. Then, very gently, he unlocked the door again and looked out. He saw Zoë at the end of the corridor, moving away from him, candle in hand. Her shoulders were drooping, beaten and crushed. Not to run after her, not to hold her in his arms, was an agony supreme. And clenching his fists, he pressed his forehead against the cool angle of the door. . . .

Zoë returned to her room, numbed. She moved about in a daze, taking off her clothes, brushing her hair, plaiting it into two tight little pigtails. But when she reached her bed, she recoiled. She moved the big armchair to the window facing the court and sat down. "I will sit up until dawn. I must see him before he goes."

Without noticing it, she fell asleep. She awoke with a start to the sound of subdued voices and the soft neighing of a horse in the court below. Dawn was creeping up fast. She sprang to her feet. With one knee on the side of the armchair and her hands on the window sill, she peered out. Poushka and Askar were leading the horses up to the house. Zoë craned her neck. She saw Prince David come out of the house with Marina-gamdeli. The old nurse gave him her parting blessing and embraced him, and Zoë thought, "Princess Anna is crying alone in her room. Later she will appear dry-eyed and composed. She is strong! Would Sasha love me better if I were more like her?"

Then she saw Sasha. She opened her mouth to call out his name,

122

but dared not in front of Prince David and the others. He looked a little pale, handsomer, she thought, than she had ever seen him before. She watched Marina-gamdeli give him her blessing. She felt almost jealous of the old hand that touched his forehead, his chest, and his shoulders. And with her whole mind spearheaded through her eyes she willed him to look up at her.

He was on his horse now, looking down, while Poushka adjusted the straps of his stirrups. But Prince David had noticed Zoë at her window. He spoke to Sasha in Russian before riding away, and Sasha looked up.

The face he saw was indeed that of a little girl, with pigtails sticking out on either side like two small sickles.

"I will be back soon, my love!" he cried, and in true Russian fashion traced the sign of the cross in her direction.

Zoë's eyes were dimmed with tears. All the girlish sentiments that were still so dominant in her came to the fore. She saw him now clad in shining armor. It was for her that he was going. And to her he would return.

13   A few miles of vineyards, orchards, and gardens separated Tsinandali from the Alazan. Prince David and Sasha, followed by Poushka and Askar, covered the distance at an easy canter, wrapped in silence, for the situation that faced them across the river was far more serious than they had led the ladies to believe. According to the latest reports, the Tchetchens, fifteen thousand strong, were descending toward the valley in two columns. Scouts had reported that the smaller column of two thousand men was led by Kazi-Mahomma, the larger one by his father-in-law, Daniel-Sultan, while Shamyl followed close behind in supreme command of the expedition.

Prince David's Auxiliary Militia consisted of about one thousand men, dispersed in three small groups over the countryside. Realizing the hopelessness of such a situation, he left thirty men to defend the small tower of Pohali, situated higher in the mountains, in the path of the invaders, hoping thereby to delay the enemy advance; and on the second of July he withdrew his remaining forces to the fortified village of Shildi, where he had the additional support of a small regular garrison. He assigned one hundred and fifty militiamen to assist the garrison in the fortress and divided the rest into small groups of ten, placing them in strategic positions around the village.

The main street leading to the fort was lined on both sides by stone walls. Behind these he placed most of his men. And they remained under arms all night, waiting for the attack.

It came at seven in the morning. Sasha, standing on the ramparts of the fort, could see the swift advance of the Tchetchens. They came at a gallop, about three thousand strong, brandishing their weapons and calling out loud invocations to Allah in their strange, guttural tongue. The attack was concentrated on the entrance to the main street. Again and again the steady volleys of the Georgians repulsed the onslaughts, and with every new volley many Tchetchens were seen to fall to the ground. But nothing seemed to daunt Shamyl's men. Toward noon they broke through and came pouring down the street into the village square at the foot of the fortress.

Sasha looked down on the fighting throng in the square below, wondering whether Kazi-Mahomma, Jemal's brother, were in it, while Poushka pelted them with bullets. Along with the soldiers and militiamen, he stood on one knee near the rampart, taking careful aim. And every time he hit a Tchetchen, he would exclaim, "Get off your horse, Shamylka! . . . Take that, Mahmutka! . . . Know your place, Danielka!"

The fighting in and around the square lasted for two hours. A heavy pall of dust hung over the entire village. Shouts of hatred mingled with the neighing of horses and the cries of dying men; and the stench of sweat and blood rose from the ground. Shamyl's men were not well organized. No leaders among them took the initiative or issued commands; every man seemed to be fighting for himself, and in the end the better-trained Georgians got the upper hand, driving them first from the square and then out of the village. At 2 P.M. the Tchetchens retreated, leaving five hundred dead behind.

Neither Prince David nor Sasha rejoiced in the victory. They knew that Shildi had been attacked by a small section of Shamyl's forces, a mere foretaste of what might come in the next twenty-four hours. Having no cavalry at their disposal, they could not pursue the enemy; and no sooner had the Tchetchens disappeared into the hills than Prince David dispatched Sasha to Colonel Kulman, asking for immediate cavalry reinforcements.

Sasha left with a heavy heart, aware of the dangers that hung over Prince David and his small body of men. But he knew, too, that their lives depended on a swift delivery of the message. Together with Poushka he galloped out of Shildi at full speed.

After a quick inspection of his men Prince David's thoughts

124

turned to his family in Tsinandali. Wishing to assure Princess Anna of his safety, he scribbled a note to her, saying, "Dearest, We were attacked this morning, but we have repulsed the enemy and they have retreated. Under the circumstances you have nothing to worry about at present." It never occurred to him that his words might be misconstrued in any way, confident as he was of the complete security of Tsinandali. But that same morning Prince Andronikoff, the commander of Telav, committed a fatal blunder. At the head of a large body of men he left Telav to reconnoiter. He crossed the Alazan at the secret Tognian Ford and, finding no one on the other side, retraced his steps across the ford back to Telav. In doing this he disclosed the fording place to Shamyl's secret scouts.

When Prince David's note reached Princess Anna late in the afternoon on the third of July, she heaved a sigh of relief. For three days now there had been wild rumors of a possible attack on Tsinandali, and she knew that no serious resistance could be offered by the villagers, since most of the able-bodied men had gone off with the militia. Only the day before, old Goulbat had sent her a message urging her to seek shelter in Telav. Goulbat's family, the messenger had said, had already left, and Goulbat himself was now in one of his villages on the Alazan, across the river from Shildi. Princess Anna had wanted to take his advice, but old Princess Tinia and Marina-gamdeli had scorned the idea. "Nonsense!" they had cried. "Such things cannot happen here! Old women's tales!" But backed by Princess Varvara, she had dispatched Adam Tchitchia, the house carpenter, to Telav to ask for post horses. He had returned that evening with the news that no horses would be available until the morning of the fourth.

The ladies had sat up late that night. From their balcony they could see whole villages burning on the other side of the Alazan. To Zoë each one of those fires represented a personal threat to Sasha, but Princess Tinia had exclaimed with scorn, "Look how far they are! Shamyl's men cannot cross the Alazan, no more than those fires can!" And to impress her listeners further, she bade them good night and went upstairs to bed.

Next morning Zoë took the children out into the park as usual. Everything around her breathed peace and quiet. It seemed almost preposterous to think of danger in this lovely, sheltered spot, and for a while she thought Princess Tinia might have been right after all. But when they returned from their walk they found Princess Anna standing on the front doorstep, a worried look on her face.

With her were Princess Varvara, Princess Tinia, Marina-gamdeli, and Marfa, the Russian maid. At the bottom of the steps stood the *natzvala*—the village elder—and beside him Zoë saw a man in drenched clothes. Salome and Marie translated to Zoë what was being said. The children sensed the tenseness of the situation. They were all excited. Adventure was in the air.

"A great calamity is hanging over us," the natzvala told Princess Anna. "They say Shamyl will attack Tsinandali!"

"Who said so?" Princess Tinia exclaimed sharply, and Marina-gamdeli asked in a sardonic voice, "If I said I would attack Shamyl, would that be a calamity!"

The natzvala tugged at the end of his long white beard. "You are old and wise, Marina-gamdeli, but you cannot swim. Shamyl's horses might, though!" He turned to Princess Anna. "The village is empty. We have taken our families to the woods. You should come with us, Princess!" His news came as a thunderbolt. They all stared at him, incredulous. "I could never look Prince David in the eye again if I left his wife and children behind." And to strengthen his plea, the natzvala pointed to the man beside him. "Listen to his story. You can trust him, he is a friend of mine. He just managed to swim across the Alazan at the Tognian Ford. See, his clothes are all wet!"

The man bowed to Princess Anna. "The place is overrun by Shamyl's horsemen!" he exclaimed. "Fifteen thousand of them! I was lucky to get away alive. They are pillaging, murdering, setting fire to everything. They spare no one!"

An exclamation of terror escaped Marfa. "How can you hesitate, Princess? They will come and murder us all!"

At this point Princess Anna was all for fleeing to the woods. The six or seven miles that separated Tsinandali from Telav were covered by a dense forest that started a hundred yards beyond the park. It had always presented serious problems when the ladies of Tsinandali went there to pick mushrooms, and now it seemed like the safest place of refuge. But once again, with the stubbornness of old age, Princess Tinia protested. "Hold your tongue, Marfa! Shamyl's men won't cross the Alazan, I tell you!" And turning to Princess Anna, "Don't let them talk you into this, Anna! The post horses will be here in the morning, and we can leave in comfort and dignity, only to return later, looking like fools!" She turned angrily on the man in drenched clothes. "Fifteen thousand, you say! I suppose they stood in a row and let you count their noses!"

The man hit his chest with his fist. "I swear it's true! When I got across the river, I saw Prince Andronikoff standing with his men this side of the Tognian Ford. Would he have come out of Telav for nothing?"

"You see, Anna, how well protected we are!"

Both Princess Varvara and Zoë took cheer at this news, but Princess Anna said with a good deal of insight, "What good can Andronikoff do by standing there? He will only show Shamyl where the ford is."

"Very well then, go to the woods!" Princess Tinia cried. "I will stay here and laugh at you when you return!" And Marina-gamdeli's old voice came cracking through the short silence that followed: "I am too old to go picking mushrooms!"

For once Princess Anna seemed full of indecision. She spoke to her sister in a whisper and then thanked the natzvala and the other man for their concern. "I promise you we will take to the woods at the slightest sign of danger!" She sent Solomon Tchitchia, the gardener, to the top of the belvedere, where there was a clear view of the valley beyond the Tognian Ford, and retired to the nursery to feed baby Lydia. And it was later that same afternoon, when Prince David's note arrived, that she heaved a sigh of relief. To her it meant that they were not confronted with any immediate danger; and Zoë and the others understood it in the same way, when Princess Anna had shown them the note, with exclamations of relief and joy.

That evening at dinner the four women were in a lighter mood than they had been for days. They laughed at their own fears and at Princess Tinia's repeated I-told-you-sos. Thoroughly pleased with herself, the old lady pointed a crooked finger at the picture over the mantel, exclaiming, "It was not for nothing that an Orbeliani escaped the Flood!"

They had just finished their dessert when the Tchitchia brothers, Adam and Solomon—the only men left in the house—rushed into the dining room, saying that a stranger was at the door asking for shelter. The memory of Hadji-Kheriett flashed through Zoë's mind. She looked at the man searchingly, anxiously, while the three princesses spoke to him. He looked harmless enough, drenched to the skin, miserable and beaten; and he told them he was a storekeeper whose property had been ransacked and burned. He had escaped with his life, he said, swimming across the river. He spoke Georgian fluently. His story was much the same as that of the natzvala's friend, and Princess Anna told the Tchitchia brothers to take him to the servants' quarters, find him some dry clothes, and give him a bed for the night. But the thought that he might be another Hadji-Kheriett kept haunting Zoë, and the knowledge that the nearby village stood empty and deserted was frightening.

She sat on the balcony with the three princesses, taking no part in the conversation, looking at the distant fires across the river. Sasha was somewhere out there, fighting, perhaps wounded; perhaps lying dead! It was his body now, not René's, that she saw flung across the meadow, the head bent at a terrifying angle, a narrow streak of blood trickling slowly out of a corner of the mouth. Unable to bear it, she excused herself and left. She ran downstairs and out into the park, hurrying down the gravel path to the bench on which she and Sasha had sat. A bright full moon was rising over the valley. The night was very still.

It was a sudden rustle in the nearby shrubs that brought her to her feet. Her eyes darted in the direction of the sound. And there, a few feet away, half hidden by the tall shrubs, she saw the fugitive storekeeper. His face stood out clear in the moonlight, and in his hands he held a musket. She stared at him, paralyzed with fear. He leered at her for a moment, then slipped away noiselessly into the ravine. With a smothered cry she ran back to the house.

"A musket!" Princess Anna cried when Zoë, panting, had told her what she had seen. "Good God!"

She summoned the Tchitchia brothers and told them to disarm the man at once. They ran out, swearing by all that was holy they would do it, but Zoë had her doubts. Adam and Solomon were small, thin, middle-aged men. She doubted their ability to cope with the armed stranger, but what else was there to be done? The four women returned to the balcony to keep a silent vigil until two in the morning. Nothing more was said. Even Princess Tinia sat quiet and subdued for a change.

Finally Princess Varvara stood up. "I think we should go to our rooms and pray. And we should try to get some sleep too. Tomorrow, with God's help, we shall reach Telav safely."

"You all go. I will stay here," Princess Anna replied. "In an hour or so it will be daylight. Attacks do not usually come by day."

Back in her room, Zoë was unable to concentrate on prayer. Her thoughts kept straying back to the edge of the ravine, to the man with the musket. And it was his moonlit face that stood out vividly before her eyes when she finally fell asleep.

128

At first Zoë thought she was still sleeping, but with the return of consciousness she knew the shot had been real, fired outside the house, over the ravine. She jumped out of bed and ran to the window that overlooked the valley. Everything seemed quiet, peaceful, and serene. But with a sudden realization of what that shot might mean, she began to dress in a frenzy of haste.

Princess Varvara had awakened earlier. She had been standing fully dressed in front of a large icon in the corner of her room when the shot cut through her prayers. She crossed herself, saying, "In Thy hands, O Lord."

Princess Tinia had not undressed that night. She had fallen asleep in a large armchair in her room, and a few strands of thin white hair had crept out from under her brown wig. The shot disturbed her slumbers sufficiently to make her open one eye and mutter, "My father, the sardar, could not have done better. . . ."

Princess Anna, exhausted by her night's vigil, did not hear it at all.

The younger nurses awoke and wondered anxiously, but Marina-gamdeli in her small room on the third floor had not slept a wink that night. She was sitting by her window, staring into space. The shot set her old heart thumping painfully, and seized with a premonition of disaster, her lips mumbled, "David, David, why aren't you here to protect your own?"

In the servants' quarters a few maids jumped out of bed, raising an alarm, while the Tchitchia brothers, who were supposed to have kept watch, woke up with a start, Adam on the belvedere and Solomon in the pantry. They ran around nervously, searching for the storekeeper, whom they had failed to disarm the night before. But the man had vanished.

Zoë and Princess Varvara met on the landing. Princess Varvara looked a little pale, but she was calm as she said, "That shot may have been a signal. I must go and wake my sister. Will you please wake the nurses and tell them to get the children ready?"

She disappeared downstairs just as the door of Princess Tinia's room opened slowly, and the old lady stuck her head out into the corridor. "Did I hear a shot?" she asked.

"Yes! It was a signal to the enemy," Zoë said. "Please come and tell the nurses to hurry!"

"Hurry? Where to?" Princess Tinia drawled, still half asleep. "Oh, how absent-minded of me! I forgot to undress last night."

"That is of no importance whatsoever. You must tell the nurses to

129

hurry! My Russian is not good enough for that." Her sharp tone brought the old lady out of her stupor, and she followed Zoë obediently to the nurseries.

Five minutes later the four nurseries were filled with noise and bustle. The younger children cried. Salome and Marie wanted to know why they were being made to get up so early.

"We are going to Telav," Zoë said.

"Why?" Salome asked sleepily.

"To visit friends. Your aunt Varvara is up and dressed, and your mamma will be ready any moment now. So hurry up!"

Princess Tinia had gone back to her room, and the nurses dawdled over everything, trying thereby to show their resentment at having a foreigner intruding in their affairs. Almost an hour went by, and the children were not yet ready.

"The horses have arrived from Telav!" Princess Varvara cried, bursting into the room. "Now we can get away!" She busied herself over her son George. She hurried the nurses. And Zoë took charge of Salome and Marie. When they were through with their breakfast, she took each girl by the hand and ran with them downstairs.

They found Princess Anna and Marfa on the balcony overlooking the front court. Two large carriages and an arba for the servants were standing below. Princess Anna from above was directing the packing of heavy cases of jewelry and other valuables into the baggage compartments of the carriages. Adam and Solomon Tchitchia and the three coachmen who had brought the post horses from Telav were carrying the loads.

"Hurry them up, Princess, for God's sake make them hurry!" Marfa kept muttering in Russian, her face deathly pale. "Let us get out of here!" And then her piercing shriek resounded through the court.

"They are coming!" one of the coachmen yelled at the top of his voice, taking to his heels; the other two followed him, and the Tchitchia brothers dropped their loads and ran after them into the park through the concealed gate in the wall.

Marfa's shriek had terrified Zoë. For a moment she stood petrified, not understanding what had happened. But when she looked in the direction of the big portals, she knew. Men on horseback, wearing turbans around their fur hats, were galloping full speed into the court.

"Into the house! Quick!" Princess Anna cried.

She pushed Zoë and the children into the ballroom and, taking

130

Marfa by the arm, gave it a sound jerk. There was no time to waste. They raced across the ballroom and up the stairs to the third floor. Eleven women of the household were rushing after them from the ground floor, screaming hysterically. Princess Varvara, her face set, came out of the corridor, followed by frightened nurses and whining children. Princess Tinia came after them, tottering a little, her wig askance. And then Marina-gamdeli appeared, led by one of the younger maids. The old woman seemed no longer able to walk alone.

"To the belvedere!" Princess Anna commanded.

The women poured down the long corridor and up the narrow wooden stairs that led to the top of the belvedere, and Princess Anna placed an arm around Marina-gamdeli's shoulders, coaxing her like a child, encouraging her to walk a little faster.

There were two small rooms and a narrow landing at the top of the belvedere. Spare mattresses, pillows, and comforters were stored in one of these rooms, while the other stood empty. And it was in this empty room that the twenty-one women and six children took refuge.

Zoë stood in a corner with her back to the wall, Salome and Marie clinging to her like two frightened little animals. The women were wailing, the smaller children screaming; only Princess Anna and Princess Varvara kept a level head, moving among them and exhorting them to be quiet. Their calm courage soon prevailed. After a while Marfa alone stood trembling from head to foot, her teeth chattering, "Today—I—will—die! Today—I—will—die," she kept stammering.

Princess Anna tried to calm her. "We have lived together, Marfa, for many years. We can die together too. Hold onto me!"

Her words had their effect, for Marfa stopped trembling and clung in silence to her mistress's skirt.

Princess Anna's eyes fell on Zoë. She came toward her with outstretched arms. "Madame Zoë-djan, what fatal destiny has tied you to us at such a moment! Forgive me if I am to blame for it in any way." She kissed Zoë. She then turned to Eliso, the thin Georgian nurse, who was holding Lydia, and took the baby. She knelt, the child in her arms, and closed her eyes in silent prayer. Princess Varvara, in the meantime, after having kissed and blessed her little George, who was asleep in the arms of Vassilissa, his buxom nurse, turned to the door and stood facing it, praying that she would be killed first and be spared the sight of the slaughter.

131

Zoë could not bring herself to think of death. Instead the silliest thoughts came cropping up in her mind: "When they find us, shall I speak to them in French or in Russian? . . . And how do I say in Russian, 'I am French'? . . ." But when Salome and Marie began to cry, she pressed the two little heads to her breast, her own eyes wandering around the room.

The housemaids were clustered together at one end. They, too, were praying. The two Russian nurses, fat Yakovlevna and buxom Vassilissa, were cooing over Sandro and George, while Eliso sat on the floor with Tamara in her lap, the child's head pressed to her heart. Marina-gamdeli was on the floor, too, her back against the wall, her eyes tightly closed. And Princess Tinia sat beside her, opening and closing her mouth and shaking her finger angrily, but not saying a word.

Slowly the minutes went by and nothing happened. Muffled sounds reached them from below, occasional screams and the crashing of furniture. At last Princess Varvara opened the door ever so gently and ventured out on the landing. The sounds became clearer. They could hear loud, discordant chords, followed by screams of surprise and raucous laughter as the Tchetchens struck the keys of the grand piano in the ballroom.

Princess Varvara returned to the room. "Perhaps," she said in a whisper to her sister, "we could venture to the third floor and lower Salome and Marie from a window. They could escape through the park into the woods!" But Princess Anna shook her head in silence.

Suddenly Princess Tinia jumped to her feet with unexpected agility and ran out of the room. Princess Anna called after her, but the old lady only waved her hand. "This has to stop!" she cried. And before anyone could stop her, she had vanished down the stairs.

The servants crossed themselves in terror. One of the maids closed the door on the hook, and Princess Varvara stationed herself again in front of it. Not another word was said.

Presently cautious steps came creeping up the stairs. Two or three men were standing outside the door, talking to each other in whispers. They went into the adjoining room, and Zoë could hear them throwing pillows and mattresses out of the windows. Having emptied the room, they returned to the closed door. A hand tugged at it gently and let go. A few more whispers, and the men retired down the stairs.

The women sighed with relief, but a few minutes later their hearts were beating wildly, for now many men were coming up the narrow

132

stairs. They paused outside the door, talking in low voices, evidently fearing an armed ambush. Someone tugged at the door. The flimsy hook held, but after a second wrench it gave way and the door flew open.

Scowling faces with high cheekbones and sharp, hawklike features peered into the room. For a moment they stood there, daggers drawn, and then a sudden roar of laughter shook the walls. With their hands on their hips they stared at the helpless women, and peal after peal of laughter resounded through the belvedere. The children shrieked in terror. The women moaned.

Zoë had no clear recollection of what happened next. Salome and Marie were torn away from her, screaming, and all she could remember was the smell of sour sweat, and of leather, and of something else indescribably stale as a pair of strong arms lifted her from the floor. . . .

She must have lost consciousness, for the next thing she knew she was down in the front court, sitting on the edge of the well. A harsh voice spoke to her in Russian, and when she looked up, a cry escaped her. Hadji-Kheriett, in a black tcherkeska, a white turban wound around his fur hat, was looking down at her, a cruel smile distorting his thin, handsome face. He thrust the reins of two horses into her hand, and she understood she was to stay there and guard his horses until he returned.

How long she remained beside the well she did not know. From her point of vantage she could see men running in and out of the house, carrying loot. The two carriages and the arba had been overturned and hacked to pieces. The post horses had vanished. At times men and horses in the court obscured Zoë's view; at others she was left an unwilling spectator of the havoc and destruction that were being wrought around her.

She saw Princess Anna being dragged out of the house, still clinging to her child. Hadji-Kheriett shouted, "That's the princess!" and ran toward her. A dozen or more men crowded around her, fighting for her possession. And when finally they had dispersed, leaving her to her original captor, Zoë almost cried out in horror. Princess Anna's clothes had been torn off, she had lost her shoes, and she was standing in her chemise, her thick black hair falling over her shoulders. But Lydia was still safe in her arms. And a few moments later, surrounded by an escort of mounted men, Princess Anna was led out of the court on foot.

Marie flashed by, a small vision of fury. She was seated on a

133

horse behind one of the mountaineers, her right arm strapped inside the man's belt; but with her free fist she was threatening her captors.

It was all like a nightmare, more gruesome for its occasional comic relief. Men were running out of the house with silver knives and forks and spoons tucked into their belts, children's caps and ladies' bonnets perched on top of their turbans, and torn window curtains wrapped around them instead of cloaks. And one man who passed close to Zoë was brandishing Princess Tinia's brown wig. Zoë felt cold all over. Had he killed the old lady? But a moment later she saw Princess Tinia on the front steps of the house. She had nothing on but her chemise. She stood there as in a trance, a fringe of white hair hanging from her bald head, her poor naked old legs shivering. She was looking up at the second-floor balcony. And when Zoë followed her eyes, she saw a procession of portraits being borne out of the ballroom. King Irakli headed this procession, his outstretched arm showing the way, and for a brief moment the Lion of Georgia stood like a conqueror on the balustrade. Then he toppled over slowly and fell to the ground. Prince David's grandparents and the proud Princess of Mingrelia came crashing after him. A minute later a Tchetchen carried the famous Charter of Nobility out of the front door. And by some queer irony of fate he threw it down at Princess Tinia's naked feet.

The old lady seemed to wake out of a dream. She looked around as though seeing things for the first time. And with a loud cry she ran down the steps and out into the park through the gate in the wall. No one stopped her; no one seemed to bother about her any more.

Zoë hid her face in her hands. Should she run too? In this bedlam she could slip away unnoticed, run through the park and out into the woods! Freedom and safety were only a few yards away, but her legs weighed a ton, and her courage failed her.

Princess Varvara's voice broke through her lethargy. Zoë looked up. Princess Varvara was passing by on a horse, seated behind the man who had captured her. Like Marie, her right arm was strapped tightly inside the man's belt. "Do not despair!" she called out to Zoë. "These men have orders to bring us to Shamyl alive. Shamyl's son was here just now and told me!"

Alive! To remain alive! What heavenly bliss! Zoë almost smiled at Hadji-Kheriett when he returned, his arms full of loot. But Hadji-Kheriett frowned and snatched the reins out of her hand. Jumping into his saddle, he gave a few brief orders to a young man who had come with him. The young man smiled at Zoë shyly; his manner was almost deferential when he lifted her and placed her on Hadji-Kheriett's horse. And then her right arm was strapped inside Hadji-Kheriett's belt.

As they passed under the portals, Zoë threw a last glance at the colonnaded house. She saw Marina-gamdeli on the front steps, standing in the same place where she had been the day of their arrival. Only now her arms were raised and she was showering curses on a crowd of men who were advancing on her with cries and threats. Zoë shuddered and closed her eyes.

15   While Prince David's house was being plundered and destroyed and its inhabitants carried away in separate groups, a battle was raging around Shildi. The second attack had come early that morning. From the ramparts of the fortress Prince David had spied the enemy through his field glasses, and again, as on the previous day, he realized that Shildi was not being threatened by the entire body of Shamyl's forces. This time the Tchetchens were about five thousand strong.

The fighting had lasted several hours, concentrating in the outskirts of the village. The steady firing of the Georgians placed in strategic positions kept the Tchetchens at bay, but by eleven o'clock half of Shildi was in flames. Prince David was beginning to be seriously alarmed about the situation, when unexpected help appeared from the river. Wild screams resounded through the air, and he saw the right flank of the Tchetchens sway, give way, and finally disperse in all directions. According to his calculations, it was still too early for Colonel Kulman's reinforcements; besides, they would not come from that direction. As his eyes took it all in, he was filled with consternation. At the head of a dozen men, old Goulbat, dressed in white as usual and seated on a white horse, was fighting his way like a demon through the ranks of the enemy. From his village on the other side of the river he had seen Shildi burning. Realizing that his kinsman was in peril, he had collected twelve men, had armed them with muskets, and had crossed the Alazan at a nearby fording place. He was charging now, brandishing nothing but a thick leather riding crop. With wild war whoops he cut into the thick of the fray, hitting the enemy right and left over bowed heads and upturned faces.

Not understanding what was happening to them, the Tchetchens thought they were being attacked by a large body of cavalry. And those among them who caught a glimpse of old Goulbat were seized with superstitious fear. Shaitan, the devil himself, had taken on the shape of Shamyl and had come to destroy them! For it was well known that Shamyl, too, rode a white horse and was often clothed in white. Panic spread like fire, and the Tchetchens fled, while old Goulbat raced up to the fortress gates, shouting at the top of his lungs, "Is my kinsman alive?"

He embraced Prince David and pounded him all over to make sure he was not a ghost. "I sent word to your family, telling them to go to Telav!" he shouted.

This was reassuring news, but there was no time to waste on talk. The Tchetchens, realizing their blunder, might return to the attack at any moment. And accompanied by Goulbat, Prince David returned to his post of observation on the ramparts.

To his surprise he saw the Tchetchens standing at a distance with no apparent intention of renewing the attack. Instead they seemed to be undergoing an inspection. Training his field glasses in their direction, Prince David recognized the man he had known at one time in Tiflis—Daniel-Sultan. Small and rotund, with thick jowls and narrow eyes, but with a smile that was amazingly gentle, almost tender, Daniel-Sultan rode past the silent ranks of Tchetchens. And at a word of command from him they turned and galloped away in the direction of the mountains.

It was unlike the Tchetchens to leave a battlefield without fighting to the bitter end, and Prince David did not know what to make of their sudden departure. He was taking council with his officers when a local peasant was brought in. The man had come with news that in the early hours of the morning a large body of Tchetchens had passed at the foot of Mount Kontzhi, headed in the direction of the Tognian Ford.

Instantly Prince David's mind was made up. Leaving the regular garrison to protect Shildi, he set out with his forces in the direction of the ford. Old Goulbat went with him. When they reached a bend in the road, from which a clear view opened across the river, they saw that the village of Tsinandali was in flames. And they knew then that they had come too late.

Prince David was faced with a bitter struggle. His duty as an officer forced him to lay an ambush for the retreating raiders, but he knew that, surprised by his men, the Tchetchens would make short shrift of any captives they might be carrying with them. The struggle was fierce but short. With a silent prayer for the safety of his family, which he still hoped was either in Telav or seeking shelter in the woods, Prince David issued his orders in a firm voice. One officer was dispatched with three hundred men to lie in ambush at the foot of Mount Kontzhi, where the invaders were bound to pass, while he himself marched with the rest of his men to the Tognian Ford to set two more traps, knowing that the Tchetchens always returned from their raids in separate groups.

In the meantime Sasha was hurrying back to Shildi at the head of a small detachment of cavalry, bringing Prince David the good news that Colonel Kulman would follow shortly with larger reinforcements.

Having learned at Shildi that Prince David was somewhere near the Tognian Ford, he hurried on to join him there. He rode swiftly, Poushka and the other men behind him, but at the bend of the road, where Prince David and old Goulbat had stopped earlier in the day, he reined in his horse and stared, horror-struck, at the burning village across the river. And in the short silence that followed only Poushka was heard to exclaim, "O-och! The dirty sons of bitches, may their mothers be damned alive or dead!"

When Sasha finally reached Prince David, old Goulbat told him that two groups of marauders had been captured and destroyed. The first one had carried nothing but loot, the second had a captive from Tsinandali.

Sasha's throat felt parched. His lips alone formulated the silent question: Who? But old Goulbat did not know, and together they turned to watch a gruesome ceremony that was being enacted by the militiamen.

Prince David sat on a mound, his face pale and drawn. The Georgians, according to an ancient custom, were throwing at the feet of their commanding officer the decapitated heads of the enemy they had slain. And when this mound had risen high, they began throwing down the loot they had found on the dead bodies. Familiar objects from the dining room, the living rooms, the bedrooms, and the nurseries of his home were piling up at Prince David's feet. Valuable silver lay alongside of trash. The pile grew rapidly, until at last it was topped by the old kettle helmet and the hatbox shield of Peter Tchilingaroff.

Sasha dared not look at Prince David, nor dared he lose himself in conjecture. "Where is the captive, for God's sake?" he almost shouted. Old Goulbat nudged him, pointing at an improvised

137

stretcher which four men were now carrying. On it lay the mutilated body of Marfa.

Sasha closed his eyes with an inward shudder. "Who else, O God!" But a light hand touched his shoulder, bringing him to with a start. Prince David was standing in front of him, calm and composed.

"There is still hope, Sasha," he said gently. "Poor Marfa was stout and she was getting old. The younger ones may have reached the woods safely. I cannot leave until Kulman arrives to relieve me, but you go to Tsinandali and see."

Unable to utter a word, Sasha saluted and turned sharply on his heel, signaling to Poushka to follow him. They mounted their horses in silence. Old Goulbat jumped into his saddle too. All three galloped to the Tognian Ford.

Night had fallen by the time they reached Tsinandali. The silence of death and devastation reigned supreme as they passed under the heavy portals and dismounted. The big house was burning like a candle. At first Sasha thought there was no one there, but presently a weak voice reached his ears, rising and falling in a cadence all its own. And Sasha caught sight of Marina-gamdeli seated on a stone near the front steps, her torn shift barely covering her naked body, her white hair falling disheveled over her face and shoulders. The women of Georgia always wailed over their dead, singing their praises in disjointed but florid, almost biblical terms. And Marina-gamdeli was singing the past glories of the big house.

"House, O House! Pride of Kahetia! I saw you grow, stone by stone, pillar by pillar! Adorned with the jewels of an empress, you shone in sparkling beauty. And your tower dominated the land! . . . I saw you born, and by all rights you should have seen me buried. Oh that my old eyes had been spared the sight of your destruction! . . . Oh, David, David, why weren't you here to protect your own!"

Old Goulbat crossed the court and placed a hand on the old woman's head. He spoke to her, but she paid no attention, continuing her mournful song.

"House, O House! House that my master Garsevan built in all his grandeur! House that my sweet Alexander loved in all his fame! Blessed you were with children, wealth, and glory! Where are you now, shelter of a noble race! . . . Cursed, cursed be the hand that rose against you, plundered you, and robbed you of your priceless treasures—the fair princesses, the flower of our land! . . . Oh,

138

David, my David, why weren't you here to protect your own!"

Old Goulbat returned to Sasha's side, his face pale. "She has lost her mind. She is demented!"

But his words were cut short by Poushka's cry. "For God's sake, Alexandr Dimitrievitch, look!"

Sasha swung around. He shouted. He ran forward, pleading, beseeching. One moment Marina-gamdeli had stood on the burning threshold, her thin arms raised above her head, and in the next she was gone.

A shrill cry. A dull thud of crumbling masonry. And millions of bright sparks flew up into the night, like giant handfuls flung toward the stars.

Part Three

The Rulers

1   "Allah is great! And Shamyl is my Imam! Men's hearts are glued to his lips, and with a breath he raises a storm in their souls!"

Such were the words Hadji-Kheriett kept crying out on his way from Tsinandali to the Tognian Ford. He was a Murid, one of Shamyl's chosen warriors, sworn to live in prayer and fasting according to the law of Islam, and to die for the Ghazavat, Shamyl's holy war. To think of a Christian woman with desire was a sin, a defilement; yet he remained disturbingly aware of Zoë's presence behind him, helpless and trembling, her right arm strapped inside his belt. And fiercely he flung his thoughts toward his god and his leader. Occasionally he would drop a few words over his shoulder to Hassan, his young attendant, who rode behind him. And Hassan, the aspirant, undergoing a period of absolute obedience before becoming a Murid himself, would repeat after his master, "Allah is

140

great! And Shamyl is my Imam! Men's hearts are glued to his lips, and with a breath he raises a storm in their souls!"

Zoë's mind refused to take it all in. Was she really seated on a horse, strapped to Hadji-Kheriett's back, riding through peaceful vineyards and orchards, listening to the guttural cries of these men? It seemed like a dreadful, horrible dream.

They had come to a clearing now. A hundred or more Tchetchens on horseback stood lined up in two long rows; beyond them Zoë caught a glimpse of the angry waters of the Alazan. Princess Varvara, Salome, Marie, the nurses, and the maids were all there seated behind their captors, all staring in the same direction, frightened and aghast. And when Zoë looked that way, she was seized with horror and pity. Princess Anna was coming toward them, her baby in her arms, her mounted escort behind her. She was naked except for her thin white chemise, and her thick black hair fell over her shoulders, covering her breasts. Her bare feet were bleeding, and she moved forward with difficulty, stumbling a little now and then. All eyes followed her in silence as she passed by them to the river. But there pandemonium broke loose. Wild shrieks and strange oaths cut through the air, and Zoë heard Princess Varvara cry out, "Oh God! She will drown in that torrent!"

Hadji-Kheriett galloped forward, and Zoë saw Princess Anna on the opposite bank. She was seated on a horse now behind one of her captors, her wet chemise clinging to her skin, her soaking hair hanging down in shreds. But the child was still safe in her left arm. Zoë heaved a sigh of relief.

Hadji-Kheriett spurred his horse, and they entered the river. The horse stepped forward carefully, almost gingerly, slipping a little now and then on the rocky bottom. The icy current stung Zoë's legs, and the muddy, churning waters tore at her clothes. She saw Marie go by, clinging to the back of her captor. "Madame Zoë-djan! You are losing your skirt!" The little girl's shocked tone added a ludicrous touch to this nightmare. And glancing down at herself, Zoë found that the angry torrent had torn away her skirt, leaving her in a drenched petticoat.

For the next few hours they traveled at a swift pace. Her arm was throbbing painfully; her whole right side ached. But at dusk they slowed down. They were climbing up a steep grade at the foot of Mount Kontzhi, heading for a narrow gorge. Zoë leaned against Hadji-Kheriett's back to release the unbearable tension in her arm and shoulder. Suddenly a volley of shots rang out from the gorge.

141

A horse stumbled and fell. A rider threw up his arms and toppled over. They had stumbled on the ambuscade placed there by Prince David.

Hadji-Kheriett swung his horse around. Under the lash of his whip the animal bounded forward, and they galloped madly away. Zoë clung to Hadji-Kheriett's shoulder. Bullets whined past her ears. The wind took her breath away. Another horse was catching up with them, and glancing over her shoulder, she saw Princess Anna, her hair a black streak behind her, her mouth wide open in a desperate scream. With slow, helpless jerks her left arm fell to her side, and the child slipped. A sickening horror clutched at Zoë's heart. She shut her eyes. When she opened them again, the child was dangling head down, the mother's hand still holding on desperately to its foot. But a second later the fingers let go, and baby Lydia dropped out of sight. Horses' hoofs pounded by, raising sparks out of the ground, and passed on to seek refuge in the nearby woods.

Zoë ducked her head. Rising suddenly out of the ground, the forest was upon them. The branches of the underbrush lashed out at her neck and shoulders, their thorns tearing off the remnants of her dress. She felt sick with pain and terror. Her strength had gone, and she pressed her forehead against Hadji-Kheriett's back.

She became dimly conscious of having come to a stop, of her arm being released, of Hassan helping her off the horse. She felt herself slipping to the ground. And she lay there on the soft moss, retching, her forehead bathed in cold sweat.

When she opened her eyes again, she found herself lying on her back, gazing up into the round face of a full moon. And somewhere very close by she heard the soothing babble of running water. Her mouth was dry, her tongue parched. She raised herself on her elbow and saw that she was lying beside a mountain stream. She leaned forward and drank avidly, swallowing the ice-cold water with loud gulps, her mouth close to the stream. She splashed water over her face and neck. Her shoulders were lacerated, striped with black streaks of caked blood, but she felt stronger. She sat up and looked around.

She discovered then that she was on a small plateau, surrounded by mountain peaks that formed a broken eggshell pattern against the dark sky. The soft sounds of munching reached her ears. Straining her eyes, she distinguished the shapes of several oxen lying in the tall grass. More cattle were grazing farther on, driven there from Tsinandali. A rustle behind her made her turn around. She saw

142

Hadji-Kheriett's horse and she saw Hadji-Kheriett standing beside it, untying a bundle from behind his saddle. Her eyes searched the plateau in vain for a sign of Hassan or anyone else. She was alone with Hadji-Kheriett.

He came up to her, the bundle under his arm. He dropped it to the ground and his fingers moved haltingly toward her bare shoulder. But when they touched her skin, he drew them sharply away, as though scorched. His face looked very white, a little drawn around the nose and mouth, but his eyes were like hot coals. And for the first time she became aware of her nakedness. The top of her flimsy chemise appeared above her corset, leaving her breasts uncovered. The sight of these small, upturned breasts was like hot burning fire to Hadji-Kheriett. He passed his tongue over his lips. Her hands flew up in a gesture of modesty, but he seized her under the arms, dragging her to her feet, his rough hands cupped over her breasts. For a brief moment he held her tight, breathing heavily, but when she began to struggle he let her go. He turned his back on her and picked up the bundle. He unrolled it, spreading it out on the ground. It turned out to be a large furry cloak on which he stretched himself out, beckoning to her to come and lie beside him. She shook her head violently. She did not know what to make of this man with his cruel, fanatical face and his advances, crude and yet furtive at the same time. Somehow she did not feel afraid, just thoroughly on the alert. And she watched his every movement, hawklike. He was crouching now. She thought he was going to spring at her, and the only two words of Arabic she had picked up, she knew not when and where, came to her mind. *Allah yah*—God exists. She repeated them twice, pointing at the moon, thinking in her ignorance that Mohammedans were moon worshipers.

Hadji-Kheriett glared at her, and she fled toward the sleeping oxen. She sank to the ground among them, throwing a last glance in Hadji-Kheriett's direction. He had rolled himself up in his cloak and lay very still, a black patch in the moonlight. She breathed a sigh of relief, nestling down among the animals and laying her head on the back of a sleeping ox. The warmth of their bodies made her feel drowsy; their slow, rhythmic breathing seemed like a part of her own existence. Zoë closed her eyes.

He came to her from the highest mountain peak: first as a small shining light gliding down the mountain, then as a pale shadow moving among the grazing and sleeping cattle. Dressed all in white, he sat down on the rump of a sleeping ox close beside her. He stretched his hand out toward her, and his hazel eyes held hers. There was patience in them almost beyond endurance, and an understanding that filled her heart with tender joy. She took her fill of those eyes, forgetting all else, until his lips began to move, pouring soundless words into her soul: "Take courage. I am watching over you." His hand moved in the direction of the forest, and again without a word she thought she heard him say, "That way. Go that way."

Zoë sat up, reaching out for his hand. But the dream had vanished. She jumped to her feet and looked around, bewildered. The moon was perched on top of the highest peak from which he had descended. The little plateau lay in deep slumber; the black patch of Hadji-Kheriett in his cloak seemed even blacker in the dark shadows that had gathered around it.

Zoë took a step forward. He had shown her the way to freedom, or to a new way of life—she knew not which—but she knew she must obey. She stepped across the stream and walked boldly into the forest. She walked without halting, without stumbling, as though she had known every tree and every stump all her life.

Presently she saw a patch of moonlight falling through the branches and heard a weak moan. Coming closer, she saw Princess Anna lying on the ground, her eyes closed. She was tossing about in delirium. The sweat was pouring down her cheeks; her thick hair was full of brambles; her neck, her shoulders and arms, even her breasts, were scratched and lacerated by the thorny bushes; and her thin chemise was ripped in several places. Without another thought Zoë took off her petticoat and wrapped it around her neck and shoulders. Princess Anna opened her eyes.

"Don't be afraid, Princess. It's me, Zoë Duval. I will take care of you."

Princess Anna sighed and closed her eyes, but now her whole body began to tremble. Zoë flung herself on the ground beside her, breathing on her to keep her warm. Gradually the trembling subsided and Princess Anna lay very still. Zoë heard her whisper, "You are kind, Zoë-djan, very kind. . . . I will never forget it. . . ."

Zoë smoothed the hair off Princess Anna's forehead. For a while the sick woman lay very still. Then she sat up abruptly. Zoë tried to force her down, but she propped herself against the trunk of a tree and looked at Zoë.

"My baby . . . Lydia . . . Did you see her . . . killed?"

But Zoë was inspired that night. "No. I saw her fall, but the ground was very soft, and the horses did not touch her."

144

Princess Anna closed her eyes. "Yes, the ground was very soft. . . ."

She lay down again, and Zoë covered her shoulders with the petticoat. And suddenly a strange, choking sound broke the silence as heavy sobs shook Princess Anna. To hear this woman cry was appalling, devastating. Zoë tried to hold back her own tears, but they came streaming down her cheeks. And she lay down beside her, rocking her gently to and fro, until, exhausted, the two women fell asleep in each other's arms.

2 Hassan had seen Zoë go into the forest. After he had carried her unconscious to the stream, Hadji-Kheriett had turned on him, ordering him out of sight. Nonplused, Hassan had retired to the edge of the forest, where he spread out his *burka*—a large furry cloak like Hadji-Kheriett's—and sat down to meditate.

Hassan had been born with a craving for truth and a compassionate heart, attributes dangerous in a youth of eighteen who hoped to become a Murid. A Murid—"the one who aspires." It was perhaps the meaning of the word rather than the rank itself that dazzled him. Until that day he had wanted to die in the cause of the holy war, for this meant glory, and glory was the ultimate truth. But that evening he was assailed by doubts. The attack on Tsinandali had been his first campaign. He had looked forward to seeing glory with his own eyes, but instead he had seen the death of little Lydia, the agony of Princess Anna, the suffering of Zoë and the other women. And he asked himself, was this the price of glory, and if so, could glory itself be perfect? He shuddered. Such thoughts, he knew, amounted to treason. And to steel himself against them he turned his mind to his leader, the Imam, the man who through his faith had risen from a humble origin to glorious heights.

The rustle of dry leaves and the crackling of a branch broke in on his reverie. Looking up, he saw Zoë entering the forest. Alarmed, he followed her stealthily, and from behind a tree he witnessed the tears of Princess Anna.

He returned to his former place more perturbed than ever. "A mother's tears are like molten lead," he thought, remembering how his own mother had wept over his brother's death. "Those who cause them to flow will have their hides scorched." But here he stopped thinking altogether. He dared not face the memory of his brother's death in his present doubting mood. It involved too much.

145

It involved the Imam Shamyl, and the customs of his people, and his own severe probation before becoming a Murid. With a heavy heart Hassan rolled himself up in his burka, willing himself to sleep.

A rough hand shook him. Startled, he jumped to his feet, and in the gray light of dawn he saw Hadji-Kheriett standing over him, his eyes mad with anger. "Where is the captive?" he yelled. "The she-devil is gone! Have you seen her, or has she bewitched you into letting her escape?"

It was unseemly for a youth to see an older man lose his temper, and Hassan lowered his eyes. "The mistress of Tsinandali slept in the hollow. She may have gone to her."

With an oath Hadji-Kheriett threw the reins of his horse to Hassan and ran into the forest.

Zoë was standing on the same spot where she had slept. Princess Anna, pale and shivering, was leaning against a tree, and the two Tchetchens, the princess's captors, stood beside them.

When Hadji-Kheriett caught sight of Zoë, he seemed to lose all self-control. His frustrated desires of the night before had turned into a thirst for revenge. She had tempted him shamelessly. She was a daughter of Shaitan. Since awakening he had repeated these words so often he had come to believe in them himself. And Zoë, glancing over her shoulder, remained stricken in terror—Hadji-Kheriett was advancing on her, brandishing his hard leather whip. Zoë covered her face with her hands.

There was a smothered cry, a rush of feet, and Hassan sprang forward. In the struggle that followed Hassan held on desperately to Hadji-Kheriett's arm, but Hadji-Kheriett, by far the taller and the stronger of the two, threw the boy to the ground. Suddenly Princess Anna stepped between them. She seemed to have regained all her strength. "How dare you!" she shouted at Hadji-Kheriett in Russian. "I will tell Shamyl you tried to beat us!"

It was a shot in the dark. She did not know of Shamyl's orders to bring them to him unharmed, but she saw at once by the frightened look in Hadji-Kheriett's eyes that she had hit the mark. And she followed it up with another threat. "If any of us are harmed, I will not spare you. This lady here is an important captive and a friend of mine. From now on she is not to leave my side."

Her imperious tone and her lack of fear had their effect. Hadji-Kheriett remained sullen, working his jaws in anger, but he said nothing. The other two men came forward with their horses, bowing to her respectfully. Zoë pointed to Princess Anna's torn chemise,

146

trying to make them understand that something should be found for her to wear. They stared back at her with dumb eyes, and it was Hassan who dashed to his horse, drew a bundle out of a bag that hung below his saddle, and came forward with a big soft shawl. He slipped it shyly around Princess Anna's shoulders. He did not know why he had done this. The shawl was part of his meager loot he intended to give to his mother. And now, seeing the gratitude in the women's eyes, he blushed and moved away, trying not to look at the other men.

But Hadji-Kheriett had found a scapegoat for his rage. He rushed up to Hassan. "These women belong to a clan that put me to shame. And you dared raise your hand against me! Kazi-Mahomma will know about this, and so will the Imam. Have you forgotten your brother's disgrace?"

All color fled from Hassan's face. He shut his eyes and clenched his fists to master his fury—the honor of his family depended on it. Hadji-Kheriett in the meantime had turned away, jumping into his saddle and ordering Hassan to put Zoë on the horse behind him.

There were tears of gratitude in Zoë's eyes as she looked at Hassan's pale face and his big almond-shaped eyes. He was lifting her onto the horse now. Her hand brushed past her ear and she felt a small hard object. By some miracle her gold earrings had escaped Hadji-Kheriett's notice. Quickly she slipped them out of her ears and pressed them into Hassan's hand. And she saw him blush again as she rode away.

This time her arm had not been strapped inside Hadji-Kheriett's belt, but for the next three hours she wished it had been, for they traveled along narrow mountain trails on the brink of precipices that seemed to draw her irresistibly to their depths. She rode most of the way with her eyes tightly closed, and when finally they came to a stop and Hadji-Kheriett ordered them to dismount, she found herself at the foot of a very high cliff.

"Too steep to ride," Princess Anna explained. "We must go on foot."

Zoë looked up at the cliff and her heart sank. It seemed to rise straight up like a wall, and from where she stood she could not see the top.

"Courage, Zoë-djan," said Princess Anna. "It is not as bad as it looks. Don't think of the mountain. Don't look up or down. Just go step by step."

To give Zoë confidence she took a few steps herself, but fell to the ground. Her captors stood over her, urging her on. With a supreme effort she scrambled back to her feet, took another step or two, and fell again, shaking her head helplessly. The men must have realized she was at the end of her strength, for one of them picked her up and swung her over his shoulder. Zoë watched him climb with an agile step, and she saw the horses, freed of their riders, go up the cliff with ease. A few loose stones rolled down. Hadji-Kheriett prodded her with the end of his whip. There was no choice.

Slowly she began to climb, clutching onto every stone, every shrub, every tuft of grass. She kept repeating Princess Anna's words, "Don't think of the mountain. Don't look up or down. Just go step by step."

They must have climbed for almost an hour. At times she was ready to give up in despair, but Hassan kept close behind her, making encouraging sounds and giving her a helpful shove now and then. And when at last, after what seemed to her like a whole eternity, she reached the summit, she heaved a deep sigh and fell to the ground, panting.

"It is safe here and we are alone," she heard Princess Anna say in a weak voice. "The men have gone behind those boulders there and have told us to rest. I feel very weak, Zoë-djan. I need your help."

Zoë looked up. They were on a narrow ridge with a solid wall of rock on one side of it. She did not get up; she crawled up to the wall on her hands and knees and sat down heavily. Princess Anna sank to the ground beside her with a groan, and Zoë saw then that she was in great pain. Her breasts were terribly swollen with milk, and one of the cuts was beginning to fester. She had shut her eyes, leaning her head against the wall. Zoë took her hand in hers and held it tight. It was all she could do, but the knowledge that this woman needed her filled her with sudden pride. She gazed at the snow-capped peaks in the distance, blinking a little—they glistened so in the sun, they hurt the eyes. "Only the day before yesterday, or was it a hundred years ago," she said to herself, "this woman was Princess Anna and I was afraid of her. Now we are alone on the top of the world, Anna and I. And Anna needs me!" And she felt she could never really be afraid of anyone again.

The head of a horse appeared suddenly in front of her; then the whole riderless animal came into sight, struggling onto the level ground. Two heavy bags dangled on either side of the saddle, and a small object, like a little black mallet, stuck out of one of them. It

148

seemed to be moving. It kicked. With a cry Zoë jumped up and ran to the horse. Princess Anna had seen it, too, and was struggling painfully to her feet. Zoë thrust her arms into the bag. There was a muffled scream and Tamara was brought out, her hair falling all over her face. She had been sound asleep and she began to cry now as Zoë anxiously felt her all over for broken bones. But the child was not hurt, only frightened. The two women fussed over her, brushing the hair away from her face and trying to console her as best they could. An angry little grunt of protest reached them from the other side of the horse. Zoë hurried around and found George Orbeliani, Princess Varvara's son, in the other bag.

"Thank God these two at least are alive!" she murmured, patting George's cheek. And the little boy, sitting up in her arms, clapped his hands and stretched them out with delight toward the snow-capped mountains.

There was the sound of falling stones, of scrambling feet, and Eliso and Vassilissa, the nurses, appeared on the scene, followed by men and horses. With screams of joy they kissed Princess Anna's hand and hugged the children. But the four women were given no time to talk. Hadji-Kheriett returned with his companions and ordered them back on their horses.

A few minutes later they were riding down a gentle incline, a far easier road than before, over which the horses could travel four abreast. Toward noon they descended into a narrow green valley, dominated by the Tower of Pohali, the fallen outpost of Prince David's militia. Zoë could see horses grazing in the distance and the carcasses of cows roasting over huge fires, the trunks of pine trees thrust through them instead of skewers. And a large, elaborate white tent had been put up near the entrance to the tower.

"Imam Shamyl!" Hadji-Kheriett explained in hushed tones, as if afraid, even at that distance, to disturb his master's peace.

As they drew nearer, Shamyl's warriors crowded around them, anxious to see these unveiled Christian women, these important captives, who, they thought, would bring them undreamed-of riches. It was Shamyl's custom to give the greater share of a ransom to those of his men who had participated in a raid, and tales about the wealth of Tsinandali had already spread, growing into fabulous proportions. The house, they said, had been full of silver and gold, and diamond flowers had grown all around it.

Princess Anna in her sorry plight passed almost unnoticed, taken for a servant, and it was on Zoë that all eyes were focused. They

149

pressed around her with raucous cries. Laughing and jeering, they tried to touch her, and one man thrust his long musket into her face. On the end of it he had stuck the hand of a woman with a gold wedding ring on its third finger. Zoë gritted her teeth and sat erect, her face stony, counting the steps that separated her from the tower.

It was a relief to find herself inside the tower, with the heavy doors tightly shut and bolted on the unruly mob. And when she grew accustomed to the semi-darkness, she saw that the round room they were in was crowded with women. The maids from Tsinandali were there, and a dozen or more peasant women from neighboring villages; and somewhere in the shadow near the wall a baby was wailing pitifully. Princess Varvara and Marie were there too. They had fared better than the others. They bore no traces of scratches or lacerations, and Princess Varvara's black dress, though torn and smeared with mud, was still in good condition.

Princess Varvara rushed forward to kiss George and then turned to her sister, tears in her eyes. She, too, had seen little Lydia's death. But before she could embrace her, Princess Anna laid a hand on her shoulder.

"There is hope, Varvara." She spoke rapidly, as if afraid someone might interrupt. "Zoë-djan saw Lydia fall. She says the ground was very soft. . . ."

Her voice trailed off into a whisper, her knees caved in, and she sank limply to the ground. They carried her across the room and laid her on some straw. But Princess Anna had not fainted. She raised herself on her elbow and peered around. "Where are the other children?"

"Salome and Sandro have not yet arrived," Princess Varvara replied, pushing Marie forward.

Marie advanced shyly, and her "Bonjour, Maman" echoed strangely through the vaulted room.

Princess Anna smiled. She tried to raise her hand, but it fell back to her side. She shut her eyes, and for a moment her face was distorted with pain, while Marie stood staring in surprise at her mother's swollen breasts.

The thin, emaciated figure of a girl of twelve rose from the shadow by the wall. She moved forward furtively, carrying a crying baby in her arms. "Have pity on us, Princess," she said in a trembling voice. "Both our parents have been killed, and my baby sister will die of hunger if you don't feed her."

150

Princess Anna sat up, her eyes glistening. She flung out both her arms. "Give her to me!"

At first the child protested, striking out with its little shriveled fist, but when the nipple touched its mouth, it fell to sucking avidly with tiny grunts of satisfaction. And Princess Anna bit her lips and closed her eyes.

3   Princess Anna experienced great relief after feeding the baby. She was reclining on the straw, the children, her sister, Zoë, and all the other women gathered around her. They had just finished eating the roast mutton that had been brought in a large earthenware pot, when the heavy door creaked on its hinges. On the doorstep stood a short fat man in a long cloak of heavy green silk and a bright blue turban from which a cocky aigrette sprouted just above his forehead. He seemed ridiculously overdressed. At first his appearance amused Zoë, but when she saw his unnaturally sweet smile, framed by heavy jowls, narrow eyes, and a small pointed beard, she felt an instinctive dislike for this gaudy, pompous little man.

He came in, blinking in the unaccustomed darkness of the room. "Where is the Princess Tchavchavadzé?" he asked in Russian, dragging out every word. His voice had an unpleasant nasal quality to it.

Princess Anna stiffened. "I am in no fit condition to receive you or anyone else, Daniel-Sultan!"

Zoë knew enough Russian by now to follow the general gist of a conversation. And at the sound of his name her mind flew back to the day Madame Tollet had discovered the Armenian merchant, Spindarian, in her husband's office. As though in answer to her thoughts, Daniel-Sultan drew out of his pocket a gold box studded with small diamonds. He opened it and offered it to the two princesses. "Peppermint fondants are very refreshing. Do have one."

They stared back at him in stony silence. With a shrug he took a peppermint out of the box and put it carefully in his mouth, laying it on the tip of his tongue. He closed his eyes, and his smile became almost beatific. Then he shut the box with a snap.

"I see you have not changed," he said. "And I can't help asking myself, 'What are these two princesses so proud of? Granddaughters of a king, stripped of their royal prerogatives, dragged down to the level of plain, ordinary subjects, they don't seem to mind licking

151

the boots of their tyrants.' The Russians tried to subjugate me in the same way, but I refused to submit!"

"Some people may prefer loyalty to prerogatives," Princess Varvara put in quietly.

"Loyalty to an oppressor?" he parried, his fingers caressing a string of amber beads he wore wound around his right wrist. "There is truth in the saying, 'One cannot account for tastes.' " He turned to Princess Anna again, his voice droning monotonously, nasally. "Hadji-Kheriett has reported the loss of your child, Princess. He claims you deliberately threw it away. Is that true?"

Princess Anna drew herself up, her eyes blazing. "How dare you ask me such a question!"

"Oh, le monstre!"

The cry escaped Zoë before she had time to think, and Daniel-Sultan looked at her with sudden interest. "Ah! A Frenchwoman in our midst!" he exclaimed, his incredible smile spreading all over his round face. "What a pleasure! How happy my daughter, my beautiful Karimat, will be when she hears of it!"

Zoë looked up at him, surprise mingling with her indignation. Little did she guess how close she had come to fitting into his ambitious schemes. Two guiding forces governed Daniel-Sultan's life —his passionate love for his daughter and his thirst for power. They were so closely interwoven, he himself could not tell which of the two predominated. In his spidery way he was spinning plans to rule over the mountain tribes of the Caucasus after Shamyl's death. With this end in view he had given Karimat in marriage to Kazi-Mahomma, Shamyl's heir, and he knew that it had been the cause of Karimat's unhappiness. She was pining for the life she had known before, for the company of worldly women she had met in her Tiflis days, and the prospect of power obtained at the cost of Karimat's happiness seemed to lose all flavor. Yet power he must have, and a way must be found to make Karimat happy. Zoë appeared to him now as a possible pawn in his game. "Perhaps this little Frenchwoman could be induced to become Karimat's companion," he speculated, looking at her with interest.

His thoughts were cut short by a loud knock on the door. A moment later Salome stood on the threshold, squinting into the dark room. But the joy of the women at seeing her alive and unhurt was short-lived. Fat Yakovlevna, the nurse, stood on the threshold now, the limp form of Sandro in her arms. With a cry Princess Anna brushed past Daniel-Sultan.

152

Yakovlevna was wailing, "Oh, Princess, my sweet Princess! The child has had nothing, nothing to eat!" Her dress was torn, her face bruised, and there was a deep gash on her right hand. She had fallen off her horse, but she seemed unaware of her injuries. She kept crying out, "Oh, God Almighty! God the Merciful! Oh, sweet saints in heaven. Sandro is dying!"

Princess Anna took her only son in her arms with a tenderness she had never shown before. She ran back to her place near the wall and, sinking to the floor, her back to the room, pressed her breast to his mouth.

At the sight of Sandro's lifeless form Daniel-Sultan looked worried. He knew that the death of another child would enrage Shamyl. It meant the loss of a bargaining point. He walked slowly to the door, but there he stopped and beckoned to Zoë. She hesitated. Then she picked up the shawl Princess Anna had dropped, wrapped herself in it, and went to him.

He was frowning, trying to remember the few words of French he had known. At last he said, *"Vous . . . tous . . . ici . . . maintenant?"*

Zoë glanced around the room, counting the women and children. Someone was missing, she knew. Then she remembered Marfa. "Princess Anna's maid is missing," she said.

Daniel-Sultan brushed this aside with a gesture of contempt. He smiled and spoke to her in Russian: "You are a subject of the French Emperor. Soon the French Emperor and the English Queen will attack the Russian Tsar. You should stay with my beautiful Karimat until they beat him. Then we can all rejoice together!" He gave her no time to answer. With a wave of his hand he was gone, and the heavy door creaked again as it closed behind him.

His words had sounded ominous. Zoë looked at the princesses and the children and she shrank at the thought of being separated from them. She was moving to Princess Anna's side with the intention of telling her about it, when the door opened again and Hadji-Kheriett came in.

For a moment he stood watching them all, a cruel smile twisting his thin lips. Sandro had taken to his mother's breast and had rallied a bit. He was back in fat Yakovlevna's lap, and Princess Varvara had torn off a strip from her petticoat and was bandaging the nurse's hand, while Princess Anna sat by, shivering a little, looking miserable. Zoë took off her shawl and slipped it over Princess Anna's shoulders.

153

Hadji-Kheriett was enjoying their plight. To him it was as good as a personal revenge against Prince David and old Goulbat. He was standing over Princess Anna now. "I don't think you will ever see your freedom again," he said brutally. "Who will pay your ransom? I hear your husband has been taken prisoner!"

"That is a lie!" Princess Anna cried. "He would never give himself up alive!"

There was no hesitation in her voice, but Zoë noticed that she shuddered slightly as she spoke. Hadji-Kheriett noticed it, too, and he seemed satisfied. He did not pursue the subject. "I have been sent to tell you," he said, "that you will leave the Tower of Pohali today. You will be taken to the Imam's seraglio in Dargo-Veden." He pointed in turn to Princess Anna and to Princess Varvara. "You and you. Your children and their nurses. The rest will remain here."

No sooner had he said this than the servant women of Tsinandali began to shriek in terror. On their knees they crowded around Princess Anna, touching her arms and shoulders, begging her not to leave them. Princess Anna did her best to calm them, but they did not seem to hear her.

A lean old man who had come in with Hadji-Kheriett and had remained unnoticed by the door, watching the scene, came forward now with raised hand and spoke to the women in Russian. "I am a mullah, a humble expounder of the holy Koran. None of you will be harmed, I promise you. You will all join your princesses in Dargo-Veden, and that is the truth. I swear to it by Allah!"

At the sound of his quiet, earnest voice the women fell silent, and a voice rose from their midst, saying, "Save us, kind old man. Tell Shamyl, if our prince has been captured, Princess Catherine will pay the ransom. She is very rich. The whole of Mingrelia belongs to her!"

Hadji-Kheriett narrowed his eyes. "Is the Princess of Mingrelia a relative of yours?" he asked Princess Anna.

Before she had time to answer, the servant women began to scream. "She is our prince's sister. She owns a whole country. A whole country all to herself!"

Hadji-Kheriett turned to the old man. "There are more riches here than we had suspected. This should be reported."

"Yes," the other replied with a sigh. "It is of importance to the Imam and to the people. Go and do your duty, my son." Hadji-Kheriett hurried out, and the mullah turned again to the women.

154

"I have no doubt the matter of the ransom will be settled soon. It will be paid, and you will all be free."

Something about this old man inspired trust. Zoë, looking up into his benevolent face, felt more confident; the princesses saw in him a pious man, for the green turban he was wearing indicated he had been on a holy pilgrimage to Mecca; the other women gazed at him with new hope.

Princess Anna smiled sadly at the mullah, and he looked down at her, stroking his thin gray beard. "I owe your family a debt," he said in a quiet voice. "Many years ago when I was robbed by bandits in Kahetia, your father-in-law, Prince Alexander, gave me shelter and sent me on my way with many a fine gift. Today, thanks to Allah, I can repay it in part. The Imam has given me permission to escort you as far as Dargo-Veden and to attend to your needs. He deems it unbefitting for women of your rank to remain here among his rough warriors."

Princess Anna smiled again—as if such things mattered now. But aloud she said, "You say that my servant women will not be harmed and will join me in Dargo-Veden, and I will take your word for it. But my friend here"—she pointed in Zoë's direction— "must come with us. She, too, is a lady of rank, the daughter of a French general. I will not leave without her."

The mullah inclined his head, a noncommittal look on his thin angular face, and Princess Anna continued: "There is a girl of twelve here with her infant sister. Please ask Shamyl to let them come with me. The child has no mother to suckle her, and I have no child to feed—any more." He inclined his head again, this time closing his eyes, and Princess Anna looked at Zoë. "My friend has nothing to wear. And I, as you see, have nothing but this shawl. We should be provided with clothes before we go."

"A friend's loyalty, a mother's grief, and a woman's modesty should be respected by all men," the mullah said gravely. "I will see what can be done."

He bowed and walked slowly out of the room.

4   Princess Anna sat wrapped in gloom. Hadji-Kheriett's words about Prince David's capture filled her with misgivings; she had no way of knowing whether it was true or not. And Zoë, realizing she might be left behind, sat beside her, clutching her trembling hands tightly around her knees.

155

Princess Varvara was saying to her: "Always take the threats of these mountaineers with a grain of salt. It is their policy to intimidate their captives. My husband, you know, was a prisoner of Shamyl some years ago. He told me, if you show any fear, they despise you and become very cruel. But if you display an indifference to suffering and death, they will respect you. They have much of the Spartan in them, and they admire it in others, even in their enemies."

Zoë swallowed hard. "But I am afraid! I'm afraid this is a plot against me personally." She told her of Hadji-Kheriett's behavior the night before, of his cruelty that morning. She reminded her of Daniel-Sultan's insinuations. And now this order that she and the servants should remain behind.

"But the Benevolent Mullah, as you call him, has promised to do his best for you, Zoë-djan."

A sigh escaped Zoë. "Can he, though? Has he any authority? After all, he is only a preacher."

Princess Varvara laid her hand on Zoë's shoulder. "I must tell you something, Zoë-djan. Not that Anna and I will ever abandon you. No! But I am not afraid for you. You can stand up for yourself. This morning that door was opened and I witnessed your arrival. I saw the ordeal you went through, the savage men mobbing you and one of them thrusting a dead hand in your face. You showed no fear; you did not even shut your eyes. You rode on with great dignity, your head high. Oh, I was very proud of you!"

Her praise did more to restore Zoë's courage than anything else could have done. And when the door opened again and Princess Varvara whispered to her, "Oh, it's Kazi-Mahomma, Shamyl's son," she was able to forget all else for a moment and look up with interest at the brother of the mysterious Jemaleddin. Broad-shouldered and slim, he held himself rather sprucely in his dark tcherkeska edged with galloons of gold. His finely modeled nose, his narrow, slanting eyes stood out clear and sharp, but the lower part of his face was blurred in softness. And he puckered his full lips in a resentful, offended way.

Somber-looking Naibs, Shamyl's highest dignitaries, dressed in black, had escorted him as far as the door but remained outside. Only Hadji-Kheriett entered the room with him. He singled out the two princesses and Zoë and then waited for his young master to speak, a mute, doglike devotion in his eyes that was strangely unbecoming to his ferocious face.

Kazi-Mahomma's voice had a rich fullness to it. He expressed himself in the flowery manner of his people, but he spoke hesitantly, bashfully, giving Hadji-Kheriett ample time to translate his words, as if hoping not to have to speak again. To Princess Varvara he said: "The noble Imam, my father, is much grieved at the news of your husband's death. He held him in great esteem. Brave and fearless warriors like Eliko Orbeliani will be accounted for in heaven, whatever their faith."

No Moslem mountaineer of his day could have said more, and Princess Varvara knew it. "Thank you, Kazi-Mahomma," she murmured. "You have a kind heart."

But a kind heart was the last thing Kazi-Mahomma would confess to—a sign of softness and weakness he despised and secretly dreaded. In spite of his youth, he had already achieved a high reputation as the most skillful rider, the most intrepid warrior among his father's men. And to many of them, like Hadji-Kheriett, he had become the subject of hero worship. They knew he fretted when forced to remain at home for any length of time, longing to be with them again, fighting in their ranks and achieving new glory. To anyone else this might have seemed strange in a young man of twenty whose bride was reputed to be the most beautiful girl in Daghestan; but to them it was a proof of manliness, of unyielding faith in the holy cause of the Ghazavat.

He now turned to Princess Anna, frowning and doing his best to appear implacable.

"Before you leave this place, you and Varvara Orbeliani are to write a letter to your friends in Tiflis."

Princess Anna drew herself up. "One of my serving-women is still unaccounted for. I want that girl there, with her baby sister, to accompany us. And I refuse to leave without our friend and companion in misfortune, Zoia Ivanovna Duval!"

Kazi-Mahomma opened his eyes in wonder. "The Imam's word is law. If you refuse to obey, we will carry you out by force."

"You have already proven your skill at it!"

When Hadji-Kheriett had translated Princess Anna's words, Kazi-Mahomma blushed to the roots of his hair. But Zoë gave him no time to speak. "Anna!" she cried. "Please don't insist. I will stay. I trust the Benevolent Mullah's word. We will all meet again in Shamyl's house."

Princess Anna rose from the floor. Taking Zoë by the hand, she turned to Kazi-Mahomma and repeated in Russian what Zoë had said. Then she added: "I admire my friend's courage, but it won't make me change my mind. If she stays, I stay!"

The Naibs shook their heads in dismay and whispered among themselves. Kazi-Mahomma looked Zoë full in the face with sudden interest, then he turned again to Princess Anna. "You are foolhardy and stubborn women. Perhaps your misfortunes have blinded you. But I advise you to collect your wits and learn to obey the Imam! And now, write your friends in Tiflis, telling them to open up negotiations for your liberation. Tell them to send you clothes and other articles you may need in your daily life. My father will offer you hospitality, but his means are limited and his house poor. He is truly a leader of men, not like those among you we have heard of who live in palaces and know not the misery of the hovel."

At a sign from him pen and ink and a sheet of paper were brought in and offered to Princess Anna. She shook her head. "Give it to my sister," she said.

Princess Varvara and Zoë guessed the reason for her refusal. Although the news of Prince David's captivity may have been a form of intimidation or just a piece of mental cruelty on the part of Hadji-Kheriett, she dared not address a letter to her husband for fear of being told once again that he was a prisoner or, worse still, dead. They, too, shared these fears. They had deliberately avoided all mention of Prince David and Sasha, and Kazi-Mahomma's words, "Write your friends," instead of "your family," had sounded ominous to them all. Princess Varvara sat on the floor, deliberating with herself whom she should write to. Finally she scribbled a hurried note to General Réad: "General, we and the whole family are in captivity. We are alive but in want of everything. Come to our assistance and inform our relatives of our situation, advising them that Shamyl is willing to open negotiations for our liberation. Communicate with us at Shamyl's house in Dargo-Veden." She gave the note to her sister, who scanned it, holding it close to her eyes, then nodded her approval and signed it. When Princess Varvara had added her own signature and was about to give the letter to Kazi-Mahomma, Princess Anna stopped her. "Not yet! Zoë-djan must sign it too!"

She disregarded Hadji-Kheriett's protests. "It will add to your prestige here," she whispered into Zoë's ear. "And there it will serve as a personal message from you."

Zoë was on the verge of tears, and Princess Varvara helped her to sign her name in Russian—"Zoia Duval."

A few minutes later, when Kazi-Mahomma and the others had withdrawn, the Benevolent Mullah came in alone. He was carrying two bundles under his arms. When he unrolled them, Zoë saw that they were katibas, the gorgeous mantles worn by Georgian women on festive occasions; one was made of purple and the other of crimson velvet. She smiled sadly. Even though the fur had been ripped off, leaving tattered edges, the katibas, with their rich velvet and elaborate trimmings, looked out of place in this dungeon-like room among women cowering on filthy straw. But the mullah seemed unaware of this. Very solemnly he laid out the purple katiba in front of Princess Anna, and in answer to the mute query in her eyes he smiled and laid the crimson one at Zoë's feet.

"The girl and the baby, can they come too?" Princess Anna asked. He inclined his head again in silence.

Zoë could have wept with joy. At first she had refrained from showing her feelings in front of the women who were to remain behind, but they apparently had become reconciled to their fate. They were crowding around their mistress, helping her into her new robe and exclaiming among themselves in Georgian. And Zoë slipped into her katiba with Princess Varvara's help. She laughed happily, turning this way and that to show herself off to an admiring group of three little girls.

When they came out of the tower, they found two long rows of armed horsemen lined up to keep the curious away; and in front of the door stood several attendants, holding saddled horses in readiness. Among them Zoë caught sight of Hassan. She was struck by the haggard look on his face. Princess Anna saw him, too, and glanced down quickly at the shawl she was carrying folded over her arm. But Zoë stopped her. "Not now, Anna. You will embarrass him."

Princess Anna gave Zoë the shawl. "Give it to him when you get a chance. That dreadful Hadji-Kheriett and he will probably be escorting you on the way."

But to Zoë's surprise Hadji-Kheriett was nowhere to be seen. Hassan came forward alone with the horse and helped her into the saddle. No one was watching them, and she tried to give him the shawl, but when he saw it, his mouth hardened and he stepped back. Smiling, she made signs to him to tie it at the back of her saddle, and this he did obligingly enough.

Zoë had never ridden astride before. The high-pommeled, well-padded saddle was uncomfortably wide and bulky, but it was a

159

relief to have this beautiful bay mare all to herself. Princess Anna shared her horse with Tamara. Princess Varvara, Salome, Marie, the nurses, and the little peasant girl, with their respective charges, each had a horse to herself. Zoë looked at them all in turn, and her eyes wandered to the big white tent. It stood grand and aloof, the abode of a man of mystery. Or was it a tabernacle that sheltered a colossus of the mountains? Who was he, what was he, this fierce Imam? They were waiting now for a signal to depart. Would he be the one to give it? She kept her eyes on the flaps of his tent. She saw them stir and held her breath. But when they were raised, only Kazi-Mahomma stepped out, followed by some of the Naibs.

They were coming straight toward her at a brisk pace, and her heart sank. For an agonizing moment she saw herself being ordered back into the tower. She clutched the pommel of her saddle, counting long minutes into the seconds that slipped by.

The men stopped in front of Hassan, and her relief turned to pity when she saw how pale Hassan's face had grown. Kazi-Mahomma was upbraiding him in a loud and harsh voice, and the eyes of all the men were upon him, cruel, merciless, ready for the kill. But for the time being no punishment followed the reprimand. Kazi-Mahomma turned his back on Hassan and gave the signal. The tension broke. Hassan swung into his saddle. The Benevolent Mullah with two other men rode ahead, and the captives moved forward, two lines of armed horsemen gliding alongside of them. And from within the tower, distant but clear, came the plaintive sounds of an old Georgian song. The women of Tsinandali were singing their farewell.

They traveled slowly through the valley, Princess Anna in the lead on a snow-white horse—a Gypsy queen in a purple mantle, her thick black hair in tangles, her feet bare, her small curly-haired daughter perched on the saddle in front of her. Zoë came next, like some wild maid of honor in a tattered crimson robe, followed by Princess Varvara and the others, bedraggled, dirty, bits of straw still clinging to their clothes and hair.

A masquerade in the wilderness, Zoë thought, smiling to herself. For the first time since their abduction she was able to think clearly, to take stock of things. Death had receded that day and, thanks to Anna, her name was on the letter—a message of survival for Sasha.

They rode on through the afternoon and early evening, a silent caravan winding its way higher and higher up, until finally it vanished, swallowed up by mountain mists.

5 Nine days later, in Tiflis, Sasha was standing at an open
   window in the small antechamber of General Réad's office.
Intense waves of heat beat back at him from the cobbled court below.
His white army tunic felt uncomfortably tight, and a stray lock of
dark hair had stuck to his damp forehead. But he stared vacantly
into space, unconscious of it all. Only his fingers drummed a swift
tattoo on the window sill.

A young officer behind him stirred in his seat.

"I wish you'd shut that window, Novoselsky, and draw the
blinds. The heat is becoming infernal!"

Almost mechanically Sasha did what he was told. He turned to
the darkened room, and his eyes fell on a row of stiff chairs lined
up against the wall. There was no one there waiting to see the
general. Why, then, was he made to wait so long?

"Have you any idea why the general sent for me? Any news from
Kahetia? From the mountains?" The young man shook his head,
and Sasha sighed. "Damn this suspense! Ten days!"

Lieutenant Nikolsky—one of the general's aides on duty that
afternoon—had been sprawling at a desk, admiring his well-polished
nails. He sat up now and stared at Sasha. "Ten days! Impossible!
Let me see . . . The attack took place on the fourth, today is the——"

"Stop counting your fingers, Nikolsky. You haven't enough to
go round! Count up the hours, and the minutes, and the seconds.
Perhaps then you'll understand." He stopped short, annoyed at
having given away so much of himself to this perfumed young
dandy. He had never liked him anyway. "A small mouse out of a
small hole with pretensions to a lion's den," he had said of him
once. Now he felt like kicking him out of his freshly starched tunic.
Instead he kicked a chair out of his way and began pacing up and
down the room.

Like everyone else in Tiflis, Nikolsky had been stunned by the
news of the attack on Tsinandali. When it had first reached town,
people had met in the streets, exclaiming, "Have you heard?" and
had gone on their way in silence. And like everyone else, he was
deeply concerned over the fate of the princesses and their children.
He looked up at Sasha again with disdain. "Novoselsky alone frets
over the Frenchwoman. As if she mattered!" In spite of Sasha's
efforts, the secret of his love for Zoë had seeped out, as such matters
always will, and had become the subject of excited speculations
and gossip among certain circles in town. Nikolsky tried to recall
what Zoë looked like. He had seen her once at a distance. "A little

161

soubrette, that's all!" He felt pleasantly superior and smug. But a thunderous "Nikolsky!" coming from the general's study shattered his importance. He jumped to his feet, flustered, and ran out of the room, straightening his white tunic.

Several minutes went by. Sasha sat down on the edge of the desk, almost sorry Nikolsky had gone. Even the company of that fop was better than none, for these days he dreaded solitude. He stared fixedly at the tip of his lacquered boot, trying to make his mind a blank, but the effort itself brought on a flood of thoughts. Thoughts, unhampered and uncontrolled, have a way of leading one by the nose. And so it was with Sasha that afternoon. The tip of his boot led him through devious ways right back to the places he dreaded most—to the burning house, to the Tsinandali woods, and to the corpses beyond the Alazan. Princess Tinia alone, poor soul, had come out of the woods, and Marina-gamdeli had gone into the burning house. And across the river lay many corpses —Marfa, slashed and mutilated, among them, and little Lydia with only a black clot at the temple. What if the others . . . Zoë! He pressed his knuckles to his temples to crush out the unendurable thought. The clinking of approaching spurs in the corridor outside cleared his mind. He shook his head at himself furiously. "If, if, if . . . If yourself, you fool! The bodies would have been found by now!"

Sasha smiled with relief when he saw Prince David coming in. He felt calmer, stronger in his company. Never before had he fully appreciated this man. Prince David's tragedy was a spectacular one—his wife, five of his six children, his home, and all his worldly treasures had vanished in the twinkling of an eye. People were beginning to refer to him as the "Modern Job." Perhaps in the silence of the night he, too, tossed miserably in his bed, stifling a deep, heartbreaking moan, but if so, he showed no signs of it. True, his deep-set eyes were no longer mischievous, no longer amused by everything they saw, but his composure and his superb self-control were a source of inspiration to Sasha throughout those hard days.

Prince David smiled back at his young friend. "Ah, Sasha! Such pleasant news. Sister Nina arrived from Mingrelia about an hour ago. She says Elena is well. Naturally they haven't told her anything, and the yellow mouse is enjoying herself with her cousins."

His eyes wandered to the general's door, and when Sasha told him Nikolsky had just been called in, he sat down at the desk.

Crossing his legs and propping his chin in his hand, he looked at Sasha with amusement and concern. "What are we to do, my friend, about Aunt Tinia's new wig? The bothersome thing won't stay on now that her head has developed a shake. Today Nina tried strapping it under her chin, but it did no good. Slowly but surely it comes creeping back over her eyes."

They both laughed, silently, sadly; but they grew serious again, hearing heavy steps coming down the corridor. The door was pushed open and General Réad's orderly stepped in. He clicked his heels and stood at attention, his round belly protruding in spite of his efforts to draw it in, his red face solemn.

"Messengers from Shamyl, sir!"

His voice went booming through the half-empty room. It must have reached the general's study, for no sooner had Prince David sprung to his feet than the door opened and the general stuck his bald head and bull-like neck into the room.

"Well done, Potap!" he exclaimed with pride. "Your voice is getting better every day—what! Bring them in." And he disappeared again, beckoning to Prince David and Sasha to come in.

The general's study was also shrouded in semi-darkness, but he ordered Nikolsky to draw the blinds aside. Bright sunlight poured over the big mahogany desk and the leather-upholstered chairs and flooded the opposite wall, on which hung two large engravings in gilt frames surmounted by imperial crowns. They were two half-size portraits engraved a quarter of a century earlier: one of Emperor Nicholas, slim and straight as a rod, looking down sternly at his subjects, and the other of Empress Alexandra, amiable, large pearls entwined in the coronet of tresses piled high above her forehead. Both were represented in the full glory of youth, their fine classical features truly Apollonian in quality and line. The general loved these portraits. To him, in a sense, they represented the whole of Russia. When some critical-minded, argumentative friend insisted on pointing out the blemishes of the administration, bribery and corruption and other such depravities, he would look up at them sentimentally and say, "With such beauty on the throne, can anything in Russia be really ugly?" And, what's more, he believed it.

General Réad settled down heavily behind his desk. His army tunic was unbuttoned, and he kept wiping the sweat off his face and neck with a large checkered handkerchief. He invited Prince David to sit beside him. Nikolsky remained near the window, and

163

Sasha stationed himself behind Prince David's chair. From there he got a full view of the entering messengers.

They came in, two of them, white turbans wound around their fur caps. They were disarmed—even their swords and daggers had been removed from their sheaths. One of them remained standing near the open door, a step or two ahead of the two soldiers who had brought them in. He spoke no Russian and he remained silent throughout the whole interview, watching; but his companion strode forward and planted himself firmly in the middle of the room. Sasha sensed at once that his appearance had startled Prince David; he saw, too, a look of triumph on the messenger's face. And a moment later he knew why. "I know this man!" Prince David exclaimed. "His name is Hadji-Kheriett!" And leaning over to the general, he added, "He is the man I told you about, sir. The spy who got away."

General Réad fixed Hadji-Kheriett with a cold and rather bulgy blue eye. "So! It's you!"

"Yes!" Hadji-Kheriett drew himself up to his full height. "Not a prisoner, but an emissary of our illustrious Imam! We came with a white flag of truce, bearing important messages, but your soldiers treated us like prisoners. They disarmed us. And you may as well know, General, we would have been here several days ago had they not held us up all down the line."

General Réad felt somewhat irritated at this unnecessary display of red tape on the part of his troops, but he was even more irritated by Hadji-Kheriett's arrogant tone. He crushed his handkerchief and clamped it down on the back of his neck. It made his eyes pop out furiously. "When you speak to me, lower your voice!" he snapped, and then, "What are your messages?"

Hadji-Kheriett drew a crumpled letter out of the side of his tcherkeska. Nikolsky stepped forward and handed it to the general.

The moment that followed was so tense and sharp, Sasha felt it like a stab. The general had unfolded the letter, and from where Sasha stood he caught a glimpse of the three signatures. They stood out, shaky and uneven, helpless, stricken, and wretched. He tore his eyes away, unable to endure the sight. But a minute later he took his fill. The general had given the letter to Prince David, saying, "This is really for you, my dear Prince!" He stuck his big finger under Zoë's name as he added, "And for you, too, Novosel-sky. This third signature must be for you—what!"

Sasha leaned over the back of the chair. He could see nothing now but that one name. It was a message, a voice, a pair of moving lips.

General Réad looked up at him, a kindly, fatherly smile hovering at the corners of his mouth, and Nikolsky, seeing it, quickly changed his own sarcastic smile to one of exaggerated concern. Sasha was too intent on the letter to notice anything, but none of it had escaped Hadji-Kheriett. He was watching Sasha closely with growing interest, not untinged by speculation, when the general's voice broke in, demanding further verbal messages if any.

Hadji-Kheriett bowed stiffly, then squared his shoulders. "The Imam, my lord and master, bade me tell you this: The captives are unhurt and unharmed. You may send a trusted man with clothes, soap, tea, a samovar, or any other articles of comfort they may require. But if you want your women and children back, you must comply with the Imam's terms."

"So! And what are his terms?"

"When the captives reach Dargo-Veden, they will write to you again. Then you will know."

"Tell Shamyl, henceforward all communications must be addressed to Colonel Prince David Tchavchavadzé. He will be in charge of negotiations from now on."

Prince David bowed to the general. He then inquired of Hadji-Kheriett about the condition of the captives.

A cruel gleam flickered in Hadji-Kheriett's eyes. "Your wife has nothing to wear. Her feet and her body are bruised. She is suffering. Her breasts are swollen with milk." Suddenly he shut up with a snap of the jaw, realizing that his desire to inflict pain on his hated enemy had led him to say more than he had intended.

The vision of Zoë, also bruised, beaten, miserable, and above all terribly frightened, flashed through Sasha's mind. But Prince David's unruffled calm made him pull himself together. The man had in no way betrayed his feelings. "You call that unhurt and unharmed?" he asked, his voice quiet, though loaded with menace.

Hadji-Kheriett drew himself up. "Your women are undefiled!"

To Shamyl's warriors, and even to Shamyl himself, this was the most important factor. A ravaged woman had no value, they argued; no one would want her, and certainly no one would pay a ransom for her liberation. Prince David knew this. He inclined his head in silence, while Sasha felt a strong, happy flow tingling through his veins.

But Hadji-Kheriett seemed intent on breaking Prince David down. "Your son," he said, "is very sick. He was sick when we took him."

"My son was in excellent health. Tell Shamyl he has killed one of my children and one of my servants. I will hold him to account for it. And if anyone else is lost during this captivity, I will break off all negotiations."

His words took Sasha's breath away—the man had nerves of steel. The general thrust his lower lip out in surprise, and Nikolsky, forgotten at his end of the room, tried to think of all the friends he could write to, bragging about his acquaintance with this "real aristocrat," as he put it. Even Hadji-Kheriett's eyes showed admiration. His hatred for Prince David may have grown, but so had his respect. And he modulated his voice accordingly when he said, "Your wife's sister suffered no injuries. Your three little daughters were in high spirits. And the young woman who signed the paper——" He seemed to pause deliberately, while Sasha leaned anxiously forward. "She is my prisoner. I carried her away from Tsinandali." He looked straight into Sasha's eyes as he added, "All she needs is a new dress. Hers was torn by the underbrush when we escaped from Mount Kontzhi."

Sasha clutched the back of Prince David's chair to steady himself, not wishing to show his relief and his joy in front of this man. But his thoughts ran wild. "A dress! Only a dress! Oh, merciful God! I'll send her six, eight, ten . . . More! As many as they will let me!"

Prince David laid a firm hand on the general's desk. "Make no mistake," he warned Hadji-Kheriett, "there will be no separate ransoms paid. I alone will bargain, and I alone will pay. And I will pay for all the captives, all or none!"

He then said he would send a trusted man with gifts. With the general's permission he would bring the man in the morning for Hadji-Kheriett and his companion to see. This, he pointed out, would enable them to identify him later when he reached Dargo-Veden.

The general stood up. "Potap!" he roared at the top of his lungs. Sasha almost laughed aloud in his newly found happiness. "He must carry on a shouting competition with his orderly," he thought.

Potap appeared in answer to the summons. He dared not praise aloud the caliber of the general's voice, but Sasha noticed that his small eyes were smiling their approval at their master as he stood at attention.

"Potap!" the general repeated in a lower voice, frowning and munching his lips. "Take these men to the servants' quarters. Give them a room and see that they are fed. But lock them up. And place

166

a guard outside their door. I will hold you responsible for them."

"How dare you lock us up!" Hadji-Kheriett shouted. "We are not prisoners! We are the emissaries of our illustrious Imam!"

His companion came to life suddenly, mumbling threats in his native tongue. General Réad thumped his desk violently. "Shut up! I am the illustrious Imam here!"

Hadji-Kheriett's eyes darted to the Tsar's portrait and then back to the general. "The Imam is supreme. You have others sitting on top of you."

The general snorted with rage. He waved him out of the room, waving Nikolsky away at the same time. He was about to give further vent to his rage, but he saw Prince David's face. It had grown a shade paler now that the tension was over, and he was wiping large beads of perspiration off his forehead with a fresh white handkerchief. The general clasped him in his arms. "You are a wonder, my dear Prince! A wonder! I will not fail to mention it in my next report to Petersburg." He turned to Sasha, clamping a heavy hand on his shoulder. "As for you, young man, off with you to Petersburg in the morning! Nikolsky will bring you your orders this evening to Prince David's house. I am glad I did not have to tell you this before the good news reached us, but I have kept you here too long. If I kept you any longer, there might be displeasure in high places!" He glanced up respectfully at the portraits and then lowered his eyes modestly to the floor. It was his way of intimating he knew Sasha's mother was influential at the imperial court and her family stood high in the imperial favors. Then he grinned. "Why should I stick out my neck for you now that a certain young lady is known to be safe—what!" He winked at Prince David and pommeled Sasha's arm. In his anxiety Sasha had paid no attention to the general's previous remark about Zoë's signature. Now he remembered it and wondered rather naïvely how the old man had discovered his secret. "If I am not mistaken," the general went on, "you have an important matter to settle before the young lady in question comes sliding down the mountain into a pair of ardent arms—what! O-ho-ho! *Very* ardent, I should say! What! What!" And throwing back his head, he gave vent to a laugh truly worthy of his high rank.

6   From General Réad's house Sasha went to the Tollets' as quickly as a horse and carriage could carry him. He could not stay long, having promised to join Prince David, but he wanted

167

to give them the good news and say good-by. During the days of anxiety and suspense he had spent every evening with them. Only in their company had he felt close to Zoë, knowing that they, too, were worrying their hearts over her.

When Madame Tollet saw him rush into her shop, she knew instantly that something terribly important had happened. Her eyes sparkled with excitement and the color rose to her cheeks. But when he shouted, "She's alive! Alive and safe!" she clutched her heart and let out a piercing "Armand!"

For many years she had not used her husband's first name, and when Monsieur Tollet heard it in his office, he thought all the catastrophes of the world were upon him. He ran into the shop, sweat oozing out of every pore, but on hearing the news, he stopped dead. His eyebrows twitched, he breathed heavily for a moment, and then a tear came trickling slowly down his cheek. "It's like finding a long-lost child, eh, my Paulette?"

He embraced his wife, but she thrust him aside. "Paulette! Am I no longer Bonbon chéri!"

"But you called me Armand first!"

"I did not!"

"You did, you did!"

"Oh! I did too!"

She stared at him openmouthed. They all laughed, and then it was "Bonbon chéri" and "Marzipan" and "Old Caramel" over and over again. And when Sasha told them Zoë was unhurt—all she needed was a new dress—Monsieur Tollet seized his wife by the waist and whirled her around, humming a gay tune.

Sasha could not bring himself to say good-by to these kind people. Farewells were distressing at all times, today they might spoil everything; he would write them a note instead. And when they had collapsed into a couple of chairs, panting and fanning themselves with their handkerchiefs, he slipped away, calling out, "*A bientôt!*"

When he reached Prince David's house he found its funereal silence of the past few days dispelled. Someone was playing a Chopin waltz on the piano in the big drawing room. He ran up the wide marble stairs three steps at a time.

Prince David had just broken the news to Nina Alexandrovna. She had dashed to the piano to give vent to her relief, while he had stationed himself behind her, humming the tune. Only Princess Tinia sat silent and unconcerned by a window, wrapped in a shawl in spite of the heat, her head shaking, shaking, shaking. Once in a while

Nina Alexandrovna or Prince David had to give her new wig a tug to get it back into place. On such occasions she would smile up at them, mumbling, "Thank you, thank you. My father, the sardar, had trouble in finding a hat to fit, his head was so large! Mine has grown very, very small." After that she would relapse into silence again. She had never been able to tell them what had taken place in Tsinandali. When asked, she managed to hold her head still for a moment and frown. Then, "It was an Orbeliani who survived the Flood!" And her head would go up and down in little jerks, as though saying, "Indeed, indeed it was!"

Nina Alexandrovna's music had served as a signal to the household. The servants came crowding outside the open door, craning their necks in surprise. She stopped playing and beckoned them in with a happy smile. They entered the room, their questioning, hopeful eyes fixed on Prince David. And some exclaimed with joy while others began to sob when he announced that the family was alive. Poushka was among the servants, towering above them all. His face was very red and his eyes all sunny with happiness. He glanced across the room at Sasha, blinking away a tear, and then made a solemn sign of the cross.

Prince David read the letter aloud to them. He would stay in Tiflis, he said, until he had further word from Shamyl, certain that they would all be on the lookout for new messengers. And when he told them he was planning to send a trusted man to Dargo-Veden, Askar stepped out from among the throng and came forward. "Prince! Let me go! I speak Tartar, and they understand Tartar up there."

He looked at his master with apprehension, afraid he might refuse his request. But Prince David laid a hand on Askar's shoulder. "You were the man I had in mind. As soon as everything is ready you can start on your way."

Askar's chest swelled with pride and a dark color suffused his brown cheeks as he lowered his head to conceal his joy, for Tartars, though reputed capable of great cruelty, have a gift for loyalty and devotion.

Nina Alexandrovna in the meantime had settled down, paper and pencil in hand, ready to make out a list of what should be sent to the captives, and Sasha went up to Prince David. "I would like to share in this. Please, David, do not refuse me. I must! I want to share in the gifts, and later in the ransom too."

Prince David smiled gratefully, but he shook his head. No, this

169

was a matter concerning his family and his household in which he could accept no help. Sasha was about to retort, when Nina Alexandrovna joined them. She had seen the disappointment in his eyes and she now turned to her brother, her expression as serene and calm as ever. "The ransom, of course, is our own private family affair. But, David, Anna and the children are yours, but Madame Zoë-djan is about to become his. You cannot refuse his gifts."

She took Sasha by the arm, and together they began to make suggestions, interrupting each other every time they thought of something specially useful to send—paper, shoes, mattresses, blankets. Prince David reminded them several times that a shipload could not be sent to the mountains, but soon he, too, got into the spirit of it. Nina Alexandrovna was sitting in a chair, writing out the list, the two men leaning over her, and they were all laughing over the absurdity of one of the suggestions—a shoehorn—when Sasha felt someone tap him on the shoulder. He looked around, and so did the others. Princess Tinia was standing close behind them, her wig almost down to her eyes.

"You are sending things to Shamyl? Then send him this and tell him to return my wig!" She tore her wig off and threw it in her niece's lap; and her bald head, with its fringe of white hair, began to shake worse than ever.

Nina Alexandrovna jumped to her feet and put her arm around Princess Tinia's shoulders. "You are tired, Aunt Tinia. You must rest. Come, I will take you to bed."

The old lady resisted. "I am tired," she complained in a peevish voice. "I'm tired of sitting up here in the belvedere, listening to those savages smashing up the furniture below. . . . Can't you do something about it? Anna! Varvara! Madame Zoë-djan! All of you—this has to stop!"

She remained silent for a moment, her eyes wandering aimlessly around the room. "Oh—— They have all been taken away!" Her stooping shoulders shivered a little and she nestled closer to her niece. "Nina, is that you? Thank God! Take me to bed, please."

The gay mood vanished. Princess Tinia's words had shed a new light on the happenings in Tsinandali. Sasha visualized all too clearly the group of terrified women and children crouching in the belvedere, and above all Zoë's frightened face. It gave him no peace. Once again he remembered the miniature Roxane had shown him—the cute little pug face and the big eyes so keen and yet a little frightened. He hardly said a word during supper, and when Nikolsky

170

brought the orders, he sent Poushka out to receive them. He retired early to his room, where he sat, tugging at a long-stemmed pipe, while Poushka packed his things. A dark wave of depression had taken possession of him. He had done nothing about the annulment. In Kahetia he had been kept too busy, then had come those ten dreadful days of waiting. And this evening a remark Prince David had made at supper had started his mind off on a new and dismal trek. Prince David had said, "When my brother-in-law, Eliko Orbeliani, was Shamyl's prisoner, Shamyl tried to force him to write to the Emperor and ask for Jemaleddin's release, but Eliko refused." The words had sent Sasha's thoughts whirling in an ever-narrowing circle. Would Shamyl ask for Jemal again? Would Jemal be called upon to sacrifice himself, and would the Tsar ever give up Jemal? Sasha could almost hear the Tsar's refusal, and with it everything seemed to plunge into a black and bottomless pit. He knew he should pull himself together, but instead, sullenly, and with a kind of morbid delight, he allowed himself to sink deeper into a state of wretchedness.

But Poushka sensed his mood. He stood up, looking down at Sasha with angry eyes, and his voice sounded gruff. "For goodness' sake, Alexandr Dimitrievitch, what's wrong now?"

"Everything is wrong. You know that yourself."

"All I know is Zoia Ivanovna will soon be free. She won't be long now among those savages!"

The word "savages" brought back the face of the miniature, with the captors standing around it, fierce and threatening, and every single one of them looking like Hadji-Kheriett. "That's just it! I keep seeing her frightened face, like the face of a small child, and it is driving me out of my mind!"

"Who said Zoia Ivanovna was a frightened child? She is an eagle!"

This unexpected comparison irritated Sasha. He kicked a footstool out of his way. "If you must speak of birds, why an eagle? You yourself said she was a little tomtit."

"And so she is when all goes well."

"Oh, go back to your packing. You are full of contradictions!"

Poushka stood his ground. "No, Alexandr Dimitrievitch. You are full of contradictions tonight. Zoia Ivanovna is a courageous and strong woman, and if you don't know it by now, you should go back and lie in your cradle!"

The thrust was well aimed. Sasha felt sheepish. He was slipping,

171

growing sentimental, he who had always made a point of despising sentimentality. He tried to think of Zoë as being strong, like Anna and Varvara, for instance. One felt less afraid for them somehow.

Poushka mistook his frown for stubbornness. He became more determined. "She wasn't afraid to come all the way to Tiflis. She wasn't afraid when she found 'Chez Michot' gone—Madame Tollet told us so. She did not hesitate to become a governess in the princess's household. Almost like a servant!" Poushka looked at him point-blank, accusingly. "You pushed her into it. And what are you doing about it now? Just sitting there getting all soft inside over an imaginary child. Shame on you, Alexandr Dimitrievitch! You should grow a couple of breasts and go suckle a baby!" Poushka stopped abruptly, growing very red in the face. "Oh, God Almighty! Now I have said too much and you will be as mad as a hornet!"

But Sasha was on his feet, hugging him. "Always speak to me like this when I deserve it. Pull me out by my hair. Make me live up to what I should be. I count on you, Poushka; you are my best friend."

Poushka turned away, his eyes moist. He was the true sentimentalist of the two. However much he might scold, Sasha would always remain the little boy he had taken care of since infancy. "He has a heart of gold, my Sashenka!" he said to himself now as he resumed his packing.

They spoke for a long time about the future. And before going to bed Sasha wrote a farewell note to the Tollets.

They left Tiflis shortly before dawn, traveling through Mtskhet. There they turned north on the Georgian military highway, the perilous road that wound its way deep into the heart of the mountains before reaching the northern plains.

7   Zoë held up a pair of red leather shoes and scrutinized them. She was sitting, her legs crossed under her, on the floor of a small flat-roofed house built into the side of a cliff. Five other pairs of shoes with sharp-pointed toes were lined up on the floor in front of her—the heelless, soft-soled type of shoe worn by the women of the mountains; a pair for Princess Anna, a pair for Princess Varvara, and a pair each for the three little girls. The pair she was holding was for herself. Her own thin summer shoes had fallen apart the morning they had climbed the steep cliff. She stuck her bare feet out from under her katiba and slipped them into the

new shoes. They fitted perfectly. And she smiled up at the old woman who had taught her the art of shoemaking.

Three weeks had gone by since the captives had left the Tower of Pohali, but they had not reached Shamyl's house in Dargo-Veden. They were living in an aoul, perched on top of a mountain that rose in a solid wall of granite a thousand feet above a narrow, barren valley. When Zoë had first seen the aoul from below, with its small flat houses stuck like swallows' nests to the side of the cliff, she had felt a little dizzy. But now she had grown accustomed to the streets that climbed up the precipitous slope like narrow, tortuous stairs, for every morning and every afternoon she had walked them in the company of the Benevolent Mullah to and from the old shoemaker's house.

The flat-roofed house in which the captives were lodged stood at the very top of the mountain, where the narrow, walled-in streets converged into a semblance of a square. Here they had waited from day to day for further orders from Shamyl. Battles were raging again in the north, the Benevolent Mullah had told them, and the Imam was away with his army. He wished to be in Dargo-Veden when they arrived. And one day the mullah had brought a large sheet of red leather, saying, "Women of your rank cannot appear in front of the Imam barefoot. One of you must go to the cobbler and learn to make shoes. But it will have to be one of the nurses. Women of your rank cannot be seen walking through the streets." Zoë could not help smiling. So much stress was being laid on rank, and yet here they were, in rags, sleeping on the floor and eating so little it almost amounted to starvation rations, for they depended on the bounty of the villagers, who had little food to spare. Zoë had argued at length, insisting on going to the shoemaker herself. And after equally lengthy protests the Benevolent Mullah had finally given in.

When Zoë had put on her new shoes, she jumped to her feet, stretching herself and shaking a few stray curls off her forehead. All hairpins had been shed on the way, most of them lost in the woods near Mount Kontzhi. Disregarding the protests of the two princesses, she had cut her hair short, just a little above her shoulders. She had done it with a clumsy pair of shears ordinarily used on sheep. And that afternoon she had found a narrow red ribbon, which she had slipped under her hair at the back, tying it around the top of her head. The ribbon had belonged to the shoemaker. After a good deal of gesticulating and a few expressive contortions of the face they had struck a bargain—the old woman gave her the ribbon in ex-

173

change for a part of the rich embroidery on Zoë's katiba. Without further ado a good foot and a half had been cut off the lower part of the robe, leaving it more tattered and torn than ever. But Zoë did not care. She felt better with her hair cut short and held more or less in place. And as she walked behind the Benevolent Mullah back to her house, she looked like a lively, sparkling vagabond in her bedraggled crimson robe, a red ribbon tied in her short curly hair, and a basket full of little red shoes slung over her arm.

She had to walk a pace or two behind him to show her respect for the male. A few young girls with handsome, solemn faces and several veiled women glided silently by, but there were never many people in the streets; and Zoë knew every stone, every crevice in the windowless walls that lined them on both sides. Soon they would come to another sharp turn, climb up a steep flight of stairs hewn out of the rock, and then emerge onto level ground, to the clearing that stood for a village square. Hassan would probably be on guard in front of their door. She had seen him there that morning and on every previous day. He looked sadder now than ever; he hardly ever smiled these days; the shadow of doom seemed to be hanging over him. Even when she had given him the shawl he had accepted it in silence, with a look of indifference, she had thought. The Benevolent Mullah alone spoke to him; other men seemed to shun him. And she did not understand why this should be so, for no one had seen hide or hair of Hadji-Kheriett since their arrival in the aoul.

But her thoughts were neither with Hassan nor Hadji-Kheriett at the moment. She was thinking of the dark pit that lay ahead. They had started up the last steep stretch, at the end of which she knew she would have to pass by the pit. She had been told that once in a while a criminal, and sometimes a Russian prisoner, was lowered into it, remaining there as long as his sentence lasted, sometimes until death. And one day, unable to restrain a morbid curiosity, she had peered into the pit. She had recoiled in disgust. It was about ten feet deep and seven feet wide, and, as far as she could make out, it had been empty; but the putrid smell of damp and decay had nauseated her. To think of a man lingering there all alone until Shamyl's clemency or a slow death came to release him from his agony filled her with revulsion. And the pit had become a creeping horror she could not get rid of. She tried not to think of it, but it would crop up every now and then. Even from the roof of their house one could see the gaping hole, like a huge black hungry mouth waiting to be fed.

As usual, that afternoon she had been all set to look the other way,

174

when she caught sight of Hadji-Kheriett. He was standing over the pit looking into it with absorption, a cruel smile on his lips. And Hassan was no longer at the door. A dreadful suspicion seized Zoë. She went up boldly to the edge of the pit and looked in. It was empty. And once again the nauseating smell made her step back in haste.

She had not noticed the look of real wonderment that had lighted up Hadji-Kheriett's eyes when they had first caught sight of her in her strange new attire. When she looked at him, the face she had seen on the moonlit plateau stared back at her across the pit—drawn and tense around the nose and mouth, the eyes hot and burning. And he passed the tip of his tongue over his lips. The Benevolent Mullah had come up to them, and Hadji-Kheriett said something to him in his native tongue. The mullah answered in an angry voice. A short but heated argument followed, and the mullah turned to Zoë. "Come!" he said in Russian. "Hadji-Kheriett must be out of his mind!"

The princesses had been coaching Zoë daily, and her Russian had improved in the last few weeks. She was now able to ask what Hadji-Kheriett wanted.

"He wants to buy you for ten rubles," the mullah replied indignantly. "He knows you are a prisoner of the Imam!"

To be bought by Hadji-Kheriett for ten rubles seemed so ridiculous she burst out laughing. But her laughter died abruptly when she saw the look in Hadji-Kheriett's eyes and the stern disapproval on the mullah's face. She followed the latter in silence across the square, and Hadji-Kheriett's harsh voice reached them, shouting in Russian, "She is a daughter of Shaitan! She drives men crazy!"

Zoë, a little breathless, ran up to the roof, anxious to tell her friends what had happened, but she stopped and looked around in silence, seeing the anguish on the faces of the two princesses. Sandro was very sick again. He lay limp and inert in Yakovlevna's lap, his eyes closed, his body wasted. The Benevolent Mullah, who had followed Zoë to the roof, looked down at him with compassion, passing his hand gently over the child's forehead.

"He is dying slowly of malnutrition," Princess Varvara said. And fat Yakovlevna began to mutter, "O God in heaven and all His sweet saints! O my Lord, Jesus Christ, the Son of God and His most holy Mother! Save this child! The boy cannot live until the morning!"

Princess Anna said nothing. She sat with lowered eyes, and it was difficult to tell whether she was praying or merely concentrating all her will power on keeping herself in hand.

The Benevolent Mullah fumbled in his pocket and then pressed a few coins into Sandro's lifeless hand. "Tell your mother not to be offended. Tell her to accept thirty kopeks. It is a very humble gift, but with it she can buy a few fowl and make you some broth."

The blood rushed to Princess Anna's face. She blushed up to her eyes with shame and mortification and was about to refuse, when Zoë snatched up the coins. "This is no time for pride, Anna! The child must be fed. I will accept the gift for him."

She remembered having seen hens in the yard across the square. She turned and ran from the roof. She raced across their own yard out into the square and pounded on a low door set in a recess of a thick stone wall. The woman who opened it was young and handsome and, like all the other women in the aoul, she wore a headdress decorated with rings and coins and other glittering ornaments. Her smile was affable. Zoë, who had become adept at sign language, managed to explain what she wanted and for whom she wanted it. The woman held up all five fingers and Zoë gave her five kopeks, and together they chased and caught a big fat hen. The woman held it up by both legs with its head down, handing it to Zoë in that position. And Zoë carried the hen out by the legs.

She stepped out into the square and heard the door being closed behind her. Suddenly she found herself confronted by Hadji-Kheriett, his face flushed, his eyes vicious. She glanced around; there was no one in sight. He stepped up close to her. She heard the word "Shaitan" hissed under his breath, and two clawlike hands shot out to strangle her. But when they touched her neck they fell limp, the tips of the fingers pressing gently on the soft skin. He said something she did not understand and, grabbing her by the left wrist, tried to drag her away. A sudden blind fury seized Zoë. She swung out her right arm and hit him across the face with the wretched fowl that gave vent to a series of terrified screeches and cackles, beating its wings over his head and shoulders. Hadji-Kheriett flung both his hands up to protect his face, and, feeling herself free, Zoë ran across the square without looking back.

The Benevolent Mullah was standing on the threshold now, ordering Hadji-Kheriett away with an imperious gesture. He let Zoë in and closed the door. She leaned against the wall to regain her composure.

The Benevolent Mullah, his thin finger wagging, shook a fatherly reprimand in her face. "You must never again leave the house alone. If you do, I will have to lock you up!" And then, looking down at the hen, "How much did you pay for it?"

"Five kopeks."

"Too much. Four would have been ample."

She shrugged her shoulder and called Eliso, the thin Georgian nurse, who had been cooking all their meager meals.

Three hours later they were gathered on the flat roof again, Zoë, the two princesses, and the Benevolent Mullah. They felt happier now; Sandro had taken some of the broth Eliso had prepared for him and had revived a little, and the other children had eaten their first good meal since their captivity. The princesses were exclaiming over their new shoes with delight, while Salome and Marie romped in the little court below.

Zoë was standing near the wall that overlooked the square. She was gazing at the chain of snow-capped mountains in the distance. Soon the last rays of the setting sun would vanish behind them and the sky would light up with the largest, brightest stars she had ever seen. From where she stood she could see the veiled women of the aoul returning from their daily trek to the river at the bottom of the rocky valley, winding their way up the narrow mountain trail with heavy earthenware jars on their heads. Suddenly she heard the tread of many feet in the square below. A tall man carrying a long ladder was approaching the pit, followed by Hadji-Kheriett and a few other Murids. Behind them, his head bent low, came Hassan, surrounded by men with muskets. Zoë gave a low gasp. She saw the tall man lower the ladder into the pit. When Hassan disappeared down it, a moan escaped her and she hid her face in her hands. Immediately the Benevolent Mullah was at her side. He saw at a glance what was happening and tried to draw her away, but she clung to the wall. They had pulled out the ladder now; the men were dispersing without a word, and the mouth of the pit remained black and gaping, insatiable.

She allowed Princess Varvara to lead her away. She sank limply to the floor beside her. "Why? Why? Why?" was all she could say in a weak, trembling voice.

The Benevolent Mullah looked sad. "Hassan has committed a grave crime," he said. "He raised his hand against his teacher."

"But he did it to protect me!" In a few broken sentences she told him what had happened in the woods.

"Poor Hassan," he said with a sigh. "He must have been born

177

under an unlucky star. When he was a child his brother died in disgrace."

He told them the story. Shamyl at the time had suffered a defeat at the hands of the Russians. Before retiring to a mosque to pray he had said to his Naibs, "We have suffered for our sins. Find those among my Murids who have transgressed, who have failed in their prayers and fastings, and have in other ways broken the law, bringing thereby death and misery to hundreds. Give me their names so that justice can be meted out and a rightful punishment descend upon their heads!" And Hassan's brother had been singled out. He had not denied his sins; he had gone to his death praying to Allah to have mercy on his soul.

"Didn't Hassan hate the Imam for it?"

The mullah frowned. "Hate the Imam!" He sounded shocked. "The Imam is just. Hassan hated his brother's sins. They had brought disgrace on his people! A few months ago he begged the Imam to admit him into the ranks of his Murids. The Imam, in his great wisdom and justice, did not refuse. He put him to a severe test, though. He made it clear he did this, not because of his brother's transgressions, but to see if Hassan had the necessary moral strength for the calling. And now Hassan has failed."

To Zoë his words were crushing. What chance did Hassan stand if kind men like the Benevolent Mullah were against him. She sat on the roof long after the others had left, thinking of Hassan, innocent and blameless, suffering in that terrifying pit. Soft tears of compassion came flowing of their own accord. And she wept, perhaps for the first time in her life, with no thought for herself.

8   Next morning Zoë was the first to rise. The air was unbearably close in the tiny cubbyhole of a room she shared with the two princesses and in the adjoining larger room in which the others slept. She went outside. She took off her clothes and performed the meager ablutions the shortage of water permitted, rubbing her body with a rag soaked in cold water. "As for you, my feet," she said, making a polite little bow of apology to her own feet, "you will have to wait until we meet Monsieur Shamyl!"

She slipped back into her clothes and went up on the roof. Pale streaks of dawn were sweeping over the eastern sky. The square below was still in darkness. She sat down, facing the distant snowy caps, rosy now in the first rays of the sun. One solitary star glistened above them, bright and luminous. The whole world seemed to hold its breath. The peace and the beauty of it struck deep. She closed her eyes. A hush had entered her soul, making it glow. It was like the sudden opening of big wide gates.

From a nearby minaret came the voice of a muezzin calling the faithful to prayer. She could see them now on the flat roofs of their houses, their faces turned toward the east, praying on their knees with arms raised to heaven. Was Hassan praying too? she wondered. Could one pray in that dark, terrifying pit? Something told her Hassan could, and she felt better for it. And Sasha. Did he ever pray, or was he like herself, capable only of silent worship when deeply moved? Sasha's sufferings, she said to herself, were harder to bear in the midst of worldly vanities. Torn away from them, with only hope and faith left to lean on, it was easier to feel detached. In this, she knew, lay her blessing. There was no room in her heart for doubts, bitterness, or jealousy. She had no recollection of ever having had any. Trash left by the roadside is soon forgotten.

She heard the others stirring below. She ran down and helped Salome and Marie get washed and dressed. The neighing of horses and the sound of many voices reached them from the square. The front door was unlocked and the Benevolent Mullah came in, bowing ceremoniously. "Messengers arrived last night from Dargo-Veden," he announced in a solemn voice. "We must leave at once."

When the captives came out of the house they found the little square crowded. At least a hundred armed Tchetchens were there on horseback, ready to escort them to Shamyl's seraglio. And most of the population of the aoul had come to see them off, flocking near the walls and crowding the low roofs. On the whole these mountain villagers had been a friendly lot, and now many of them waved to Princess Anna and Princess Varvara as they rode away.

Ignoring Hadji-Kheriett's impatient signs, Zoë remained with Salome and Marie while the little girls were being strapped to their saddles. Marie protested vigorously, "Knights are never tied to their horses!" But she submitted grudgingly to it after Zoë had patted her on the shoulder. "That is all right, Peter Tchilingaroff. You are a captive knight now."

With the children safely on their way, Zoë turned at last to face Hadji-Kheriett. She noticed that her horse was held by a stranger. She stopped in front of Hadji-Kheriett and glanced in the direction of the pit. "Hassan?" she asked.

He waved her away angrily and was about to help her into her

179

saddle, but she brushed him aside. She took hold of the saddle with both hands and raised her left foot. The man who was holding her horse slipped her foot into the stirrup and held it there. It was her polite "Thank you" that must have enraged Hadji-Kheriett. He leaped forward, ordering the man to let go, but by then she had bounced herself off the ground with such vigor she almost overshot the saddle. She heard laughter in the crowd and a few voices calling out, *"Djiggit!"* the Caucasian word for an intrepid rider, a bold performer of dangerous horseback stunts. Hurriedly she arranged the end of her robe under her seat and around her legs and rode away, smiling and waving to the crowd but not daring to look back at Hadji-Kheriett.

Zoë and Hadji-Kheriett had been the last to leave the aoul. They were traveling now over a flat rocky ridge almost a mile long which connected the aoul to a high snow-capped mountain. The others were all far ahead, some of them almost at the other end of the ridge. Hadji-Kheriett rode behind her with head bent, scowling at her from under his thick eyebrows. His thoughts were in a turmoil, dark and sinister and muddled. He hated this woman because he desired her, and because he desired her she must be a witch, a daughter of Shaitan. She had cast a spell over him that very first time he had seen her on the steps of the big house in Tsinandali. She was so small, so slender; there was nothing to her, yet the touch of her soft white skin made him tremble. And in the moonlight on the plateau she had allowed him to look at her tilted breasts until they had driven him out of his mind. Why, he asked himself now, had she been so frightened when he carried her away from Tsinandali, and where did her present arrogance and daring come from? She must have trembled then at the thought of death. Nothing could be worse than death to a child of the devil. And now, confident she would be allowed to live, she had become brazen and bold. She had even cast a spell over the crowd in the aoul, and this to him was a final proof of her witchcraft. No! Better to face the Imam's wrath, better for the people never to get their rightful ransom, than to allow one accursed witch to walk free over the face of the earth! He clutched the handle of his thick leather whip, and Zoë, glancing over her shoulder at that moment, saw the fanatical look in his eyes and spurred her horse nervously. It was this frightened gesture of escape, the folding back of the hare's ears, that brought out the final lust to kill. With a loud cry Hadji-Kheriett raised his whip and slashed it down with all his might across the flanks of her horse.

180

The horse bolted, almost throwing Zoë to the ground. Desperately she tugged at the reins, but the horse had taken the bit between its teeth and was careening madly ahead, its ears folded back. She saw a man—the one who had helped her into the saddle—come galloping to her rescue, but her horse swerved and dashed headlong in the direction of a precipice. Horror-stricken, she watched the edge of the precipice come closer in leaps and bounds, yet to throw herself out of the saddle onto the hard rocks seemed almost as terrifying as the certain death that lay ahead of her. She shut her eyes and clung to the front pommel of her saddle. A horse was catching up with her, a man was shouting, but she heard nothing, saw nothing. Suddenly she knew she had left the saddle. She thought she was falling to her death. But a moment later she found herself flying through the air by the side of a horse, a strong arm holding her in an iron grip. And out of the corner of her eye she saw her own horse rear and stop dead at the very brink of the precipice.

When her rescuer came to a stop and his arm relaxed, she slid to the ground, gasping, her face and neck bathed in cold sweat.

Princess Anna galloped up to Hadji-Kheriett, her face pale, her eyes livid. "I warned you in the woods, now it shall be done! Shamyl will know about this the moment we get to Dargo-Veden!"

Hadji-Kheriett's neck seemed to shrink a little into his shoulders. He, too, looked pale. When he had seen the horse make straight for the precipice, he had remained frozen in his saddle. A superstitious fear had clutched at his heart the moment he had realized to what kind of death he had sent Zoë. And he remained petrified, with only one thought in mind, "Oh, Allah! She will perish the way Mariam did!" If Zoë had vanished over the brink at that moment, he would have whipped up his horse and jumped in after her. But now, with her safe on the ground, he only felt fear of Shamyl's possible anger. "She is alive and unhurt; there is nothing more to be said," he growled, turning his horse and riding away a few paces, where he remained with his back turned to the others.

Zoë, still trembling a little, was unable to tear her frightened eyes away from her horse. Her rescuer had captured it and was leading it up to her, its flanks all foamy with sweat. For a wild moment she wanted to beg the Benevolent Mullah to have her placed behind one of the men, but she saw the stern eyes of the Tchetchens upon her and she remembered Princess Varvara's words: "If you display an indifference to suffering and death, they will respect you." She knew she must overcome her fear, force herself to get back on that horse.

181

"Pat it! Show the horse you are not afraid of it!" Princess Anna called out.

Zoë stretched out her hand timidly. The horse shied, and every muscle in its body trembled at her touch. But gradually, as she continued to pat and stroke it, the animal quieted down; and when she laid her cheek against its neck, mutual confidence was restored.

9   When they reached the top of the snow-capped mountain, Zoë drew a deep breath of amazement. There was no trace of snow on the other side. They rode down a gradual slope covered with bright green grass and a multitude of flowers, finally coming to a valley rich in semi-tropical vegetation. They traveled along the banks of a swift mountain river until the valley had narrowed down to a gorge. Here they had to pass through a tunnel, large, round, and smooth. It looked like a perfect engineering feat, but when Zoë, expressing her surprise, asked who had built it, the Benevolent Mullah said, "Allah did."

The "Tunnel of Allah" was about half a mile long, with cavelike apertures looking out on the river, which here flowed deep and undisturbed. When they came out at the other end, the narrow gorge was behind them, and the river broke furiously over shallow rapids. They had entered a broad, tall canyon. And in the distance, high up on a rocky ledge, they saw a pair of massive gates flanked on both sides by narrow towers.

"Karaty," the Benevolent Mullah said, "the house of Kazi-Mahomma. From there, if you know the mountain trails, it is but a day's ride to the first Russian fortifications. But you must know the way," he added in a hurry, afraid perhaps that the women might try to escape.

Princess Anna and Princess Varvara glanced at Karaty and rode on, but Zoë could not tear her eyes away from it. "Gates of Freedom!" she said to herself, not knowing why the words had come to her mind. Somehow those gates stood linked to her dream. The man on the moonlit plateau, she mused, must live in just such a place as this. She called it a fantasy. She tried to laugh it off and shrug it away, but it kept returning during the rest of the journey. And not until they had come in sight of Dargo-Veden, close to four that afternoon, did she forget the sunlit gates of Karaty.

The aoul of Dargo-Veden seemed earthy and plebeian by comparison. It sprawled over a lofty plateau, solid, well rooted behind

182

a wooden stockade and a moat. On the wooden drawbridge they were met by a group of Murids on horseback, led by an old Naib with a very thin face and a long thin beard.

"Kahjio, the Imam's treasurer," the Benevolent Mullah said by way of introduction. And the ladies acknowledged the treasurer's salute with a bow.

Zoë noticed at a glance that everything in this aoul was built of wood. Wooden houses and wooden walls stood everywhere, separated by gardens and plowed fields. A wide street led from the wooden gates to the high wooden walls of Shamyl's seraglio that rose in the center of the aoul, dominating the scene. They rode into a huge outer court with covered galleries running the full length of the walls, leading into rooms in which two hundred selected Murids were lodged at all times. Everything here breathed austerity. The walls were unadorned, the wooden columns supporting the galleries were plain and severe in line, and all the men were dressed in black. No joy, Zoë thought, could ever enter this place.

But a moment later her whole attention was riveted to the second, inner wall that rose high in the center of the vast court, enclosing the seraglio proper—the home of Shamyl and his family. On a small balcony to the right of the big central doorway she saw the figure of a man—or was it a vision of snow and fire? High above the court he stood, gigantic in his tall white turban and his long white robe; and his fiery beard appeared like a burning bush against the snow-white purity of his garments.

"Oh, mon Dieu!" she exclaimed in an awed whisper. "The monster himself!"

Princess Anna was too near-sighted to see clearly, Princess Varvara strained her eyes to get a better look, but none of them had a chance to see his features, for when the big doors were finally thrown open and they were told to ride in, Shamyl had gone.

The Benevolent Mullah and the other men remained outside. Kahjio, the treasurer, alone rode into the inner sanctum with them. They found themselves in a small enclosure separated from the rest of the court by a wooden partition. Immediately a dozen young girls surrounded them, helping them to dismount and showing them the way with polite gestures and low bows. They rounded the partition and entered the inner court proper. It was a smaller replica of the outer court, with covered galleries lining the walls. And at the far end stood a small house, also surrounded by a covered gallery. This, Zoë was soon to learn, was the house in which Shamyl lived. "Like a box in a box in a box," she whispered in French, making the children laugh.

The room they were finally brought to was dark and narrow. As Zoë later announced, after having measured it, "twenty-six 'shoes' by twelve!" It was situated close to the wooden partition and, like all the other rooms in the seraglio, it opened out on the gallery. A large portion of the room was occupied by an open fireplace built between the door and a small window two feet square, and the floor was covered with white felt and small rugs of native manufacture. But when they entered it a cry of joy escaped every throat. Everywhere around the room and on the shelves that protruded from the walls were the gifts Prince David and Sasha had sent: mattresses, pillows, blankets, soap, and towels; a samovar, a tea set, plates, knives, forks, and spoons; dresses, stockings, shoes, underwear, brushes, combs, hairpins, and mirrors, and in a corner a portable zinc bathtub. Everything had been carefully thought out. Even the sunbonnets had long dark veils that could be lowered over the face to comply with the customs of their captors. They rushed from one object to the other with small cries of joy, embracing one another in their excitement.

"The first thing for me," Zoë cried, "is off with this katiba!"

She found the things that were marked with her name, and a few minutes later she stood fully clothed in a dark gray dress with a long full skirt, small black cuffs, and a little black collar.

The children were delighted, but Princess Anna said severely, "I hope you will let your hair grow now. It is positively indecent for a woman of your age to walk around with short hair."

"*Oui, patronne!* But admit it is easier to keep your neck clean this way. Let us compare necks and see!"

"Get away from me, you impossible creature!" Princess Anna laughed, pushing her away. And Zoë thought, marveling at their changed relationship, "Just such a remark as this, and in that tone of hers, would have crushed me a few weeks ago!"

She heard the murmur of voices outside and looked around. Several women were crowding onto the gallery, craning their necks to peer into the room, while one of them, a tall and stately woman of thirty, stood on the threshold, bowing stiffly. She was wearing a long white shirt strapped around the waist and falling below the knees over white balloon-like trousers that were caught up at the ankles. Her headband was somewhat similar to those worn by Georgian women, but her long veil, in which she could shroud herself at will, was of white linen instead of tulle. "I am Shouanet, wife of the

184

Imam," she said in Russian. "Not the Great Wife who was the mother of his children. The Great Wife died some years ago, may Allah rest her soul in peace." She hesitated and then added, "I was born in Russia. I am an Armenian. That is why I can speak Russian." And after another short hesitation, "I was a captive, too, once upon a time."

The princesses and Zoë rose to greet her, and when they had settled down again on the floor Shouanet looked around the room. Her movements and gestures had a natural well-rounded grace to them, but there was something studied, almost artificial, about her smile and the tone of her voice, as though she were weighing every word she said. "All your things are here, I believe," she said at length. "Is there anything else you need?"

When Princess Anna had expressed her anxiety about the child she was feeding, confiding that her milk was dwindling unaccountably away, Shouanet smiled. "Allah must have sent that baby to us. Kahjio, the treasurer, has a widowed sister-in-law living with him. Her baby died a few days ago. I am sure she will want to feed the child. I will speak to her about it." A frightened cry escaped the thin little peasant girl at the thought of being separated from the other captives. Shouanet turned to her. "Don't be afraid, child. Kahjio lives right here in that corner tower." She pointed in the general direction of the big front door.

She then made a sign to someone outside, and two maids carried in large trays with refreshments—tea, honey, cheese, white bread, and, to the consternation of the two princesses, a large box of sweets from Tollet. Zoë smiled sadly at the box. Spindarian's big offer must have been too tempting for Monsieur Tollet after all, and he had double-crossed Madame Tollet. But she said nothing, while the children, seeing the sweets, went wild with joy. All three little girls stuck their hands into the box, picking out their favorite sweets. And Tamara, after she had swallowed hers, danced a jig around the room, pressing the tip of her finger to the top of her head.

A clear, bell-like laugh resounded through the room. Looking up, Zoë saw a girl leaning against the side of the door. A delightful young creature with a small nose slightly retroussé, white even teeth, bright red lips, and a pair of large gray eyes. She was dressed like Shouanet, only her long shirt was blue and her trousers red. Shouanet, turning around, introduced her: "Aminet, the Imam's youngest wife."

That this girl, still in her teens, should be Shamyl's wife seemed

185

incredible. Zoë looked at her with pity, while Aminet stepped forward and bowed low. Then she resumed her former position by the door, looking out into the court, but Zoë could see she was listening intently to every word that was being said.

"We appreciate your kindness," Princess Anna said to Shouanet, "but unfortunately I have a complaint to make. Our friend, Zoia Ivanovna Duval, barely escaped being killed, thanks to the brutality, the criminal brutality of one of your Murids—Hadji-Kheriett!" She gave Shouanet a detailed account of Hadji-Kheriett's actions from the first night in the woods to the mad episode on the ridge.

Shouanet raised her eyebrows. "You surprise me! Hadji-Kheriett is known as a good Moslem and a chaste man. Only once has he loved a woman. He was married to her, but she, poor thing, loved his younger brother. She threw herself off a high cliff, and his brother was killed in battle soon after. Hadji-Kheriett has never been known to look at a woman since!"

Suddenly Aminet leaned forward, scowling. She spoke haltingly in Russian, but her tone was forceful. "Hadji-Kheriett is no good! He always says to Kazi-Mahomma, 'Go to war!' "

Shouanet laughed, artificially, it seemed to Zoë. "Pay no attention to Aminet. She hates everyone who is close to Kazi-Mahomma."

Hearing this, Aminet grew very red in the face and ran out of the room, shooting an angry look at the older woman, while Shouanet got up to take her leave.

"I was promised I would find my servants here," Princess Anna said. "Where are they?"

"They are in Dargo-Veden. There was no room for them in the seraglio, but you can ascertain for yourself that they are being well taken care of."

"I wish to go and see them at once!"

"You must send one of your nurses. A woman of your rank cannot be seen outside the seraglio."

The question of rank was forever cropping up. But again, as in the other aoul, Zoë protested. One of them must go. She would. And after a moment's hesitation Shouanet agreed to this.

Zoë put on her new bonnet and lowered the long veil. The princesses laughed. She looked like a Quaker girl hiding behind a short curtain. And Shouanet glanced at her in surprise.

A quarter of an hour later Zoë was walking behind the Benevolent Mullah again, crossing the big outer court. They went out into the wide main street and followed it for a while. They turned left into a very narrow lane in which the branches of trees hung gracefully over the walls. She smiled to herself, amused at the startled looks of the passers-by. But when she turned a corner and came out into a square, her smile froze. At the other end of the square was the black open mouth of a pit. "Oh, God! They have those dreadful things everywhere!" And looking the other way, she kept as close to the Benevolent Mullah as she could.

The house in which the Tsinandali servants were kept stood on this square. During the next half hour or so while she spoke to the women, who seemed to have no complaints to make, the pit faded out of Zoë's mind, but when she came out of the house again, she stopped dead, her heart beating wildly. A solemn procession was crossing the square, headed by a man carrying a long ladder. This time they were leading a young woman, who walked with a heavy tread, her face a tragic white mask. Zoë clutched the mullah's arm.

He shook her off. "Never touch a man!" he said sharply, brushing his arm off with his fingers as though it had been soiled. "And now come!"

But Zoë remained rooted to the ground. "Why? Why?" she kept repeating weakly, pointing at the condemned woman.

"She is a criminal. She killed her husband."

Zoë refused to think of the woman's crime. It had never occurred to her until then that they might put a woman into the pit. The ladder had been lowered, and she saw them pushing the resisting woman toward it. A sudden ungovernable terror took hold of her. She trembled in every limb, and her hands flew up, pressing the veil to her eyes and cheeks.

The acute agony lasted but a moment. The Benevolent Mullah was growing impatient. He raised his voice, commanding her to come. And, clenching her fists, not daring to look back, she followed him with head bent.

10   That same evening around eight o'clock Shouanet, flustered,
        rushed into the captives' room to say the Imam wished to see the children. One of the women, she said, but not the princesses, could come and watch over them, provided she did not cross the Imam's threshold. And Princess Anna pressed Sandro into Zoë's arms, begging her to watch over him closely, for though he had gained a little in strength, he was still a sick child.

A light fell through Shamyl's opened door. Zoë approached it, her curiosity mingled with a certain amount of trepidation. What she found there took her completely by surprise.

In a long narrow room lit by several tallow candles Shamyl sat on the floor, his legs crossed under him. Opposite him at a low table sat a plain black-and-white alley cat. The cat watched him hungrily while he prepared a meal for her in a small earthenware bowl. His fiery beard seemed less flamboyant now against a long black robe, and he spoke to the cat in purring tones, his narrow eyes half closed. All his movements were measured and dignified. He looked majestic in his white turban, wound in an intricate fashion around a fez, the ends hanging loose at the back. And the edge of black fur around the forehead gave it the appearance of a colossal white crown.

He placed the bowl on the table in front of the cat and scratched her behind the ear. Salome, Marie, and Tamara, who had stood hand in hand watching all this with wide-open eyes, now broke into peals of delighted laughter. He smiled at them. Aminet was hovering behind him, ready to serve him his supper, but he waved her aside and nodded to Shouanet.

She put George Orbeliani on a big red pillow beside him and told the three little girls to come closer. Shamyl patted them all. Then he reached into his pocket and brought out a handful of hard caramels which he stuffed into their mouths.

Sandro's turn came next, and Shouanet took him from Zoë.

Shamyl had not looked at Zoë once. She was glad of this; it gave her time to take in every detail of his surroundings. Except for bright rugs and a few big red cushions on the floor, the room was austere —a few daggers and sabers on the whitewashed walls, several large leather-bound books on a shelf, and that was all. Even the supper Aminet held in readiness for him was frugal—a glass of dark brown tea, milk, cheese, and two small loaves of white bread.

Shamyl was leaning over Sandro, a deep furrow knitting his eyebrows. The child was lying in his lap, thin and pale. He shook his head and for the first and only time looked straight at Zoë. His eyes were half closed as usual, but the look in them was intense. Zoë was grateful for her veil. He stared at her for a full moment and then turned away, apparently disliking her clothes and bonnet. He said a few words to his wives in a harsh voice and waved the children away. Shouanet brought Sandro back to Zoë and picked up George. "The Imam says we cannot afford any more deaths. We must take good care of Sandro. He wants me to bring him here every day.

188

Alone." She herded the little girls out of the room, and the audience was over.

Early next morning Shouanet slipped quietly into the captives' room. Alone with them, her manner was no longer forced and artificial. Her big brown eyes looked at them with sympathy; her smile was open and kind. She crouched on the floor beside the two princesses and Zoë, speaking in a hurried whisper. "I wanted to tell you. Last night I spoke to the Imam about Hadji-Kheriett. The Imam said it is lucky for all concerned that no one was hurt. There is nothing more to be said at present, though justice will take its course in due time!"

"Justice!" Zoë exclaimed indignantly. "A man tries to kill a defenseless woman and goes unpunished. He calls it justice!"

Shouanet opened her eyes wide and put her finger to her lips. "Never, never say a word against the Imam! I shudder to think of the punishment that may come to you. And if you do, I will never help you again. The Imam is a great and wonderful man. I love him!"

She stood up, her face flushed, and led the peasant girl and her baby sister to the door. "Come," she said abruptly, "I will take you to Kahjio's tower." And then, in a gentler voice, "Don't be afraid, you can come and visit your princesses whenever you like."

No sooner had she left than Hadji-Kheriett came to their door, carrying a three-legged stool which he placed outside in the gallery. "Cover your faces," he said. "The Illustrious Imam is coming to call on you."

The princesses and Zoë put on their bonnets and lowered their veils. The nurses and the children stood up.

Shamyl appeared in the doorway, dressed as he had been the night before in a long black robe and a white turban. He was leading a girl of seven by the hand, a child with fine, delicate features. She wore the same kind of clothes as the grown-up women of the seraglio, only her head was bare.

Shamyl spoke to Hadji-Kheriett in a low voice, and the latter said in Russian, "The Illustrious Imam says your children should play with Najabat, his youngest daughter."

Najabat smiled at Salome and Marie and beckoned to them and, taking them by the hand, ran with them into the court. Shamyl ordered the nurses to take the other children out.

Hadji-Kheriett then said, "The Imam wishes to know if you enjoyed your morning meal."

"Yes, thank you," Princess Anna replied. "All but the greasy crust on the bread. We are not accustomed to grease."

Shamyl smiled back at her in complete understanding. "I don't like it either. I will tell Shouanet to bake you the same bread she bakes for me."

The three women had not expected such kindness and affability. They sat on the floor of their dark room, not daring to formulate even to themselves the hopes that had risen suddenly in their hearts. The conversation that followed was a slow one, both sides having to wait while Hadji-Kheriett translated their words.

Shamyl had settled down on the three-legged stool. "You made me wait a long time, Anna," he said. "I had to send my scouts out many times before they reported your arrival in Tsinandali."

When the full meaning of his words dawned on her, Princess Anna exclaimed in horror, "Do you mean to say you pillaged half a province and sent hundreds of people to their death just to capture us!"

"How else could I get my son back? The pitiful cries of a king's granddaughter and great-grandchildren are bound to be heard by the powerful Russian Tsar." He turned to Princess Varvara. "That you and your son should have been there was a pleasant surprise to me. I admired and respected your husband." For a moment he looked at them steadily from under his eyebrows, then he smiled. "You need not be alarmed. No one will harm you here. You will be treated like members of my family, provided you obey me implicitly." Here he frowned and raised a finger. "Your children are free to play with mine, and their nurses may follow them wherever they go." He raised a second finger. "As long as I am at home you three must remain in this room until dusk. After that you can sit on the bench outside your door." He raised a third finger. "When I am away the woman of France is free to walk in the court and visit my wives in their apartments, but for women of your rank, Anna and Varvara, such behavior would be unseemly. You must never go beyond the bench."

As he spoke his words gathered momentum and his voice became louder. "Listen to me carefully, that is not all. If any of you attempts to carry on a secret correspondence with your relatives, or if they write secretly to you, I will spare neither you nor your children. I will kill you as I killed ten Russian officers who received a letter baked in a loaf of bread, or I will give you as slaves to my Naibs!" He pointed a threatening finger at them. "I will also tell you the story of

190

a wealthy Russian girl my men took prisoner several years ago when she was on her way to church to be married. Her family were willing to pay a high ransom for her, but I would listen to none of their offers because she had presumed to set me at defiance. Instead I gave her away as a slave, and thus she will remain to her dying day! The same fate will befall you and your children, Anna and Varvara, and you, Woman of France, if I don't kill you first!"

His manner had remained calm, heightening the brutality of his words. Following immediately upon his suave amiability, the threats came like blows. Cold shudders ran down Zoë's spine. Princess Anna, outraged, turned her back on him, trying to control the furious retorts that crowded the tip of her tongue. Princess Varvara alone remained calm. She got up and stepped closer to the door.

"You must not threaten us, Shamyl. We have no intention of disobeying you. As for letters addressed to us, we cannot be responsible for their contents nor for the way in which they are sent."

He gave her a long searching look. "Nevertheless," he said at last, "what I have said will be done, whatever the circumstances, whatever the cost to me. If any of you receives a single secret message, you will never see your freedom again. And remember! My threats are never idle ones!"

He remained silent, allowing his words to sink in. Then his manner changed abruptly. He smiled again. "Now that we understand one another, you, Anna, will write your husband and send your letter to me for my approval. General Réad has put him in charge of all negotiations."

Princess Anna's anger vanished and her eyes filled with tears of happiness. It was the first official intimation she had had that Prince David was alive and well. The gifts had implied it, though no certainty had come with them; his family, she knew, would have sent them anyway. "Yes, Shamyl," she said almost humbly, "I will write whatever you say."

"Very well then. Write and say this: For himself Shamyl wants his son Jemaleddin, for his people one million rubles in silver!"

The women gasped. In their day and age, with the high value of silver coinage and the low cost of living, few people owned such a fortune. "A million rubles!" Princess Anna repeated, hoping she had not heard right. "Why, we do not own that much. Nothing approaching such a sum!"

"I have been told innumerable riches were found in your house."

"Yes, Shamyl. We lived well. We had a beautiful home in which

191

we entertained friends, and people considered us rich. But all this is gone now. We never had much money. We lived on the produce of our lands, most of which you have destroyed."

Shamyl narrowed his eyes. "Your husband's sister, the Princess of Mingrelia, could pay us a million."

"I doubt it. Besides, whatever fortune she may enjoy came from her late husband. She is merely holding it in trust for her young son."

He turned to Princess Varvara. "Eliko Orbeliani was a rich man. You could raise a good part of the ransom if you wanted to."

"No, Shamyl," Princess Varvara replied sadly. "My husband's fortune was mostly in land. He left it to our son, and according to our laws, it cannot be touched until George comes of age."

Shamyl shook his head impatiently. "In that case, Anna, write your husband as I told you to. My people must have a million rubles!"

He stood up abruptly and left. Princess Anna hid her face in her hands, and Princess Varvara, her shoulders drooping, sat staring dully at the floor in her despair. A million rubles in silver were worth almost four times that much in paper currency. They knew their families would never be able to raise such a sum. But Zoë could not bear to see these two strong women crushed. Tearing off her bonnet and throwing it on a shelf, she glanced around the room and snatched up a deck of cards that had been sent with the other gifts. "Wait and see what Madame Désirée has to say about it!" she exclaimed, laying out the cards on the floor in even rows. "Anna! Varvara! Look! The cards are all in your favor! I have never seen such lucky, lucky cards. And it must be true. Everything that has already happened is shown correctly here. The cards say you have had a change of residence. They say you went to the mountains to get some fresh air. They say Anna had to masquerade in a katiba and Varvara got her dress torn and soiled. And here General Réad says to Prince David, 'I put you in charge of negotiations—what!' This king of diamonds next to the knave of diamonds means Shamyl will get his son. And all these clubs here are Prince David's words to Shamyl— 'A fig for your million, my good man! Give them back to me without a million, and Zoë-djan will give you five kopeks for a fowl!' "

Suddenly Princess Varvara smiled and Princess Anna's silvery laugh resounded through the room. She gave Zoë a pat on the shoulder, exclaiming, "You are so right! We all know even five kopeks is too much for an old fowl!"

11   Four days went by. Zoë got to know all the inhabitants of
       the seraglio by sight if not by name. In addition to Shamyl's
family and servants and Kahjio's young wife and sister-in-law, there
was a guest residing in the seraglio at the time—Kahjio's motherless
granddaughter, Zulma. Mysterious little Zulma, Zoë called her. She
had seen her only once, crossing the court in a hurry, a wisp of a
girl of fifteen with enormous eyes. Yet Zoë was very conscious of
her presence, for at dusk Zulma would sit in one of the tower windows, singing to the accompaniment of a string instrument. And her
voice was very beautiful.

Zoë knew nothing else about Zulma. Aminet alone seemed to be
on intimate terms with her, but Aminet had ignored the captives
since the first day of their arrival. When Zoë asked why this was so,
Shouanet said she was a wild and untamed creature. In the two years
Aminet had spent in the seraglio she had made friends with no one
except Zulma. Sometimes of an evening, Shouanet said, Aminet
would drop into her room, asking her to teach her Russian. "There is
nothing else to do," she would say on such occasions. "Life is dull
here. You are dull, too, but you are better than the others."

But early on the fifth morning Aminet appeared in the captives'
room with Shouanet. She was smiling brightly, and her large gray
eyes were dancing with merriment.

"Aminet has come for you, Zoë-djan," Shouanet said. "Fatima,
one of my maids, is getting married today, and the Imam has allowed
her to take you to see the bride."

Zoë jumped to her feet, exclaiming with joy. She snatched her
bonnet off the shelf and followed Aminet down the gallery to Shouanet's room.

It was a long narrow room, larger than the one occupied by the
captives, but furnished in much the same way, with rugs on the felt-
covered floor, shelves on the walls, and a large open fireplace between the door and the window. Fatima sat on the floor, surrounded
by her trousseau: two mattresses, several tin plates, a couple of
kettles, a few frying pans, a metal dish, and a wooden chest filled
with clothes. Her long tunic and wide trousers were of brightly
colored linen, but her face had been whitened with chalk, and all
superfluous hair had been plucked out of her eyebrows to make them
regular and even. The face looked like a mask, yet it seemed vaguely
familiar to Zoë. It reminded her of someone. She was trying to think
who it could be, when she noticed a merry twinkle in Aminet's eyes.
Aminet pointed at Fatima, passed a finger around her own face, and

193

then thrust her finger straight at Zoë, as much as to say, "She resembles you, doesn't she?"

Zoë looked at the bride closely. Something about the eyes, perhaps, but the rest of the face, no! It was too thin and the nose and chin were much too pointed. She shook her head.

Aminet ran to a shelf and brought back a small mirror. It was then that Zoë realized for the first time how thin her face had grown, the features standing out sharp and pointed.

"When Fatima is happy, she laughs just like you," Aminet said in a weighty tone, as though in this lay the bride's greatest endowment. "That is very good!"

Almost against her will Zoë looked at Fatima again. A pair of dark, haunted eyes were staring at her now reproachfully out of the white chalked face, as though saying, "Why were you ever born? Why did you come here?" Feeling uncomfortable and self-conscious under the steady gaze, Zoë went to the door. Fatima did not move, but her eyes never left Zoë's face until Shouanet entered the room, followed by a few maids, and covered her from head to foot with a large white veil. The maids then led Fatima into Shouanet's bedroom. "She will remain there all day fasting," Shouanet explained, "while the other women will eat a great meal in her honor. At dusk they will lead her to the outer court to meet the bridegroom."

Zoë could not forget Fatima's haunted eyes. "Who is the bridegroom?" she asked.

She and Aminet were standing outside Shouanet's door now. Aminet looked at her out of the corner of her eye and then turned her head away. "Hadji-Kheriett," she said casually.

"Ha-dji-Kheriett!" Zoë's involuntary cry was indignant, scandalized. But unable to express all she felt, she had to be contented with a cold "Why Hadji-Kheriett?"

Aminet looked down at the pointed end of her blue leather shoe. She turned her foot in and out, her tongue in her cheek. "Bad to be alone," she said at last. "He needs a wife. Oh, the Imam is very wise!" Then she bubbled over with mischievous laughter. "The other night I told him to do it."

"Louis Quatorze Shamyl, Shouanet de la Vallière, and Aminet de Montespan!" Zoë thought, trying to laugh it off, but inwardly she was fuming with rage. That they should honor Hadji-Kheriett by giving him a bride out of Shamyl's household was in itself an insult, but to choose one who resembled her was an outrage. Zoë brooded over it that day.

194

Next morning when she went to her door she saw the younger women of the seraglio gathered near the wooden partition, peeking through its holes and cracks. Shouanet, Aminet, and Shamyl's four daughters had the best gaps all to themselves, while the others, crowding behind them, had to manage as best they could.

Presently Aminet detached herself from the partition and walked away, a blissful smile hovering around her bright red lips. She saw Zoë and ran up to her. "Zoë-djan," she whispered breathlessly. "*He* has arrived! Kazi-Mahomma!" And to cover up her embarrassment she added in a hurry, "And Daniel-Sultan too! They are in the council chamber with the Imam, discussing a very important matter. Oh yes, very important to you!" And she skipped down the gallery, humming a little tune.

Zoë watched her until she had disappeared into her room. Strange girl, she thought. In love with her husband's son, a hopeless love that could never come to anything, yet she seemed to derive all the joy she could out of it. And gradually, as she turned the matter over in her mind, the full meaning of Aminet's last words dawned on her— the men in the council chamber were discussing her, Zoë! Puzzled, intrigued, and somewhat alarmed, she was pondering over this when Shouanet burst into the room.

"I told you justice would take its course," she exclaimed in an excited voice. "Zoë-djan, you must come and see the punishment of your offender. Hadji-Kheriett is to be tried this morning!"

Zoë stared back at her, unable at first to comprehend it all. Were they going to punish him the day after his wedding, these strange, unpredictable people? And why did they want her there? She had no wish to witness his punishment. But Shouanet was firm. "The Imam's orders!" she said. And turning to the two princesses, "You must all come."

She led the way across the court to Shamyl's council chamber, situated to the left of the big entrance door. Like all the other rooms in the seraglio, this one was long, narrow, and bare. And much to Zoë's surprise there was no one in it.

Shouanet took them to a window. It looked out on the vast outer court, which was full of people. On a raised platform, with his back turned to the wall so that the women at the window were unable to see his face, sat Shamyl in a stiff thronelike armchair, a large white parasol held high above his head by an attendant. Daniel-Sultan stood on his right and Kazi-Mahomma on his left; facing them were several silent ranks of Murids. In the center of the court Zoë saw

Hadji-Kheriett and Hassan. Hadji-Kheriett stood very erect, his face pale, his thin nostrils quivering, but Hassan's face she could not see. His head was bowed.

"So they are to be tried together, the criminal and the innocent," Zoë exclaimed in French. "Really, the ways of these people are incomprehensible!"

Shouanet was translating every word that was being said in the court below. First Kazi-Mahomma stepped down from the dais and went to Hadji-Kheriett's side. He spoke at length, eulogizing his friend's piety and bravery. He stressed his words with expressive gestures, and when he was through he bowed and returned to his father's side.

The Benevolent Mullah came forward next. Zoë had not seen him, for he had been standing beneath their window. He moved across the court and laid an encouraging hand on Hassan's shoulder. He spoke with dignity in a quiet, even voice. He extolled Hassan's piety, but instead of his bravery he stressed the boy's modesty, humility, and his spirit of sacrifice. Then he in turn bowed to all those present and retired to his former place near the wall.

It was Shamyl's turn to speak now. He did not raise his voice, yet every word could be heard distinctly in all four corners of the big court. "Speak, Hassan! What wisdom has Allah granted you during your penance?"

Zoë held her breath, wondering whether Hassan could overcome his shyness. But when he raised his head, her fears vanished. His face, though pale, was composed, his eyes steady, and his voice clear and even. "Oh, great and Illustrious Imam. I have seen my actions face to face, and I know now that they were evil. To raise a hand against one's teacher is a sin. I should have allowed his deeds to take their course and bear their own fruit."

Shamyl turned to the other defendant. "And you, Hadji-Kheriett?"

Hadji-Kheriett drew a deep breath. His thin cheeks seemed to cave in, and his eyes were ablaze. "Great Imam! I swear by all that's holy, by your life, by your immortal soul, I was not myself. I was bewitched. That woman is a daughter of Shaitan! In Tiflis I saw a strong man, a Russian officer, become all weak and soft at the mere mention of her name. And here, in our own mountains, a whole crowd fell under her spell!"

When Shouanet had translated Hadji-Kheriett's words, the blood rushed to Zoë's face, spreading over her neck and tingling in her ears. Princess Varvara, noticing her acute embarrassment, pressed

196

her hand reassuringly. Together they moved closer to the window and saw that Daniel-Sultan was whispering in Shamyl's ear. Shamyl inclined his head and then said, "Hadji-Kheriett, what you took for witchcraft was but a trait peculiar to a distant race of infidels known as the French."

Zoë and Princess Varvara exchanged glances, smothering their involuntary smiles. But a moment later they were all attention again, for Shamyl was proclaiming the verdicts in a flowery speech. Hassan, for his failure to live up to the test of obedience imposed upon him, would have his apprenticeship suspended until such time as Shamyl decided to give him a new teacher. In the meantime he was to remain in the seraglio, working in the Imam's stables. As for Hadji-Kheriett, Shamyl turned to him, his voice cold and stern. "For having come so close to defiling yourself, you a brave Murid of long standing, I banish you from my presence for a year. You will go to Karaty and serve Kazi-Mahomma. And even when you accompany my son to Dargo-Veden, remember, you are never to cross those portals!" And his long finger pointed to the great outer gates.

At dusk that day Zoë and Princess Varvara went out to the bench outside their door. Princess Anna, complaining of a headache, had retired early. They sat in silence, listening to Zulma's song, sad and mournful, like an ancient Hebrew chant. The voice that sang it, full of mature, well-controlled emotion, was pure, clear, and true.

"Where, where does that thin, shy little girl get such a voice?" Zoë murmured, clasping her hands. "Oh, what I wouldn't give to have a voice like that!"

She fell silent again, and when the last notes had died away she heaved a deep sigh. "If I could sing like that I would sing to the whole wide world, and Sasha in Petersburg would hear me! That, at least, is how I would feel while I was singing."

She smiled, embarrassed at her sudden outburst, and then turned to her friend with an earnest look. "Varvara, tell me about Sasha. I mean, tell me what his home in Petersburg is like. I know nothing, nothing about it! I would so much like to be able to close my eyes sometimes and imagine it."

Princess Varvara cleared her throat, and Zoë leaned forward eagerly. "It is a big, big house, Zoë-djan. Almost a palace, one might say, painted dark red on the outside. It has several entrances. If you come through the main entrance you will find yourself in a marble hall, and the first things you will see there are two tremendous stuffed bears holding out round silver trays for calling cards. Then you will go up an impressive marble staircase, with busts of Roman emperors standing in niches all the way up. But if you look at them closely you will find they have no tips to their noses. And you know who did that? Sasha! When he was about ten or twelve, with a few friends. They said they were bashi-bazooks, the little vandals!"

"And the busts were never replaced?"

"No. They just stand there with chopped-off noses."

They laughed over this a little, and then Zoë urged her to go on. "What happens when you get upstairs, Varvara?"

"Upstairs there is a ballroom and a whole enfilade of drawing rooms—a pink one, a yellow one, a green one. The last one you come to is blue, and that is his mother's favorite room."

Zoë shook her head. "But I don't see Sasha there, except on the staircase!"

"Oh, Sasha has an apartment of his own in one of the wings, with his own entrance. There he has his own dining room and a large comfortable study."

"Yes! Tell me about his study. Tell me . . ." And Zoë shut her eyes, the better to visualize every detail.

"Well, there are many shelves there with books, and an open fireplace, but what always impressed me most of all was his map of the world. My dear, it covers an entire wall! Sasha uses a step-ladder to reach the higher spots. And believe it or not, he has little flags on pins which he sticks into this map. Some are white, and some are green. The white ones are all over Russia and western Europe, in all the places he has visited. The green ones are every-where else, and they have a small anchor drawn on them. I remem-ber asking him why, and he said, 'Green is the color of hope, and an anchor is a symbol of hope. With these I mark the places I hope to visit someday.' "

"What places?" Zoë asked breathlessly. Here, she felt, was a glimpse into Sasha's inner self. And indeed, Princess Varvara's next words disclosed a vivid, if somewhat chaotic, longing for adventure and knowledge.

She chuckled as she began, "Not what one would expect. Not the pyramids and places like that, I mean. Though I do remember seeing a few green flags stuck into Africa, farther along the coast. He said he wanted to see the Bedouins and travel in the Sahara on a camel. There were plenty of green flags in India too. There he wanted to see a fakir, and ride an elephant, and kill a tiger. Also, he said, he wanted to stay there sometime to find out if Jesus Christ

198

really went to India to preach, as some people claim He did. And let me see . . . Ah, yes! I was quite surprised to see one or two green flags stuck into the United States of North America. Sasha told me he wanted to catch a wild buffalo and also find out for himself how a nation born of a revolution managed its affairs!"

12 "Where is that new flag, Poushka? Haven't you made it yet? Hurry up!"

Sasha sat perched on his stepladder in front of his map, and Poushka's answer reached him from the next room—a small dressing room that connected the study with the bedroom. "One more minute, Alexandr Dimitrievitch. Just one little minute!"

Poushka's eyes and nose and beard—in fact, the whole upper half of his huge frame—were concentrated on a tiny black object in his hands. His big clumsy-looking fingers were shaping it and pasting it together with extraordinary agility. From time to time he would glance at the original model lying on a small table in front of him and then go to work again, sticking his tongue out to ease the effort.

At last he stood up. For a moment he admired his handiwork. Then he went into the study and presented Sasha with a minute replica of Zoë's black widow's bonnet stuck on a pin.

Sasha opened his eyes in surprise and laughed. "Did you make that?" He turned the little bonnet over in his hand. "Why, you old devil, it's a wonderful little piece of work."

"Naturally! And it will look well in the mountains of the Caucasus."

"Yes! We will stick it in right here. Right in the heart of the Daghestan, where I think Dargo-Veden is!"

"And may it stick right under Shamylka's tail!" was Poushka's solemn rejoinder.

It had taken many weeks for Princess Anna's letter to reach Prince David and for General Réad's full report on the subject to get to St. Petersburg. September was coming to a close, but Sasha was in a happy mood that day. He had just heard that the Tsar had raised no objections over Jemaleddin's release, provided the latter agreed to return to his father; Jemal himself had been sent for and was due to arrive in town any day now. Prince David was carrying on energetic *pourparlers* with Shamyl from a small town on the northeastern slopes of the Caucasus known as Hassaf-Yourt; and everyone felt confident he would succeed in breaking the mountain-eers down to a more reasonable sum for the ransom. One thing only marred Sasha's happiness—the Holy Synod had taken no steps as yet toward the annulment of his marriage. But Zenaida Pavlovna, his mother, had written about it to the procurator of the Synod—the Tsar's agent in the affairs of the Church, with a portfolio of cabinet minister—and he felt confident her letter would carry weight and some action would be taken soon.

He smiled up at Poushka. "What do you say, old man? Things seem to be brightening up, eh?"

"Yes, Alexandr Dimitrievitch. And as soon as Shamylka lets Zoia Ivanovna go we will open up a few more rooms in this wing and have a whole enfilade of our own!"

"Oh no! As soon as this damned war is over"—for rumors had recently reached St. Petersburg of an attack on the Crimea by the British and French forces—"Zoia Ivanovna and you and I will visit some of these other places!" Sasha pointed at random to different parts of the world.

But Poushka shook his head dubiously. "If you go looking for our Lord and Saviour in that pagan land of India, leave me behind. It's heresy! As for the land of the redskins"—he glanced at the Atlantic Ocean on the map and shuddered—"uh-uh! I'll wait for you here! The sight of a boat, even when I am standing safely on the shore, turns my insides out and I have to run for the nearest privy."

Sasha was still laughing over this when Hélène came in, cool and well groomed as ever, bringing a whiff of perfume into the room. "Sasha," she exclaimed, "Mamma sent me to tell you. She has received a reply from the procurator. He promises to attend to the matter at once." She squeezed his arm and kissed him. And her big gray eyes, shaded with dark lashes, were merry. "From now on everything is going to be so wonderful, Sasha, so wonderful!"

Sasha hugged her. "That is good news!" he cried. "I hope he gives that clergy of his a good prodding so they can keep from snoring into their beards long enough to grant me an annulment!"

Sasha shared with many of his Russian contemporaries a certain contempt for the priesthood which in no way detracted from their deep-rooted acceptance of the Church as such. But Hélène, who was profoundly orthodox in all matters concerning her religion, looked at him with reproach. "I wish you wouldn't speak that way about the clergy, Sasha."

200

And Poushka said severely, "Shame on you, Alexandr Dimitrievitch. Those beards are ordained!"

"All right, all right." Sasha laughed. "I promise to bow low to all the bishops of the Synod and kiss their pudgy little hands if only they will give me my freedom. Ah! More good news," he added, turning to a footman who had appeared at that moment in the doorway. But he frowned slightly when the footman announced that the Tsarevna Anastasia was due to arrive at any moment and Zenaida Pavlovna wished them to meet her in the front hall.

Sasha and Hélène exchanged a bored look. Tsarevna Anastasia of Georgia, the mother of Princess Anna and Princess Varvara, was of pure Russian stock, a native of Moscow and Zenaida Pavlovna's first cousin. She had invited herself to their house, announcing her arrival from Moscow on the new railroad that connected the two capitals of the Russian Empire. And she had asked Zenaida Pavlovna to arrange an audience for her with the Empress, and if possible with the Tsar, too, saying in her letter, "I feel it my sacred duty to implore them in person to give up Shamyl's son and do everything possible to liberate my daughters and grandchildren. I also feel, my dear Zenaida, that this would offer me a golden opportunity to present to Their Majesties my own sad plight and that of my younger children; the sudden death of the tsarevitch, my beloved Elijah, coming on top of the abduction of Anna and Varvara, was a terrible shock, an irreparable loss to me, for my poor dear husband departed to a better world, leaving his earthly affairs in a frightful tangle."

It was this last sentence in the tsarevna's letter that had alarmed Zenaida Pavlovna and her children. "The Emperor has agreed to give up Jemal. She will only annoy him and spoil matters with her everlasting tears and complaints," Sasha was saying as he walked swiftly with Hélène down the long, labyrinthine corridors that connected his wing to the main body of the house.

While they were hurrying to the great central staircase with its line of noseless Roman emperors, a small, solemn procession was coming in their direction from the opposite end of the big house. Zenaida Pavlovna formed its nucleus, preceded by her old majordomo who opened the doors for her, and followed by an old housekeeper and two elderly maids—the supervisor of the household linen and the head of the sewing room. She walked leisurely, a tall, massive figure, but her step was surprisingly light and her movements full of quiet, dignified grace. She was dressed all in black, with a widow's peaked cap and a long crepe veil that she had worn ever since her husband's death, changing the whole attire to gray on family birthdays and name days, and to pure white on great festive occasions.

She was returning from an inspection of the rooms prepared for her guest. She had gone into every detail meticulously, examining the large bed, the bed linen, the towels, the washstand, the cupboards, and passing the tip of her finger now and then over the surface of a table or the back of a chair to make sure no trace of dust had been left anywhere. And although she did not scold or even frown when she came across some signs of negligence, her servants had hovered around her on tenterhooks, knowing well that not a single detail would escape her eagle eye.

When they all finally met at the top of the marble stairs they found that the tsarevna had arrived. Large and heavy, she was climbing the stairs slowly, puffing and blowing as she went. And out of this heaving mountain of black crepe a round face burst forth like a sunflower in bloom.

The tsarevna was a woman who always complained of the futility of her efforts. It was said of her that when she chaperoned her numerous daughters and nieces to a ball she would climb the stairs, muttering to herself, "Mon Dieu! Mon Dieu! What is the use of it all? Driving oneself to death trying to find them husbands! And then they get married and find lovers for themselves!" And on this occasion she came muttering, "Mon Dieu! Mon Dieu! What is the use of it all? Driving oneself to death in these devilish new inventions of steam! And at the end one finds oneself back in the comfort and ease of an old-fashioned horse and carriage!" And aloud, as she neared the top of the stairs and Sasha ran to meet her and offer her his arm, "No, Zenaida, my darling! No more trains for me! Whether you like it or not, you must send me back to Moscow in one of your lovely soft carriages, where I can stretch myself out and sleep as much as I like and have the soles of my feet scratched by my maid!" But when Zenaida Pavlovna had embraced her, expressing her condolences, the tsarevna burst into a flood of tears. "Ah, Zenaidochka! You don't know how I have suffered all these weeks!"

Her emotions got the better of her, and Zenaida Pavlovna was obliged to lead her through the long enfilade of reception rooms to her little blue-and-white sitting room with its graceful Louis XV furniture, while Sasha and Hélène followed them. On the way she told the tsarevna they were to be received by the Empress at five the next afternoon. The news helped to restore the tsarevna's spirits, and by the time she had settled down in one of the armchairs she had regained her composure. She regaled her listeners with tidbits of Moscow gossip, complaining bitterly about the existence of a certain "dreadful woman" who had "enslaved" one of her sons. "And he, poor dear, is cursed with one of those Georgian temperaments! So what am I to do? Ah! Before I married the tsarevitch, my father-confessor told me, 'Brace yourself, my poor dove. Georgians are passionate.' And how right he was! Not a moment's respite—twelve children one after the other, not counting those I lost. Mon Dieu! Mon Dieu! And what is the use of it all? Driving oneself to death, trying to give them a decent upbringing, and then they squander it on—on something unmentionable!"

Zenaida Pavlovna raised her eyebrows. "You would be surprised to know, my dear, what unmentionable things I would do if I were a man!"

The tsarevna looked astounded, but Sasha and Hélène burst out laughing. It was the kind of remark that had always endeared their mother to them, always coming out of the blue, a bold statement of her own firm though somewhat naïve outlook on life.

The tsarevna turned a watery eye on Sasha. "Ah, Sashenka"—she liked to use diminutives—"I hear you, too, have a sentimental attachment in the mountains of the Caucasus!"

Zenaida Pavlovna drew herself up. "Not a sentimental attachment, Anastasia! His future wife! Zoia Ivanovna, the daughter of our famous Colonel Chabout."

A wave of gratitude and deep affection for this big woman who was his mother swept through Sasha. He strode up to her, raised her large hand to his lips, and kissed it three times in succession. Then he excused himself and left the room. As fond as he was of his cousins Anna and Varvara, he always found himself irritated in the presence of their mother, who was so different from them in every respect. And later that evening, when Hélène told him the tsarevna had promised Zenaida Pavlovna to refrain from mentioning her reduced circumstances to the Empress but to address a written petition on the subject to the Emperor, he shrugged his shoulders, unconvinced. "I hope she keeps her word. She is never quite able to get over being sorry for herself."

A few minutes before five on the following afternoon Zenaida

Pavlovna and the tsarevna arrived at the Winter Palace and were conducted to the Empress's private apartments. The aura and tradition of majesty surrounding the imperial couple was such in those days that even Zenaida Pavlovna never failed to experience a certain feeling of awe and trepidation when she approached their presence, even though she had known them intimately for years and had, so to speak, grown up with them. But she knew how to disguise her feelings. She walked with composure through the magnificent halls, looking very impressive all dressed in white crepe, several strings of large pearls wound around her neck, for she considered a visit to the Empress equal to a festive occasion. The tsarevna, on the other hand, was puffing and blowing. Her round face, its thickset features somewhat blurred by years of solid food and shallow thoughts, seemed ready to burst with the force of her pent-up emotions; and in her hands she clutched almost convulsively a large reticule covered with black sequins.

On entering the Empress's private drawing room, the first impression of a nervous visitor such as the tsarevna was of red velvet brocade and of a profusion of potted plants. In a haze the tsarevna went through the ceremony of curtsying and kissing the Empress's hand, after which she found herself seated in a heavy gilt armchair opposite her dreaded sovereign's wife.

Empress Alexandra was no longer the young beauty of the engraving in General Réad's office. Her features had grown sharper and her forehead more pronounced, but the fine bone structure was still there, and she held her head high on a long, well-rounded neck. A gracious, faded background to a powerful autocrat.

Before she had time to exchange a few words with her guests, the big ornate doors were flung open and Nicholas himself walked into the room. Zenaida Pavlovna and the tsarevna sprang to their feet and swept down to the floor in a low curtsy.

Nicholas, too, was no longer the handsome, slender youth of his former days. There were pouches under his eyes, and a fleshiness had crept over his body, though not enough to make his six feet four appear fat. His carriage was proud and erect, unbending. And the look in his eyes was heavy. So heavy, in fact, that many people claimed they could not endure it, and women, they said, had been known to faint under its weight. But if anyone had dared to look deep into those gray eyes they might have found there the despair of a dreamer who had lost his dream. For Nicholas, the soldier, the disciplinarian, the martinet, the man one did not talk back to, the "Iron Tsar," as some people called him, who believed implicitly in his own divine right as an autocrat, had pinned his faith on a grand illusion. To him all Christian monarchs were beings set apart, whose words and deeds must always be inspired by sentiments based on traditions of medieval chivalry. This had been the substance of his dream. The fact that it had crumbled did not affect his outward aspect, for he possessed a will of iron that made him carry on, whatever the circumstances might be. But his inner world had been shaken to its roots. The treachery of Francis Joseph of Austria, whose throne had been saved and made secure at the point of Russian bayonets, the alliance of Victoria with the Moslem Turk, and the fact that Christian nations were fighting on the side of Turkey were to Nicholas as shattering at the age of fifty-eight as the disillusionments in love and religion can sometimes be to other far younger men.

But all Zenaida Pavlovna and the tsarevna saw that afternoon was the Tsar, the embodiment of "Holy Russia," coming toward them with outstretched hand. And they quivered a little as they touched it and then rose to their feet to listen respectfully to what he had to say.

Nicholas had turned to a young officer who had followed him unobtrusively into the room and was standing now at rigid attention near the door; very young, very slim, very modest.

"You remember Jemaleddin, my dear."

The Tsar was speaking to the Empress, but his words electrified the tsarevna and Zenaida Pavlovna. They gazed at the young man with hope. He was of medium height, with a slightly oriental cast to his sharp and well-modeled features; there was nothing remarkable about his outward appearance except for the disturbing clarity of his eyes and the bright, feverish red of his cheeks which his friends mistook for a sign of health but which in reality was a seal of death.

The tsarevna clutched her heart as she watched him bowing low over the Empress's hand, and then the Tsar spoke again: "Tsarevna, I present to you Cornet Jemaleddin Shamyl! Who never hesitated when he learned all the circumstances. He will return to his native land to liberate your daughters and your grandchildren!"

For a moment the tsarevna forgot her surroundings. All she saw now was a very young man willing to give up the civilized world, his friends, and all the ties and interests he had created for himself to return as a stranger to the wild country of his birth for the sake of her family. She embraced him, murmuring, "Brave! Noble! Self-sacrificing knight! How can I ever, ever express my gratitude?"

It was perhaps overacted, but nevertheless sincere, and Jemal bowed to her respectfully. Now the strange part about this incident was that all four witnesses were later confused on the subject of Jemal's answer to the tsarevna. The tsarevna herself told her friends he had spoken at length about self-sacrifice with a magnificent, fiery eloquence; Zenaida Pavlovna said he had consoled the tsarevna in a few simple but very moving words; and the Tsar and the Empress quoted him as saying, "Don't thank me, Tsarevna. I am only doing my duty." Either they were all embroidering on the story to make it more sensational, which was likely only in the case of the tsarevna, or else they had all fallen victim to an oral hallucination, each one having heard words that were in accordance with his or her conception of Jemal's character; for the actual truth lay in the fact that he had said nothing at all. After bowing to the tsarevna in silence, he had gone back to his former place near the door, and it was the Tsar who had spoken in his clipped way, as though every sentence were an abrupt but important pronouncement. "Tsarevna! I must congratulate you! You have a splendid son-in-law! Today I have made Prince David Tchavchavadzé my honorary aide-de-camp! A reward for his brave defense of Shildi and his unswerving duty to his Tsar and country!"

The tsarevna must have considered this a propitious moment to present her own petition, for she snatched out of her large reticule a piece of parchment-like paper tied up into a roll, and plunged once again into a deep curtsy at the Tsar's feet. "Sire, your kindness knows no bounds! And I implore Your Imperial Majesty to accept this humble petition of a helpless, heartbroken widow."

The Tsar frowned and took the paper, laying it aside on a table. "I will look into it, Tsarevna!" he said while she rose to her feet, murmuring her thanks and perspiring a little after the effort.

They had all been speaking French, as was customary at court, especially in the presence of the Empress, whose French was far more fluent than her Russian. But the Tsar's frown had grown deeper. "What are we? A crowd of foreigners?" he said in Russian. "We have a beautiful language of our own!" And turning to Zenaida Pavlovna, "Your son has submitted a petition to the Synod for an annulment of his marriage. I hear he has done this with your consent."

206

"Yes, sire. As Your Majesty knows, his wife has been hopelessly insane for years. I want Sasha to be happy, and he has found a good woman whom he loves."

"The Frenchwoman who is held captive with the tsarevna's daughters?"

"Yes, sire."

The whole weight of his eyes was upon her now. "I can understand a young man losing his head when in love, but I am surprised at you, Zenaida Pavlovna! Encouraging a marriage between your son and an enemy subject!"

The blood rushed to Zenaida Pavlovna's face, but she stood her ground. "Your Majesty will recall how my mother saved the life of a Frenchman in 1812. We were at war with France then, but everyone, including the late Emperor, your brother, thought her act a noble one. Sasha's fiancée is that Frenchman's daughter!"

Nicholas' eyes glistened dangerously. "To save the life of an enemy is an act of Christian mercy! We shall save this woman's life. But no officer of mine will marry a Frenchwoman! Your son's petition will be rejected by the Synod!"

Zenaida Pavlovna held her head high, but her lips were quivering and her heart was crushed. The whole of the Russian Empire had descended on Sasha, forbidding his happiness.

13   When Zenaida Pavlovna, with tears in her eyes, told Sasha what had happened, he was shaken by the violence of his feelings. Although he had foreseen the possibility of certain obstacles to his marriage in case of a war with France, he had not expected this deadly blow from the one man with whom no one could argue. The shock was such that for a moment he lost all self-control. He dashed out of his mother's room and ran down endless corridors, past gaping servants, until at last he stood in his own study. With a shaky hand he poured himself a stiff drink of cognac and gulped it down. He slumped into a chair and pressed the tips of his fingers to his eyes, remaining there for a long time stilling all thoughts.

He was aroused by several voices and opened his eyes to find himself in the company of his two best friends, one of them being Jemal, the other a young man named Prince Ivan Saltykoff. Poushka was opening a bottle of champange. Sasha heaved a sigh. "Thank you for coming. And now talk, you devils, talk!"

"If talk is what you want, here you are." Saltykoff raised a glass and declaimed in English:

> *"The Saltykoff, and the Gorchakoff, and the Menshikoff,*
> *'Twas a very great cough that carried them off,*
> *And 'twas a very great coffin they carried them off in!*

My English nurse used to say that, but she never mentioned the Novoselsky, so Novoselsky will live and prosper!" And for the benefit of Jemal, who understood no English, he added in Russian, "That means most of us will perish young, but Novoselsky will carry on to tell the story!"

Saltykoff was Sasha's childhood friend, one of the boys who had helped mutilate the Roman emperors. He was remarkable for three things: he was one of the richest men in Russia; contrary to tradition, he was making no career for himself either in the army or in any branch of the government service; and his greatest passion in life was his carriages and horses. He was happiest when he could drive them at full speed over the highways around St. Petersburg dressed as a *yamstchik*, or postilion, in a long, thick, padded coat tied at the waist by a bright sash, and a high four-cornered hat with a couple of peacock feathers stuck in it. He had been known to bribe the transportation authorities and take the place of a regular yamstchik, and on such occasions he accepted a tip with pride, handing it later to the regular postilion he had replaced, saying, "Here, my good friend, try and top this one!" His friends laughed at his oddities and made fun of them, but they always wound up by exclaiming with real feeling, "Oh, Ivan Saltykoff—the soul of a postilion and a heart of gold!" And in these affectionate words lay reflected the whole of Saltykoff's nature.

The three friends had dinner together and then returned to the study. By eleven o'clock Saltykoff had helped Sasha empty several bottles of champagne. His spirits were high, his face aglow, and his tongue a little thick. But Sasha remained glum. Seeing that nothing helped to distract him, Saltykoff suggested a visit to the Gypsies or some fun with women; not that he himself wanted it particularly, but, as he said, "it will divert our Sasha. He is the only true profligate of us three!" But Sasha shook his head. The sad songs of the Gypsies would make him feel worse, he said, and as for women . . . "I must confess I can think of only one. I have tried others, but nothing seems to work somehow. They are all flat! Flat! Flat!"

"Ah! The impotence of true love!" Saltykoff exclaimed. "I know,

I know! I feel like that about my glossy horses and my shiny carriages. I even gave up that luscious, buxom Thereska, the French girl, on their account. She was always jealous of them, and in the long run she did not compare." He made a sour face and then looked at Jemal. "And our friend here, isn't he a victim of the impotence of true love? He has kept himself pure, oh so pure, because when the time comes for him to give, he must give all. He is a virgin sword that refuses to be drawn out of its scabbard except to kill!" He was so amused by his own words that he threw his head back and laughed.

Jemal had drunk nothing that evening. In fact, he never drank, and his friends did not seem to mind. In any other young man they would have considered it a deficiency, but his sincere enjoyment of their fun made up for the discrepancy, and often, toward the end of a spree, his companions would be convinced he had had his full share and were apt next day to credit him with witticisms and pranks he had neither said nor done.

Saltykoff raised his glass. "To your health, Jemal. Look at him, Sasha. Not a drop to drink and his cheeks as rosy as any maiden's!" He made a sly face. "You know what I think? I think every time Jemal comes to a feast or to a spree he performs a little miracle. Something like the one—— You know what I mean, at the wedding in Cana of Galilee!" Jemal blushed a deep red, but Saltykoff gave him no time to speak. "Wine is inspiration, my friend!"

"Yes, it is!" Sasha broke in with sudden animation. "It has inspired me tonight. I know now what must be done! I must leave Petersburg. I will get myself transferred to the Caucasus, where I can breathe freely. People there are dignified and independent. Not like our courtiers here, crushed by their nearness to—the deity!" Saltykoff looked startled, Jemal opened his eyes in surprise, but Sasha hurried on: "With my mother's connections, the transfer might be arranged in five days. Then I will leave with you, Jemal!"

Jemal's face brightened, but Saltykoff shook his head. "I don't think I would like the Caucasus. High mountains everywhere. No place to drive a horse and carriage! Besides, I have no girl sitting under Mount Kazbek, waiting for me to clasp her in my arms."

Sasha frowned. "I will never dare clasp her in mine again," he muttered darkly.

"Oh yes, you will! Remember our Russian saying—'After much grinding you get flour.' You will get it in the end. Before you know it, you'll be kneading the dough of matrimonial bliss and baking cakes like mad. Little cakes with currants, little cakes with dill! But I, I will remain here as I am, driving my troika up and down the Kolomna road. What a road! What a troika!" He raised his glass again and squinted at it. "Ah, the pretty little bubbles. Do you know what they are? Each one is a beautiful troika galloping straight to heaven!"

Jemal laughed. "Planning to drive your chariot to heaven like the prophet Elijah?"

"Not yet. Not yet, Jemal. But when I do, I will drive it all over the sky. And all you poor devils down below, whenever you hear thunder rumbling in the distance, you will say, 'Ah! There goes Ivan Saltykoff!' "

Suddenly Sasha sat up. His lips were smiling, but his eyes were cold. "That's all very well, you and your troikas. Driving around, pretending to be a yamstchik, fooling a lot of insignificant people. You have never dared fool anyone of importance! The Tsar, for instance!"

Jemal looked at Sasha narrowly, while all color left Saltykoff's cheeks and then rushed back again until his face became as red as a poppy. He jumped to his feet, his arms working like a windmill. "By God! I never thought of it. By God! Of course I must drive the Tsar. The Tsar's yamstchik, Ivan Saltykoff! Sounds wonderful! By God! I will do it tomorrow!"

"Listen to him. Tomorrow he will drive the Tsar."

"I will, too! Tomorrow morning the Tsar is traveling down the Kolomna road on an inspection tour. My friends, the yamstchiks, told me so. I will drive him part of the way!"

"Who are you trying to fool, Ivan? One look at the Tsar and you will take to your heels!"

A devil had taken hold of Sasha. His bitterness had mingled with his wine. To fool the Tsar seemed a wonderful revenge, and he was not going to miss it. Jemal, guessing what was at the back of his mind, got up and crossed the room. "Don't make him do it, Sasha. You will both get into trouble and it won't be worth it." But Sasha waved him away. Afraid Saltykoff might give up the idea, he continued to dare him until the latter thumped a frenzied fist on a table. "How much, how much will you bet me?"

"A thousand rubles!"

"A thousand! Good! It's a bet!" They clasped hands, and Salty-koff turned to Jemal. "Witness it! And tomorrow you must come with Sasha and admire the skill of Ivan Saltykoff, yamstchik to the Tsar!"

Jemal seemed to hesitate, and Sasha turned to him with derision. "Afraid, Jemal?"

Jemal shook his head sadly. "I have little to lose, you know."

Suddenly Sasha blushed to the very roots of his hair. He tore his hand out of Saltykoff's clasp. Jemal was giving up everything to sacrifice himself for people he had never seen, and no one was fussing over him or trying to console him. And here *he* was, planning petty revenges, while his own future still held plenty of hope. For the first time he saw it all clearly. The war would not last forever, and the Tsar was not eternal. Even if the Tsar lived on for years and refused to relent, once the war was over, Sasha could resign from the army and marry whomsoever he pleased. He felt ashamed of himself. He threw his arms around his friend and hugged him. "Forgive me, Jemal, forgive me!"

But Saltykoff would have none of it. "No, no!" he cried. "First he must witness our bet, then he can forgive you!"

Sobered, Sasha had no heart left for the bet. "Let us call it off, Ivan. The whole thing is absurd." But by now Saltykoff was thrilled with the idea of driving the Tsar. He would do it tomorrow at all costs, he said, and if Sasha did not stick by his bet, he just had no guts. There was nothing to be done. The two men clasped hands again, and Jemal pretended to cut them apart—a sign that the bet was on.

Saltykoff sobered up too. He paced up and down the room, laying out the plans of action for the morning. Some other yamstchik, he said, would drive the monarch to the first station, where his horses would be changed. There Saltykoff would take over and drive Nicholas to the next station, thirty versts away, a distance equivalent to some twenty-odd miles. He gave them the name of the place and added, "I should get there around noon. You must be there earlier. And you, Sasha, be sure to bring those thousand rubles with you!"

On this the three men parted. And early next morning Jemal came to fetch Sasha, looking disappointed. He had been to Saltykoff's house in the hope of talking him out of his foolishness but had missed him. And Saltykoff's old valet, who had served his father before him, had said, raising his eyes to heaven, "His Serene Highness is playing yamstchik this morning. Yes, sir, if you could find

211

him a wholesome bride, you'd be doing us all a favor. Only children, a lot of little Saltykoffs, will help him grow up!"

Sasha and Jemal left, feeling like two conspirators. They did not even tell Poushka where they were going. They slipped out of the side door and climbed into Sasha's carriage. "It's almost like going to a duel," Sasha said with a short laugh, looking at the long red façade of his home. "I am taking it all in as though I were never to see the old place again!"

Shortly after eleven they arrived at their destination, driving into a vast courtyard with the main one-story building at one end and the stables at the other. A generous tip made the stationmaster place at their disposal the long narrow waiting room reserved for travelers of distinction. Being so close to St. Petersburg, this waiting room was less shabby than those Sasha had seen in other parts of the country. The plaster on the walls still held, though it was peeling here and there, and only a few dusty cobwebs hung from the ceiling; the plush seats on the chairs were only partly worn out, the scraggly potted palms in the corner of the room were not quite dead, and a colored woodcut of Tsar Nicholas hanging on one of the walls reminded the two young men forcibly why they were there.

They settled down at one of the windows, Jemal quiet and composed. Things were beyond his control now, and he sat back, prepared to watch the show. But Sasha was all on edge. He counted the minutes and glanced nervously from time to time at the highway that could be seen beyond the courtyard gates.

In the courtyard itself everything looked somnolent. Several yamstchiks, waiting for their turn to take to the road, leaned lazily against the walls, cracking sunflower seeds and spitting out the shells; the stationmaster's children poked about lazily in the mud; and when some carriage drove in, its lean horses would be replaced by equally lean ones in a slow fashion, as though time were of no account. But shortly before noon the whole place suddenly sprang to life. Men began to hurry about, gesticulating; a woman rushed out of the main building and shooed the children away; and the stationmaster shouted orders in a loud, strained voice, his face red, his chest puffed out to its ultimate capacity. The Tsar's approach was being felt by all. Three handsome prancing horses were led out of the stables and held in readiness—no delay was permissible in the royal progress. And in the distance Sasha caught sight of a cloud of dust. With beating heart he leaned closer to the windowpane. He saw a light open carriage drawn

212

by three horses approaching from the direction of St. Petersburg at a terrific pace. Closer and closer it came without slowing down. Sasha could distinguish now the stern profile of the Tsar under a tall helmet, and he recognized one of the Tsar's aide-de-camps seated beside him, looking insignificant next to Nicholas' imposing figure. But was the yamstchik on the box Saltykoff? he asked himself. Jemal, unable to resist the tension, stood up to see better. At full speed the troika clattered through the gates and came to a smooth stop. And on the box they saw Ivan Saltykoff, grinning from ear to ear.

At that particular moment he was the happiest man on earth. Everything had gone right, and he had surpassed himself in his driving. He had covered the thirty versts in less than forty minutes. Once during the trip he had heard the Tsar's voice saying, "Not so fast," and he had felt the imperial fingers tap him on the shoulder. But he had shouted back, "Do not worry, Your Majesty. I know what an exalted personage I am driving!" And to show off his skill he had stopped his horses—his own beautiful black horses—and had made them walk slowly past a large log on the road. Then he let go again, speeding them up, faster and faster, until the wind sang in his ears and the little bells on the harness rang out to all four corners of the earth.

Sasha and Jemal saw the Tsar step out of the carriage, looking pleased with his trip. "He has done it!" Sasha exclaimed, squeezing Jemal's arm in his excitement. "Good old Saltykoff!" But a moment later, seized with anxiety, his face was glued to the window again. Something had gone wrong outside. Poor Saltykoff had done too well.

The Tsar had told his aide to give the yamstchik twenty-five rubles for his excellent driving, and turning to the stationmaster, he said, "The best yamstchik I have ever had! What is his name?"

It was then that the blow fell. "Prince Ivan Saltykoff, Your Imperial Majesty!"

A frown darkened the imperial countenance. The Tsar turned to the culprit. "Come here!" And Saltykoff scrambled off the box.

He approached the Tsar, trembling in every limb, his hands fumbling awkwardly at the folds of his long padded coat. Nicholas' heavy eyes were upon him, boring through him, until he wished he could have crumbled through the earth. His ordeal was intensified by the knowledge that, above all, the Tsar disliked young noblemen who did not serve their country and, like Ivan, led an idle life off

213

the revenues of their estates. He held his breath now for fear of letting out a loud, plaintive gasp, and his face grew redder with every passing second.

At last Nicholas spoke in a cold, intransigent voice. "Saltykoff! I suggest you give up these pranks and whimseys! It is time you served me and your country! Leave at once for the Caucasus! I appoint you to the Nijegorodsky Regiment! May you serve your fatherland as all Saltykoffs have done before!"

The new horses had been harnessed, a new yamstchik had taken his place on the box, and Nicholas turned away, leaving a sweating Saltykoff staring vacantly at the world, his mouth wide open.

The Tsar was leaving, and Sasha dashed out of the room, out of the building, rushing to Saltykoff's side. But to his misfortune, precisely at that moment the Tsar looked back to get a last glimpse of Saltykoff. When he caught sight of Sasha, he stopped the carriage.

Sasha's heart gave a bound and stood still. The Tsar was coming toward them, his frown deeper than ever. Sasha drew himself to attention, staring straight ahead past the Tsar's shoulder to avoid those heavy gray eyes. "It is the end, it is the end," was all he could think of.

But suddenly something so strange happened, so staggering to all those present, that even the Tsar stopped short and raised his eyebrows. One of the windows of the station building flew open and Jemal was seen, perched for a second on the window sill. Then he jumped to the ground, ran to Sasha's side, and stood there at rigid attention.

The Tsar was close to the three young men now. "What is this? Officers sprouting out of the ground! Officers flying out of windows!" There was a touch of humor to his voice. He spoke to Jemal. "What are you doing here, Jemaleddin? On your way already? I thought you were leaving at the end of the week!"

He was offering Jemal a way out. But Jemal refused to take it. He looked straight into the Tsar's eyes without fear. "No, Your Imperial Majesty. I came to see if Saltykoff would dare drive you here, Your Majesty."

"So!" The Tsar's eyes shifted to Sasha. "And you too?"

"Yes, Your Majesty."

"A bet?"

"Yes, Your Majesty."

There was a long pause. Then Nicholas said, "Such shameful be-

214

havior is unbefitting to a guardsman! Novoselsky! I demote you from the guards! You, too, will join the Nijegorodsky Regiment! You will be more useful to me there, fighting for your country!"

He looked at Jemal, and his anger seemed to dwindle away. He must have guessed what had prompted him to commit such an unseemly act. He had wanted to draw the whole of the monarch's anger on himself, hoping thereby to soften the punishment of his friends. And in a way he had succeeded in this, for Nicholas turned to Sasha, saying, "For Jemaleddin's sake, and out of regard for your mother, whom I respect, you may remain in Petersburg under house arrest until Jemaleddin's departure. You will accompany him to Hassaf-Yourt, and you will then report to the Nijegorodsky Regiment!" And turning to Jemal for the last time, he added, "Good-by, Jemaleddin. May God be with you!"

With that the Tsar left them for good.

Sasha remained motionless, not knowing whether to cry or to laugh. To be demoted from the guards was a disgrace, to be sent to the Caucasus a joy. And it was Saltykoff who put his thoughts into words: "It's all very well for you. You will be close to the one you love. But what in hell am I going to do in the Caucasus?" He sighed and shook his head. "Oh well! I suppose I must go home now and pack."

But Saltykoff was not to see his home again for a long time. He found himself confronted by a tall gendarme in a blue uniform, a saber dangling at his side. His walrus mustache bristled, his face was stern, and his speech almost as clipped as that of the Tsar. "Your Serene Highness! Your carriage is ready!"

"My carriage?" Saltykoff looked around in confusion. All he could see was a cart with a rough plank laid across it instead of a seat.

"His Majesty's orders! You are to leave at once for the Caucasus under my tutelage!"

"But, my good man—not in these clothes!"

"Yes, Your Serene Highness, just as you are. Orders is orders!"

Saltykoff rushed up to Sasha. "The thousand rubles! Have you the thousand rubles? For heaven's sake, give them to me! I did not bring mine, I was so sure to win. And the little I had I spent on bribes."

Sasha had the money ready. He pressed a thick roll of treasury notes into his friend's hand, and the gendarme bundled Saltykoff into the cart unceremoniously, though not forgetting to address him by his full title while he was doing it. And the last Sasha and Jemal saw of him was Ivan riding out of the gates in his yamstchik outfit, seated beside the tall gendarme, headed for the Caucasus two thousand miles away.

14   Sasha spent the next four days under house arrest. Although he did not leave his rooms, he seldom found himself alone. His mother and sister were with him constantly, and Jemal had moved in to keep him company. On the morning of the fifth day they left, first for Moscow, where Jemal had promised to pick up letters and gifts from the tsarevna to her daughters, and then on to Hassaf-Yourt and the Nijegorodsky Regiment.

Zenaida Pavlovna bid them farewell at the top of the big main staircase. She embraced Jemal. She blessed Sasha with a broad sign of the cross and clung to him for a moment. Then she turned away abruptly and hurried down the long line of reception rooms to her own apartments, where in the privacy of her bedroom she could give vent to her sorrow. And Hélène accompanied the two young men down the stairs, her arm linked tightly in Sasha's.

But in the front hall they met with an unexpected delay. Poushka was nowhere to be found. "He has been acting strangely these last few days, as if he had lost his mind," Sasha said, his irritation rising out of the tenseness of the moment rather than from any real annoyance with Poushka. And while servants were being dispatched to look for the big man, Sasha glanced at the two stuffed bears. His eyes softened. They held many childhood memories, standing there stiff and erect, one of them grinning and the other snarling fiercely. Long ago Hélène had nicknamed them "La Belle Ursule" and "The Beast."

"I think this occasion should be commemorated by depositing cards on the bears." He laughed suddenly, picking a calling card out of his wallet. On the back of it he scribbled the date and then wrote, "Alexander Novoselsky, leaving home, disgraced but happy." He read it aloud to the others and deposited it on The Beast's tray. "You must give yours to La Belle Ursule," he said to Jemal, handing him a gold pencil and another calling card. After a moment's hesitation Jemal wrote down hurriedly, "Jemaleddin Shamyl, going to another world." And Hélène, with tears in her eyes, dropped his card into La Belle Ursule's tray.

Poushka, in the meantime, had been taking leave of his uncle, the

216

old major-domo, Klementi Pamfilitch. The old man had been ailing for the last two days. He was reclining on his bed, propped up by many pillows and wearing a sumptuous dressing gown that had once belonged to Sasha's father. A folded handkerchief dipped in vinegar covered his forehead, half hiding his eyes from view. The room was small and meagerly furnished—a table, a chair, a wooden coffer near the wall, and in one corner of the room a large icon in front of which flickered the tiny flame of a float light. Klementi Pamfilitch did not believe in fresh air, and the atmosphere in his room was heavy, the sour smell of an aging body mingling with the vinegar used for the compresses.

Poushka was sitting on the chair at the foot of the bed, clasping and unclasping his big bony fingers. He was saying, "I figured it out this way—no one in this world is as great as our Tsar, and therefore no man's sin is as great as the Tsar's sin!"

Klementi Pamfilitch stirred uneasily and spoke in a weak voice. "To figure out something is one thing. To proclaim it to the world is another."

"Yes, Uncle. That is why I am saying it to you alone. I know it won't go beyond these walls. To my ignorant way of thinking, the Tsar sinned when he forbade the annulment of our Sashenka's marriage, and the Tsar should be saved from his own sin." Poushka cracked the joints of his fingers and went on: "It isn't right to keep two young people apart. Their love should be sanctioned, otherwise their passions will drive them into bad ways. Now if our Sashenka were free, he could go ahead and marry Zoia Ivanovna. Nothing much would happen. They would be banished to one of his estates for a year or two, but that would do them no harm!"

"But that is just what the Tsar wants to avoid," Klementi Pamfilitch replied with irrefutable logic. "Our Tsar is a thorough man. He does not want his subjects to marry Frenchwomen. The French have always been treacherous to us."

"But Zoia Ivanovna is not like other Frenchwomen. She is Colonel Chabout's daughter."

The old man sighed. Like all the older servants in the house, he remembered Zoë's father. He had liked him. Moreover, he was proud of him in the way a faithful family retainer becomes proud of a family ghost or a family legend. But to disobey the Tsar was wrong. He shook his head and sighed again. "All the same, I say it is a pity for our Sashenka to love a Frenchwoman, even if she is Colonel Chabout's daughter. Why couldn't he fall in love with a young Rus-

217

sian lady of noble birth, nicely trimmed, pink and rosy, as though fresh from the oven!"

"Love is not a potato, Uncle!"

"That is true." The old man remained lost in thought for a few seconds. "What is she like, this Zoia Ivanovna?" he asked at length.

"Small and thin, but strong inside. Once she gets into her stride, she will rule this household as efficiently as the lady Zenaida Pavlovna has done."

"Small and thin. That isn't good!" Klementi Pamfilitch said severely, viewing the problem now from a breeding angle. He raised himself on his pillows and looked around with an air of superiority. "Our lords have always carried their asses high!"

Poushka straightened his shoulders and smiled with pride. "Yes! A magnificent sight! But remember, Uncle, her father was a big man. And you should see her three aunts. Giantesses, all of them. Especially the one called Mam'selle Roxana! Oh no! Zoia Ivanovna will not lower the race!"

Grudgingly Klementi Pamfilitch gave in. "Very well, Nephew! I will tell the household what you told me. They might as well know it. After all, big or small, Zoia Ivanovna will be their mistress someday. Our Sashenka is a stubborn one. Either the madwoman will die or the Tsar will relent."

"Thank you, Uncle." Poushka stood up. "And now I want your blessing. My father is dead. You are my godfather. Give me your blessing. From now on my path will be a thorny one."

He knelt by the side of the bed. The old man propped himself up on his elbow and raised his hand. "If I read your thoughts correctly, little Nephew, there is much in them I cannot sanction. But the ways of the Almighty are devious at times. I will give you my blessing, for when you come back I will no longer be here." And he laid his hand on Poushka's head, murmuring a prayer.

There was a loud knock on the door, and one of the footmen thrust his head into the room. "The gentry are waiting for you in the front hall, Poushka. They are ready to leave!"

Poushka embraced his uncle, bowed to the icon in the corner, crossing himself devoutly, and then hurried out of the room.

From then on he seemed to regain his old good humor. Throughout their trip to Moscow and during their three days' stay in that city he went about his work merrily, cracking jokes and giving Sasha encouragement when he saw his spirits were low.

On the eve of their departure Sasha returned to his hotel room

218

late. He and Jemal had spent the evening with the tsarevna and her family, and he felt tired and out of sorts. Poushka helped him to undress and slip into a dressing gown, and instead of bidding him good night and leaving, as he always did, he remained standing motionless in the middle of the room. Sasha glanced at him over his shoulder. "What is the matter now, Poushka?"

Poushka made a solemn face. "The time has come, Alexandr Dimitrievitch, for us to part."

Sasha thought he was joking. He even laughed nervously. "Have you gone mad?" But to his consternation he soon discovered that Poushka was in dead earnest.

"What? Leave me for good? Why—why, that's impossible!"

"Oh, not for good. What would you do without me?" Poushka smiled. "No. For two or three months at the most. After that I will join you in the Nijegorodsky Regiment." He went on to explain how much he had neglected his daughters and his grandchildren all these years. "We are going to war now," he said. "Who knows? I might be killed. I must go to Romantzevo and see my three daughters and their children!"

"But why didn't you tell me this sooner? You might have gone there while I was in Moscow!"

Poushka shook his head. "A couple of days would not be enough. They would not make up for my neglect. I must spend at least a month with them. My nephew, Sidor Poushka, is in town. You remember him. A good, honest, hard-working lad! I have taken the liberty of fitting him out with a soldier's uniform. He can be your orderly and take care of you until I return."

Sasha sat down on the edge of the bed. "You have thought of everything," he said bitterly. As long as he could remember, Poushka had always been at his side. He had never before expressed a wish to go to Romantzevo to see his family unless Sasha were going there too. Why should he do it now, at this difficult moment in Sasha's life? "There must be something at the back of it all," he said to himself. "But what?" He could not make it out. And he sat there, feeling dejected. Without Poushka the loneliness, the dreadful void that was facing him now would be harder to bear.

Poushka must have guessed his thoughts, for he said, "You won't be lonely, Alexandr Dimitrievitch. You will be traveling with Cornet Jemaleddin Shamyl, and in the regiment you will have Prince Ivan Saltykoff. Please let me go."

219

"How can I stop you? You are a free man now!" Sasha cried out in despair.

"No, Alexandr Dimitrievitch, no man is free who cares much. I love you as if you were my own flesh and blood."

He was by the door now. Sasha jumped to his feet and ran across the room. He grabbed Poushka by the shoulders and looked deep into his eyes. "You won't fail me, Poushka? You will return?"

A stifled sob escaped the big man. He pressed the back of Sasha's hand to his forehead for a second and then let it go. "I will never fail you. I will return to serve Zoia Ivanovna and you for the rest of my born days!"

15   Zoë moved uneasily in her sleep. She could hear Sasha's voice in the distance. It was indistinct, but she knew he was speaking French. Then suddenly it cut sharply through the darkness that surrounded her, saying, *"Ce drôle ne semble pas s'apercevoir que nous lui offrons la possibilité d'une indépendance complète du Tsar!"* The words were so loud and clear they awakened her with a start. She sat up on her mattress, hugging her blanket close to her shoulders. The early November nights were cold, but the door had to be kept open to give enough air for the eleven occupants of the small narrow room. The others were all fast asleep around her. Bright moonlight flooded the court of the seraglio, and Zoë guessed it must be close to midnight. At first she thought she was still dreaming, for the words she had heard had actually been spoken, not by Sasha, but by a live Frenchman somewhere outside, not far from the room. Another man's voice answered, speaking French with a strong English accent, *"Ces montagnards sont très méfiants. Shamyl ne croit pas en notre sincérité!"* And then the Frenchman again, "Yes. He said, 'How can I lay my trust in you? Your two Christian tsars have allied themselves with the Sultan to conquer a third Christian tsar. When they have beaten him, as you say they will, what assurance have I they won't turn against us Moslems?' "

There was no doubt left in Zoë's mind. Incredible as it seemed, a Frenchman and an Englishman were in the seraglio, discussing Shamyl. Swiftly she rose to her feet and began to dress, listening intently to what was being said outside. The Frenchman bemoaned Shamyl's reluctance to engage himself in a campaign large enough to draw more Russian troops away from the Turkish front and to synchronize his plans of action with those of the allied forces that were

220

now laying siege to Sevastopol in the Crimea. The Englishman said, "He wants more proof of our ability to cope with the Russians before joining hands with us. Remember, *cher collègue*, how he said, 'The Sultan has created me Viceroy of Georgia. I am appreciative of the honor, but the title will remain an empty one so long as the Sultan himself is unable to reach that province.' "

Zoë moved silently to the door and stopped on the threshold in surprise. The two men were standing in the shadow of the gallery, halfway between her door and the wooden partition; and they were dressed like ordinary mountaineers in dark tcherkeskas and high peaked fur caps. She crept toward them, hugging the wall, and when she was close behind them she whispered, *"Au nom du ciel, messieurs, dites moi, qui êtes-vous?"*

They looked around, startled. This slender young woman in her long gray dress and her sunbonnet must have seemed like an apparition from another world. But when Zoë explained who she was and how she came to be there, they moved closer to her, asking eager questions and telling her about themselves. They had both been stationed in Russia for a number of years in the consular services of their respective countries and had learned to speak Russian fluently. Now, on a secret mission to Shamyl, they had been smuggled from the Black Sea by friendly mountain tribes. That evening the two men had had an hour's session with Shamyl in his little house and had been told to wait outside while he discussed their proposals with Kazi-Mahomma and Daniel-Sultan.

"If he asks you to wait until he gets his Council of Naibs together, you will stand a chance of success; otherwise you might as well give up hope of getting help from him," Zoë said, proud of being able to give them an inkling into the way Shamyl handled his affairs. She felt elated. The news that Europe was at war was overshadowed by her joy at hearing a Frenchman talk, at seeing two men from the great outer world she had lost. For a moment she craved to be back in Paris, settled safely at Roxane's side, saying to herself, "All I have been through was but a dream." "Oh, when you get back to Paris," she said to the Frenchman, "please look up my aunts and tell them I'm alive and well." She gave him their name and address. To write anything down would be unsafe, he said, repeating the name "Chabout" and the address she had given him several times to memorize them.

Zoë and the two men, intent on what they were saying, never noticed Daniel-Sultan until he appeared in their midst. For once he

221

had discarded his gorgeous blue-and-green attire and was dressed in a gray tcherkeska richly decorated at the edges with gold; a small white-and-gold turban was wound around his gray fur cap. When Zoë saw him she felt cold all over. If he chose to accuse her of sending a secret message to her people, it would be the end of her. But he flashed one of those strange blissful smiles at her, saying in Russian, "Don't go!"

Zoë lowered her veil and remained motionless, wondering what was coming next, not in the least reassured by his treacherous smile.

Daniel-Sultan spoke to the Frenchman, his unpleasant nasal voice drawing out every syllable. "As you see, Sir Envoy from France, we have a compatriot of yours in our midst. By a concurrence of unfortunate circumstances she is our prisoner, but she will tell you we are treating her well. However, she would be treated even better if she gave up the idea of returning to the Russians, our common enemies. There would be no question of her being a prisoner then. She would live as an honored friend and ally, under the protection of my daughter, Kazi-Mahomma's wife, until the war came to an end."

It was not the first time Daniel-Sultan had tried to persuade her to remain with his daughter. What his purpose was in doing this, she did not know, but the thought terrified her. She dared not express her feelings aloud in front of him, and she murmured in a strained voice, "Oh no! I cannot leave my friends." The Frenchman must have understood, for he smiled and nodded to her encouragingly before following his English colleague and Daniel-Sultan to Shamyl's house.

Zoë returned to her room. She undressed and slipped under her blankets, but sleep did not return. For more than an hour she lay there staring at the ceiling, turning Daniel-Sultan's words over and over in her mind. He had seen her talking to the Frenchman. She knew she was in his power now. That this should happen now, when all their troubles seemed to be coming to an end, filled her with anguish. For Isaak Gramoff, Prince David's emissary, was getting close to a final settlement with Shamyl and his Naibs. They had come down in their demands to two hundred thousand rubles, and, as Princess Anna had said only the other day, "Soon they will accept the forty thousand David has offered them. They have no real sense of the value of money." Jemaleddin, they had been told, was with Prince David in Hassaf-Yourt, waiting for the exchange. Freedom, happiness, all she wanted most in life seemed almost within reach. And now this! Cold fear clutched at Zoë's heart.

In the meantime Daniel-Sultan was talking to Shamyl. The envoys had been dismissed with a vague promise to have their proposals reconsidered at some later date, and Kazi-Mahomma had accompanied them to the guest room situated to the right of the main entrance. There they were to be given a meal and allowed to sleep until the morning. Shamyl had expected Daniel-Sultan to take his leave, too, but the latter had remained seated on his red cushion.

"I must speak to you of the Frenchwoman, O Imam!" Shamyl frowned, and Daniel-Sultan hurried on: "The French envoy has seen her. He, too, is of the opinion that she should not be returned to the Russians!" The Frenchman had said nothing of the kind, but Daniel-Sultan had no scruples about lying as a means to an end.

Shamyl made a wry face. The subject was distasteful to him. "We have discussed this before, Daniel-Sultan. You know the circumstances. The Frenchwoman must be returned with Anna and Varvara. I have accepted David Tchavchavadzé's terms. I never break my word. Why do you trouble me with this again?"

Daniel-Sultan lowered his eyes and bowed his head respectfully. "Fatherly love prompts me, O Imam! I have but the happiness of our children at heart—your son and my daughter." Shamyl knew of Daniel-Sultan's great love for his daughter Karimat and his face relented a little. "Imam, your eyes have seen and your heart has told you that our children are not happy in their married life. My Karimat is not accustomed to the life here. She feels discontented and miserable. She was brought up among worldly women who read books and can discuss many subjects. If this Frenchwoman—Zoë-djan, as they call her—were to become her companion, she would be much happier. And I am sure she would then find a way of making Kazi-Mahomma happy too!"

Shamyl's face became stern again. "Your Karimat is a willful girl. She must find a way without such inducements!"

Daniel-Sultan had been toying with his string of amber beads. Now he raised both hands to heaven. "How can she, O Imam, when your son deserts her all the time? And do you know why he does it? Because he feels humiliated by Karimat's superior knowledge of the world! Ah! I lay great hopes in Jemaleddin! He, too, has acquired a knowledge of the outside world. He will be able to enlighten his brother." He looked at Shamyl out of the corner of his eye. "And speaking of Jemaleddin, O Imam, again the Frenchwoman, Zoë-djan, comes to my mind."

223

Having said this in a tone calculated to arouse Shamyl's curiosity, Daniel-Sultan lowered his eyes and toyed with his beads.

Shamyl looked at him keenly. "And why does the name of my son make you think of the Frenchwoman?"

Daniel-Sultan sighed. "You have been longing for your son's return, O Imam. You have been making plans for his happiness. You have gone so far as to choose a wife for him, and your choice has been a wise one. Kahjio's granddaughter Zulma will make him a gentle wife." He sighed again and shrugged his shoulders. "But will she give him happiness? No. Like my Karimat, he will feel lonely, empty inside. Ah! How different it would be if the Frenchwoman were to find favor in his eyes! And if she embraced the faith of Islam, as Shouanet did when she discovered the greatness of your soul, she could become his second wife. Yes, things would be different then. Just as they have been with you, Imam, ever since Shouanet became your wife."

Shamyl stood up, perturbed. His face was flushed, his eyes glistening. "Why do you tempt me in this way, Daniel-Sultan? Your words are idle. My promise cannot be broken!"

Daniel-Sultan was standing, too, with bowed head. "What promise, Imam? Will you keep your promise if I give you proof the Frenchwoman sent a secret message to her people?"

Shamyl's conflicting emotions showed clearly in his face. Daniel-Sultan's words about Jemaleddin had sunk deep. He would have liked to detain Zoë, but to stoop to the low level of intrigue was distasteful to him. He knew Daniel-Sultan's scheming nature. In his heart he despised him, though he did his best to conceal it. He needed Daniel-Sultan as an ally. "Has she?" he asked at length, looking down at the fat little man.

"Yes, Imam, yes. I caught her whispering to the French envoy."

If he had wanted to, Shamyl could have accepted this as a proof of Zoë's guilt, but his dignity forbade him to do so. "What they said to one another is beyond our knowledge, Daniel-Sultan. Besides, her people are very far away."

Daniel-Sultan bowed over his beads, as though concentrating on a reverent prayer. "Oh, Allah!" he murmured. "Help me to forget this moment! Oh, had I never witnessed the weakness of so great a man!"

His words stung Shamyl to the core. He turned his back on Daniel-Sultan and went to the door leading to his bedroom. There he stopped. "Search the envoys!" he commanded abruptly. "If you find any written proof of her guilt, the woman will be your slave!"

224

And thus the danger that had hung over Zoë's head was temporarily dispelled. The envoys were made to strip; their clothes were searched. And when the Frenchman remarked with sarcasm, "Even if there were such a note, how would you know it? It would be written in French," Daniel-Sultan smiled at him gently. "I know the Latin alphabet. I know she is called either Duval or Chabout. I would recognize the names." But convinced at last of the futility of his search, he lost his suave manner and stamped out of the room.

16   A few days later Shamyl left for a prolonged stay with his troops. He rode out of the seraglio on a white horse, looking austere and yet magnificent in a white tcherkeska edged with black fur, high red leather boots, and a white turban wound around a black fur cap.

A long, dreary winter set in. With his departure, life in the seraglio seemed to have come to a standstill. Shouanet remained friendly but a little aloof, spending most of her time in her rooms. Aminet had offered Zoë some diversion at first, amusing herself at the expense of old Kahjio and making Zoë go up to him and touch his hand. The old man would then spit on the ground and rush back to his rooms to wash his hand seven times. But when Zoë heard that his shrewish young wife kept him out of her bed for seven consecutive nights, claiming he was still unclean, she refused to do it again; and Aminet turned her back on her, exclaiming, "You are dull!" From then on she spent most of her time in Zulma's tower, listening to Zulma's songs and dreaming of Kazi-Mahomma. "She is happy that way," Zoë said with sudden insight into Aminet's wild, capricious nature that despised everything within reach and adored the unattainable.

The cold had become intense, and when the fire was lit, it either scorched the captives or smoked them out of their room. As a result, the two princesses fell seriously ill and the children and the nurses were constantly ailing. Zoë alone did not succumb, marveling at times at her own iron constitution. The whole weight of those dreary weeks fell on her shoulders. At times she felt so disheartened and depressed that she was ready to throw everything up and sob like a child. And on such occasions she would sit down, pressing the back of her head against the wall and closing her eyes. "Don't think of the mountain, Zoë-djan. Don't look up or down. Just go step by step!"

225

Zoë was not the only one whose spirits were low that winter. The whole of Russia and most of western Europe were caught in a thick mesh of depression. Englishmen, Frenchmen, and Russians were dying in the Crimea, and Balaklava, Malakoff, Sevastopol were the tragic names of the day. In his Winter Palace in St. Petersburg, Emperor Nicholas spent restless nights on the narrow army cot he used for a bed. Like his brother Alexander before him when Napoleon had invaded Russia, Nicholas had sworn not to make peace so long as enemy forces remained on Russian soil. But as the months dragged by it became more and more evident he could not live up to his word. His spirit was in a turmoil.

And in faraway Paris, in the stuffy little living room of the Chabout sisters, Emilie, Clotilde, Roxane, and Auguste Tresor, dressed all in black, stood at rigid attention in front of the mantel. Through some error the postal authorities in Tiflis had returned Roxane's last letter to Zoë marked, "Unable to deliver. Addressee killed in a raid." Solemnly Roxane moved to the mantel and hung Zoë's miniature on the wall under General Chabout's portrait. And around the miniature she placed a tiny laurel wreath with a bow of black crepe tied to it. For a second or two they stood in silence, their heads bowed. Then Roxane stepped back, lining herself with the others, and Emilie's bugle call resounded through the house.

But back in the Caucasus, not far from Zoë, at the foot of the mountains, it was Sasha who had given in to the gloom of depression. Ivan Saltykoff's company was of no help; nothing in the Caucasus pleased him. Sasha and he were billeted together in a small peasant hut. They spent most of their evenings alone, a bottle between them —cognac when such was available, vodka when nothing else was to be had. Saltykoff would raise his glass, saying in a lugubrious voice, "The slough of Despond, friend Sasha, was a merry little place compared to this vaunted Caucasus of yours!"

And Sasha would reply, "You have nothing to complain about, my friend. You have your carriage and your horses now. What else do you want?"

The fact that he had been permitted to buy a carriage and horses and drive them around made Saltykoff all the more homesick for the Kolomna road among its spacious fields and forests. And to tell the truth, there was little to enliven the spirits of two disgruntled, disheartened young men in the small settlement in which the Nijegorodsky Regiment was stationed at the time. It lay on a bleak plain at the foot of the mountains, and over it hung a constant pall of dust that

settled down slowly but mercilessly over the roofs of the low buildings, over the dry mud roads, and over the only two trees in the
settlement that grew outside the regimental headquarters. And when
it rained, one waded in mud up to one's knees. Since Saltykoff
and Sasha had reported for duty nothing had happened, not
even a skirmish with the enemy, to enliven the monotony of their
existence.

"Where is that fool Sidor?" Sasha cried, thumping his fist on the
table. Sidor Poushka appeared on the threshold. "How many times
must I tell you to watch the bottle? Never let it stand empty in front
of us!"

A vague smile spread over Sidor Poushka's good-natured face. He
opened his round eyes wide, muttering, "Oh! I did not understand!"

"You never understand anything I say. To think that this oaf is
Poushka's nephew!" Here his real grievance came to the fore and he
vented his spleen on Poushka, complaining bitterly about his long
absence.

But the day came, shortly before Christmas, when Poushka finally
showed up. Sasha was so happy to see him that he could have cried
with joy, but for a little while, luxuriating in his grievance, he feigned
indifference. It did not last long, however. When he had read the
letter Poushka had brought, he forgot everything. He sat stunned,
staring dully into a corner of the room, the letter dropping out of his
hand to the floor. He did not look at Poushka, nor did Poushka look
at him. He stood in front of Sasha with bowed head, his face drawn,
his cheeks twitching a little. Tears came suddenly to Sasha's eyes.
And bending down, he picked up the letter and read it over again. It
was from Hélène, written in Romantzevo early in November.

Darling Sasha,
I am at a loss how to begin this letter, knowing the conflicting emotions
it will bring you; for the past can never be quite wiped out, can it? And
the future is still so uncertain! Natalie is no more, may God rest her tor-
mented soul. But to explain the strange circumstances of her death I must
start from the very beginning. You know how she was, poor thing, always
vacillating between adoration and hatred for those who surrounded her.
Well, she developed *un de ces béguins* for Poushka soon after his arrival
in Romantzevo. She would go on her daily rides only if Poushka drove the
horses; she refused to eat unless Poushka served her. Then one afternoon
they went for a sleigh ride—it had snowed heavily the night before. Natalie
insisted on going alone with him, refusing to allow her maid to accompany
her. They say Poushka got worried. He begged her to take her maid along,

but she grew so agitated they decided to humor her. And it was in this state of mind that poor Natalie went on her last ride. Several hours passed, and they did not return. It was past five and night had fallen when a search party was sent out. They found Poushka sitting in the snow, dazed and half frozen. The sled had overturned and Natalie lay dead, a deep gash over her left temple, where they say the sled must have hit her. . . . That is all I can tell you, Sasha dear, except that Mamma called Poushka into her room and remained closeted with him for over an hour. After that he went to confession and communion. Later he said to me, mysteriously, "The ways of the Almighty are often devious. Now Alexandr Dimitrievitch is free and the Tsar has been cleansed of his sin."

Poushka gave Sasha no time to speak. He had read his emotions in his face and was afraid he might break down. He said gruffly, "You must pull yourself together, Alexandr Dimitrievitch. You have been behaving badly while I was away. You were unfair to poor Sidor. He is a good, willing lad. And you and Prince Saltykoff have been moping together over solitary, melancholy bottles. That is not good!" Sasha wanted to put in a word, but Poushka stopped him. "We will keep Sidor with us, Alexandr Dimitrievitch. I will train him, and he will make a good valet for you someday when I am gone. And now you must go over to the officers' mess and get good and drunk with young men who have no chips on their shoulders!" He stopped suddenly and looked around. "What time is it, Alexandr Dimitrievitch?"

It was almost four. Without another word Poushka turned to an icon that hung in a corner of the room. He crossed himself, bowed low from the waist, and began to mumble a prayer.

"Poushka, what are you doing?" Sasha exclaimed in surprise.

For a full moment Poushka remained silent, his back rigid. Then he said, without turning around, "The priest gave me a prayer to say at this hour. I must say it every day of my life wherever I am. And now run along to the mess hall, Alexandr Dimitrievitch, and get nicely, wholesomely drunk. Tomorrow all will be well again!"

As Sasha tiptoed out of the room, closing the door gently behind him, he saw Poushka bow to the icon again, and he heard the words, "God have mercy on my sinful soul!"

Things began to brighten up after Poushka's return, and the new year brought new hope. Early in January, Isaak Gramoff, Prince David's emissary, paid his last call on Shamyl and won a final settlement. Prince David could have chosen no better man to carry on the negotiations. Gramoff possessed to a nicety the knowledge of the

Tchetchen language and of the manners and customs of the mountaineers. From the very start Shamyl had taken a liking to this quiet man with his dark serious face and dignified manners. He called him "Isai-bek" and sometimes, affectionately, "My Isai-bek."

On that day Shamyl sat enthroned in his council chamber, Kazi-Mahomma, Daniel-Sultan, Kahjio, and all the Naibs squatting on the floor along the walls. Isaak Gramoff stood facing Shamyl. "Bring a cushion for my Isai-bek. Let him be seated!" Shamyl exclaimed suddenly. It was a sign that Prince David's offer of forty thousand rubles in silver had been accepted. Kahjio had been the last to raise an objection, to show that the honor of a matrimonial alliance with Shamyl had not blinded him to the interests of the people. He had rubbed his hooked nose and had said, "Isai-bek, you and your prince amaze me, offering us only forty thousand! Why, if the Imam required it, he could have a whole arba full of silver!"

"Do not be amazed, Kahjio," Gramoff replied with a polite bow. "The forty thousand rubles the prince offers you will fill two whole arbas!" The Naibs looked at him incredulously, but his reply had clinched the matter.

Shamyl's next words might have seemed inconsistent to anyone unacquainted with the ways of the mountaineers, but Gramoff knew they were leading up to something important. And he listened attentively. "Isai-bek, now that you have seen our country, tell us what you think of our roads and of the reception we have given you."

Gramoff looked straight at Shamyl. "If you will allow me to speak candidly, Imam, I will say this. Your roads are very bad and very dirty, made almost impassable by your woods, your rivers, and your defiles. But the hospitality of Your Highness is everything that could be desired."

Shamyl nodded his approval. "I am glad to hear you say this. Now you can understand why the powerful Tsar, who refuses to submit to three other tsars, can do nothing with me, though he never ceases to send his armies against me. I ought to anoint all my trees with oil and mix the mud of my roads with fragrant honey!" He looked around with a smile that was returned by all those present. Then his face became serious again. "Isai-bek, I have decided to build a road over which I can conduct my honored guests, the princesses, in comfort to the border and bring my son back to Dargo-Veden. It will take some time and we must all be patient a little longer. Tell Prince Tchavchavadzé to have everything ready for the exchange early in

March!" He leaned forward eagerly in his chair. "Tell me, Isai-bek! What has my son been doing all these months?"

"Your son, Imam, has been studying his native tongue. As you know, he had almost forgotten it during his years in Russia. But he said, 'I must be able to converse with my father when I see him again.' "

Shamyl raised his hands and looked up at the ceiling. "Allah be praised! Then the delays have not been in vain!"

The glad news of the forthcoming liberation of the captives spread rapidly in all directions, reaching Tiflis two weeks later. When Madame Tollet heard about it from Nina Alexandrovna, she remained gasping for breath, a fish out of water. It took all of Nina Alexandrovna's serenity and tact to calm her. "My heart! My poor old heart!" Madame Tollet kept muttering. But a few happy tears relieved the strain, and before leaving Nina Alexandrovna her joy had turned to apprehension. "Everyone will be happy," she said anxiously, "everyone but poor little Zoë-djan."

The news that the Tsar had forbidden Sasha to marry Zoë had reached Tiflis long ago. And on her way home from Prince David's house Madame Tollet kept repeating to herself, "Zoë-djan does not know it. What a shock it will be for the poor child!" She kept thinking of it all day, saying to Monsieur Tollet that evening at supper, "Poor Zoë-djan! I am sure she does not even know she will soon be free. Those wily mountaineers will probably keep it a secret from her to the very last minute. And then, when free, she will learn there can be no happiness for her with Captain Novoselsky! I'm afraid the sudden shock will be too much for her."

When Monsieur Tollet protested, pointing out the absurdity of her fears, she lost her temper. "*Mais voyons, espèce do nougat!* Don't you understand? We should try to warn the child and tell her she will be welcome in our home!"

Monsieur Tollet thought it wiser to drop the matter. "There is no way of sending a message," he said to himself. "She will soon forget about it."

But he had underestimated Madame Tollet's tenacity. The busybody side of her nature was working overtime. She kept weighing the problem in her mind, thinking of it by day, dreaming of it by night, until it had acquired distorted proportions, and the necessity of warning Zoë of the blow that awaited her had become a matter of life and death. She did not even get angry when three days later Monsieur Tollet introduced old Spindarian into her storeroom, say-

230

ing, "You must discuss the matter with my wife," and left. She merely fixed her visitor with a cold eye. "I thought I made it quite clear we did not wish to do business with you, Monsieur Spindarian!"

Old Spindarian was sitting on the edge of his chair, his podgy hands folded in a gesture of supplication. "Have a heart, dear Madame Tollet. My customer demands your sweets, nothing but your sweets. It's a big order, and you will run no risks. Absolutely none! I will provide you with boxes so that your name will not even appear anywhere." The tip of his long fleshy nose seemed to rest in the curve of his smile. "Think of those poor, noble captives pining away in the mountains among those wild men! Wouldn't this be a golden opportunity to send them a gift, a small message of consolation?"

Was this good sales talk, or had a devil prompted him? No one will ever know. The fact remains, his words left Madame Tollet breathless. She stood up precipitately and paced up and down the room. For one moment only did she hesitate, glancing at old Spindarian out of the corner of her eye. "How could the bon Dieu send such an ugly messenger?" But, "Beauty is skin deep, and the bon Dieu knows best," she rebuked herself, coming to a stop in front of him. "I will accept your order for the very last time and on one condition only!" She raised a warning finger and looked at him severely. "There will be a box tied with a pink ribbon. It must be delivered into the hands of my friend, Zoia Ivanovna Duval."

Madame Tollet was kept busy next morning filling the boxes Spindarian had sent her. And when she got to the one intended for Zoë, her heart began to beat faster. She filled it with sweets, carefully avoiding the cherub wings. When the box was full, she picked up a pair of cherub wings, a pink strawberry one, Zoë's favorite. She turned it over and held it upside down between thumb and forefinger. She frowned, she smiled, she frowned again. And seizing a small pastry tube, she squeezed out the white frosting carefully, tracing a capital N to stand for "Novoselsky." Then she added, in a minute but clear hand: "is not for you. Come to us when you have been freed."

She waited until the frosting had hardened. Then she laid the pink cherub wings tenderly on top of the other sweets and closed the box.

231

17   In one respect only Madame Tollet had been right. The
       captives were not told about their forthcoming liberation.
The seraglio knew how to keep a secret when secrecy was the order
of the day. Not until the eighth of March—three days before the
final date set for the exchange—did Shamyl, accompanied by Shouanet, come to their door to announce the good news. "On the
eleventh you will be free and I will have my son!"

The women sat in dead silence, afraid to break down and sob
with joy. And for the next two days Zoë walked on air, hardly noticing what was going on around her. Only two episodes stood out
clearly in her mind, both of them connected with Karimat.

First there had been her arrival that same afternoon. At one time or
another Zoë had heard her praises sung by most of the women in the
seraglio, their voices acquiring a special tone when they exclaimed,
"Ah, Karimat! Beautiful! Lovely! Gracious!" And Zoë stood outside
her door now, together with the other captives, curious to see what
this young woman was like. She heard the old creaky doors being
opened, and her eyes remained glued to the end of the wooden partition. Kazi-Mahomma rode in first, wearing a white fur cap and a
white cloak. Behind him came Karimat, sitting gracefully on a
golden-brown mare and followed by the servant maids who had met
her at the door. An involuntary "Oh!" escaped Salome and Marie.
They had never seen such a resplendent costume. A mantle of gold
brocade lined with sable fell from her shoulders, and her face was
covered with a thin veil embroidered in gold. Zoë gazed at her,
entranced. It was like something out of *A Thousand and One
Nights.*

The maids helped Karimat to dismount, and while her horse was
being led away to the stables by Hassan she stood there, taller than
the other women, receiving ceremonious bows, first from Shouanet
and then from Aminet. She bowed back with ease and grace, and the
ceremony over, Shamyl's four daughters surrounded her, embracing
and kissing her. They led her to a guest room on the other side of
the court, and Karimat was seen no more that day.

The following afternoon Karimat sent a message to Zoë, asking
her to come and see her. Zoë found Karimat alone in her room, sitting on a cushion, busy embroidering a soft red leather belt. When
she saw Zoë, she rose to her feet. Smiling, she took a step forward
and held out her hand. "Thank you so much for coming and giving
me this opportunity of making your acquaintance," she said in Russian. She picked up something from a nearby shelf and, to Zoë's

amazement, held up the ruby-and-diamond pendant with the miniatures of Zoë's parents. "A sale was held this morning of valuables
taken from Tsinandali," she explained. "I bought this. I believe it is
yours. Do you mind my having it?"

"Oh no," Zoë exclaimed. "I am glad it is yours now." And to
herself she added, "A present from Roxane to the Caucasus!"

She did not know what to admire most, Karimat's polished manners or her majestic beauty. She stood, slender and graceful, her
white teeth flashing with every smile; and when she spoke, the tip
of her small, straight nose bobbed up and down a tiny bit in a most
beguiling manner. Her hair was long and black, her hands pale and
delicate. She wore a long white chemise that touched the floor, con-
cealing her feet, and on top of it a knee-length tunic of dark crimson
lined with green taffeta and trimmed with satin ribbons of the same
color. The slashed sleeves of the tunic were held together with loops
and buttons of gold, revealing the long, white, tight-fitting sleeves of
the chemise. A small black silk handkerchief was tied around her
head, and over it a white muslin veil hung in loose folds down her
back. The front of her bodice was adorned with gold loops and buttons similar to those on her sleeves, and her gold crescent-shaped
earrings and the elaborate gold buckle on her belt were studded with
precious stones.

She offered Zoë a cushion and sat down again, picking up the belt
she had been embroidering. "I am making it for Jemaleddin," she
said casually. "All the women of the family have to give him a
present."

Zoë wanted to tell her she had heard a great deal about him, that
he was Sasha's best friend, but somehow she dared not mention
Sasha's name aloud—the joy of seeing him soon was too intense.
And she gazed for a while in silence at the red belt in Karimat's delicate hands.

They talked for a long time, of Paris, of Tiflis, of books they had
both read. Listening to her, Zoë forgot her surroundings. The Daghestan mountains and Shamyl's seraglio melted away, giving her a
foretaste of the world she was to regain so soon.

It had grown dark and a maid brought in a few tallow candles.
Zoë stood up reluctantly. Karimat stood up too, taking both Zoë's
hands in hers. "You were like a breath of fresh air to me. Oh, how
lucky you are to be leaving this place! You will meet people again
with whom you can talk, and I—never!"

Her voice broke. Zoë felt infinitely sorry for her, but there was

233

little she could say. She lowered her eyes, and they came to rest again on the red belt lying forgotten on the floor.

While Zoë and Karimat were spending the afternoon together, Daniel-Sultan was busy at the other end of the aoul, in the house he always occupied when he came to Dargo-Veden. He was sitting on a low divan among soft silk cushions, and around him were boxes of Tollet sweets that had been delivered that day. He was looking thoughtfully at a small box tied with a pink ribbon. Slowly he undid the ribbon and raised the lid. The pink cherub wings lay vivid against the dark background of chocolate candy. Laying them aside, he went through the whole box, examining every piece of candy meticulously. At last he threw them all back pell-mell. He was about to throw the cherub wings in, too, when something made him change his mind. He turned them over slowly in his hand, and his eyes lit up.

When he reached the seraglio he hurried to Karimat's room, but on the threshold he paused, his face puckered up with sudden anxiety. Karimat was on the floor, crying bitterly, her face buried in the cushion. Instantly he was on his knees beside her, murmuring tender words, demanding to know who had offended her.

"No one, Father." She sat up, wiping her eyes with her handkerchief. "The Frenchwoman, Zoë-djan, spent the afternoon with me, and now I feel lonelier than ever!" He drew up another cushion and sat down. "I am unhappy, Father! No one here likes me. The Imam was horrid to me today. He said, 'I am sorry to see that you are as vain as ever. Your gold mantle is vulgar and ostentatious, especially here in my house, where sobriety and simplicity are the rule!' "

Daniel-Sultan was about to say something, but he fell silent under the compelling look in her eyes. "It is all your fault, Father! You brought me here; you gave me in marriage to Kazi-Mahomma!"

There was real misery in Daniel-Sultan's eyes. "But, my child, what would your life have been like in Russia? There were no young men there of our faith and of our rank. You would have remained unmarried."

"Better that than living with Kazi-Mahomma! He is not even aware of me. I might be a piece of furniture for all he cares!"

"Be patient, Karimat. Shamyl won't live forever. As Kazi-Mahomma's father-in-law, I will be the real ruler. I will draw priceless metals out of our granite rocks. I will establish trade with other countries. I will bring culture to this land, make it prosperous, civilized. And you will be a real queen then, surrounded by a brilliant court!"

234

"But I don't want to be a queen! I want friends!"

With Karimat, Daniel-Sultan was always gentle. He spoke to her at length now, finding words that soothed, until at last, with a sigh, she rested her cheek on his knee. He stroked her head tenderly. "Everything will be all right, darling, everything will be all right. Just trust your old father." He remained silent for a moment and then smiled. "And now, Karimat, try to remember all the French you used to know and tell me what is written here."

Out of his pocket he drew his gold box studded with diamonds. He opened it and gave her the cherub wings. She looked at them closely, a little puzzled, reading the words slowly one by one. Finally she said, "I don't understand it. It says, 'N is not for you. Come to us when you have been freed.'" She sprang to her feet. "It must be for Zoë-djan! Oh, Father, let me run over and give it to her!"

He shook his head and replaced the cherub wings carefully in the box. "No, my dear. She will have plenty of sweets from now on. You know how greedy your old father is. I want to enjoy this one. But I will deliver the message. That is why I asked you to read it to me." He kissed her on the forehead and left the room.

Ten minutes later he was seated opposite Shamyl in the latter's house. Shamyl was looking at him in alarm, confused and a little bewildered. "If only you had listened to me long ago, O Imam, when I told you about the French envoy! It is all so clear now. She sent a message through him and this is the reply. N stands for Nicholas, the Tsar, and the whole message is a reminder of where her loyalty should lie. The Tollet candymakers are also French, you know." He looked boldly into Shamyl's eyes. "Your word is law, Imam. And you never break your word!"

Shamyl bowed his head in silence. His cat hopped into his lap, and absent-mindedly he scratched it behind the ears, lost in thought. For once he felt beaten. Daniel-Sultan was bound to spread the news about this secret message. The entire seraglio, the whole of Dargo-Veden knew what Shamyl had threatened to do in such a case. If he did not live up to his threat now, he would lose face with his people. And there was Daniel-Sultan to be considered too. He was capable of anything if Karimat continued to be unhappy. He might even go back to the Russians. The Russians, he said to himself, whatever they might do to Daniel-Sultan later, would accept his services as long as he was useful to them.

Furious, his fingers scratched harder. The cat stretched out its neck and miaowed with annoyance. Shamyl stroked it gently, apologizing in the purry tones he always used with his pet. Then he shook his head at Daniel-Sultan. "We have twenty-three prisoners here from Tsinandali, and twenty-three we must return. That is my agreement with Prince Tchavchavadzé. I never break my word!"

Daniel-Sultan's smile was full of indulgence. "Any child could solve that one," it seemed to say. "Release the officer we captured in the Tower of Pohali, O Imam. An officer is worth more than a woman."

To Shamyl this was an irrefutable argument. But he put up a last protest. "There must be no further delays. My son must be with me the day after tomorrow. If Anna and Varvara hear of this, they will refuse to leave!"

"That can be easily arranged." And leaning forward, Daniel-Sultan whispered at length into Shamyl's ear.

Shamyl put the cat down on the floor and stood up, picking the cherub wings off the small table beside him. He had regained all his composure now, all his dignity. "We must seal this bargain," he said disdainfully. He broke the cherub wings in two and handed one half to Daniel-Sultan. "Eat it, my friend, as a token of my regard!"

Daniel-Sultan smiled blissfully as he put his half of the cherub wings into his mouth. He chewed on it once or twice with relish and smacked his lips. And bowing respectfully, he waited for Shamyl to swallow his half. But with a sardonic smile Shamyl held it up for a second and then gave it to his cat.

18   That night Zoë fell asleep, happy, but in the early hours
       of the morning she awakened in terror. She had been dreaming of Karimat's red belt. It had come floating through the air, coiling itself around her neck, choking and strangling her. She tried to scream, but she could not. She thrashed about, clawing at her neck in a vain effort to free herself. Then all of a sudden she was free, and with a scream she awoke, or at least she thought she did. She sat up, her heart beating wildly, her face turned to the open door. On the threshold she saw a man in a long white tunic, like a tcherkeska, only plain, with none of its usual trappings. Not even a dagger dangled from the belt, and the belt he wore was Karimat's red belt. She could not see his face, his eyes were like two dark blotches, yet she knew he was the man of her dream. He raised

236

his hand, saying in a whisper that she alone could hear, "Take courage. I am watching over you!"

It was then that she opened her eyes. The doorway stood empty. She was wide awake now, her heart pumping slowly, ominously. No strength, no promise of security had come with the dream. From his words she had drawn nothing but disquieting auguries. For a wild moment she felt like waking Princess Varvara, but what could she tell her that wouldn't sound childish and absurd? She glanced around the room. They were all sleeping, the sound sleep that comes before dawn. She looked at them wistfully—Princess Anna with her arm thrown behind her head, Princess Varvara as still as an effigy, the children curled up like kittens, and the three nurses sprawled across their mattresses, fat Yakovlevna on her back, her mouth wide open, snoring like a trooper. It was their last night together. Tomorrow they would all be free, sleeping in their beds, each one to her own slumbers and in her proper place. Tonight was the closing of a long, hard chapter. It saddened her. She got up stealthily and began to dress.

Outside, with the gray dawn creeping through the court of the seraglio, her forebodings seemed to vanish. She breathed deeply of the cold, fresh air, sighing with relief. Yet somewhere deep inside of her the question remained unanswered: Why had he appeared to her that night? Why had he said, "Take courage. I am watching over you"? Why?

Shortly before seven three arbas, drawn by horses instead of oxen, were brought into the court; the first one for Princess Anna, her children, and their nurses, the second for Princess Varvara, George, Vassilissa, and Zoë. Zoë gazed at it, her eyes big with happiness. The women of the seraglio were milling around it now, hiding it from view, and she glanced at the third arba, which was to carry the maids. She searched the court for them and saw Daniel-Sultan coming toward her. He spoke to her in his suavest manner: "Isn't it time you went to fetch the maids?"

She complied willingly. It seemed quite natural—the maids had been her special charge throughout their stay in Dargo-Veden. Daniel-Sultan walked with her to the main entrance, his eyes never leaving Zoë. And when Zoë stepped into the outer court, she heard him call out, "Au revoir, madame." She glanced over her shoulder, but the big doors had closed.

Instead of the Benevolent Mullah, six silent Murids dressed in black were waiting to escort her. This filled her with sudden alarm.

She hesitated and turned back, but the Murids ranged themselves into a silent semicircle, blocking the way to the door. She had no choice. She walked ahead briskly, nervously, consoling herself with the thought that they would not dare do anything to her at this point.

The main street was lined with people waiting to see the departure of the princesses. They watched her curiously as she passed by in her gray dress and gray bonnet, a long veil hanging down over her face, her silent escort behind her. She turned left into the narrow lane, the Murids following her. She knew the way by heart. Without hesitating she took a right and then a left turn. Soon she would pass by a door in the wall, and after that she would come to the square. She was almost running now, anxious to join the maids; the silence of the Murids behind her was becoming oppressive. At last she saw the square ahead of her. She began to breathe more freely. But at that very moment the door in the wall flew open. A few more Murids stepped out, blocking the way. And Hadji-Kheriett appeared in front of her.

At the sight of him her blood ran cold. "Have the maids been moved to another house?" she asked in a feeble, trembling voice. But she got no answer, nor was she given time to think. Silently the Murids closed in on her, pressing her closer to the open door; and Hadji-Kheriett pushed her in.

She was standing in a garden now. She heard the door bang behind her, and someone lifted her veil, pulling off her bonnet. It dangled by its ribbon from her neck. Mechanically she tugged at the end of the ribbon and the bonnet fell to the ground. She stooped to pick it up, but Hadji-Kheriett shouted, "Stand still!"

They blindfolded her, and a hand grabbed her by the wrist. She tried to ask where they were taking her, but her voice failed her. Instinctively she knew they had entered a house and had gone through several rooms, and when finally the handkerchief was removed from her eyes, she saw she was alone in a small room with Hadji-Kheriett.

"What does this mean!" she exploded, regaining her powers of speech. "Where are the maids?"

His smile, showing a row of sharp teeth, was like a snarl. "You are not a princess, you need no maids!" And he left her, closing the door behind him. She heard the key turn in the latch.

The walls of the room were hung with Persian rugs, and in a corner stood a low divan covered with soft silk cushions. She was shaking from head to foot. She sat down, clutching her hands together to stop them from trembling. Never in her life had she been so scared. The silence of the Murids, the gaping door, and now this silent room. "No! This cannot be happening to me!" she cried. "Let me out! Let me out!" She rushed to the door. She pounded on it and rattled the handle. She thought she heard a chuckle on the other side, and then all was silent again.

Slowly she dragged herself across the room. Her feet weighed a ton; she sat down heavily. She shut her eyes and pressed her knuckles to her temples. "Don't lose your head! Something is bound to happen. Don't lose your head!" She tried to think rationally. Anna and Varvara would notice her absence. They would refuse to leave without her. Perhaps even now they were protesting, demanding her return. She opened her eyes again. The low divan was across the room from her. She stared at it blankly, unable to realize at first what she was sitting on. Accustomed as she had become to sitting on the floor, she felt perched unusually high. And for the first time she noticed the chairs—dainty gilt chairs, the likes of which were found in Western ballrooms. She was sitting on one, and beside her stood a large round table inlaid with different kinds of wood. She knew then that she was in Daniel-Sultan's house. Who else in the Daghestan would have such furniture? And a silver bowl stood on the table, filled with Tollet sweets. The hopelessness of her situation overwhelmed her. With a moan she fell forward on the table, sobbing.

An hour went by, maybe more. Zoë could not tell. Very gradually she became conscious of the rumbling of many voices. She listened intently. A voice was shouting nearby, somewhere on the other side of the wall. Quickly she glanced around the room. High up, close to the ceiling, she saw a small window with iron bars in it. She dragged the table across the room, pushing it against the wall. She put a chair on the table and scrambled onto the chair. She could see out of the window now. There was a garden wall in front of her, and beyond it the main street. People were waving and shouting, craning their necks in the direction of the seraglio. The first arba came in sight. She could see the children in it, and the nurses and Princess Anna, her face veiled. She was standing, looking around, searching the crowd. Zoë tried to open the window, but it stuck. Desperately she tugged at it several times. Finally it flew open, almost throwing her to the floor, and she grabbed the iron bars with both hands. The arba was passing by. She tried to scream, but her voice was weak and shaky.

The second arba was approaching now with Princess Varvara, George, and Vassilissa in it. That was where she belonged. In her agony Zoë prayed, "O God! Let them hear me!" And suddenly, as though piercing a membrane, her voice came tearing, shrieking out: "Help! Varvara! Help! Save me!"

She saw Princess Varvara look around, startled. She screamed again. But now men were cursing behind her and the chair was knocked out from under her feet. For a moment she clung to the bars, still screaming. A pair of arms grabbed her around the legs, hands were tugging at her, and she let go. She fell. And a rough hand clamped down on her mouth.

The Murids carried her, unresisting, through the garden and out into the narrow street. There was no question in their minds as to what should be done. To them she was but a rebellious slave for whom no punishment could be too severe.

Zoë lay very still. Nothing mattered any more. Let them carry her to the very ends of the world. But when she saw it—the black, gaping mouth of the pit—her whole body stiffened. A sudden mad frenzy took possession of her. She hit out. One of the Murids, taken by surprise, let go of her leg, and she kicked him with all her might. She heard him groan as he doubled up. She did not scream, she did not think; she was like one possessed. She scratched, she bit, she drew blood. It was a dreadful, silent struggle between a crazed woman and half a dozen panting men. They held her down, dragging her mercilessly on. Dimly she saw the face of Hadji-Kheriett close to hers, distorted, quivering. With a sharp twist of her body she freed an arm and dug her nails into his eye. She heard him scream in agony and rage. Someone grabbed her by the hair, shook her violently. The black mouth of the pit danced in front of her eyes; the putrid smell hit her nostrils. The sky swung low; the earth heaved. And she fell, unconscious, to the ground.

Part Four

The Friend

1 Emperor Nicholas lay dead in his Winter Palace. Some said
he had taken his life, leaving the way clear for his son and
heir, Alexander, to patch up a peace, which his solemn oath had
forbidden him to consider. At the outbreak of the war he had
boasted grimly, "Generals January and February will be my strong-
est allies"; but the two "generals" proved to be impartial. Furthermore, Russian troops that had been ordered to recapture Eupatoria
—the first Crimean town taken by the allied forces—had made a
poor showing and had failed in their objective; and the snowbound
roads of Russia were strewn with the bodies of Russian soldiers
who had died of cold and hunger on their way to the Crimea. It was
the realization of his failure that broke the spirit of the Iron Tsar;
and when "General February" hit him, he flung away a life that
with a little care might have been saved.

For almost thirty years Nicholas had held Russia in an iron grip.
Haunted by the memory of December 1825, when at the very out-

set of his reign he had crushed an army uprising led by men demanding a constitution, he resorted to rigid discipline and repressions to keep his subjects under control. The preservation of autocracy, which alone, he thought, could bring true happiness to his people, became his life's aim, and in this he proved to be indefatigable. His energies seemed unlimited, and in the end he succeeded in building up a frontage of strength and order. The death of such a ruler in the midst of an unsuccessful war was bound to be followed by overtures of peace, for war held no interest to Alexander, his son. It was well known that Alexander's aims were of a different fiber and he needed peace to put them into effect. He was dreaming of freedom and human rights, of the abolition of serfdom and the establishment of a new order in which Tsar and people could work together for the betterment of their country. An epoch of great reforms hung over Russia.

All this and much more went through Sasha's mind as he stood lined up with the rest of the regiment on the parade ground outside the small settlement, every man beside his horse. The news of Nicholas' death had reached them early in March; and the regiment, after taking an oath of allegiance to Alexander II, was attending a Requiem Mass for the dead Emperor. At an improvised altar draped in black, the priest in his black-and-silver vestments intoned the service for the dead while the regimental choir sang the responses. The sad, melodious chants of the Russian Orthodox funeral service were stirring, and Sasha, listening to the strong, clear voices of the choir, felt tears stinging his eyes and throat. Regimental banners were lowered, and the choir sang an "Eternal Remembrance." A gust of wind whipped up small, whirling clouds of dust, chasing them past the silent immobile regiment and scattering them across the wide plain. Dust, and the dying notes of a prayer for immortality.

When finally the regiment broke ranks and Sasha had returned to his billet with Saltykoff, he found a short note from Jemal. "I want to be the first to wish you a long life of happiness," Jemal wrote. "On the eleventh of March, early in the morning, the captives will be free, and with them, of course, the one you love best on earth." It was characteristic of him not to say a word about his own future, except to wind up with "Good-by, Sasha, and thank you for your friendship, the memory of which I will always treasure." And there was a postscript, saying, "Give my regards to Saltykoff, and tell him not to drive his horses and carriage too close to my father's lands."

When Sasha read this aloud, Saltykoff roared with laughter. "I will not have to suffer these roads and mountains much longer. With Alexander Nicolaievitch on the throne you will soon have your Zoë-djan and I will have my Kolomna road!" He poured himself a drink. "To steady my joy," he explained, adding somewhat wistfully, "One thing I will say for this filthy hole of a place. I will leave it, thanking heaven for the existence of our brigadier, Baron Wrangel!"

Saltykoff was the problem child of the regiment. Everyone liked him for his good nature, but ever since the day he arrived dressed as a yamstchik and accompanied by the tall gendarme in blue, no one really knew where he belonged and what to make of him. A brief written confirmation had come through from St. Petersburg, stating that until further orders Saltykoff was to be considered a junior officer of the Nijegorodsky Regiment. That was all the official information they received. But General Wrangel had known his father and had taken him under his wing. It was through his intercession that Saltykoff had been granted permission to buy himself a carriage and horses, and later arrangements had been made for him to act as messenger between the regiment and the brigade headquarters. Three times a week he carried the messages, and the only thing that dimmed his pleasure was the fact that he was not permitted to dress as a yamstchik. He had to drive his horses in his officer's uniform, with Sidor Poushka, now his temporary orderly, sitting behind him in the carriage. "A fine passenger indeed, this Sidor," he would complain. "Takes orders from his coachman and gives no tips!"

He was about to raise his glass when he noticed a faraway look in Sasha's eyes. "I see you are thinking of something. I bet I know what it is, and I think you are right. You should be present when the exchange of captives takes place. And, damn it all, I should be the one to drive you there!" He clamped a hand on Sasha's shoulder. "Wait here, friend Sasha, while I go and stir up the powers that be and see what can be done about it."

He succeeded in stirring up the regimental commander's sense of humor, which did the trick. To obtain a leave for Sasha was not difficult. Every officer in the regiment had heard of his love for Zoë; they thought it romantic and sympathized with it. But there was no reason for Saltykoff to go, and the regimental adjutant to whom he had applied told him so bluntly. Whereupon Saltykoff grinned. "There is every reason, my friend. You see, I am in love too!"

The adjutant had a somewhat mordant sense of humor. He said, "I didn't know Shamyl was releasing a captive horse."

Saltykoff threw back his head and laughed. "Oh no! I'm in love with the open road. All open roads! An open road is like a woman, smooth and easy at first, then suddenly beware! The Kolomna road is my wife, of course, but I have been torn away from her. The road to Baron Wrangel's headquarters—— Oh well!" He waved his hand in mock despair. "I know every dainty curve, every little dent. I know when to hold my horses and when to go full speed ahead. After a while it becomes monotonous, you know. Variety, variety is the essence of happiness! I must have my fling with a new road!"

When the regimental commander heard of this, he laughed till the tears ran down his cheeks, and a short leave of absence was granted to both Sasha and Saltykoff.

They reached Hassaf-Yourt on the ninth of March. Saltykoff drove all the way. Seated on the box, he spoke encouragingly to his horses and sang sad yamstchik songs to them. Sasha occupied the back seat, with Poushka at his side and Sidor opposite him on the bracket seat. Poushka, with his nepotic tendencies, was forever promoting Sidor. And since he ran the Novoselsky-Saltykoff household with undisputed authority, it was he who had decreed that Sidor would be Saltykoff's orderly. He had said, "The untidiness of His Serene Highness and his princely pranks need special attention. It will be a good experience for Sidor."

They were traveling eastward, skirting the foothills of the Daghestan, and Sasha, with an eye on the mountains that were to release the captives, talked and laughed with Poushka all the way. He avoided all mention of his forthcoming meeting with Zoë; the joy of it was almost more than he could bear. And only when the small town of Hassaf-Yourt appeared on the horizon, with its low wooden structures and its gardens and orchards, did he grow silent. He said to Poushka in a low voice, "Just think! The day after tomorrow she will be with us!" And Poushka replied with his usual insight into Sasha's character and with a bluntness that had become even sharper since his return from Romantzevo, "Now that it is all over, Alexandr Dimitrievitch, I will say this. You have a restless nature. Faithfulness to women is not your strong point. It is good that Zoia Ivanovna was out of reach for so long. It has made you value her all the more. And if it were not for her sufferings, I would say let her stay there a while longer!"

A sudden inexplicable panic seized Sasha. He turned on Poushka furiously. "A curse on your tongue, Poushka! Nothing is over yet! One more word out of you, and I'll hit you. Honest to God I will!"

244

"Say 'My name is Alexandr Dimitrievitch Novoselsky' ten times before you do it," Poushka replied with a grand air.

A small dark cloud obscured the sun and hung there for a minute or two. Then it sped on its way, driven by the wind in the direction of the mountains, changing its shape as it went, until it looked like a long thin belt ready to enlace the nearest mountain peak. And by the time they had reached Prince David's house in Hassaf-Yourt, Sasha had almost forgotten the incident.

This was the day on which Zoë spent the afternoon with Karimat.

Sasha had been looking forward to a long talk with Jemal, but the moment he saw him he knew this could not be. Jemal had grown thinner, the color in his cheeks had become brighter, and there was a new look of resignation in his eyes, and of detachment too. A heart-to-heart talk with Sasha would only disturb the peace he had found within himself. Nor did the opportunity arise for a talk that day. Callers kept streaming in to congratulate Prince David on the forthcoming return of his family and to wish Jemal Godspeed. And that evening they all went to the house of Prince Bagration-Moukhransky, the commanding general of that sector, who gave a farewell dinner for Jemal. Ladies were present in low-cut evening gowns and men wore their orders and decorations. Sasha watched Jemal closely—it was the last time he would attend a function of this kind. Jemal remained calm, a little aloof, perhaps, but his manner was natural and he spoke with quiet courtesy to the other guests. Only toward the end of dinner did he betray any emotion. Prince Bagration had stood up, his lanky figure towering over the dinner table, his long thin nose and his droopy mustache accentuating the solemnity of his face. He made a short speech in Jemal's honor and, going to a small table near the window, picked up a sword. He drew it out of its scabbard. The blade, richly decorated by the hand of an ancient Persian craftsman, had belonged to the prince's ancestor, one of the Bagratide kings of Georgia. He gave the sword to Jemal, saying, "Accept this as a token of my affection and my esteem, but do not draw it against us."

Jemal rose to his feet. He held the sword in both hands, his head bowed, the muscles of his face twitching slightly. All eyes were upon him, expectant and a little anxious. But when at length he spoke, his voice resounded through the room, steady and firm. "I will obey my father in all things. All things but one! I hope and pray he will not command me to go and fight my friends, for in that case I will have to refuse. I have sworn never to wear arms again as long as I live. And I thank Your Excellency from the bottom of my heart. Your sword will always remain with me as a sword of peace."

Bagration smiled. "And what is a sword of peace, Jemaleddin?"

"One which is drawn only to be admired by friends."

It was very simple and moving. Little lace handkerchiefs fluttered around the table as the ladies wiped their eyes and blew their noses; and Prince Bagration was heard to make a low rumbling sound in his throat. Then he led the way into the adjoining room.

It was a large room, almost the size of a ballroom. The furniture had been pushed aside and an army band was playing a waltz. But Sasha did not feel like dancing. A full realization had suddenly come upon him that Jemal was moving out of their lives for good. And it was Sasha who retired into a corner, sad and lonely, while Jemal danced with every woman present. Next morning, leaving Saltykoff and the two Poushkas behind, Sasha and Jemal left for the outlying fort of Kourinsk. Prince Bagration and Prince David rode swiftly ahead, but Jemal, anxious to remain in Kourinsk as short a time as possible, suggested traveling with the cavalry escort that was to accompany the slow arbas with the ransom money and Jemal's belongings; for Jemal was taking with him many books and a few other objects he valued most. Sasha went with him, and they set out of Hassaf-Yourt, riding in front of three arbas, two of which were loaded with sacks of silver rubles, while the third carried Jemal's possessions.

This was the morning on which three arbas left Dargo-Veden without Zoë.

Jemal rode beside Sasha, holding his reins loosely. The soldiers of the escort sang cavalry songs, but Sasha and Jemal traveled in silence. There was nothing they could say—words at such a time would have sounded shallow and empty.

It was almost five o'clock and the little fort of Kourinsk could be seen in the distance, when Jemal raised his head. "Sasha!" he said abruptly. "They say only foolish old women believe in dreams. But some dreams are like life, aren't they?"

Sasha had not expected such a question, and he looked at Jemal in surprise. "Perhaps they are, Jemal. I really don't know."

"Neither do I, really. Yet some dreams are like life, and sometimes life is like a dream. I seem to be living in a twilight. And today I am full of strange presentiments I cannot get rid of. Whatever may happen, Sasha, you know you can count on me."

It sounded weird. Jemal might have been asleep or in a semitrance. And Sasha, whose realistically inclined nature followed and accepted the pattern of life without prying too deeply into what lay beneath it, felt almost shocked. He had never seen his friend in such a mood before. "But for God's sake, Jemal!" he cried. "What could happen?"

Jemal shook his head sharply, as if chasing away a vision or trying to wake up. "Nothing. Pay no attention. I must be tired after last night. When we get to Kourinsk I will go to bed and sleep until it is time for me to meet my father."

He kept his word, leaving Sasha to spend the evening with the two princes. After supper Isaak Gramoff arrived in Kourinsk and Prince Bagration called him in, wishing to hear all the details of tomorrow's ceremony as worked out by Shamyl.

In accordance with these, at seven o'clock sharp the next morning two troops of cavalry stood lined up on a knoll a hundred yards from a shallow mountain river called Mitchik—a somewhat arbitrary border line between the Russian Empire and Shamyl's domains. Prince Bagration was there, and Prince David, seated on their horses, the latter wearing his new gold braids of honorary aide-de-camp to the Tsar. Sasha and Jemal were behind them, while to the right stood the three arbas, with Gramoff keeping watch over them. On the other side of the river the terrain ran even and flat for almost a mile, ending abruptly at the foot of the mountains; and on a hillock they could see Shamyl's big white tent, a group of men clustered in front of it. Prince David trained his field glasses in their direction, exclaiming, "Yes, that is Shamyl, all in white, sitting under a big white parasol."

He passed the field glasses to Prince Bagration, who scrutinized Shamyl with interest. But Sasha's whole attention was directed to the left of the big tent, where he could discern three arbas filled with women, and he felt his blood pulsating through his veins.

For almost an hour they were forced to watch the *djiggitovka* of the mountaineers—their stunt riding, in which they indulged on festive occasions. With bloodcurdling yells hundreds of them galloped at full speed one by one past the tent. Some of them jumped off their saddles, hitting the ground with their feet, and jumping back again; others picked small objects off the ground as they galloped by or rode standing on their heads. Ordinarily such exercises were accompanied by shooting, but not a single shot was heard on this occasion. Shamyl had forbidden it, saying, "My warriors might get overexcited and attack the Russians. Today I am at peace with the Russian Tsar."

At last the wild celebrations came to an end, and the mountaineers formed themselves into ranks, headed by Kazi-Mahomma, his standard-bearer close behind him. The three arbas moved slowly forward, a man on horseback riding alongside the first arba. Prince Bagration was still watching it all through Prince David's field glasses when he exclaimed, "That rider looks like a Russian officer in a torn and bedraggled uniform!" There was surprise in his voice. He handed the field glasses back to Prince David.

For a second or two Prince David scrutinized the approaching procession. When he tore his glasses away, there was blank amazement on his face. He turned to Bagration. "That is a kinsman of mine who was in command of the Tower of Pohali!"

"So! They are returning an additional captive. Shamyl is certainly generous today," Bagration muttered in a low voice.

Nothing more was said, but the silence that followed his words was ominous. A heavy threat seemed to hang in the air. Jemal sat very still on his horse, his face pale and drawn, his shoulders stooping slightly. And Sasha was seized by an uncontrollable anxiety; his heart beat very slowly now, making it hard to breathe. Unable to bear the suspense any longer, he asked Prince David for the field glasses and trained them on the approaching vehicles. The first arba appeared within the circle of the lenses, coming toward him. He saw the children, the nurses, and a veiled woman standing in it. "Must be Anna," he said to himself. He shifted the glasses and the second arba came into sight. It was almost empty—just a nurse carrying a child and a veiled woman. That must be Varvara. The third arba was crowded with women, and none of them was veiled. Sasha could not distinguish their faces, for his eyes had become blurred, yet he knew Zoë was not among them. He knew it, but his mind refused to take it in. And he kept repeating to himself stubbornly, "She is among these women. Of course she is!"

Prince David, Gramoff, and the three loaded arbas moved toward the river. Suddenly Jemal seized Sasha by the shoulders and looked deep into his eyes. He threw his arms around him and pressed him to his heart. "Forgive us, Sasha, and have faith!" he whispered. He then saluted Prince Bagration, shook hands with him, saluted again, and rode away after Prince David.

Sasha had dismounted. He watched the proceedings, turned to stone; yet every instant stood out separate and clear, impressing itself on his mind, distinct and sharp, as if seen through a narrow slit. He saw the three arbas with the captives come to a halt on the other side of the river. He saw Prince David dismount, handing the reins of his horse to Gramoff, and the voices of Salome and Marie rang clearly through the silence—"Mamma! Look! That is Papa!" He saw Jemal ride across the river and hand a letter to Princess Anna. She said something to him. He turned back sharply, but Kazi-Mahomma embraced him and drew him away. A bird flew by close to the ground, its bright blue plumage striking Sasha in the eye, and the thought flashed through his mind, "This evening there will be rain." Then he saw Anna standing silently in front of her husband. The children were running to their father, and Varvara was coming slowly up the hill. She paused for a moment to let Prince Bagration kiss her hand, kissing him on the forehead in return. And then she stood in front of Sasha. In her sad, soft eyes he read the whole grim truth, and his hand flew up to his throat. He saw her lips move, but he could not hear a sound. Years of training and military discipline came to his rescue. Like an automaton, he stepped up to General Bagration and drew himself to attention. He heard his own voice saying, "Your Excellency, I beg your permission to return to Hassaf-Yourt!" Bagration gave his permission, patting Sasha kindly on the arm. Sasha saluted, turned sharply on his heels, and, leaping into the saddle, let his horse go full speed.

The wind sang in his ears. His military cap got blown off. He did not stop. He galloped past the fort of Kourinsk and down the dusty road to Hassaf-Yourt. He galloped for hours. Furies tore at his soul; a madness, a frenzy to kill, to destroy. His horse was covered with foam. Its flanks were heaving, it snorted, but he spurred it on. They thundered through the streets of Hassaf-Yourt, sending chickens, ducks, and geese scattering in all directions. And a pig rolled squealing under a fence. People followed Sasha with anxious eyes, wondering what calamitous news this messenger had brought.

In Prince David's yard he came to an abrupt stop. He jumped to the ground and for a brief moment stood there, his hand on the saddle to steady himself. It was the sight of Poushka, rising from the doorstep with an anxious smile, a nosegay for Zoë in his big hand, that broke Sasha down. He rushed up the steps four at a time, down a long corridor, and into the room he had slept in two nights before. And slamming the door behind him, he flung himself face down on a divan, his body racked by sobs.

249

2   There was a tree on the plain halfway between the river
     Mitchik and Shamyl's tent. Under it a few old Naibs stood
beside their horses, waiting for Jemaleddin. He rode up to them with
Kazi-Mahomma and dismounted.

A Naib came forward, carrying a dagger richly inlaid with gold.
Behind him Kahjio, the treasurer, held a sword to match. And when
Jemal bowed and looked into the Naib's archaic face, with its long
hooked nose and black curly beard, he did not know he was looking at his future father-in-law. For this was Naib Taljik, the father
of Zulma.

Six other Naibs each held an article of clothing. Jemaleddin,
Kahjio explained, could not appear before the Imam in the uniform
of a Russian officer. And the Naibs formed a circle around him to let
him change his clothes with the help of Kazi-Mahomma.

When the circle broke open again and Jemal stepped out, he was
like a man transformed. The streamlined effect of his white tcherkeska broadened his shoulders and narrowed his hips, while his tall
white fur cap added inches to his height. He wore soft red leather
shoes with tight-fitting red leather gaiters; his hazel eyes were half
closed like those of his father, and the gold on his sword and dagger
glittered in the sun.

Jemal swung into his saddle. The others followed suit, riding behind him to the place where Shamyl sat in state. Like a figure carved
in chalk and touched up here and there with vermilion, he sat in
studied outward grandeur and majesty; but his whole heart shone
through his eyes as he watched his long-lost son dismount a few
paces away and come toward him on foot. When he finally clasped
him in his arms, tears rolled freely down his cheeks and beard and
his lips murmured a prayer of thanks to Allah.

A few minutes later Jemal sat on a rug inside the big white tent,
facing Shamyl. Father and son were alone, taking stock of one another. Jemal, according to the laws of civility of his native land, did
not look straight into his father's face, but studied it surreptitiously;
and it was Shamyl who first broke the silence. "Today I have much
to thank Allah for, my son. And my heart is full of gratitude to the
Russian Tsar for giving you back to me."

"The Tsar is dead, Father."

The news seemed to stun Shamyl. He exclaimed with feeling,
"Such a strong and powerful monarch dead! It touches my soul!"
Then, narrowing his eyes, "Did he at any time try to convert you to
Christianity, my son?" When Jemal had answered in the negative,

250

Shamyl asked his next question, which lay closest to his heart: "Are you still true to the faith of Islam?"

"I am, Father." There was no hesitation and no artificiality in Jemal's tone. "But I have also learned that truth lies in every human heart, whatever faith it may belong to. In some it lies buried and dormant; in others it is alive and throbbing. And the teachings of Jesus are indeed a living seed. If men followed them, there would be peace on earth."

He had referred to Jesus as Issa, in the Moslem fashion, and Shamyl frowned. "Issa was a prophet, but not as great as Mohammed. The proof of it lies in the fact that Issa's followers do not live according to the truth. They admire wealth and riches; a few among them have power and privileges, while all the others are downtrodden. And they worship and tolerate tyrants and slaves in their own race. That is an abomination!"

Jemal inclined his head respectfully. "They do not live according to the teachings of Issa, Father. Just as we do not live according to the higher ways of Islam, the *Tarikat* and the *Hadikat*—the Path and the Truth."

His words seemed to impress Shamyl. He pondered over them before replying, "Mysticism is for individuals, my son. It cannot guide the destinies of nations."

"I am an individual, Father. My destiny is not to rule. That belongs to my brother, Kazi-Mahomma."

"But you are the wiser of the two, Jemaleddin."

They talked for more than an hour. Jemal gave Shamyl a detailed description of the Russian Empire, urging him at the same time to sign an advantageous peace with the new Emperor. "This is a propitious moment to do so," he said.

Shamyl listened attentively. He asked many pertinent questions, but when Jemal spoke of peace, he shook his head. "Our war is a holy war, my son. It cannot be terminated by diplomatic parleys!" And with a good deal of sagacity he added, "Nor will the Russians live up to such a peace treaty. It could be nothing more than an armed truce at best. They will never rest contented until they have subjugated us and drawn us into the orbit of their power!"

It was apparent to Jemal that Shamyl did not wish to pursue the subject, and he remained silent. It was then that Shamyl told him he had chosen a wife for him. He looked narrowly at his son as he said this, but contrary to his expectations, Jemal showed no surprise.

"I was prepared for this," he said quietly, "and I am ready to

251

obey you, Father. I will obey you in all things, but do not ask me to take up arms against my friends. I have sworn a sacred oath to Allah never to carry arms again and to spend my life praying for peace."

He stood up. Taking off his dagger and his sword, he laid them at his father's feet.

Shamyl sat for a long time, gazing in silence at the sword and the dagger. When he raised his head again, there were tears in his eyes. "I will respect your wishes, my son. Your wisdom has moved my heart. Your brother, Kazi-Mahomma, will learn to rule and govern my people, but you will be their supreme judge."

It was Jemal's turn to be moved. He stood in front of Shamyl, the color rising slowly to his cheeks. "Father, I feel humbled. But I cannot accept this high mission without telling you all that lies in my heart. It grieves me that you did not return the Frenchwoman with the other captives as you had promised to do."

Shamyl stiffened. Flames of anger flickered in his eyes. "That Frenchwoman again! I am tired of hearing her name! And how dare you accuse me of breaking my word! I promised to return the same number of captives as I took. I gave them an officer, a kinsman of Prince Tchavchavadzé, instead of this woman. What more could they ask of me?" He gave Jemal a piercing look, but the latter did not lower his eyes, though he listened to his father respectfully. "I gave the captives a fair warning. They knew what would happen to them if they carried on a secret correspondence with their friends. This woman defied me! She sent out a secret message and received one in return. My threats are never idle ones, Jemaleddin. The woman is now a slave of Daniel-Sultan."

Whatever Jemal's feelings may have been, he remained outwardly unperturbed. "I cannot accept the high mission you offer me without telling you the whole truth. When you have heard it, you may change your mind about me, and I will submit gladly to any decision you may make concerning my future. The woman we are discussing was to be married to my best friend. His people always treated me as one of their own. By your act, Father, you have mortally wounded a man who is like a brother to me."

Shamyl stood up, his anger rising. "I have said I will respect your wishes, Jemaleddin, but you must respect mine! Listen to me carefully, for I mean every word I say. You will judge my people and teach them to live in peace and harmony with one another. But you must never take the law into your hands. The law belongs to me! You can pass judgment and refer the case to me, and I will take your

252

judgment into consideration. But you cannot punish or liberate of your own free will. Such prerogatives belong to me alone. If you disobey me in this, I will not spare you. I will banish you to the wildest, the farthermost end of my mountains, and you will never see a living soul again!"

His fiery temper had got the better of him. But it was not his temper alone that had prompted him to make this threat. Somewhere deep inside himself he felt he could not fully trust this son of his; a son who had been brought up by his enemies and had formed brotherly ties among them. To entrust him with the law would be to toy with danger. Jemal may have understood this, for he bowed his head obediently, saying, "I will respect your wishes, Father."

Suddenly Shamyl opened his arms and clasped him to his heart. "Oh, Jemaleddin, my son! Rulers are forced to make compromises with their conscience, but yours will remain forever free. I beseech you to remember my words and obey them!"

He then took Jemal by the hand and led him out of the tent. Kazi-Mahomma, Daniel-Sultan, the Naibs, and behind them rows and rows of silent warriors stood waiting for a word from their Imam. Still holding Jemal by the hand, Shamyl presented him to his people. "Let the word be carried to all the tribes of the Daghestan," he cried. "Jemaleddin, my son, will be their supreme judge. He will travel among them unarmed and unguarded, for his mission will be one of peace!" He waited for the murmur of acceptance to subside. Then he said, "A man of peace should have a servant of peace." His eyes wandered over the ranks of Murids and warriors and their attendants, finally coming to rest on Hassan, who stood holding his horse and gazing at Jemal with wide-open eyes. "Come here, Hassan!"

Hassan heard the call and his heart began to throb, even though at first he dared not trust his own ears. "The Imam," he said to himself, "must mean some other Hassan," for the name was a common one among the mountaineers. But Shamyl's eyes were upon him, and when the order was repeated impatiently, he came forward, leading his horse behind him.

He stood in front of Shamyl with downcast eyes, and the latter turned to Jemal. "This is Hassan, your standard-bearer." He paused to lend a dramatic effect to his next words and exclaimed, "Hassan! In front of all my Naibs, my Murids, and my warriors I tell you this —you shall not draw your arms except to protect the life of Jemaleddin!"

A standard inscribed with Arabic letters had been prepared for

Jemal. It was handed now to Hassan, who lowered it in front of his new master.

3   Three times the sun had risen over the pit in Dargo-Veden.
To Zoë time had ceased to exist. All feeling had fled. The tower of human dignity had crumbled, and her soul lay bare. Oblivion had come to her from time to time. A blessed torpor that for hours had rendered her insensible to the slime and the human excrements around her and, above all, to the black heap of putrid horror that lay at the other end of the pit. Her mind had refused to identify it until in an agonizing moment, her brain tortured by fever, she had thought she saw the "thing" stir and heard it giggle as it whispered, "Scratch me, friend. The maggots tickle so." And with a shudder she had crumpled unconscious to the ground.

During her waking hours she would sit motionless, leaning against the side of the pit. She had found an earthenware pitcher of water beside her and a chunk of stale bread. She had drunk some of the water, but she had not touched the bread, and she sat, her head thrown back, her eyes tightly closed, waiting for the few rays of sunshine that at high noon touched her face. They were her only source of hope, her prayer, her sole reason for existence.

On that third day, as she sat waiting for the light to come and bathe her face, wishing she could find a way to capture it and retain it in the depths of her soul, she suddenly heard a man's voice calling her name: "Zoë-djan!" She looked up. High above her she saw the head and shoulders of Hassan peering over the edge of the pit. He was holding something in his hand. She saw him take aim once or twice, and then a small ball of paper landed in her lap. With trembling fingers she picked it up, unrolling it and smoothing it out. The rays of light were traveling down the side of the pit. They were just above her head now. She raised the piece of paper to the light, and the words, written in French, leaped to her eyes, bold and clear: "Take courage. I am watching over you."

Hassan was saying something to her. All she could understand was the name "Jemaleddin." Then his head vanished, but she did not mind. The light she had hoped to capture was in her heart now, and the rays of sunshine were warming her face. Suddenly she felt strong, purposeful, inspired. "If I could sing, I would rise above myself." No sooner had the thought flashed through her mind than she remembered a song she had often heard as a child. It was a very old song, dating back to the days of Henri IV of France, with a simple, easy, haunting little tune that kept repeating itself over and over again. And before she knew it, she heard herself singing:

> "*Aux marches de Palais, aux marches de Palais,*
> *Y à une tant belle fille, lonlà!*
> *Y à une tant belle fille.*
>
> "*Elle a tant d'amoureux, elle a tant d'amoureux,*
> *Qu'elle ne sait lequel prendre, lonlà!*
> *Qu'elle ne sait lequel prendre.*"

At first her voice had sounded like a foghorn humming a lullaby. But as she went on, it grew in volume, becoming firm and clear. She hit the notes squarely. All hoarseness vanished. It was as if someone else were singing for her while she listened intently, opening her mouth and supplying the words.

> "*C'est un petit cordonnier, c'est un petit cordonnier,*
> *Qui a-z-eu sa préférence, lonlà!*
> *Qui a-z-eu sa préférence.*
>
> "*C'était en la chaussant, c'était en la chaussant,*
> *Qu'il lui fit sa demande, lonlà!*
> *Qu'il lui fit sa demande!*"

She sang all the verses through and then started all over again from the beginning. The rays of sunshine were creeping up the side of the pit now, and she followed them, rising slowly to her feet. By the time she had come around again to the last verse she was standing with her back to the damp wall, the sunlight out of reach above her head. She fell silent for a moment and looked up. The eager faces of several children were peeking at her over the edge of the pit. They laughed and clapped their hands. They shouted, "Lolà! Lolà!" trying to pronounce lonlà, the only word of the song they had caught onto. Zoë smiled and began to sing for them alone, the children chiming in with "Lolà" every time she came to the end of the second line.

> "*La belle si tu voulais, la belle si tu voulais,*
> *Nous dormirions ensemble, lonlà!*
> *Nous dormirions ensemble.*
>
> "*Dans un beau lit carré, dans un beau lit carré,*
> *Orné de taies blanches, lonlà!*
> *Orné de taies blanches.*

> *"Aux quatre coins du lit, aux quatre coins du lit,*
> *Un bouquet de pervenches, lonlà!*
> *Un bouquet de pervenches."*

She did not know it, but her voice resounded through the small square, coming out of the dark mouth of the pit like the voice of some spirit trapped in a subterranean cavern. The square was rapidly filling with people. They were coming from all directions down the narrow lanes, looking at each other in amazement. Such a thing had never been heard of—a prisoner singing in the pit! They did not know what to make of it. Some frowned and shook their heads, saying it was the voice of a devil; others smiled, waving a finger in time to the tune. A few men ran up to the edge of the pit, threatening to silence the voice by force, but it rose out of the depths louder and louder, a defiance to their threats.

> *"Dans le mittant du lit, dans le mittant du lit,*
> *La rivière est profonde, lonlà!*
> *La rivière est profonde.*

> *"Tous les chevaux du roi, tous les chevaux du roi,*
> *Pouraient-y boir ensemble, lonlà!*
> *Pouraient-y boir ensemble."*

There was a commotion in the crowd now. Men were hurrying to the pit, pushing the people aside—the Benevolent Mullah and Hassan, followed by a few Murids and preceded by a tall man carrying a long ladder.

When the ladder appeared in front of Zoë, she clutched it with a cry and clung to it, hardly daring to breathe. For a moment she thought she was too weak to climb, but her song came back to her, and with it her strength returned. She climbed up the ladder slowly, step by step. She was standing on solid ground now. She saw the faces of the Benevolent Mullah and Hassan. She saw them make a step in her direction to support her, but she walked straight ahead for a few paces, singing the last verse of her song, while the children followed her, still chanting, "Lolà! Lolà!"

> *"Et là nous dormirions, et là nous dormirions,*
> *Jusqu'à la fin du monde, lonlà!*
> *Jusqu'à la fin du monde . . ."*

She stopped and looked around in bewilderment. She took a deep breath. Suddenly all things began to swim in front of her eyes, and darkness descended, obliterating consciousness.

256

Zoë did not know, when she fell, that she had given birth to a legend. For from that day on her story grew and grew, spreading itself among the people of the Daghestan. The story of a beautiful young girl, the spirit of the mountains, whom Shaitan himself, jealous of her loveliness, had imprisoned in a subterranean cavern, rolling a heavy rock in front of the entrance. She had been there so long that people had forgotten her name. And so she sang it day and night until the children of the villages heard her and went to look for her. And when they had rolled away the heavy rock, she came out into the light of day, singing her name to the world, "Lolà! Lolà! Lolà!"

4   For more than three weeks Zoë lay unconscious, hovering between life and death. At times she became aware of an excruciating pain in her head, of fiery flashes that seemed to end in silent, burning explosions. She would thrash about, moaning in her agony; then a cool hand would touch her forehead and she would sink back into oblivion.

But the day finally came when all pain left her and she experienced an indescribable relief. Her body seemed weightless, as though drifting lightly through cool water, an almost imponderable substance, dissolving itself gradually into the gentle stream. And she was aware of bright sunlight around her.

For a long time she lay very still, her eyes closed, afraid to lose the sense of bliss that permeated her whole being. When at last she decided to look up, she saw a white ceiling above her and a light sunlit wall to her right. She was lying on a low divan between clean white sheets, her head resting on a soft pillow. And beside her, on top of a quilted blanket, lay somebody's arm. It could not be hers, she thought; it was too thin, too emaciated, and the long white sleeve of a nightgown that partly covered it did not belong to her.

Slowly, carefully, she turned her head to the left, and her eyes rested on a Persian rug that covered the floor. She took in every detail, rejoicing at the bright coloring and the delicate intricacy of the design. It was like a physical touch, like a caress; a pattern of beauty, of life regained.

She allowed her eyes to feast on it for a while and then glanced at the other end of the room. She recognized the tall, slender figure of Karimat standing near an open window in the recess of the thick stone wall. And when she saw the blue luster of the sky a deep sigh of contentment escaped her.

257

Karimat heard it. She turned around swiftly and hurried to Zoë's side. "Oh, you are alive, you are conscious. Thank God!" She sank to the floor, taking Zoë's hand in hers.

Zoë's voice scarcely rose above a whisper. "Where am I, Karimat?"

"In my house in Karaty."

"Karaty!"

The memory of the tall gates flanked by two slender towers flooded her mind. For a moment she was back in the high-pommeled saddle, emerging from the Tunnel of Allah and gazing up at them. Now she was behind those golden gates. "How did I get here?" she asked at length.

But Karimat would not let her speak. "You have been very ill. Tomorrow I will tell you about it. Now you must sleep and regain your strength." And Zoë slept for almost twenty-four hours.

Under Karimat's constant care her strength returned rapidly in the next two weeks. At first she got up for a few minutes at a time and walked around the room, supported by Karimat. Maids came to take her measurements, for Zoë's clothes, Karimat explained, had been so filthy they had to be destroyed. And then came the day when she felt strong enough to stay up an entire afternoon.

The maids brought in the new clothes, modeled after Karimat's dresses. First a long white chemise with tight-fitting sleeves, then the knee-length tunic of thick dark blue silk lined with peach-colored taffeta. Its long sleeves were split and held together by gold loops and buttons. A belt with a gold buckle was strapped around her waist. They tied a little black handkerchief around her head and laid a thin veil on top of it that fell in graceful folds down her back. In the past Zoë would have been excited about this new, exotic costume, but on that day she stood very still, disinterested, allowing the women to dress her. Karimat gave her a pair of gold crescent-shaped earrings, and although Zoë protested at first, Karimat finally made her wear them. And leaning on Karimat's arm, she went out to a porch. No parapet here to keep one from falling, no glass to protect one, just a wide-open space with a glorious view. Narrow gorges and deep canyons cut through a chain of mountains, black with dense forests; above them towered the thousand snow-capped peaks Roxane had read about in Paris long, long ago. Their majesty and grandeur were almost too much for the eye to bear. A casual glimpse was as good as a long look. Days, even weeks, might go by before one could absorb it all; and by then, as sure as not, one would get so accustomed to it one might not even see it any more. Zoë felt this as she glanced in the direction of the mountains and then turned her head away. In her weakened condition she said to herself, "I wish it were more restful. A walled-in garden with a nice shady tree."

The porch itself was lined with oriental rugs; soft divans with multicolored cushions stood along the walls, and in front of each divan there was a low octangular table inlaid with mother-of-pearl. It was strange to find such luxury in the heart of this wild country, yet it seemed a proper setting for Karimat, and somehow Zoë had not expected it to be any different. She glanced wistfully at the crystal salvers on the tables, filled with Tollet sweets, for she knew by now that a pair of cherub wings had been her undoing. She wondered vaguely what sudden misplaced wave of affection and concern had prompted Madame Tollet to do such a thing, but she felt no bitterness. All that belonged to another life she had lived long ago and could think of now only as belonging to someone else she had known very well.

She sat down, propping herself up among the many cushions of a divan, and when Karimat asked her if she wanted anything, she blushed a little. "I want to see what I look like, Karimat."

Karimat brought her a hand mirror, and she gazed into it for a long time. The face that looked back at her seemed to be all eyes. The nose had become sharp and pointed, and there were a few small lines at the corners of the mouth. But what Zoë could not see was the look deep in her eyes that was both questioning and discerning, as though the riddle and the answer were there, wrapped in one. And those who could see it felt uncontrollably drawn to it.

"I look like a marmoset," she said at last with a sigh, laying the mirror on the table. "I can see now how ill I must have been. It is surprising I did not die when you had me transported in a litter to Karaty. Life must be holding back a few more things for me to see!" Not wishing to carry on the conversation in this vein, she changed the subject. "From all you tell me, Karimat, Jemaleddin's wedding must have been a resplendent affair."

"Yes, especially if one thinks of Shamyl's stinginess and austerity!" There was a touch of resentment in Karimat's voice. But she brightened up, and a look of satisfaction came into her eyes as she added, "I think, though, that his choice of a wife for Jemaleddin was a wise one. Zulma is a good little girl."

The words were simple but deadly. Zoë looked away. She did not care to show all she had guessed, all that Karimat had left unsaid in the past two weeks. She had seen the happiness in Karimat's eyes and the color that rose to her cheeks whenever she spoke of Jemal. And she spoke of him as often as she could. She knew that Jemal and Zulma were also living in Karaty, and she could sense, though she had seen no one but Karimat and her maids, that there was a tenseness in the atmosphere.

Karimat occupied a whole wing to herself. Besides the room in which Zoë lived, she had three rooms on the other side of the porch. They were bright rooms. All the windows looked out on the mountains, while the doors that faced them led to an arched gallery supported by massive stone columns. As in Dargo-Veden, this seraglio had an inner court, and across it were Zulma's rooms. They were dark and gloomy, Karimat had told Zoë, with no outside windows; but from her flat roof Zulma could see the outer court, where Kazi-Mahomma's Murids lived, and the steep, narrow, tortuous streets of the aoul beyond it. When she had first been brought there she had hidden in the darkest recesses of her rooms, speaking to no one, trembling and staring like a wild animal at those who came in. But Jemal had succeeded in taming her. She answered him now in little frightened whispers, and of an evening she would go out on her roof and sing, to the enchantment of all the inhabitants of Karaty. When Jemal was at home he would sometimes sit there with her. "It is the closest she will ever come to enchanting him, the poor little mite!" And a look of triumph had crept into Karimat's eyes when she had said this.

Zoë knew that Kazi-Mahomma was away and that Jemal had recently returned from a three weeks' journey, during which he had visited many aouls of the Daghestan, riding unarmed, as he had sworn to do, with Hassan as his sole attendant bearing his standard behind him. Before returning to Karaty he had reported to Shamyl in Dargo-Veden, and during their interview he had tried to talk his father into abolishing the horror of the pit. But so far he had succeeded in only one respect. Shamyl had said, "I will issue orders that no captive Russian officers be treated in this way. And if you find any man disobeying my orders, send him to me and I will have him beheaded." Jemal had begged his father to make the law applicable at least to all prisoners, irrespective of their rank, but Shamyl had refused to listen. "No! Officers, I am told, are in some ways like my Murids. They are supposed to live up to a code of honor. Besides, some of them are your friends, my son, and have been kind to you. This law will apply to officers only!" And Zoë, on hearing it, had smiled sadly. "It is a step in the right direction, anyway. We must not think of the mountain. We must just go step by step."

The words had brought back Anna to her mind and the morning she had sat with her at the top of the world. It was the only moment in Zoë's past that still appeared real and vivid. That and the thought of Anna and Varvara refusing to leave Dargo-Veden when they discovered she had been detained. Karimat had told her about it. The women of Tsinandali had shrieked and fallen on their knees, pleading with the princesses to leave at once; the children had cried, but Anna and Varvara had stood their ground, saying Shamyl would not see his son unless Zoë was returned immediately. Anna had actually thrust a finger into Shamyl's chest, calling him a liar and a deceiver. She had been forced into the arba. And when Zoë had heard all this, she had remained silent for a long time, filling her soul with the loyalty of her friends.

That afternoon as she sat on the porch with Karimat, she sensed that the latter was perturbed. Karimat had opened her mouth several times to say something and had changed her mind, turning her head away with a frown.

"What's worrying you, Karimat? What is it?" she asked at length.

Karimat gave her a long, searching look. "Is it true that the man who loves you is Jemaleddin's best friend?"

"The man who loves me!" Zoë repeated the words to herself several times. Had she not heard them before? Had she not spoken them many times in the past that now seemed like a distant puppet show? Yes, and later there had been her love for him, by which she had lived and grown. She had held a shining pebble in her hand, but it had been knocked roughly away and lay now at the bottom of a clear pool. She could make out its shape, dimmed and blurred. To retrieve it she must dive, yet to dive she had no will. Let it lie there, shimmering in the rays of light. Too much had happened. Threads had been torn. She had reconciled herself to her fate.

She said nothing. She only nodded her head in silence, and it was Karimat who spoke again: "As I told you before, Jemaleddin asked after you every day when he was at home. Today he is coming to see you."

An anxiety took hold of Zoë, growing in intensity as Karimat went on: "His father told him, if you pleased him and were willing to embrace our faith, he should marry you. He has even allowed Jemaleddin to see you and talk to you, a thing unheard of in this land!"

Karimat fell silent, trying to master her emotions. Not indignation

261

at the trampling of customs but jealousy was tormenting her. And Zoë's mind was in a turmoil. To think of Jemal wanting to marry her was unbefitting somehow. To think of marrying him was in a way even worse. And when Karimat said in a strained voice, "If you married him, we would become sisters and I would grow to hate you," Zoë shook her head and closed her eyes.

They heard a soft step outside. Karimat whispered his name and stood up. And the agitation that seized Zoë was almost more than she could bear. She was breathing heavily, her eyes widened, and her hand flew up to her lips. Yet when she actually saw him in the doorway, standing as in her last dream, wearing a white tcherkeska, with no dagger, no sword, and Karimat's red belt strapped around his waist, she suddenly grew calm. All that had once been real had become a dream; all that had been a dream had become reality.

He looked at her keenly, eagerly. They knew one another so well they needed no words of welcome. She smiled. He strode across the porch to prevent her from rising. He took both her hands in his and said, "Sasha loves you."

His simple words conveyed a message, but they also must have held an invocation, for Sasha seemed to rise up in their midst; he might almost have walked in and stood behind Jemal's back. And to Zoë at that moment only two things stood out alive and real in a dream-spun world—her love for Sasha and her dream. Withdrawing her hands gently from his clasp, she replied, "I love him too."

She knew at once when she said this that her words held no longer the same meaning as before. No burning flames, no sweet turmoil underlined them, only a gentle flow of iridescent tenderness. And some of the strength she used to derive from her dream was in them too. From Jemal to her, from her to Sasha. A circle bound them, yet held them apart. And she knew Jemal understood this. Words were more than words to one who listened with his soul.

He said, "Sasha died a thousand deaths at the river Mitchik."

A thousand deaths they had suffered together to survive and live. "My own pain rendered me senseless," she murmured, for now she could see Sasha's face, pale and haggard. He was sitting on the floor at her feet, looking at her with all the pain that lay in his heart. A miracle had taken place. The shiny pebble had risen of its own accord and was floating on the surface of the water. She snatched at it and held it tight.

"Emperor Nicholas forbade him to marry a Frenchwoman," Jemal was saying. "The Emperor is dead, and I don't know what the new

262

Emperor will do about it, but Sasha has always been faithful to you."

Strange how this man could always find the words one wished to hear most; how he could bring out one's deepest feelings and make them pulsate. Sasha had laid his head in her lap, a black, unruly lock falling over his forehead. She wound it tenderly around her finger, his faithfulness around her heart. "If we are destined to meet again," she said aloud, not certain whether she was speaking to Sasha or Jemal, "emperors won't have to give their permission and churches won't have to grant annulments. We will be together."

And it was then that Jemal leaned forward, saying in a half whisper, "His wife is dead."

Sometimes when we are dreaming we know we are asleep, and when the inexplicable comes to us during waking hours all things seem to be woven of a dreamlike tissue. And so it was with Zoë that afternoon. She did not notice how Karimat had slipped away. Jemal was sitting on a cushion across the low table from her, and Sasha was no longer with them. It seemed to her Jemal was saying, "On that last night in Dargo-Veden you did not wear these clothes, yet I saw you in them. And you saw me dressed like this. It is a fact, isn't it, that we have always known one another as we are today?" When she thought of it later, she could not be sure that any words had actually been said. Perhaps it had been his silence that had grown eloquent. But one thing she knew. She had asked him if he had ever seen her before that night, and he had replied, "Yes, but never as clearly, nor did I know who you were until then. Before I seem to have been driven; that night I went of my own free will." And Zoë suddenly felt limp and tired. She remembered getting up and going to her room. She slipped the veil off her head, and when she lay down she fell fast asleep.

She awakened again at dusk. At first she could not remember where she was. Then the memory of the porch came back to her. She ran across the room to the door that stood ajar. When she opened it she stopped dead on the threshold. Jemal and Karimat were standing with their backs to her, shoulder to shoulder. She saw Karimat take his face between her hands, drawing it closer. But before her lips touched his he covered her hands with kisses. "Oh, Karimat, my beloved sister!"

The words had been a mere whisper, but Zoë heard them distinctly. And Zulma's song broke through the silence that followed them, sweet and gentle. Jemal tore himself away. "Good-by, Karimat. I have a child entrusted to my care."

He was gone. And Karimat sank onto the nearest divan, her hand on her heart, her eyes dilated, staring at the chain of snow-capped peaks.

5   Jemal's soul was in a turmoil. Temptations that had passed him by until then were lashing at him with sharp talons and claws. Hot blood ran in his veins, and all the passion that had lain dormant in him for so long had surged up when he met Karimat. From the very first day in Dargo-Veden, when she had bowed low handing him the red belt, he had carried the image of her delicate beauty with him wherever he went. And more disturbing than all was the knowledge that she, too, was ripe with love for him.

But Karimat belonged to his brother. A brother who from the very start had shown nothing but respect and shy admiration for him; whose sad, frustrated, yet proud soul he could understand and pity. The shadowy presence of his brother had always been there, and yet on that particular afternoon it was not Kazi-Mahomma who had risen between him and Karimat. Zoë had stepped into his life, tearing out of him the words, "Oh, Karimat, my beloved sister!" For Zoë was the one he had known forever, for whose sake he must either linger on the way or climb to greater heights. All lives are interwoven, coral-bound and coral-built; where one falls, another must rise; where one infringes, another must recede. He had read this in her eyes, in the question-answer he had seen in them. And he had read it right. She loved him for what he was—the man who never claimed, who knew how to recede while giving; she loved Sasha for what he was—the man who always claimed, taking all the gifts she had to offer. And thus it had to be. Every new revelation, every shade of tenderness and understanding she drew from Jemaleddin she would store away to shower on Sasha. And with sudden fierceness Jemal spun the large terrestrial globe he had brought with him from St. Petersburg.

In Karaty the house in the center of the inner court was larger than the one occupied by Shamyl in Dargo-Veden. It contained six rooms. Three of these, facing Karimat's apartment, belonged to Kazi-Mahomma; the other three were Jemaleddin's. And every time Jemal looked out of his window he saw Zulma's door. He gazed at it now, the look of patience and resignation creeping back into his eyes. Poor, lonely, frightened child he must take care of as long as he could; for when he had said to Karimat, "A child has been entrusted

264

to my care," he had meant it in more ways than one. Zulma, whose voice had matured and developed until it brought joy to all those who heard it, had the body and mind of a child of ten. And as far as Jemal could tell, she would remain that way as long as she lived. He had succeeded in gaining her confidence. She would sing for him alone, her face becoming transformed at such moments into an object of beauty, like a holy, shining vessel of inspiration. But touch her he dared not. He had told his father about it, asking Shamyl to place Zulma under Shouanet's care should anything happen to him. And Shamyl had promised to do it, speaking to him at the same time of Zoë.

Jemal spun the globe again, gently this time, and stopped it with his finger. He leaned forward. The tip of his finger lay on the Caucasus, covering the Daghestan—the place of his destiny. Strange that so much could conglomerate in Karaty, a tiny speck of a place he could not even identify on the globe. "But then," he said to himself, "the globe is made up of such tiny specks, and in each one men receive what they have earned."

He heard a door open and, glancing over his shoulder, saw Kazi-Mahomma standing on the threshold. As usual, he was looking in wonder at the globe his brother seemed to ponder over so often.

"I have just returned home," he said apologetically, afraid of intruding on his brother's mysterious studies. "I wanted to know how you were."

Suddenly Jemal's mind was made up. At all costs he must make Kazi-Mahomma stay at home this time and pay court to Karimat. Everything depended on it. He invited him in, and Kazi-Mahomma sat down on a cushion, his eyes wandering over the numerous books that lined the walls of Jemal's room. He liked to come here and listen to his brother. Sometimes, with almost childish curiosity, he would ask him about the outside world, about the beliefs, the customs and habits of other people. Jemal knew this. He described to him now in detail the life led by well-to-do women in other countries; their deportment, their behavior, the clothes they wore, and the attentions they received from their men. Kazi-Mahomma listened attentively, marveling. He muttered to himself from time to time, as if to make sure he had heard right, "Sitting at the same table with men, eating and drinking with them! Men and women dancing together! Low-cut gowns! A man's arm around a woman's waist!" And then with sudden humor, "Why, none of those people will ever go to heaven; they have paradise on earth!"

265

Jemal laughed. "A man's best paradise," he said at length, "is to find a true companion in his wife. I suppose you will be staying at home now for a while?"

Kazi-Mahomma shook his head. He was leaving again the next day, he said. There was a short campaign planned and his men needed him. It was then that Jemal grew eloquent. "The bravest men are not always those who go to war," he exclaimed. "It sometimes takes a lot of courage to stay at home!" He spoke for several minutes without stopping. His words were calculated to sting and provoke, and finally, carried away by his own emotions, he painted a vivid picture of Karimat's gentleness and loveliness. But Kazi-Mahomma looked sulky. He frowned and his lips pouted. "That is how she appears to others. When she is alone with me she looks as if she had smelled something bad. And the last time I was with her she said I was a clumsy, uncouth bear and that I should stay away from her!"

The brothers fell silent. With the tip of his finger Jemal turned the globe slowly halfway around. Then he said in a low voice, "Karimat is a woman who needs much attention. She is accustomed to it. She expects it." He turned and looked Kazi-Mahomma in the eye. "You have never even given her a present. I have been told quite a few pieces of jewelry were your share of the plunder of Tsinandali. Why don't you give her one of them? Our father gave Shouanet a diamond ring. Give Karimat something too. Keeping those treasures hidden in your room is a total loss. You will derive more pleasure by seeing them on Karimat." Before Kazi-Mahomma could answer, Jemal took him by the hand and led him to his side of the house. And somewhat unwillingly Kazi-Mahomma brought out a small leather box filled with pieces of jewelry. Jemal picked out a ring with a beautiful pigeon-blood ruby. "How lovely it would look on her finger," he murmured dreamily. He pressed the ring into Kazi-Mahomma's hand. "Give it to her and stay with her for a while."

"It belonged to Princess Anna," Kazi-Mahomma said morosely.

"It belongs to you now. Give it to your wife."

"Princess Anna could sting like a viper. Karimat has plenty of venom. She needs no more."

With sudden warmth Jemal took his brother by the shoulders. "You have so much gentleness and kindness in your soul. You must find an outlet for it. That is why a beautiful wife has been given you." He looked searchingly into Kazi-Mahomma's eyes. "Promise you will stay and find a way to her affections. Make her appreciate your company."

266

Kazi-Mahomma looked away, sulky. "She does not need my company. She has the Frenchwoman!"

Jemal's arms fell to his sides. He was crushed by the sense of his own failure. He returned silently to his room, blaming himself, not his brother. His own passion for Karimat had stood in the way. His words had been full of falsehood. Only some action coming from the heart would ring true. But what was it to be? His inspiration had left him, and he fell asleep, turning the matter over and over in his mind.

Early next morning, after Jemal had finished his breakfast, Hassan came in to report for duty. "Kazi-Mahomma and Hadji-Kheriett are leaving," he said. "The women are outside bidding them farewell."

Jemal sprang to his feet, his face pale, his thin nostrils quivering. "Saddle our horses, Hassan. Today we will lead men into battle!"

He hurried out. He saw Karimat and Zoë standing in the gallery, but he did not stop. Kazi-Mahomma and Hadji-Kheriett had already vanished behind the stone partition at the other end of the court. Jemal ran toward it, calling out Kazi-Mahomma's name.

Beyond the partition were the guest rooms of Karaty, and to the left was a big door leading to the outer court and to the tall gates Zoë had seen from the canyon below. Hearing Jemal's voice, Kazi-Mahomma reined in his horse in front of the big door, but he did not look around. Hadji-Kheriett alone glared out of one eye at Jemal, for his right eye had been blinded during the wild struggle at the edge of the pit. And the black patch Jemal had made for him gave him a sinister air.

"Where are you going, Kazi-Mahomma, my brother?" Jemal cried. "Get off your horse at once!"

The imperative tone of his voice brought a look of surprise to Hadji-Kheriett's face. There was a momentary silence, and Kazi-Mahomma jumped to the ground, throwing his reins to Hadji-Kheriett, who had dismounted too. He came toward Jemal now, a furtive look in his eye. "I cannot do it, Jemaleddin. Last night she was cruel to me. I did not give her the ring. Here, take it!" He fumbled in his pocket and held out the ring. But Jemal put his hands behind his back.

"You are a brave man, Kazi-Mahomma. You will stay here and give it to her yourself. I will lead your men to war!"

Hadji-Kheriett stepped forward, his face distorted with fury. "You cannot stop a warrior from doing his duty, Jemaleddin!"

Hassan had brought the horses, and Jemal was in his saddle now. He looked down at Hadji-Kheriett, his head high. He sounded very much like his father when he said in a withering tone, "Did I hear you raise your voice when the sons of your Imam were speaking? Go!"

Hadji-Kheriett slunk away, muttering something to himself, while Kazi-Mahomma ran forward, full of sudden concern for his brother. "You cannot go like that, Jemaleddin. You are unarmed. Here, take my dagger, my sword!"

"I need no arms, Kazi-Mahomma."

At a sign from Jemal attendants opened the big door and he rode out, followed by Hassan.

Zoë had seen Hassan lead the horses from the stables situated behind Kazi-Mahomma's house, and she had noticed the agitation that had suddenly taken hold of Karimat. At first she had not understood what was happening, but when Karimat tore herself away from her place and ran precipitately across the court, she knew Jemal must be leaving. She ran after Karimat, entreating her to come back, afraid her friend would give herself away in front of Kazi-Mahomma and the other men. But Karimat did not seem to hear. She did not stop until she had reached the partition. And Zoë, running up to her, saw Jemal refuse Kazi-Mahomma's arms and ride away.

A pang of anxiety cut through her heart, but she was given no time to think about it or to analyze her feelings. Karimat was clinging to her arm, trembling from head to foot, her face pale, her eyes agonized. "He has gone, Zoë-djan! Unarmed, he has gone to war!" Karimat's voice sounded like a plaintive moan.

Zoë saw Kazi-Mahomma coming toward them, looking down thoughtfully at the ruby ring he held in his fingers. And suddenly she knew. She could almost hear Jemal's voice whispering to her, "Show her the way. Tell her what to do."

"You must pull yourself together, Karimat," she said almost roughly. "Your husband is bringing you a gift." Taking Karimat by the hand, she looked at her, an earnest appeal in her eyes. "You must be strong, Karimat. You must be tender. You must be attentive and solicitous. You must find a way to your husband's heart. It is Jemaleddin's parting wish. His command!" She left her. And from the gallery she saw the strained and self-conscious expression on Kazi-Mahomma's face as he slipped the ring on Karimat's finger.

For a whole week after that Zoë saw very little of Karimat. She tried to avoid her as much as possible, though she noticed with satisfaction the sudden interest Karimat had developed in all things concerning her husband's welfare. She supervised the cooking of his meals; she served him his breakfast and his dinner, as the dutiful wife of a mountaineer should do. She invited him in the afternoons to sit with her on the porch, and Zoë knew he spent every night in Karimat's room.

Her own thoughts were all with Jemal during that week. There was no place in them for anyone else, not even for Sasha. Jemal was the one who needed all her prayers now. That he had gone in search of death, she did not doubt. And with her newborn intuition she guessed the reason why. Her evenings she spent on Zulma's roof, listening to Zulma's songs, for somehow only in the company of this strange half woman, half child did she feel the close presence of Jemal. "He must be thinking of her," she said to herself, "anxious for her fate in case he died." The thought of Jemal's death held no sadness. Death meant liberation to him. Only the knowledge that he had sought it was disquieting. Suicide should not be his end. And she put up a silent prayer for his safety.

On the seventh day Karimat came to Zoë's room and stood in the recess of the window, gazing at the distant mountains. There was a new light in her eyes, and a look of well-being permeated her whole person. "Is he alive, I wonder?" she whispered. "Seven days and no news! It is only a day's ride from here to the nearest Russian fortifications."

"If he were dead I think we would know it."

"Yes."

Zoë came up to the window. The sun was setting, bringing a new softness, a new glow to the mountains, as though blood were flowing through their veins. "Are you happy, Karimat?"

Karimat did not answer at once. She kept her eyes on the sunset, and when she spoke at last, her voice sounded distant. "There is a strange likeness between Kazi-Mahomma and his brother. A superficial one, I suppose. Or is it a light that Jemaleddin sheds on all he touches?" For the first time she looked straight at Zoë, an enigmatic smile hovering around her lips. "Zoë-djan," she said, a faraway look in her deep blue eyes. "If I had a child now, it would be Jemaleddin's."

6   Jemal had courted death, but death refused to claim him, and life brought him fame among his people. The men he had led returned home singing his praises. Wherever they went they told stories of his bravery and fearlessness. Unarmed, they said, he

led them into battle, inspiring them with words of encouragement, and his knowledge of military tactics won him battles. In awed tones they spoke of the day they won a decisive victory, chasing the Russians way out into the northern plains. His men had gathered around Jemal to cheer him, when a volley of shots rang out from a secret enemy ambush. A bullet went clean through Jemal's fur cap; another hit his standard held by Hassan, splitting it in two. And Jemal, taking his cap off and sticking his finger through the bullet hole, had said to Hassan, "That settles it, my friend. The Russian bullets do not like us."

His men were ready to attack and destroy the ambush, but he had stopped them. "You have achieved sufficient glory to rest awhile in peace. Your mission has been accomplished. Return home now to receive your awards from the Imam and from Kazi-Mahomma, your true leader, whose place I have temporarily usurped."

When Zoë saw him again, she was shocked by his appearance. His body looked wasted, his eyes glittered feverishly, and the redness of his cheeks had become even more pronounced. He paid a formal call on Karimat and Zoë, staying only a few minutes. He complained of a chill he had caught during the campaign, but he did not tell them of the dry cough that at times racked his whole body and of the blood he had been coughing up of late.

For days after that Zoë saw him only at a distance, when on a sunny afternoon he lay warming himself on Zulma's roof. Karimat never spoke of him now; she even avoided looking up at the roof when he was there. She seemed intent on holding and retaining the semblance of happiness she had found with Kazi-Mahomma, and perhaps, though she may not have fully realized it herself, the animal side of her had been repelled by the disease that was ravishing the body she had longed for. Hassan alone took care of Jemal with a devotion that could not be surpassed. Jemal had said to him one day, "Hassan, you are not a dweller among men. Someday when the time is ripe I will send you to the old hermit we visited together. Then the greatest wish of your life will be fulfilled—the holy man will teach you the higher aspects of your faith." Hassan had grown a shade paler when he heard these words. "Not as long as you live, master." But Jemal had shaken his head. "That is not for us to determine. When the time comes, you will go." And Hassan, knowing now that he might be separated from Jemal at any time, had redoubled his care and attention.

Zoë, of course, did not know this, but she had sensed the spiritual growth in Hassan, and she felt almost envious of his closeness to Jemal. She wished she could claim Jemal as her husband to take care of him and be by his side too. With his life ebbing away, the bond that united them had tightened, bringing her even closer to him. Something told her Sasha was destined to live, and it was to Jemal that all her feelings flowed. She was blinded in a sense by her willful desire for sacrifice, not realizing that he was still destined to give more than she could give. She wanted to sit at his feet, worshiping in silence, offering him the companionship she feared he missed. And one day, unable to bear it any longer, she sent him a message through Hassan, written in French: "You have watched over me so long, I wish I could watch over you now." The answer came promptly: "You are, and it gives me courage." The words opened up secret inner shutters. The light of sudden understanding flooded her heart and soul. The harmony of their relationship needed no solidifying, no physical closeness. And now, when he rested on Zulma's roof, she would come out into the court for a minute or two, looking up at him, and he would smile back, waving his hand. And Zoë felt happy.

But a storm was brewing in the peace and quiet that seemed to have descended over Karaty. Hadji-Kheriett's tortured soul could find no rest, now more than ever, since Kazi-Mahomma was no longer anxious to be drawn to the smoke and rage of battle. Hadji-Kheriett had never liked Fatima, the young wife Shamyl had given him. He, too, had seen her casual resemblance to Zoë, and it had only served to whip up his passion and his fury. The sight of Zoë gave him no peace. The daughter of Shaitan, as he still persisted in calling her, always seemed to get the upper hand. He had hoped to find satisfaction at the sight of her sufferings, but instead she had not only mutilated him but was living now in honor and splendor by the side of Kazi-Mahomma's wife. If that were not the power of a witch, he argued, then what could be? In a futile effort to run away, more from himself, perhaps, than from anyone else, he was forever thinking up new campaigns, new raids into enemy territory, anything to get away from Karaty. When he was there he lived in a house with a big yard just outside the walls of Kazi-Mahomma's seraglio. People said he treated Fatima badly. Sometimes when he was away she would pay a call on Zulma, and Zoë had seen her walking slowly through the court, heavy with child, her shoulders drooping, her head bowed. But she had not seen her now for more than two weeks, for Hadji-Kheriett had remained in Karaty all that time.

Late one afternoon several days after Jemal's return he presented himself at Kazi-Mahomma's door. Kazi-Mahomma invited him in, and the two men sat on cushions, facing one another across the room. Hadji-Kheriett's only eye was staring at Kazi-Mahomma reproachfully, and Kazi-Mahomma sat in silent embarrassment. He guessed what was on Hadji-Kheriett's mind—a new raid or some bold attack on the enemy. He was loath to tear himself away from his newly found happiness, yet he felt a little ashamed of himself, fearing that his other men, like Hadji-Kheriett, might be disapproving of his sudden inactivity. He could almost hear them whispering among themselves, "Kazi-Mahomma is enslaved by his wife. His sword is idle; his hand is growing soft." But he said nothing, waiting for his guest to speak first.

Hadji-Kheriett's eye strayed over the sabers and daggers and other weapons that decorated the walls. "How is the health of your illustrious brother?" he inquired by way of beginning the conversation with the usual oriental courtesy. And when Kazi-Mahomma shook his head sadly, Hadji-Kheriett sighed. "Jemaleddin was not born to fight battles. You are the Imam's true warrior son! Jemaleddin soars high, but you understand the needs and requirements of our fierce men. You know what is needed to keep them satisfied." He leaned a little forward, continuing in a confidential tone, "I cannot hide it from you; there is a good deal of unrest among them. They feel bitter about the small ransom received for the two princesses. All that trouble, all those lives lost, and only forty thousand rubles in return!"

Kazi-Mahomma drew himself up. "The Imam accepted it. Do they presume to criticize him?"

"Oh no! Allah forbid it! We all know the Imam has our interests at heart. The Georgian prince could pay no more, and what was the use of milking a dry goat? But I have heard of another prince who, they say, is the richest man in Russia, outside of the Tsar, of course. If we captured him, we would be sure to get a million!" He saw interest in Kazi-Mahomma's eyes, and he moved his cushion closer, speaking almost in a whisper. "His name is Prince Saltykoff. He is an officer in the Nijegorodsky Regiment. Our spies have been watching him. Three times a week he goes to General Wrangel's headquarters and back. Incredible as it may seem, he travels in a carriage, unguarded, driving his own horses like a common coachman! You would be right in saying, 'Beware! There may be some trickery in this.' I thought so myself, but we have been watching him now for over three weeks. There is nothing wrong, except that he must be a little deranged in the head. As you know, in one place the road he takes runs close to our territory, through a narrow gorge. He goes by there early in the morning and again around four in the afternoon. An easy catch!" And leaning forward again, Hadji-Kheriett expounded his plan in detail.

Kazi-Mahomma heaved a sigh of relief. This small raid was not worthy of his personal leadership, yet it would demonstrate his good will toward his men. He gave his consent gladly, saying, "It must be understood, all the men of Karaty will profit by it, not just those who take part in the capture. And I appoint you in charge of the expedition. My father has called for me. I am leaving for Dargo-Veden in the morning. I will be away for five or six days. Capture this prince during my absence. Bring him here. Treat him well. And send me a message of your success. I will then tell the Imam. Perhaps I can obtain a pardon for you at the same time." And Hadji-Kheriett, happy with his success, hopeful now of regaining Shamyl's favor, bowed low to Kazi-Mahomma before leaving the room.

Late next afternoon Saltykoff, unaware of the danger that hung over his head, rushed into his billet, his face jubilant. He brandished a piece of paper in front of Sasha's nose. "It has come! My reprieve! Our good Emperor Alexander Nicolaievitch—may he live long—has read my petition and has given me permission to return to Petersburg and resume my former life. It's the Kolomna road for me!"

"Isn't there anything besides that stupid road you would be glad to see there?" Sasha exclaimed with irritation.

"Of course there is. I will be glad to see my friends, the yamstchiks. I will have something to brag about when I tell them what skill is required to drive fast on our road here. And God forgive me for calling it a road. It's not a road at all. It's just an approach to Wrangel!" He threw his arms out in mock ecstasy. "Ah! Tomorrow will be my last trip over that bouncing alley!"

Sasha looked morose. He had changed considerably since his wild ride from the river Mitchik to Hassaf-Yourt. There were lines around his eyes and mouth that had not been there before; a few gray hairs had appeared over his temples, and there was a disillusioned, almost cynical look in his eyes. Saltykoff grabbed him by the shoulders and shook him. "Can't you be happy for my sake, you son of melancholy?"

"I am very happy for you," Sasha replied almost peevishly, "but stop shaking me!"

273

Saltykoff threw his head back and laughed. "Oh, Sasha! You Monster of Solitude! You Old Man of the Caucasus! Rejoice with me, you son of a bitch!"

His good humor was irresistible. Sasha smiled, and some of his old self returned as his smile broadened into a boyish grin. "Thanks be to Allah!" Saltykoff cried. "And may old Allah rejoice at the merriment of a good Christian. Don't you know there's a feast on tonight, Sasha? All the drinks in the officers' mess are on me. And we will have the regimental choir singing there. By imperial displeasure a yamstchik was raised to the dizzy heights of a cornet. The displeasure is no more. Now the demotion of a cornet to the glorious status of a yamstchik must be celebrated by all!"

All night the officers of the regiment made merry. Only those on duty listened with envy to the sounds of laughter and singing that came from the officers' mess hall. Saltykoff's farewell party was turning out to be a huge success. Far more than his return to freedom was being celebrated that night. News had reached the regiment that fighting had ceased in the Crimea and Alexander II had made overtures of peace to the West. The regimental choir sang soldiers' songs and Russian folk songs. Wine and cognac flowed freely, and even champagne, a few cases of which Saltykoff had had brought from his cellars in St. Petersburg to while away his exile. Everyone was talking, laughing, singing. Sasha alone remained silent and glum. Of late wine made him quarrelsome, and, if all the truth be told, he was becoming unpopular among his comrades for the shortness of his temper. On that night in particular dark thoughts kept torturing his brain—Natalie was dead, Tsar Nicholas was dead, the war with France and England was coming to an end, and what was the use of it all? And he wandered aimlessly through the big room, ungracious and morose.

He came to a stop beside a group of younger officers. In their midst stood Saltykoff, a little unsteady, gesticulating in all directions. Sasha heard one of the officers say, "Shamyl, that sly old fox, built a road to take the two princesses to freedom and bring his son back to his home. And now they say he has destroyed it, afraid we might use it to invade his mountains."

Saltykoff caught sight of Sasha. He winked at him, exclaiming, "What a pity! And here I was planning to take a quick ride up that road to pay my respects to Zoia Ivanovna Duval!"

The joke was a thoughtless one, but it had been said in Saltykoff's usual good-natured manner, with no intention to offend. But Sasha suddenly grew livid. He stepped up to Saltykoff with clenched fists. His face looked cruel; his eyes were burning with drunken rage. "How dare you make light of such a matter, Prince Saltykoff? If you had not been a friend of childhood, I would provoke you to a duel. As it is, I wash my hands of you. I never wish to see you again!"

Saltykoff's eyes almost popped out of his head, and his mouth sagged. "But, Sasha, friend of my heart! I meant no harm! I am a drunken fool. Forgive me!"

Sasha had turned his back on him and was walking away. Saltykoff looked around miserably. "I have offended my best friend. Now all I need is oblivion!" He filled a large glass with cognac, raised it to Sasha's receding back, and drank it at a gulp.

Sasha staggered out of the mess hall. His brain was befogged, his reactions thwarted. He was still fuming with rage. But when he reached his room he threw himself on his bed and fell sound asleep.

Poushka's hand shook him by the shoulder. "Alexandr Dimitrievitch! Wake up, Alexandr Dimitrievitch! For God's sake, wake up, it is getting late!"

"Oh, go to hell," Sasha murmured through his sleep, and turned over to the wall.

"All hell will break loose if you don't wake up, Alexandr Dimitrievitch!" Poushka gave Sasha another prod. "We cannot wake the prince. You must do something about it. The carriage is at the door. The regimental adjutant has an important verbal message for the general!"

Sasha rolled over on his back and squinted up at Poushka. Behind Poushka's back he could discern Sidor's face with its perpetual grin, a little dismayed now but still grinning. The sunlight falling through the window hurt his eyes, and with the light came the recollection of his quarrel with Saltykoff. It hurt even more. His heart sank. He felt dreadfully ashamed of himself. And he closed his eyes again, pretending to fall asleep.

Poushka was becoming desperate. "Wake up, wake up!" he shouted, and pointing to the other end of the room, where Saltykoff lay on his bed, snoring, "Look at the princely corpse!"

"Corpse!" Sasha sat bolt upright, rubbing his eyes. "What time is it?"

"Past eight."

"Holy Mother!"

He jumped out of bed and ran across the room. Saltykoff was

275

lying fully dressed; only his feet were bare. Sasha shook him violently, but Saltykoff only mumbled a few indistinct words and then fell to snoring again louder than ever.

"I tried it, it's no use," Poushka said. "His Serene Highness got home after five. And you should have seen the state he was in. Noah himself would have turned green with envy! All Sidor could do was pull off his boots and socks."

The words made Sasha glance down at himself. He noticed for the first time that he was in his underwear. "Did you undress me?"

"Sidor did. You were recalcitrant, Alexandr Dimitrievitch. I had to sit on top of you."

Sasha gave him a sidelong glance, but there was no time to be lost. Saltykoff should have left an hour ago. They went to work on him. Sidor was made to tickle the soles of his feet; Poushka performed a kind of artificial respiration, jerking Saltykoff's arms up and down, while Sasha wet a towel and slapped it across Saltykoff's face a few times. But even that did not help. Finally they gave up. Sasha ran to the washstand and brushed his teeth with fierce determination. He brushed his hair in front of a small mirror on the wall, and less than two minutes later, with Poushka's help, he was fully dressed. "Get ready," he shouted as he ran out of the room. "We will have to take the dispatches to headquarters!"

It did not take Sasha long to get permission to go to Baron Wrangel's headquarters instead of Saltykoff. He rushed to the adjutant's office to get the dispatches and the verbal message. He was to give the general the name of the place and the exact time at which the regiment would attack the mountaineers early next morning. When he returned to his billet he found Poushka seated on the box, ready to drive him to headquarters. Sasha jumped into the carriage. "Let 'em go, Poushka!" And the bells on the harness rang out as their carriage vanished down the road in a cloud of dust.

They reached General Wrangel's headquarters by noon, and shortly after one Sasha was ready to leave again. When he saw Poushka on the box, he laughed. "Scramble down, Poushka. I will drive this time. I'll be damned if I will stop and wait while you make your penance at four o'clock!"

For almost three hours they traveled in silence. Sasha kept his horses going at an easy trot. He was in no hurry to get back. The prospect of facing Saltykoff troubled him. And when they had turned a bend in the road and the narrow defile through which they had to pass appeared ahead of them, Sasha was saying to himself,

"I insulted Ivan in front of all the officers. I must apologize in front of them too. Only in that way can I really atone for it."

Poushka was so silent he might have been asleep. Glancing back, Sasha saw him sitting in the carriage with his head bent and eyes shut, muttering a prayer. "Yes, it must be four o'clock," Sasha thought with a smile, looking up at the sun.

They were entering the gorge now. A draft of cold air hit Sasha in the face. The sunlight vanished; it was almost dark there, and the humidity oozed out of the rocky walls on both sides of the road. Involuntarily Sasha whipped up his horses. As far as Sasha could remember, there were three bends in the road and then a clearing where the narrow defile widened for a short space. He was counting the bends as he rounded them, when all of a sudden wild yells resounded through the gorge. He saw about fifty armed mountaineers on the road, blocking his way. He reined in his horses. There was shouting behind him. He glanced hurriedly over his shoulder. A band of mountaineers were galloping toward him. One of them, with a black patch over his eye, was ahead of the others, close to the carriage. Over his head he was twirling a long rope with a noose at the end of it. Sasha stood up reaching for his pistol. But the rope whined past his ears, pinning his arms down to his sides. And with a violent jerk he was thrown to the ground, hitting his head as he fell.

It was then that a cry escaped Poushka. A cry of agony and despair. He sprang to his feet, leaning forward in the carriage. Sasha's unconscious form was being dragged along the road at the end of a rope. "Brigands! Murderers!" Poushka yelled at the top of his lungs, seizing his musket. But before he could cock it, a bullet pierced his chest. Slowly, very slowly, he toppled over and the earth came up to meet him.

A few brief minutes, a mad melee, and all was over. The mountaineers vanished, carrying Sasha with them. The frightened horses careened down the road, dragging an upset carriage behind them. And Poushka lay alone in the narrow gorge. Life receded slowly. A dark blotch appeared on his white soldier's shirt, the blood trickling down drop by drop to the dusty road. He tried to move, but he could not, though he felt no pain. He opened his eyes, and a smile lit his face. "Sashenka!" he murmured. He could see a little dark-haired boy running toward him through the park of Romantzevo, a toy gun in his hand. And a moment later it was the same boy, grown a little older, brandishing a real saber, leading his friends up a great staircase in a wild attack on the marble busts of Roman emperors. A wisp of a sigh escaped Poushka. "Ach, Sashenka!" He saw a young officer now with love-happy eyes fixed on the dark slender bride at his side. And then the scene switched to Paris, where a more mature man courted a young widow. He saw Roxane standing in the doorway and Zoë coming down the stairs. He heard his own voice shouting, "For God's sake, Alexandr Dimitrievitch, look!" And there was the burning house in Tsinandali and Sasha running toward it, calling out the name of Marina-gamdeli. And there was Sasha arrested by the Tsar. And Sasha, with agonized eyes, standing beside his horse in the yard of Prince David's house in Hassaf-Yourt. He saw it all. For it was Sasha's life that flashed by him with his last, rasping breath. The big man lay very still now on the deserted road. A vulture circled in the skies above.

7 When Hadji-Kheriett realized his mistake, his fury knew no bounds. All he had been able to see during the turbulence of the melee was the young Russian officer seated on the box of his carriage, driving his own horses. But when they came to a halt in the forest and he recognized Sasha, he saw red. His own blunder enraged him. Instead of a rich prince, he had captured this man who, for all he knew, might be a penniless army captain.

Sasha was standing in front of Hadji-Kheriett, his arms bound behind him, the side of his head throbbing painfully. Hadji-Kheriett seized him by the front of his army tunic, ripping off a few buttons, and pushed him against a tree. Sasha saw a dagger glisten in Hadji-Kheriett's hand, and with a silent prayer he closed his eyes. But the blow did not fall. When he looked up again, the hand with the dagger was still raised in mid-air. And once again, without any conscious effort on his part, the years of military training came to his assistance, the training that had drilled into him since early boyhood, "When you face death, die like a soldier." And Sasha's voice was calm and steady when he said, "Kill me and get it over with."

A blind, superstitious fear had stopped Hadji-Kheriett's hand. The infernal witchery of the Frenchwoman was at work again. It had been the cause of this inexplicable subterfuge. She was drawing her allies around her. And the thought had flashed through his brain, "If I kill him, Shaitan himself may rise to avenge her and inflict a thousand tortures on my soul!" Slowly he replaced the dagger in its sheath. Sasha saw the look of fear in his eyes, and though he could not guess the reason for it, he knew it had won him a temporary reprieve.

Hadji-Kheriett turned to the other men. "This is not the rich prince. We have made a mistake. But we must not despair. Let us find out more about this man. Perhaps he, too, can fetch a good price. Kazi-Mahomma entrusted the prisoner to my care. He will remain in my house until Kazi-Mahomma's return to Karaty." Hadji-Kheriett, who was always seeing Shaitan lurking around every corner, did not see the black wing hanging over his head now, for in sparing Sasha and taking him to his house he had sealed his own doom.

Shortly before dawn Fatima, Hadji-Kheriett's young wife, had awakened with a start. She heard her husband's harsh voice calling her and she shuddered a little. She had not expected him back so soon. She dressed hurriedly, wrapped herself in her veil, and crossed the yard. Hadji-Kheriett came to the door of his room, scowling at her. "Hurry up! I am tired and hungry. I have captured a Russian officer and have ridden all night. Get me some food."

She went to the covered shed that served her as a kitchen, while he turned back into the room. It was bare, with a few bright rugs, woven by Fatima, on the floor. Sasha stood near the opposite wall, his arms still bound behind his back. With his disheveled hair a mass of furious dark locks, and a day's growth of beard on his chin, he looked stronger somehow, undaunted, even a little formidable.

"I know who you are," Hadji-Kheriett said in Russian, sizing him up. "Your name is Novoselsky. Do you recognize me?"

"Yes. You are Hadji-Kheriett, the spy."

"Not a spy, an emissary of the Imam!"

"A spy," Sasha repeated firmly.

"You are a prisoner," Hadji-Kheriett hissed angrily. "Better be careful what you say!"

"Take me to Jemaleddin!" Sasha replied in a tone of command.

Hadji-Kheriett looked at him narrowly. "So, you are a friend of Jemaleddin's! But don't forget you are my prisoner. Jemaleddin can't help you. If your people do not pay a ransom, you will be my slave. That is the law of our land."

Sasha was thinking, "This man was afraid once; he can be made to be afraid again. I can cow him." And aloud he said, "Even if I were your slave, you would still fear me. You were afraid of killing me in the forest; you are afraid of unbinding me now."

Hadji-Kheriett came a step closer, his eye menacing. "You think

Jemaleddin can protect you and you grow arrogant. But I warn you again, his friendship won't save your skin. Just as your wish to see the Frenchwoman again will never be granted!"

"Where is she?" The question came as a cry torn out against Sasha's will.

A cruel smile twisted Hadji-Kheriett's lips. "She defied the Imam. I put her in a pit. Now she is a slave!" Sasha struggled in a vain effort to free his arms, and the smile on Hadji-Kheriett's face turned into a smirk. "Yes, I put her in a pit and I let her rot there in hunger and filth. I treated her like the accursed witch that she is!"

Sasha grew dangerously still. "You coward," he said in a low voice laden with hatred. "You dirty, yellow, low-down coward! You fight women and you dare not even kill a man!" And he spat at Hadji-Kheriett's feet.

The insult was a deadly one, far worse in a way than if he had spat in Hadji-Kheriett's face. With a cry of hate Hadji-Kheriett seized Sasha by the collar. His right fist crashed against Sasha's jaw. He hit him again. And Sasha fell to the floor. From the corner of the room Hadji-Kheriett snatched up his thick leather whip. The blows fell over Sasha's head and shoulders. He gritted his teeth. "Coward and dog!"

Suddenly Hadji-Kheriett threw the whip away. He grabbed Sasha under the shoulders and dragged him to the door.

Hadji-Kheriett lived in a house that had once belonged to a Naib. All such houses had a pit at the back of the yard, for it was the Naibs who meted out such punishments to their people. Hadji-Kheriett threw Sasha to the ground at the edge of the pit. He ran across the yard for the ladder. He slipped it into the pit. Sasha was struggling to his feet. Hadji-Kheriett knocked him down again.

"You are afraid of untying my arms," Sasha cried out in an impotent, stubborn rage. "You know I would kill you!"

Hadji-Kheriett took him by the scruff of the neck and forced him to climb down the ladder. When Sasha had gone a few steps, Hadji-Kheriett pushed him in. He drew the ladder out and threw it aside, panting a little.

The peaceful voice of a muezzin came from the minaret, calling the faithful to prayer. It was the hour of Allah, the hour in which Shaitan had no power. Quickly Hadji-Kheriett rinsed his hands and feet, took his prayer mat, and went up on the roof. And for a long time he prayed on his knees, bowing to the ground, murmuring

280

the prescribed words. But the peace of Allah was not in his heart; the fury of Shaitan still raged in it.

When he came down into the yard again, he glanced at the pit and hesitated. For the first time he remembered Shamyl's new order. But the memory of the insult returned to burn him anew, and his mind, searching for a possible alibi, whispered, "He threatened to kill you. You did it out of self-protection."

From her kitchen Fatima had seen it all. She, too, had heard of Shamyl's new order; and she had heard what the penalty was for breaking it. She felt frightened. If an ignominious death came to Hadji-Kheriett, what would be her own fate and that of her unborn child. They would share in the disgrace. She dared not speak about it to Hadji-Kheriett while she served him the cheese made of sheep's milk and the roast lamb she had prepared for his breakfast. Nor did Hadji-Kheriett speak to her. He ate in somber silence; and, the breakfast over, he lay down to sleep.

She went about her daily chores, the thought of what might happen to them all never leaving her mind. When the neighboring women brought her her daily supply of water from the river, she was tempted to tell them about it, but again she dared not. "He would kill me if he found out," she said to herself. She sat in her room, hoping that sleep would bring Hadji-Kheriett wisdom and he would free the Russian officer from the pit. But when he awoke in the late afternoon he went out, locking the front door behind him. Worried, perplexed, she went up to her roof. The granite wall of Kazi-Mahomma's seraglio was behind her. In front of her lay the aoul, descending in terraces down the steep slope of the mountain. For more than an hour she gazed despondently at the narrow street that led to the gates in the wall. It was growing dark when she caught sight of Hassan coming up the street. She had known him in their Dargo-Veden days. The thought flashed through her mind, "He can tell Jemaleddin! And then the Imam will hear about it, and he might remember me and be magnanimous to me and my child!"

"Hassan," she called out in a timid voice. He stopped and looked up. She glanced nervously around to make sure no one was there to hear her. "It's Fatima. Shouanet's former servant. Hadji-Kheriett's wife," she said. And in a few breathless words she told him what Hadji-Kheriett had done. She saw a man coming out of the seraglio gates. With a frightened gasp she ran down into the yard. Almost

281

afraid of her own shadow now, she crept into her room and hid in the darkest corner, her heart beating wildly.

Sasha lay at the bottom of the pit. His arms and shoulders were numb. He could hardly bear to move. The pit itself had been in disuse for a long time. Whatever filth it had contained had dried up, and the stench had left it. But once in a while a cold, slimy body passed over Sasha's hands and face, and it took all his will power not to shudder and cry out. He had lain there, watching the daylight fade away, until a merciful sleep brought him oblivion.

He was awakened by the sound of loud voices above. He looked up. The flickering light of several torches lit the edge of the pit. And suddenly, as in a dream, he heard Jemal's voice. He could not understand what was being said, but he knew Jemal was speaking in the yard. With difficulty Sasha scrambled to his feet, shouting, "Jemal! Is that you, Jemal? This is Sasha! Sasha Novoselsky! For God's sake, get me out of this filthy hole!"

There was a short silence. Then he heard Jemal's voice exclaiming in surprise. He heard him give some brief orders, and the ladder was lowered into the pit. "I cannot climb it," Sasha shouted. "My arms are bound behind my back."

As nimble as a young cat, Hassan slid down the ladder. With his dagger he cut the rope that held Sasha's arms, and Sasha almost groaned with relief. He rubbed his shoulders; he bent his arms and clasped and unclasped his hands several times. And then slowly he climbed up the ladder.

A cry of dismay escaped Jemal when he saw Sasha's head appear over the edge of the pit. His beard had grown still longer, there was mud on his hair and cheeks, caked blood at the corners of his mouth, and the sweat poured freely down his forehead. He stepped off the ladder unsteadily. He would have fallen had Jemal not rushed to his aid. He led Sasha away from the pit. And with his arm still around Sasha's shoulders he turned to Hadji-Kheriett. "You said you did it out of self-protection. What threat was there in this man? His arms were bound behind his back. Do you acknowledge your guilt, Hadji-Kheriett?"

"I do."

Hadji-Kheriett hung his head, the muscles of his thin face twitching, his jawbones working. Jemal spoke to the three men who stood behind Hadji-Kheriett with lighted torches. "Take him to Dargo-Veden. And tomorrow tell my father Hadji-Kheriett has pleaded guilty; the law must take its course." He looked at Hadji-Kheriett again, and there was pity in his eyes. "And tell the Imam I plead that Hadji-Kheriett's life be spared. He was not in his sane mind when he committed the crime."

Sasha was watching Hadji-Kheriett closely. He saw him draw himself up to his full height and look straight at Jemal. "I need no pity, Jemaleddin, from you or anyone else. I would rather die than live in disgrace!"

Sasha saw him turn and walk away, followed by the three men. And the light of their torches traveled through the dark yard, falling for an instant on the veiled face and terrified eyes of Fatima crouching behind her door.

8   The smallest of Jemal's three rooms was his dressing room. Here stood a European washstand, a large old-fashioned wardrobe, and the zinc tub Princess Anna and Princess Varvara had left behind in Dargo-Veden. Hassan had brought several buckets of hot and cold water from the kitchen, and while Sasha luxuriated in shaving and taking a warm bath, Jemal in his study drew Hassan aside, speaking to him in a low voice.

"Tomorrow, before dawn, have four horses in readiness at my door. You will guide my Russian friend and Zoë-djan to the border. When you come in sight of the Russian fort, let them go their way. And you must follow yours, Hassan. Do not return to me."

"And you, master?"

"The time has come, Hassan."

Hassan grew very pale. He seemed to shiver slightly. He seized Jemal's hand and pressed it to his forehead. But when he drew himself up again, he looked calm and composed. He stood waiting while Jemal remained lost in thought. Jemal knew he had to find a way to tell Zoë about her forthcoming liberation without arousing Karimat's suspicions. For the time being, he said to himself, Karimat must remain in ignorance of the true facts, just in case his father chose to question her later. And finally, having settled on a plan, he said, "Knock at Karimat's door, Hassan. Tell her I must see her and Zoë-djan at once on a very important matter."

A few minutes later Jemal stood in Karimat's living room. It was a chilly night. He stood with the two young women in the circle of light thrown by the burning logs in the large open fireplace. The rest of the room remained in darkness. For a moment he hesitated. For the first time in his life he was about to tell a deliberate lie, and it was important for the success of his plan that Karimat should believe it and that Zoë should guess the truth. He looked deep into Zoë's eyes as he said, "My father has summoned me to Dargo-Veden. I am leaving before dawn. You must come with me, Zoë-djan. It is time for you to make a profession of faith, since you have done me the honor to become——" He hesitated again and then added, "My soul's companion."

The subtlety of his remark escaped Karimat. She only heard what was in her own mind. Had she been asked about it, she would have sworn he had said, "My life's companion, my wife." And the involuntary toss of her head brought a smile to Jemal's lips. "Do not blame Zoë-djan for not telling you about this sooner. I swore her to secrecy. This was decided long ago, at our first meeting."

Zoë held her breath. She had guessed the truth, but in front of Karimat she dared not betray the conflicting emotions that had assailed her, for her joy at the thought of freedom mingled with sorrow. She lowered her eyes and remained silent.

Karimat frowned into the fire. "And if I protested?" she asked in a hollow voice.

"That would be in the true nature of things," he replied musingly, half in earnest, half in jest. "The world is built on protests. Sons protest against their fathers. New orders arise in protest against the old." He, too, was looking into the fire now, only his face had grown serious. "Land protests against the sea, peace against war, love against hate, life against death. Protest we must and protest we will, yet in the end what is there left but uniformity?" He stretched his hands out to the fire and smiled at Karimat. "Haven't we achieved a certain harmony, you and I, Karimat? Is there any real protest left between us?"

She swallowed hard and shook her head. And he left, telling Zoë to be ready at the appointed hour and begging Karimat not to wake up anyone to see him off. He wished to leave, he said, quietly and unobtrusively.

For a long time the two women remained silent. At last Karimat stirred. "He is right," she murmured. "There is no protest left in me."

Zoë looked up at her. "You said you would grow to hate me if I ever married Jemaleddin. Was that just once upon a time?"

"Yes, just once upon a time." Karimat's eyes were full of wonder. "How could I have known then I would miss Kazi-Mahomma so! Oh, it is all so strange!"

She hurried out of the room, returning a few minutes later carrying Zoë's pendant with the miniatures of her parents. She clasped it around Zoë's neck. "Let this be my wedding gift." And the two women embraced one another, a sigh close to a sob escaping Zoë, for she knew she was parting with Karimat forever.

It was Karimat who woke her up shortly before five. She had placed a lighted candle on the table beside Zoë's bed and was helping her to put on the clothes she had prepared for her. Instead of the long chemise, unsuited for horseback riding, there was a pair of white balloon-like trousers caught up at the ankles. Over these came a knee-length tunic of dark red silk strapped around the waist with a gold belt. Once again Karimat clasped the pendant around Zoë's neck and held out the gold crescent-shaped earrings. "Wear them," she insisted. "A bride should be properly adorned."

Over Zoë's head she placed a thin gold-embroidered veil, like the one she herself had worn on the day of her arrival in Dargo-Veden. She fixed it so that it covered the lower part of Zoë's face. "Daughters-in-law protest against fathers-in-law." She laughed, paraphrasing Jemal's words. "This is a protest against Shamyl's austerity!" And last of all came the white sheet, the *tchadrah* of thick silk, in which Zoë could shroud herself. They heard a discreet knock on the door, and Zoë held out both her hands to Karimat. "That must be Hassan coming to fetch me."

"Be happy, Zoë-djan, and come back soon."

Zoë tore her hands away and hurried across the room. At the door she glanced back. Karimat stood there like some graceful phantom in her long white nightgown, holding the lighted candle shoulder-high. Zoë turned away sharply. She wrapped herself in her tchadrah and slipped out of the room, closing the door behind her.

In the gray light of early dawn she recognized the figure of Hassan a few paces away, with two saddled horses behind him. He beckoned to her, and she followed him across the silent court. At a whispered word from him the big doors opened and she found herself in the outer court. She was standing now behind the gates of Karaty, the two tall towers on either side of them silhouetted against the dimly lit sky. The gates opened, and Zoë stepped out on the rocky ledge.

Two men were there, one dressed in white, the other in a black tcherkeska, a white turban wound around his black fur cap. They stood talking in low tones, holding their horses by the reins. The one in white she recognized at once as Jemal. She was about to speak to him, when he stepped aside, leaving her with the other man. And it was then that she saw Sasha's face. Just his face at first, standing out clear, sharp, alive; a little drawn, a little older, every line in it impressing itself on her mind for the rest of her life. Something within her gave a leap. The world revolved around them. He lowered her veil to see her face better. She stroked his hands gently with her fingers, rejoicing at the touch of his skin, at the light bristles of hair she had not even noticed there before. And all of him was regained in that brief moment.

But words did not come to either of them. She heard herself saying, her voice a little choked, "Good morning, Sasha." And his answer came back to her, tense and vibrant, "Good morning, Zoëdjan."

He helped her into her saddle and fixed her stirrups. There was a certain instinctive formality in their demeanor. And when Sasha had mounted his horse, Jemal rode up to them, followed by Hassan.

"It is getting late," he said. "You must leave at once. Hassan will conduct you as far as the border. You should reach it sometime this afternoon. When you come out of the forest and see the Russian fort, raise a white flag and gallop toward it. But do not forget, so long as you are on my father's territory you are a Naib traveling with his wife. Behave accordingly, act accordingly. And if anyone stops you, Hassan has my badge of office. It will serve as a pass."

Without a word Hassan took to the narrow trail. Whatever treasures he had acquired he carried with him; he did not need to look back. But Zoë did. She hesitated. She was coming to the end of her dream, walking on an edge between two realities. And seeking for the last time the propelling force that always lay behind his spoken word, she said, "Where are you going, Jemaleddin?"

His plan had been to flee into the wilderness, to which his father had threatened to banish him. But now he knew he must stay to face Shamyl and allow his destiny to take its course. Escape was but a snare; banishment would bring fulfillment. "I must go to my father." His eyes strayed to the snow on the mountains, pink now in the first rays of the sun. And he raised his hand in a last gesture of farewell. "May the peace of this hour be with you always."

Sasha turned his horse abruptly to hide his tears. He rode away down the trail. It descended a steep slope for a few hundred yards and then turned sharply. Zoë followed him. At the sharp bend the trail widened. Horses could stand there two abreast. Hassan had gone ahead, but Sasha reined in his horse. And Zoë stopped beside him.

286

The canyon was still in darkness. The murmurings of the forest, alive with ancient, gigantic trees, reached them from below. Above, the gates of Karaty stood rosy in the light of dawn. And Jemal on his horse looked like a figure carved of stone.

With all her heart Zoë longed to capture the vision and hold it. She gazed up at him until her sight became blurred. Sasha's half-forgotten words came back to her. "Someday you will meet him and then you will understand." She looked at Sasha now, tears of gratitude and humility shining in her eyes. "Yes, Sasha, I have understood." And speaking almost in a whisper, half to herself, she added, "A lofty tower of granite is his soul. From it passers-by pick cornerstones on which to lean, and build, and dwell."

Sasha bowed his head. His hand closed on hers, and Zoë dreamed no more.